THE

PRICE OF

SPRING

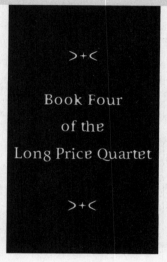

>+<

Book Four
of the
Long Price Quartet

>+<

Daniel
Abraham

TOR®

A Tom Doherty Associates Book
New York

THE PRICE OF SPRING: BOOK FOUR OF THE LONG PRICE QUARTET

Copyright © 2009 by Daniel Abraham

Edited by James Frenkel

Maps by Jackie Aher

A Tor Book
Published by Tom Doherty Associates, LLC
175 Fifth Avenue
New York, NY 10010

www.tor-forge.com

Tor® is a registered trademark of Tom Doherty Associates, LLC.

Library of Congress Cataloging-in-Publication Data

Abraham, Daniel.
  The price of spring / Daniel Abraham. — 1st ed.
      p. cm.
  "A Tom Doherty Associates book."
  ISBN-13: 978-0-7653-1343-0
  ISBN-10: 0-7653-1343-X
  I. Title.
  PS3601.B677P75 2009
  813'.6—dc22   2009001508

First Edition: July 2009

Printed in the United States of America

0 9 8 7 6 5 4 3 2 1

To Scarlet Abraham

ACKNOWLEDGMENTS

For the last time on this project, I reflect on the people who have helped me get to the end of it. I owe debts of service and gratitude to Walter Jon Williams, Melinda Snodgrass, Emily Mah, S. M. Stirling, Ian Tregillis, Ty Franck, George R. R. Martin, Terry England, and all the members of the New Mexico Critical Mass Workshop. I owe thanks to Connie Willis and the Clarion West '98 class for starting the story off a decade ago. Also to my agents Shawna McCarthy, who kept me on the project, and Danny Baror, who has sold these books in foreign lands and beyond my wildest dreams; to James Frenkel for his patience, faith, and uncanny ability to improve a manuscript; to Tom Doherty and the staff at Tor, who have made these into books with which I am deeply pleased.

Thank you all.

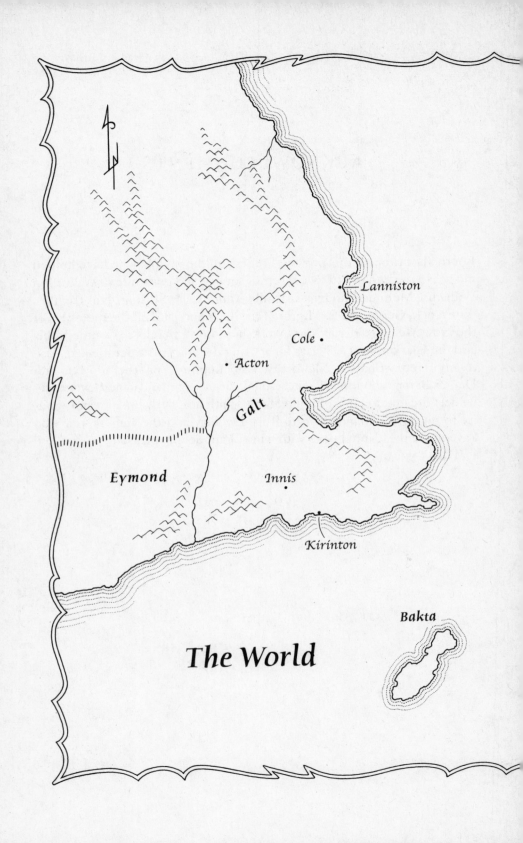

Lanniston

Cole

Acton

Galt

Eymond

Innis

Kirinton

Bakta

The World

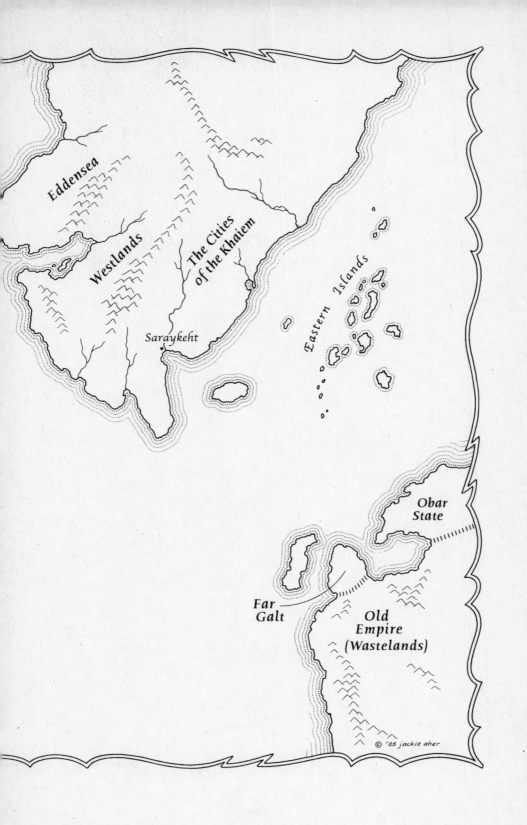

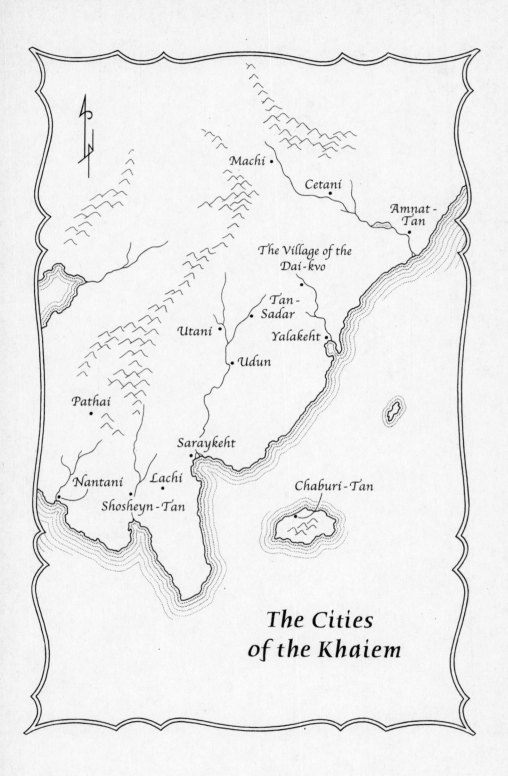

Machi •

• Cetani

Amnat-
Tan

The Village of the
Dai-kvo

Tan-
Sadar

Utani •

Yalakeht •

• Udun

Pathai
•

Saraykeht
•

Chaburi-Tan

Nantani   Lachi
•   •

Shosheyn-Tan

The Cities
of the Khaiem

THE
PRICE OF
SPRING

PROLOG

>+< Eiah Machi, physician and daughter of the Emperor, pressed her fingers gently on the woman's belly. The swollen flesh was tight, veins marbling the skin blue within brown. The woman appeared for all the world to be in the seventh month of a pregnancy. She was not.

"It's because my mother's father was a Westlander," the woman on the table said. "I'm a quarter Westlander, so when it came, it didn't affect me like it did other girls. Even at the time, I wasn't as sick as everyone else. You can't tell because I have my father's eyes, but my mother's were paler and almost round."

Eiah nodded, running practiced fingertips across the flesh, feeling where the skin was hot and where it was cool. She took the woman's hand, bending it gently at the wrist to see how tight her tendons were. She reached inside the woman's sex, probing where only lovers had gone before. The man who stood at his wife's side looked uncomfortable, but Eiah ignored him. He was likely the least important person in the room.

"Eiah-cha," Parit, the regular physician, said, "if there is anything I can do . . ."

Eiah took a pose that both thanked and refused. Parit bowed slightly.

"I was very young, too," the woman said. "When it happened. Just six summers old."

"I was fourteen," Eiah said. "How many months has it been since you bled?"

"Six," the woman said as if it were a badge of honor. Eiah forced herself to smile.

"Is the baby well?" the man asked. Eiah considered how his hand wrapped his wife's. How his gaze bored into her own. Desperation was as thick a scent in the room as the vinegar and herb smoke.

"It's hard to say," Eiah said. "I haven't had the luck to see very many pregnancies. Few of us have these days. But even if things are well so far, birthing is a tricky business. Many things can go wrong."

"He'll be fine," the woman on the table asserted; the hand not being squeezed bloodless by her man caressed the slight pooch of her belly. "It's a boy," she went on. "We're going to name him Loniit."

Eiah placed a hand on the woman's arm. The woman's eyes burned with something like joy, something like fever. The smile faltered for less than a heartbeat, less than the time it took to blink. So at least some part of the woman knew the truth.

"Thank you for letting me make the examination," Eiah said. "You're very kind. And I wish the best of luck to you both."

"All three," the woman corrected.

"All three," Eiah said.

She walked from the room while Parit arranged his patient. The antechamber glowed by the light of a small lantern. Worked stone and carved wood made the room seem more spacious than it was. Two bowls, one of old wine and another of fresh water, stood waiting. Eiah washed her hands in the wine first. The chill against her fingers helped wash away the warmth of the woman's flesh. The sooner she could forget that, the better.

Voices came from the examining room like echoes. Eiah didn't listen. When she put her hands into the water, the wine turned it pink. She dried herself with a cloth laid by for the purpose, moving slowly to be sure both the husband and wife were gone before she returned.

Parit was washing down the slate table with vinegar and a stiff brush. It was something Eiah had done often when she'd first apprenticed to the physicians, all those years ago. There were fewer apprentices now, and Parit didn't complain.

"Well?" he asked.

"There's no child in her," Eiah said.

"Of course not," he said. "But the signs she *does* show. The pooled blood, the swelling. The loss of her monthly flow. And yet there's no slackening in her joints, no shielding in her sex. It's a strange mix."

"I've seen it before," Eiah said.

Parit stopped. His hands took a pose of query. Eiah sighed and leaned against one of the high stools.

"Desire," Eiah said. "That's all. Want something that you can't have badly enough, and the longing becomes a disease."

Her fellow physician and onetime lover paused for a moment, considering Eiah's words, then looked down and continued his cleaning.

"I suppose we should have said something," he said.

"There's nothing to say," Eiah said. "They're happy now, and they'll be sad later. What good would it do us to hurry that?"

Parit gave the half-smile she'd known on him years before, but didn't look up to meet her gaze.

"There is something to be said in favor of truth," he said.

"And there's something to be said for letting her keep her husband for another few weeks," Eiah said.

"You don't know that he'll turn her out," he said.

Eiah took a pose that accepted correction. They both knew it was a gentle sarcasm. Parit chuckled and poured a last rinse over the slate table: the rush of the water like a fountain trailed off to small, sharp drips that reminded Eiah of wet leaves at the end of a storm. Parit pulled out a stool and sat, his hands clasped in his lap. Eiah felt a sudden awkwardness that hadn't been there before. She was always better when she could inhabit her role. If Parit had been bleeding from the neck, she would have been sure of herself. That he was only looking at her made her aware of the sharpness of her face, the gray in her hair that she'd had since her eighteenth summer, and the emptiness of the house. She took a formal pose that offered gratitude. Perhaps a degree more formal than was needed.

"Thank you for sending for me," Eiah said. "It's late, and I should be getting back."

"To the palaces," he said. There was warmth and humor in his voice. There always had been. "You could also stay here."

Eiah knew she should have been tempted at least. The glow of old love and half-recalled sex should have wafted in her nostrils like mulled wine. He was still lovely. She was still alone.

"I don't think I could, Parit-kya," she said, switching from the formal to the intimate to pull the sting from it.

"Why not?" he asked, making it sound as if he was playing.

"There are a hundred reasons," Eiah said, keeping her tone as light as his. "Don't make me list them."

He chuckled and took a pose that surrendered the game. Eiah felt herself relax a degree, and smiled. She found her bag by the door and slung its strap over her shoulder.

"You still hide behind that," Parit said.

Eiah looked down at the battered leather satchel, and then up at him, the question in her eyes.

"There's too much to fit in my sleeves," she said. "I'd clank like a toolshed every time I waved."

"That's not why you carry it," he said. "It's so that people see a physician and not your father's daughter. You've always been like that."

It was his little punishment for her return to her own rooms. There had been a time when she'd have resented the criticism. That time had passed.

"Good night, Parit-kya," she said. "It was good to see you again."

He took a pose of farewell, and then walked with her to the door. In the courtyard of his house, the autumn moon was full and bright and heavy. The air smelled of wood smoke and the ocean. Warmth so late in the season still surprised her. In the north, where she'd spent her girlhood, the chill would have been deadly by now. Here, she hardly needed a heavy robe.

Parit stopped in the shadows beneath a wide shade tree, its golden leaves lined with silver by the moonlight. Eiah had her hand on the gate before he spoke.

"Was that what you were looking for?" he asked.

She looked back, paused, and took a pose that asked for clarification. There were too many things he might have meant.

"When you wrote, you said to watch for unusual cases," Parit said. "Was she what you had in mind?"

"No," Eiah said. "That wasn't it." She passed from the garden to the street.

A decade and a half had passed since the power of the andat had left the world. For generations before that, the cities of the Khaiem had been protected by the poets—men who had dedicated their lives to binding one of the spirits, the thoughts made flesh. Stone-Made-Soft, whom Eiah had known as a child with its wide shoulders and amiable smile, was one of them. It had made the mines around the northern city of Machi the greatest in the world. Water-Moving-Down, who generations ago had commanded the rains to come or else to cease, the rivers to flow or else run dry. Removing-the-Part-That-Continues, called Seedless, who had plucked the seeds from the cotton harvests of Saraykeht and discreetly ended pregnancies.

Each of the cities had had one, and each city had shaped its trade and commerce to exploit the power of its particular andat to the advantage of its citizens. War had never come to the cities of the Khaiem. No one dared to face an enemy who might make the mountains flow like rivers, who might flood your cities or cause your crops to fail or your women to miscarry. For almost ten generations, the cities of the Khaiem had stood above the world like adults over children.

And then the Galtic general Balasar Gice had made his terrible wager and won. The andat left the world, and left it in ruins. For a blood-soaked spring, summer, and autumn, the armies of Galt had washed over the cities like a wave over sandcastles. Nantani, Udun, Yalakeht, Chaburi-Tan. The great cities fell to the foreign swords. The Khaiem died. The Dai-kvo and his poets were put to the sword and their libraries burned. Eiah still remembered being fourteen summers old and waiting for death to come. She had been only the daughter of the Khai Machi then, but that had been enough. The Galts, who had taken every other city, were advancing on them. And their only hope had been Uncle Maati, the disgraced poet, and his bid to bind one last andat.

She had been present in the warehouse when he'd attempted the binding. She'd seen it go wrong. She had felt it in her body. She and every other woman in the cities of the Khaiem. And every man of Galt. Corrupting-the-Generative, the last andat had been named.

Sterile.

Since that day, no woman of the cities of the Khaiem had borne a child. No man of Galt had fathered one. It was a dark joke. Enemy nations locked in war afflicted with complementary curses. *Your history will be written by half-breeds*, Sterile had said, *or it won't be written*. Eiah knew the words because she had been in the room when the world had been broken. Her own father had taken the name Emperor when he sued for peace, and Emperor he had become. Emperor of a fallen world.

Perhaps Parit was right. Perhaps she had taken to her vocation as single-mindedly as she had because she wanted to be something else. Something besides her father's daughter. As the princess of the new empire, she would have been a marriage to some foreign ward or king or lord incapable of bearing children. The degraded currency of her body would have been her definition.

Physician and healer were better roles to play. Walking through the darkened streets of Saraykeht, her robes and her satchel afforded her a measure of respect and protection. It was poor form to assault a healer, in part because of the very real chance of requiring her services one day. The toughs and beggars who haunted the alleys near the seafront might meet her eyes as she walked past, might even hail her with an obscenity or veiled threat, but they had never followed her. And so she didn't see that she had any need of the palace guard. If her work protected her, there was no reason to call upon her blood.

She stopped at the bronze statue of Shian Sho. The last emperor gazed out wistfully over the sea, or perhaps back through the ages to a time when his name had been important. Eiah pulled her robe tight around herself and squatted at his metalwork feet, waiting for the firekeeper and his steamcart. In daytime, she would have walked the streets north and uphill to the palaces, but the seafront wasn't the worst part of Saraykeht. It was safer to wait.

To the west, the soft quarter was lit in its nightly festival. To the east, the bathhouses, the great stone warehouses, rarely more than half-filled now. Beyond that, the cohort houses of the laborers were darker, but far from unpeopled. Eiah heard a man's laugh from one direction, a woman's voice lifted in drunken song from another. The ships that filled the seafront docks stood silent, their masts like winter trees, and the ocean beyond them gray with a low mist.

There was a beauty in it, and a familiarity. Eiah had made her studies in places like this, whatever city she'd been in. She'd sewn closed the flesh of whores and thieves as often as soothed the coughs and pains of the utkhaiem in their perfumed palaces. It was a decision she'd made early in her career, not to be a court physician, not to care only for the powerful. Her father had approved, and even, she thought, been proud of the decision. For all their differences—and there were many—it was one reason she loved him.

The steamcart appeared first as a sound: the rough clatter of iron-bound wheels against the bricks of the street, the chuff of the boiler, the low rumble of the kiln. And then, as Eiah stood and shook the dirt and grime from her robe, it turned into the wide street they called the Nantan and came down toward the statue. In the light of the kiln, she saw seven or perhaps eight figures clinging to the cart's side. The firekeeper himself sat on the top, guiding the cart with a series of levers and pedals that made the most ornate loom seem simple. Eiah stepped forward as the cart trundled past, took one of the leather grips, and hoisted herself up to the cart's side runner along with the others.

"Two coppers," the firekeeper said without looking at her.

Eiah dug in her sleeve with her free hand, came out with two lengths of copper, and tossed them into the lacquer box at the firekeeper's feet. The man nodded rather than take any more-complex pose. His hands and eyes were occupied. The breeze shifted, a waft of smoke and thick steam washing her in its scent, and the cart lurched, shuddered, and turned again to the north along its constant route. Eiah sighed and made herself comfortable. It would take her almost the time for the moon to move the width of her hand before she stepped down at the pathway that led to the palaces. In the meantime, she watched the night city pass by her.

The streets nearest the seafront alternated between the high roofs of warehouses and the low of the tradesmen's shops. In the right season, the clack of looms would have filled the air, even this late at night. The streets converged on wide squares where the litter of the week's market still fouled the street: cheeses dropped to the cobbles and trod into mush, soiled cabbages and yams, even a skinned rabbit too corrupt to sell and not worth hauling away. One of the men on the far side of the steamcart stepped down, shifting the balance slightly. Eiah watched as his red-brown cloak passed into darkness.

There had been a time, she knew, when the streets had been safe to walk down, even alone. There had been a time beggars with their boxes would have been on the corners, filling the night with plaintive, amateur song. She had never seen it, never heard it. It was a story she knew, Old Saraykeht from long ago. She knew it like she knew Bakta, where she had never been, and the courts of the Second Empire, gone from the world for hundreds of years. It was a story. Once upon a time there was a city by the sea, and it lived in prosperity and innocence. But it didn't anymore.

The steamcart passed into the compounds of the merchant houses, three, four, five stories tall. They were almost palaces in themselves. There were more lights here, more voices. Lanterns hung from ropes at the crossroads, spilling buttery light on the bricks. Three more of Eiah's fellows stepped down from the cart. Two stepped on, dropping their copper lengths into the firekeeper's box. They didn't speak, didn't acknowledge one another. She shifted her hands on the leather grip. The palaces of the utkhaiem would be coming soon. And her apartments, and bed, and sleep. The kiln roared when the firekeeper opened it and poured in another spade's worth of coal.

The servants met her at the gateway that separated the palaces from the city, the smooth brick streets from the crushed marble pathways. The air smelled different here, coal smoke and the rich, fetid stink of humanity displaced by incense and perfume. Eiah felt relieved to be back, and then guilty for her relief. She answered their poses of greeting and obeisance with one of acknowledgment. She was no longer her work. Among these high towers and palaces, she was and would always be her father's daughter.

"Eiah-cha," the most senior of the servants said, his hands in a pose of ritual offering, "may we escort you to your rooms?"

"No," she said. "Food first. Then rest."

Eiah suffered them to take her satchel, but refused the sable cloak they offered against the night air. It really wasn't that cold.

"Is there word from my father?" she asked as they walked along the wide, empty paths.

"No, Eiah-cha," the servant replied. "Nor from your brother. There have been no couriers today."

Eiah kept her pleasure at the news from her expression.

The palaces of Saraykeht had suffered less under their brief Galtic occupation than many others had. Nantani had been nearly ruined. Udun had been razed and never rebuilt. In Saraykeht, it was clear where statues had once been and were gone, where jewels had been set into the goldwork around the doorways and been wrenched out, but all the buildings except the Khai's palace and the library still stood. The utkhaiem of the city hadn't restored the damage or covered it over. Like a woman assaulted but with unbroken spirit, Saraykeht wore her scars without shame. Of all the cities of the Khaiem, she was the least devastated, the strongest, and the most arrogant in her will to survive. Eiah thought she might love the city just a little, even as it made her sad.

A singing slave occupied the garden outside Eiah's apartments. Eiah left the shutters open so that the songs could come through more clearly. A fire burned in the grate and candles glowed in glass towers. A Galtic clock marked the hours of the night in soft metallic counterpoint to the singer, and as she pulled off her robes and prepared for sleep, Eiah was amazed to see how early it was. The night had hardly exhausted its first third. It had seemed longer. She put out the candles, pulled herself into her bed, and drew the netting closed.

The night passed, and the day that followed it, and the day that followed that. Eiah's life in Saraykeht had long since taken on a rhythm. The mornings she spent at the palaces working with the court physicians, the afternoons down in the city or in the low towns that spread out from Saraykeht. To those who didn't know her, she gave herself out to be a visitor from Cetani in the north, driven to the summer cities by hardship. It wasn't an implausible tale. There were many for whom it was true. And while it couldn't be totally hidden, she didn't want to be widely known as her father's daughter. Not here. Not yet.

On a morning near the end of her second month in the city—two weeks after Candles Night—the object of her hunt finally appeared. She was in her rooms, working on a guide to the treatment of fevers in older patients. The fire was snapping and murmuring in the grate and a thin, cold rain tapped at the shutters like a hundred polite mice asking permission to enter. The scratch at the door startled her. She arranged her robe and opened the door just as the slave outside it was raising her hand to scratch again.

"Eiah-cha," the girl said, falling into a pose that was equal parts apology and greeting. "Forgive me, but there's a man . . . he says he has to speak with you. He has a message."

"From whom?" Eiah demanded.

"He wouldn't say, Most High," the slave said. "He said he could speak only with you."

Eiah considered the girl. She was little more than sixteen summers. One of the youngest in the cities of the Khaiem. One of the last.

"Bring him," Eiah said. The girl made a brief pose that acknowledged the command and fled back out into the damp night. Eiah shuddered and went to add more coal to the fire. She didn't close the door.

The runner was a young man, broad across the shoulder. Twenty summers, perhaps. His hair was soaked and sticking to his forehead. His robe hung heavily from his shoulders, sodden with the rain.

"Eiah-cha," he said. "Parit-cha sent me. He's at his workroom. He said he has something and that you should come. Quickly."

She caught her breath, the first movements of excitement lighting her nerves. The other times one or another of the physicians and healers and herb women of the city had sent word, it had been with no sense of urgency. A man ill one day was very likely to be ill the next as well. This, then, was something different.

"What is it?" she asked.

The runner took an apologetic pose. Eiah waved it away and called for a servant. She needed a thick robe. And a litter; she wasn't waiting for the firekeeper. And now, she needed them now. The Emperor's daughter got what she wanted, and she got it quickly. She and the boy were on the streets in less than half a hand, the litter jouncing uncomfortably as they were carried through the drizzle. The runner tried not to seem awed at the palace servants' fear of Eiah. Eiah tried not to bite her fingernails from anxiety. The streets slid by outside their shelter as Eiah willed the litter bearers to go faster. When they reached Parit's house, she strode through the courtyard gardens like a general going to war.

Without speaking, Parit ushered her to the back. It was the same room in which she'd seen the last woman. Parit sent the runner away. There were no servants. There was no one besides the two physicians and a body on the wide slate table, covered by a thick canvas cloth soaked through with blood.

"They brought her to me this morning," Parit said. "I called for you immediately."

"Let me see," Eiah said.

Parit pulled back the cloth.

The woman was perhaps five summers older than Eiah herself, dark-haired and thickly built. She was naked, and Eiah saw the wounds that covered her body: belly, breasts, arms, legs. A hundred stab wounds. The woman's skin was unnaturally pale. She'd bled to death. Eiah felt no revulsion, no outrage. Her mind fell into the patterns she had cultivated all her life. This was only death, only violence. This was where she was most at home.

"Someone wasn't happy with her," Eiah said. "Was she a soft-quarter whore?"

Parit startled, his hands almost taking a pose of query. Eiah shrugged.

"That many knife wounds," she said, "aren't meant only to kill. Three or four would suffice. And the spacing of them isn't what I've seen when the killer had simply lost control. Someone was sending a message."

"She wasn't stabbed," Parit said. He took a cloth from his sleeve and tossed it to her. Eiah turned back to the corpse, wiping the blood away from a wound in the dead woman's side. The smear of gore thinned. The nature of the wound became clear.

It was a mouth. Tiny rosebud lips, slack as sleep. Eiah told her hand to move, but for a long moment her flesh refused her. Then, her breath shallow, she cleaned another. And then another.

The woman was covered with babies' mouths. Eiah's fingertips traced the tiny lips that had spilled the woman's lifeblood. It was a death as grotesque as any Eiah had heard in the tales of poets who had tried to bind the andat and fallen short.

Tears filled her eyes. Something like love or pity or gratitude filled her heart to bursting. She looked at the woman's face for the first time. The woman hadn't been pretty. A thick jaw, a heavy brow, acne pocks. Eiah held back from kissing her cheek. Parit was confused enough as it stood. Instead, Eiah wiped her eyes on her sleeve and took the dead woman's hand.

"What happened?" she asked.

"The watch saw a cart going west out of the soft quarter," Parit said. "The captain said there were three people, and they were acting nervous. When he hailed them, they tried to run."

"Did he catch them?"

Parit was staring at Eiah's hand clasping the dead woman's fingers.

"Parit," she said. "Did he catch them?"

"What? No. No, all three slipped away. But they had to abandon the cart. She was in it," Parit said, nodding at the corpse. "I'd asked anything unusual to be brought to me. I offered a length of silver."

"They earned it," Eiah said. "Thank you, Parit-kya. I can't tell you how much this means."

"What should we do?" Parit asked, sitting on his stool like a fresh apprentice before his master. He'd always done that when he felt himself at sea. Eiah found there was warmth in her heart for him even now.

"Burn her," Eiah said. "Burn her with honors and treat her ashes with respect."

"Shouldn't we . . . shouldn't we tell someone? The utkhaiem? The Emperor?"

"You already have," Eiah said. "You've told me."

There was a moment's pause. Parit took a pose that asked clarification. It wasn't quite the appropriate one, but he was flustered.

"This is it, then," he said. "This is what you were looking for."

"Yes," Eiah said.

"You know what happened to her."

"Yes."

"Would you . . ." Parit coughed, looked down. His brow was knotted. Eiah was half-tempted to go to him, to smooth his forehead with her palm. "Could you explain this to me?"

"No," she said.

AFTER THAT, IT WAS SIMPLE. THEY WOULDN'T REMAIN IN SARAYKEHT, NOT WHEN they'd so nearly been discovered. The Emperor's daughter asked favors of the port master, of the customs men on the roads, of the armsmen paid by the city to patrol and keep the violence in the low towns to an acceptable level. Her quarry weren't smugglers or thieves. They weren't expert in covering their tracks. In two days, she knew where they were. Eiah quietly packed what things she needed from her apartments in the palace, took a horse from the stables, and rode out of the city as if she were only going to visit an herb woman in one of the low towns.

As if she were coming back.

She found them at a wayhouse on the road to Shosheyn-Tan. The winter sun had set, but the gates to the wayhouse courtyard were still open. The carriage Eiah had heard described was at the side of the house, its horses unhitched. The two women, she knew, were presenting themselves as travelers. The man—old, fat, unpleasant to speak with— was posing as their slave. Eiah let the servant take her horse to be cared for, but instead of going up the steps to the main house, she followed him back to the stables. A small shack stood away at an angle. Quarters for servants and slaves. Eiah felt her lips press thin at the thought. Rough straw ticking, thin blankets, whatever was left to eat after the paying guests were done.

"How many servants are here now?" Eiah asked of the young man—eighteen summers, so four years old when it had happened—brushing down her horse. He looked at her as if she'd asked what color ducks laid the eggs they served at table. She smiled.

"Three," the servant said.

"Tell me about them," she said.

He shrugged.

"There's an old woman came in two days ago. Her master's laid up sick. Then a boy from the Westlands works for a merchant staying on the ground floor. And an old bastard just came in with two women from Chaburi-Tan."

"Chaburi-Tan?"

"What they said," the servant replied.

Eiah took two lengths of silver from her sleeve and held them out in her palm. The servant promptly forgot about her horse.

"When you're done," she said, "take the woman and the Westlander to the back of the house. Buy them some wine. Don't mention me. Leave the old man."

The servant took a pose of acceptance so total it was just short of an open pledge. Eiah smiled, dropped the silver in his palm, and pulled up a shoeing stool to sit on while she waited. The night was cool, but still not near as cold as her home in the north. An owl hooted deep and low. Eiah pulled her arms up into her sleeves to keep her fingers warm. The scent of roasting pork wafted from the wayhouse, and the sounds of a flute and a voice lifted together.

The servant finished his work and with a deferential nod to Eiah, made his way to the servants' house. It was less than half a hand before he emerged with a thin woman and a sandy-haired Westlands boy trailing him. Eiah pushed her hands back through her sleeves and made her way to the small, rough shack.

He was sitting beside the fire, frowning into the flames and eating a mush of rice and raisins from a small wooden bowl. The years hadn't been kind to him. He was thicker than he'd been when she knew him, an unhealthy fatness that had little to do with indulgence. His color was poor; what remained of his hair was white stained yellow by neglect. He looked angry. He looked lonesome.

"Uncle Maati," she said.

He startled. His eyes flashed. Eiah couldn't tell if it was anger or fear. But whatever it was had a trace of pleasure to it.

"Don't know who you mean," he said. "Name's Daavit."

Eiah chuckled and stepped into the small room. It smelled of bodies and smoke and the raisins in Maati's food. Eiah found a small chair and pulled it to the fire beside the old poet, her chosen uncle, the man who had destroyed the world. They sat silently for a while.

"It was the way they died," Eiah said. "All the stories you told me when I was young about the prices that the andat exacted when a poet's binding failed. The one whose blood turned dry. The one whose belly swelled up like he was pregnant, and when they cut him open it was all ice and seaweed. All of them. I started to hear stories. What was that, four years ago?"

At first she thought he wouldn't answer. He cupped two thick fingers into the rice and ate what they lifted out. He swallowed. He sucked his teeth.

"Six," he said.

"Six years," she said. "Women started appearing here and there, dead in strange ways."

He didn't answer. Eiah waited for the space of five slow breaths together before she went on.

"You told me stories about the andat when I was young," she said. "I remember most of it, I think. I know that a binding only works once. In order to bind the same andat again, the poet has to invent a whole new way to describe the thought. You used to tell me about how the poets of the Old Empire would bind three or four andat in a lifetime. I thought at the time you envied them, but I saw later that you were only sick at the waste of it."

Maati sighed and looked down.

"And I remember when you tried to explain to me why only men could be poets," she said. "As I recall, the arguments weren't all that convincing to me."

"You were a stubborn girl," Maati said.

"You've changed your mind," Eiah said. "You've lost all your books. All the grammars and histories and records of the andat that have come before. They're gone. All the poets gone but you and perhaps Cehmai. And in the history of the Empire, the Second Empire, the Khaiem, the *one* thing you know is that a woman has never been a poet. So perhaps, if women think differently enough from men, the bindings they create will succeed, even with nothing but your own memory to draw from."

"Who told you? Otah?"

"I know my father had letters from you," Eiah said. "I don't know what was in them. He didn't tell me."

"A women's grammar," Maati said. "We're building a women's grammar."

Eiah took the bowl from his hands and put it on the floor with a clatter. Outside, a gust of wind shrilled past the shack. Smoke bellied out from the fire, rising into the air, thinning as it went. When he looked at her, the pleasure was gone from his eyes.

"It's the best hope," Maati said. "It's the only way to . . . undo what's been done."

"You can't do this, Maati-kya," Eiah said, her voice gentle.

Maati started to his feet. The stool he'd sat on clattered to the floor. Eiah pulled back from his accusing finger.

"Don't you tell that to me, Eiah," Maati said, biting at the words. "I know he doesn't approve. I asked his help. Eight years ago, I risked my life by sending to him, asking the Emperor of this pisspot empire for help. And what did he say? No. Let the world be the world, he said. He doesn't see what it is out here. He doesn't see the pain and the ache and the suffering. So don't you tell *me* what to do. Every girl I've lost, it's *his* fault. Every time we try and fall short, it's because we're sneaking around in warehouses and low towns. Meeting in secret like criminals—"

"Maati-kya—"

"I *can* do this," the old poet continued, a fleck of white foam at the corner of his mouth. "I *have* to. I *have* to retrieve my error. I have to fix what I broke. I know I'm hated. I know what the world's become because of me. But these girls are dedicated and smart and willing to die if that's what's called for. Willing to *die*. How can you and your great and glorious father tell me that I'm wrong to try?"

"I didn't say you shouldn't try," Eiah said. "I said you can't do it. Not alone."

Maati's mouth worked for a moment. His fingertip traced an arc down to the fire grate as the anger left him. Confusion washed through his expression, his shoulders sagging and his chest sinking in. He reminded Eiah of a puppet with its strings fouled. She rose and took his hand as she had the dead woman's.

"I haven't come here on my father's business," Eiah said. "I've come to help."

"Oh," Maati said. A tentative smile found its way to his lips. "Well. I . . . that is . . ."

He frowned viciously and wiped at his eyes with one hand. Eiah stepped forward and put her arms around him. His clothes smelled rank and unwashed; his flesh was soft, his skin papery. When he returned her embrace, she would not have traded the moment for anything.

1

>+< It was the fifth month of the Emperor's self-imposed exile. The day
had been filled, as always, with meetings and conversations and ap-
preciations of artistic tableaux. Otah had retired early, claiming a headache
rather than face another banquet of heavy, overspiced Galtic food.

The night birds in the garden below his window sang unfamiliar
songs. The perfume of the wide, pale flowers was equal parts sweetness
and pepper. The rooms of his suite were hung with heavy Galtic tapestries, knotwork soldiers slaughtering one another in memory of some
battle of which Otah had never heard.

It was, coincidentally, the sixty-third anniversary of his birth. He hadn't
chosen to make it known; the High Council might have staged some further celebration, and he had had a bellyful of celebrations. In that day, he
had been called upon to admire a gold- and jewel-encrusted clockwork
whose religious significance was obscure to him; he had moved in slow
procession down the narrow streets and through the grand halls with their
awkward, blocky architecture and their strange, smoky incense; he had
spoken to two members of the High Council to no observable effect. At
this moment, he could be sitting with them again, making the same points,
suffering the same deflections. Instead, he watched the thin clouds pass
across the crescent moon.

He had become accustomed to feeling alone. It was true that with a
word or a gesture he could summon his counselors or singing slaves, scholars or priests. Another night, he might have, if only in hope that this time
it would be different; that the company would do something more than
remind him how little comfort it provided. Instead, he went to the ornate writing desk and took what solace he could.

Kiyan-kya—
I have done what I said I would do. I have come to our old enemies, I
have pled my case and pled and pled and pled, and now I suppose I'll plead

some more. The full council is set to make their vote in a week's time. I know I should go out and do more, but I swear that I've spoken to everyone in this city twice over, and tonight, I'd rather be here with you. I miss you.

They tell me that all widowers suffer this sense of being halved, and they tell me it fades. It hasn't faded. I suspect age changes the nature of time. Four years may be an epoch for young men, to me it's hardly the space between one breath and the next. I want you to be here to tell me your thoughts on the matter. I want you here. I want you back.

I've had word from Danat and Sinja. They seem to be running the cities effectively enough in my absence, but apart from our essential problem, there are a thousand other threats. Pirates have raided Chaburi-Tan, and there are stories of armed companies from Eddensea and the Westlands exacting tolls on the roads outside the winter cities. The trading houses are bleeding money badly; no one indentures themselves as an apprentice anymore. Artisans are having to pay for workers. Even seafront laborers are commanding wages higher than anything I made as a courier. The high families of the utkhaiem are watching their coffers drain like a holed bladder. It makes them restless. I have had two separate petitions to allow forced indenture for what they call "critical labor." I haven't given an answer. When I go home, I suppose I'll have to.

Otah paused, the tip of his pen touching the brick of ink. Something with wide, pale wings the size of his hands and eyes as black and wet as river stones hovered at the window and then vanished. A soft breeze rattled the open shutters. He pulled back the sleeve of his robe, but before the bronze tip touched the paper, a soft knock came at his door.

"Most High," the servant boy said, his hands in a pose of obeisance. "Balasar-cha requests an audience."

Otah smiled and took a pose that granted the request and implied that the guest should be brought to him here, the nuance only slightly hampered by the pen still in his hand. As the servant scampered out, Otah straightened his sleeves and stuck the pen nib-first into the ink brick.

Once, Balasar Gice had led armies against the Khaiem, and only raw chance had kept him from success. Instead of leading Galt to its greatest hour, he had precipitated its slow ruin. That the Khaiem shared that fate took away little of the sting. The general had spent years rebuilding his broken reputation, and even now was less a force within Galt than once he had been.

And still, he was a man to be reckoned with.

He came into the room, bowing to Otah as he always did, but with a wry smile which was reserved for occasions out of the public eye.

"I came to inquire after your health, Most High," Balasar Gice said in the language of the Khaiem. His accent hadn't lessened in the years since they had met. "Councilman Trathorn was somewhat relieved by your absence, but he had to pretend distress."

"Well, you can tell him his distress in every way mirrors my own," Otah said. "I couldn't face it. I've been too much in the world. There is only so much praise I can stand from people who'd be happy to see my head on a plate. Please, sit. I can have a fire lit if you're cold. . . ."

Balasar sat on a low couch beside the window. He was a small man, more than half a head shorter than Otah, with the force of personality that made it easy to forget. The years had weathered his face, grooves at the corners of his eyes and mouth that spoke as much of laughter as sorrow. They had met a decade and a half ago in the snow-covered square that had been the site of the last battle in the war between Galt and the Khaiem. A war that they had both lost.

The years since had seen his status in his homeland collapse and then slowly be rebuilt. He wasn't a member of the convocation, much less the High Council, but he was still a man of power within Galt. When he sat forward, elbows resting on his knees, Otah could imagine him beside a campfire, working through the final details of the next morning's attack.

"Otah," the former general said, falling into his native tongue, "what is your plan if the vote fails?"

Otah leaned back in his chair.

"I don't see why it should," Otah said. "All respect, but what Sterile did, she did to both of us. Galt is in just as much trouble as the cities of the Khaiem. Your men can't father children. Our women can't bear them. We've gone almost fifteen years without children. The farms are starting to feel the loss. The armies. The trades."

"I know all that," Balasar said, but Otah pressed on.

"Both of our nations are *going* to fall. They've been falling, but we're coming close to the last chance to repair it. We might be able to weather a single lost generation, but if there isn't another after that, Galt will become Eymond's back gardens, and the Khaiem will be eaten by whoever can get to us first. You know that Eymond is only waiting for your army to age into weakness."

"And I know there are other peoples who weren't cursed," Balasar said. "Eymond, certainly. And the Westlands. Bakta. Obar State."

"And there are a handful of half-bred children from matches like those in the coastal cities," Otah said. "They're born to high families that can afford them and hoarded away like treasure. And there are others whose blood was mixed. Some have borne. Might that be enough, do you think?"

Balasar's smile was thin.

"It isn't," he said. "They won't suffice. Children can't be rarer than silk and lapis. So few might as well be none. And why should Eymond or Eddensea or the Westlands send their sons here to make families, when they can wait a few more years and take what they want from a nation of geriatrics? If the Khaiem and the Galts don't become one, we'll both be forgotten. Our land will be taken, our cities will be occupied, and you and I will spend our last years picking wild berries and stealing eggs out of nests, because there won't be farm hands enough to keep us in bread."

"That was my thought as well," Otah said.

"So, no fallback position, eh?"

"None," Otah said. "It was raw hell getting the utkhaiem to agree to the proposal I've brought. I take it the vote is going to fail?"

"The vote is going to fail," Balasar said.

Otah sat forward, his face cradled in his palms. The slight, acrid smell of old ink on his fingers only made the darkness behind his closed lids deeper.

Five months before, he had wrestled the last of the language in his proposed treaty with Galt into shape. A hundred translators from the high families and great trading houses had offered comment and correction, and small wars had been fought in the halls and meeting rooms of his palace at Utani, sometimes resulting in actual blows. Once, memorably, a chair had been thrown and the chief overseer of House Siyanti had suffered a broken finger.

Otah had set forth with an entourage of hundreds—court servants, guards, representatives of every interest from Machi in the far, frozen north to the island city of Chaburi-Tan, where ice was a novelty. The ships had poured into the harbor flying brightly dyed sails and more banners and good-luck pennants than the world had ever seen. For weeks and months, Otah had made his arguments to any man of any power in the bizarre, fluid government of his old enemy. And now, this.

"Can I ask why?" he said, his eyes still closed.

"Pride," Balasar said. Otah heard the sympathy in the softness of his voice. "No matter how prettily you put it, you're talking about putting our daughters in bed under your sons."

"And rather than that, they'll let everything die?" Otah said, looking up at last. Balasar's gaze didn't waver. When the old Galt spoke, it was with a sense of reason and consideration that might almost have made a listener forget that he was one of the men he spoke of.

"You don't understand the depth to which these people have been damaged. Every man on that council was hurt by you in a profound, personal way. Most of them have been steeping in the shame of it since the day it happened. They are less than men, and in their minds, it's because of the Khaiem. If someone had humiliated and crippled you, how would you feel about marrying your Eiah to him?"

"And none of them will see sense?"

"Some will," Balasar said, his gaze steady as stone. "Some of them think what you've suggested is the best hope we have. Only not enough to win the vote."

"So I have a week. How do I convince them?" Otah asked.

Balasar's silence was eloquent.

"Well," Otah said. And then, "Can I offer you some particularly strong distilled wine?"

"I think it's called for," Balasar said. "And you'd mentioned something about a fire against the cold."

Otah hadn't known, when the great panoply of Khaiate ships had come with himself at the front, what his relationship with Balasar Gice would be. Perhaps Balasar had also been uneasy, but if so it had never shown. The former general was an easy man to like, and the pair of them had experienced things—the profound sorrow of commanders seeing their miscalculations lead loyal men to the slaughter, the eggshell diplomacy of a long winter in close quarters with men who had been enemies in autumn, the weight that falls on the shoulders of someone who has changed the face of the world. There were conversations, they discovered, that only the two of them could have. And so they had become at first diplomats, then friends, and now something deeper and more melancholy. Fellow mourners, perhaps, at the sickbeds of their empires.

The night wore on, the moon rising through the clouds, the fire in its grate flickering, dying down to embers before being fed fresh coal and coming to life again. They talked and they laughed, traded jokes and memories. Otah was aware, as he always was, of a distant twinge of guilt at enjoying the company of a man who had killed so many innocents in his war against the Khaiem and the andat. And as always, he tried to set the guilt aside. It was better to forget the ruins of Nantani and the bodies of the Dai-kvo and his poets, the corpses of Otah's own men scattered like scythed wheat and the smell of book paste catching fire. It was better, but it was difficult. He knew he would never wholly succeed.

He was more than half drunk when the conversation turned to his unfinished letter, still on his desk.

"It's pathetic, I suppose," Otah said, "but it's the habit I've made."

"I don't think it's pathetic," Balasar said. "You're keeping faith with her. With what she was to you, and what she still is. That's admirable."

"Tends toward the maudlin, actually," Otah said. "But I think she'd forgive me that. I only wish she could write back. There were things she'd understand in an instant that I doubt I'd ever have come to. If she were here, she'd have found a way to win the vote."

"I can't see that," Balasar said ruefully.

Otah took a pose of correction that spilled a bit of the wine from his bowl.

"She had a different perspective," Otah said. "She was . . . she . . ."

Otah's mind shifted under him, struggling against the fog. There was something. He'd just thought it, and now it was almost gone again. Kiyan-kya, his beloved wife, with her fox-sharp face and her way of smiling. Something about the ways that the world she'd seen were different from his own experience. The way talking with her had been like living twice . . .

"Otah?" Balasar said, and Otah realized it wasn't the first time.

"Forgive me," Otah said, suddenly short of breath. "Balasar-cha, I think . . . will you excuse me? There's something I need to . . ."

Otah put his wine bowl on the desk and walked to the door of his rooms. The corridors of the suite were dark, only the lowest of servants still awake, cleaning the carpets and polishing the latches. Eyes widened and hands fluttered as Otah passed, but he ignored them. The scribes and translators were housed in a separate building across a flagstone square. Otah passed the dry fountain in its center before the thought that had possessed him truly took form. He had to restrain himself from laughing.

The chief scribe was so dead asleep that Otah had to shake the woman twice. When consciousness did come into her eyes, her face went pale. She took a pose of apology that Otah waved away.

"How many of your best calligraphers can work in Galtic?"

"All of them, Most High," the chief scribe said. "It's why I brought them."

"How many? How many can we put to work now, tonight?"

"Ten?" she said as if it were a question.

"Wake them. Get them to their desks. Then I'll need a translator in my apartments. Or two. Best get two. An etiquette master and a trade specialist. Now. Go, now! This won't wait for morning."

On the way back to his rooms, his heart was tripping over, but his mind was clearing, the alcohol burning off in the heat of his plan. Balasar was seated where Otah had left him, an expression of bleary concern on his face.

"Is all well?"

"All's excellent," Otah said. "No, don't go. Stay here, Balasar-cha. I have a letter to write, and I need you."

"What's happened?"

"I can't convince the men on the council. You've said as much. And if I can't talk to the men who wield the power, I'll talk to the women who wield the men. Tell me there's a councilman's wife out there who doesn't want grandchildren. I defy you to."

"I don't understand," Balasar said.

"I need a list of the names of all the councilmen's wives. And the men of the convocation. Theirs too. Perhaps their daughters if . . . Well, those can wait. I'm going to draft an appeal to the women of Galt. If anyone can sway the vote, it's them."

"And you think that would work?" Balasar asked, incredulity in his expression.

In the event, Otah's letter seemed for two full days to have no effect. The letters went out, each sewn with silk thread and stamped with Otah's imperial seal, and no word came back. He attended the ceremonies and meals, the entertainments and committee meetings, his eyes straining for some hint of change like a snow fox waiting for the thaw. It was only on the morning of the third day, just as he was preparing to send a fresh wave of appeals to the daughters of the families of power, that his visitor was announced.

She was perhaps ten years younger than Otah, with hair the gray of dry slate pulled back from an intimidating, well-painted face. The reddening at her eyelids seemed more likely to be a constant feature than a sign of recent weeping. Otah rose from the garden bench and took a pose of welcome simple enough for anyone with even rudimentary training to recognize. His guest replied appropriately and waited for him to invite her to sit in the chair across from him.

"We haven't met," the woman said in her native language. "Not formally."

"But I know your husband," Otah said. He had met with all the members of the High Council many times. Farrer Dasin was among the longest-standing, though not by any means the most powerful. His wife Issandra had been no more than a polite smile and another face among hundreds until now. Otah considered her raised brows and downcast eyes, the set of her mouth and her shoulders. There had been a time when he'd lived by knowing how to interpret such small indications. Perhaps he still did.

"I found your letter quite moving," she said. "Several of us did."

"I am gratified," Otah said, not certain it was quite the correct word.

"Farrer and I have talked about your treaty. The massive shipment of Galtic women to your cities as bed servants to your men, and then hauling back a crop of your excess male population for whatever girls escaped. It isn't a popular scheme."

The brutality of her tone was a gambit, a test. Otah refused to rise to it.

"Those aren't the terms I put in the treaty," he said. "I believe I used the term *wife* rather than *bed servant,* for example. I understand that the men of Galt might find it difficult. It is, however, needed."

He spread his hands, as if in apology. She met his gaze with the bare intellect of a master merchant.

"Yes, it is," she said. "Majesty, I am in a position to deliver a decisive majority in both the High Council and the convocation. It will cost me all the favors I'm owed, and I have been accruing them for thirty years. It will likely take me another thirty to pay back the debt I'm going into for you."

Otah smiled and waited. The cold blue eyes glittered for a moment.

"You might offer your thanks," she said.

"Forgive me," Otah said. "I didn't think you'd finished speaking. I didn't want to interrupt."

The woman nodded, sat back a degree, and folded her hands in her lap. A wasp hummed through the air to hover between them before it darted away into the foliage. He watched her weigh strategies and decide at last on the blunt and straightforward.

"You have a son, I understand?" Issandra Dasin said.

"I do," Otah said.

"Only one."

It was, of course, what he had expected. He had made no provision for Danat's role in the text of the treaty itself, but alliances among the Khaiem had always taken the form of marriages. His son's future had always been a tile in this game, and now that tile was in play.

"Only one," he agreed.

"As it happens, I have a daughter. Ana was three years old when the doom came. She's eighteen now, and . . ."

She frowned. It was the most surprising thing she'd done since her arrival. The stone face shifted; the eyes he could not imagine weeping glistened with unspilled tears. Otah was shocked to have misjudged her so badly.

"She's never held a baby, you know," the woman said. "Hardly ever seen one. At her age, you couldn't pull me out of the nursery with a rope. The way they chuckle when they're small. Ana's never heard that. The way their hair smells . . ."

She took a deep breath, steadying herself. Otah leaned forward, his hand on the woman's wrist.

"I remember," he said softly, and she smiled.

"It's beside the matter," she said.

"It's at the center of the matter," Otah said, falling reflexively into a pose of disagreement. "And it's the part upon which we agree. Forgive me if I am being forward, but you are offering your support for my treaty in exchange for a marriage between our families? Your daughter and my son."

"Yes," she said. "I am."

"There may be others who ask the same price. There is a tradition among my people of the Khai taking several wives. . . ."

"You didn't."

"No," Otah agreed. "I didn't."

The wasp returned, buzzing at Otah's ear. He didn't raise a hand, and the insect landed on the brightly embroidered silk of his sleeve. Issandra Dasin, mother of his son's future wife, leaned forward gracefully and crushed it between her fingers.

"No other wives," she said.

"I would need assurances that the vote would be decisive," Otah said.

"You'll have them. I am a more influential woman than I seem."

Otah looked up. Above them, the sun burned behind a thin scrim of cloud. The same light fell in Utani, spilling through the windows of Danat's palace. If only there were some way to whisper to the sun and have it relay the message to Danat: Are you certain you'll take this risk? A life spent with a woman whom you've never met, whom you may never love?

His son had seen twenty summers and was by all rights a man. Before the great diplomatic horde had left for Galt, they had discussed the likelihood of a bargain of this sort. Danat hadn't hesitated. If it was a price, he'd pay it. His face had been solemn when he'd said it. Solemn and certain, and as ignorant as Otah himself had been at that age. There was nothing else either of them could have said. And nothing different that Otah could do now, except put off the moment for another few breaths by staring up at the blinding sun.

"Very well," Otah said. Then again, "Very well."

"You also have a daughter," the woman said. "The elder child?"

"Yes," Otah said.

"Does she have a claim as heir?"

The image appeared in his mind unbidden: Eiah draped in golden robes and gems woven into her hair as she dressed a patient's wounds. Otah chuckled, then saw the beginnings of offense in his guest's expression. He thought it might not be wise to appear amused at the idea of a woman in power.

"She wouldn't take the job if you begged her," Otah said. "She's a smart, strong-willed woman, but court politics give her a rash."

"But if she changed her mind. Twenty years from now, who can say that her opinions won't have shifted?"

"It wouldn't matter," Otah said. "There is no tradition of empresses. Nor, I think, of women on your own High Council."

She snorted derisively, but Otah saw he had scored his point. She considered for a moment, then with a deep breath allowed herself to relax.

"Well then. It seems we have an agreement."

"Yes," Otah said.

She stood and adopted a pose that she had clearly practiced with a specialist in etiquette. It was in essence a greeting, with nuances of a contract being formed and the informality that came with close relations.

"Welcome to my family, Most High," she said in his language. Otah replied with a pose that accepted the welcome, and if its precise meaning was lost on her, the gist was clear enough.

After she had left, Otah strolled through the gardens, insulated by his rank from everyone he met. The trees seemed straighter than he remembered, the birdsong more delicate. A weariness he only half-knew had been upon him had lifted, and he felt warm and energetic in a way he hadn't in months. He made his way at length to his suite, his rooms, his desk.

Kiyan-kya, it seems something may have gone right after all. . . .

2

>+< Ten years almost to the day before word of Otah's pact with the Galts reached him, Maati Vaupathai had learned of his son's death at the hands of Galtic soldiers. A fugitive only just abandoned by his only companion, he had made his way to the south like a wounded horse finding its way home. It had not been the city itself he had been looking for, but a woman.

Liat Chokavi, owner and overseer of House Kyaan, had received him. Twice, they had been lovers, once as children, and then again just before the war. She had told him of Nayiit's stand, of how he had been cut down protecting the Emperor's son, Danat, as the final assault on Machi began. She spoke with the chalky tones of a woman still in pain. If Maati had held hopes that his once-lover might take him in, they did not survive that conversation. He left her house in agony. He had not spoken to her since.

Two years after that, he took his first student, a woman named Halit. Since then, his life had become a narrow, focused thing. He had remade himself as a teacher, as an agent of hope, as the Dai-kvo of a new age.

It was less glamorous than it sounded.

All that morning he had lain in the small room that was presently his home, squinting at the dirty light that made its way through the oiled-parchment window and thinking of the andat. Thinking of thoughts made flesh, of ideas given human form and volition. Little gods, held tight to existence by the poets who knew them best and, by knowing, bound them. Removing-the-Part-That-Continues, called Seedless. Water-Moving-Down, called Rain or Seaward. Stone-Made-Soft who had no other name. And his own—Corrupting-the-Generative, called Sterile, whom Maati had not quite bound, and who had remade the world.

The lessons he had learned as a boy, the conversations he had had as a man and a poet, they all came back to him dimly. Fragments and moments, insights but not all the steps that had led him there. A mosquito whined in the gloom, and Maati waved it away.

Teaching his girls was like telling the story of his life and finding there were holes in it. He knew things—structures of grammar and metaphor, anecdotes of long-dead poets and the bindings they had made, occult relationships between abstractions like shapes and numbers and the concrete things of the world—without remembering how he'd learned them. Every lecture he gave, he had to half-invent. Every question he answered, he had to solve in his mind to be sure. On one hand, it was as awkward as using a grand palace as a lesson on how to build scaffolding. And on the other, it was making him a better poet and a better teacher than he would ever have been otherwise.

He sat up, the canvas cot groaning as his weight shifted. The room was tiny and quiet; the stone walls wept and smelled of fungus. Half-aware of his surroundings and half in the fine points of ancient grammars, Maati rose and trundled up the short flight of stairs. The warehouse stood empty, the muted daylight and the sound of light rain making their way through the high, narrow windows. His footsteps echoed as he crossed to the makeshift lecture hall.

Benches of old, splintering wood squatted near a length of wall smooth enough to take chalk. The markings of the previous evening still shone white against the stone. Maati squinted at them.

Age was a thief. It took his wind, it made his heart race at odd times, and it stole his sleep. But the worst of all the little indignities was his sight. He hadn't thought about the blessing that decent vision was until his eyes started to fail. It made his head ache a bit, but he found the diagram he'd been thinking of, traced it with his fingertips, considered, and then took a rag from the pail of water beside his little podium and washed the marks away. He could start there tonight, with the four categories of being and their relationships. It was a subtle point, but without it, the girls would never build a decent binding.

There were five of them now: Irit, Ashti Beg, Vanjit, Small Kae, and Large Kae. Half a year ago, there had been seven, but Umnit had tried her binding, failed, and perished. Lisat had given up and left him. Just as well, really. Lisat had been a good-hearted girl, but slow-witted as a cow. And so, five. Or six, if he counted Eiah.

Eiah had been a gift from the gods. She spent her days in the palaces of Utani, playing the daughter of Empire. He knew it was a life she disliked, but she saw to it that food and money found their way to Maati. And being part of the court let her keep an ear out for gossip that would serve them, like a dispute over the ownership of a low-town warehouse that left both claimants barred from visiting the building until judgment was passed. The warehouse had been Maati's for two months now. It was beginning to feel like his own. He dropped the rag back into its pail, found the thick cube of chalk, and started drawing the charts for the evening's lecture. He wondered whether Eiah would be able to join them. She was a good student, when she could slip away from her life at the palace. She asked good questions.

The crude iron bolt turned with a sound like a dropped hammer, and the small, human-size door beside the great sliding walls intended for carts and wagons opened. A woman's figure was silhouetted against the soft gray light. It was neither of the Kaes, but his eyes weren't strong enough to make out features. When she came in, closing the door behind her, he recognized Vanjit by her gait.

"You're early, Vanjit-cha," Maati said, turning back to the wall and chalk.

"I thought I might be able to help," she said. "Are you well, Maati-cha?"

Vanjit had been with him for almost a year now. She had come to his covert school, as all the others had, through a series of happy accidents. Another of his students—Umnit—had fallen into conversation with her, and something had sparked between them. Umnit had presented Vanjit as a candidate to join in their work. Reluctantly, Maati had accepted her.

The girl had a brilliant mind, no question. But she had been a child in Udun, the only one of her family to survive when the Galts had come, and the memory of that slaughter still touched her eyes from time to time. She might laugh and talk and make music, but she bore scars on her body and in her mind. In the months he had spent working with her, Maati had come to realize what had first unnerved him about the girl: of all the students he had taught, she was most like him.

He had lost his family in the war as well—his almost-son Nayiit, his lover Liat, and the man he had once thought his dearest friend. Otah, Emperor of the Khaiem. Otah, favored of the gods, who couldn't fall down without landing on rose petals. They had not all died, but they were all lost to him.

"Maati-cha?" Vanjit said. "Did I say something wrong?"

Maati blinked and took a pose of query.

"You looked angry," she said.

"Nothing," Maati said, shifting the chalk to his other hand and shaking the ache from his fingers. "Nothing, Vanjit-kya, my mind was just wandering. Come, sit. There's nothing that you need to do, but you can keep me company while I get ready."

She sat on the bench, one leg tucked under her. He noticed that her hair and robe were wet from the rain. There was mud on her boots. She'd been walking out in the weather. Maati hesitated, chalk halfway back to the stone.

"Or," he said slowly, "perhaps I should ask if you've been well?"

She smiled and took a pose that dismissed his concerns.

"Bad dream again," she said. "That's all."

"About the baby," Maati said.

"I could feel him inside of me," she said. "I could feel his heartbeat. It's strange. I hate dreaming about him. The nightmares that I'm back in the war—I may scream myself awake, but at least I'm pleased that the dream's ended. When I dream about him, I'm happy. I'm at peace. And then . . ."

She gestured at the childless world around them.

"It's worse, wishing I could sleep and dream and never awake."

Maati's heart rang in sympathy, like a crystal bowl taking up the ringing of a great bell. How many times had he dreamed that Nayiit lived? That the world had not been broken, or, if it had, not by him?

"We'll bring him," Maati said. "Have faith. Every week, we come closer. Once the grammar is built solidly enough, anything will be possible."

"Are we coming closer?" she asked. "Be honest, Maati-cha. Every week we spend on this, I think we're on the edge, and every week, there's more after it."

He tucked the chalk into his sleeve and sat at the girl's side. She leaned forward, and he thought there was something in her expression—not despair and not shame, but something related to both.

"We are coming near, and we are close," he said. "I know it isn't something you can see, but each of you knows more about the andat and the bindings right now than I did after a year with the Dai-kvo. You're smart and dedicated and talented. And together, we can make this work. It sounds terrible, I know, but as soon as Siimat failed her binding and paid the price . . . I won't say I was pleased. I can't say that. She was a brave woman, and she had a wonderful mind. I miss her. But that she and all the others died means we are very close."

Ten bindings, ending in ten failures and ten corpses. His fallen soldiers, Maati thought. His girls who had sacrificed themselves. And here, wet as a canal rat and sad to her bones, Vanjit impatient to make her own try, risk her own life. Maati took her small hand in his own. The girl smiled at the wall.

"This *will* happen," he said.

"I know it," she said, her voice soft. "It's just so hard to wait when the dream keeps coming."

Maati sat with her for a moment, only the tapping of raindrops and the songs of birds between them. He stood, fished the chalk from his sleeve, and went back to the wall.

"If you'd like, you could light a fire in the office grate," Maati said. "We could surprise the others with some fresh tea."

It wasn't called for, but it gave the girl something to do. He squinted at the figure he'd drawn until the lines came into focus. Ah, yes. Four categories of being.

The rain slackened as the others arrived. Large Kae checked the coverings over the windows, careful that no stray light betray their presence, as Irit fluttered sparrowlike lighting the lanterns. Small Kae and Ashti Beg adjusted the seats and benches, the younger woman's light voice contrasting with her elder's dry one.

The scents of wood smoke and tea made their warehouse classroom seem less furtive. Vanjit poured bowls for each of his students as they took their places. The soft light darkened the stone so that the chalk marks almost seemed written on air. Maati took a moment to himself to think of his teachers, of their lectures. He willed himself to become one of their number.

"The world," Maati began, "has two essential structures. There's the physical"—he slapped the stone wall behind him—"and there's the abstract. Two and two are always four, regardless of whether you're talking about grains of sand or racing camels. Twelve could always be broken into two sets of six or three sets of four long before anybody noticed the fact. Abstract structure, you see?"

They bent toward him like flowers toward the sun. Maati saw the hunger in their faces and the set of their shoulders.

"Now," Maati said. "Does the physical require the abstract? Come on. Think! Can you have something physical that doesn't have abstract structure?"

There was a moment's silence.

"Water?" Small Kae asked. "Because if you put two drops of water together with two drops of water, you just get one big drop."

"You're ahead of yourself," Maati said. "That's called the doctrine of least similarity. You're not ready for that. What I mean is this: is there anything real that can't be described by its abstract structure? Any of you? No one has a thought about this? I answered that one correctly before I'd seen ten summers."

"No?" suggested Irit.

"No. How many of you think she's right? Go on! Take a stand about it one way or the other! Good. Yes. Irit's right," Maati said and spat at the floor by his feet. "Everything physical has abstract structure, but not everything abstract need be physical. That's what we're *doing* here. That's the asymmetry that lets the andat exist."

In all their faces, turned to his, there was the same expression. Hunger, he thought, or desperation. Or longing halfway forged into something stronger. It gave him hope.

After the lecture, he made them run through grammar exercises, and then, as the moon rose and the lanterns smoked and the rats came out to chuff and chitter at them from the shadows, they considered the failed bindings of the women who had gone before them. Slowly, they were developing a sense of what it was to capture an andat, to take a thought and translate it into a different form. To give it volition and a human shape. To keep the binding present in your mind for the rest of your life, holding the spirit back from its natural state of nothingness like holding a stone over a well: slip once, and it is gone. Maati could see the knowledge growing in the set of their poses and hear it in the questions they asked. He had almost reached the end of his night's plan when the small door to the street flew open again.

Eiah strode in, her breath labored. She wore a drab cloak over a silk robe rich with all the colors of sunset. The others fell silent. Maati, standing before a wall now covered in white, ghostly notations and graphs, took a pose that expressed his alarm and asked the cause of hers.

"Uncle Maati," she said between gasps, "there's news from Galt. My father."

Maati shifted toward several poses at once, managing none of them. Eiah's expression was grim.

"That's all for tonight," he said. "Come back tomorrow."

He had intended to assign exercises, translation puzzles for them to work in their time away from class. He abandoned the idea and shooed them out the door. All of them left except Eiah, sitting on a low chair in the warehouse office, her face lit by the shifting flames in the grate.

The letters had arrived by fast courier. Against all expectation, the Emperor's benighted mission to Galt had borne fruit. Danat was to be married to a daughter of the Galtic High Council. Terms were being arranged for the transport of a thousand Galtic women of childbearing age to the cities of the Khaiem. Applications would be taken for a thousand men to leave their lives among the cities of the Khaiem and move to Galt. It was, Eiah said, intended to be the first exchange of many.

There were protests and anger in only a few cities. Nantani and Yalakeht, hit hard by the war, were sending petitions of condemnation. In the low towns, the anger burned brighter. Galt was still the enemy, and there were rumors of plots to kill whomever of them dared set foot on Khaiate soil: talk and rumor, drunken rhetoric likely to come to nothing.

The greater mass of the utkhaiem were already gathering their best robes and most garish jewelry in preparation for the journey south to Saraykeht to greet the returning fleet and see this Galtic girl who would one day be Empress. Maati listened to it all, his frown deepening until his mouth began to ache.

"It doesn't change anything," he said. "Otah can sell us to our enemies if he wants. It doesn't affect our work here. Once we have the grammar worked through and the andat back in the world—"

"It changes everything," Eiah said. "Danat is marrying a Galt. The utkhaiem are either going to line up like sailors at a comfort house to follow the example or resist and restart a war we'll never win. Or worse, both. Perhaps he'll divide the utkhaiem so deeply that we turn on each other."

Maati took the tea from the fire and filled his bowl. It was bitter and overbrewed and scalded his tongue. He drank it anyway. Eiah was looking at him, waiting for him to speak. The fire danced over the graying lumps of coal.

"The women's grammar won't matter if the world's already passed us by," Eiah said softly. "If it takes us five more years to capture an andat, there will already be a half-Galt child on its way to becoming Emperor. There will already be half-Galt children born to every family with any power, anywhere in the cities. Will an andat undo that? Will an andat unmake the love these fathers feel for their new children?"

If it's the right one, yes, Maati thought but didn't say. He only stared down into his bowl of tea, watching the dark leaves staining its depth.

"He is remaking the world without us," Eiah went on. "He's giving his official seal to the thought that if a woman can't bear a child, she doesn't matter. He's doing the wrong thing, and once a wound has healed badly, Uncle, it's twice as hard to put right."

Everything she said made sense. The longer it took to bring back the andat, the harder it would be to repair the damage he'd done. And if the world had changed past recognition before his work was complete, he wasn't sure what meaning the effort would have. His jaw ached, and he realized he'd been clenching it.

"So what then?" Maati said, taking a pose that made his words a challenge. "What do you want me to do I'm not doing already?"

Eiah sat back, her head in her hands. She looked like Otah when she did it. It was always unnerving when he caught a glimpse of her father in her. He knew what she would say before she spoke. It was, after all, what she'd been steering him toward from the conversation's start. It was the subject they had been arguing for months.

"Let me try my binding," Eiah said. "You've seen my outlines. You know the structure's sound. If I can capture Returning-to-Natural-Equilibrium . . ."

She let the words trail away. Returning-to-Natural-Equilibrium, called Healing.

"I *don't* know that," Maati said, half-ashamed by the peevishness in his voice. "I only said that I didn't *see* a flaw in them. I never said there wasn't one, only that I couldn't see it. And besides which, it might be too near something that's been done before. I won't lose you because some minor poet in the Second Empire bound Making-Things-Right or Fix-the-Broken or some idiotically broad concept like that."

"Even if they did, they hadn't trained as physicians. I know how flesh works in ways they wouldn't have. I can bring things back the way they're meant to be. The women that Sterile broke, I can make whole again. If we could only—"

"You're too important."

Eiah went silent. When she spoke again, her voice was heavy and bitter.

"You know you've just called all the others unimportant," Eiah said.

"Not unimportant," Maati said. "They're all important. They only aren't all irreplaceable. Wait, Eiah-kya. Be patient. Once we have a grammar that we know can work, I won't stop you. But let someone else be first."

"There isn't time," Eiah said. "We have a handful of months before the trade starts in earnest. Maybe a year."

"Then we'll find a way to move them faster," Maati said.

The question of how that might be done, however, haunted him the rest of the night. He lay on his cot, the night candle hissing almost inaudibly and casting its misty light on the stone ceiling. The women, his students, had all retired to what quarters Eiah had quietly arranged for them.

Eiah herself had gone back to the palaces of the Emperor, the great structures dedicated to Otah, while Maati lay in the near-dark under a warehouse, sleep eluding him and his mind gnawing at questions of time.

Maati's father had died younger than he was now. Maati had been an aspiring poet at the village of the Dai-kvo at the time. When the word came, he had not seen the man in something near a decade. The news had stung less than he would have anticipated, not a fresh loss so much as the reminder of one already suffered. A slowing of blood had taken the man, the message said, and Maati had never looked into the matter more deeply. Lately he'd found himself wondering whether his father had done all that he'd wished, if the son he'd given over to the poets had made him proud, what regrets had marked that last illness.

The candle had almost burned itself to nothing when he gave up any hope of sleep. Outside, songbirds were greeting the still-invisible dawn, but Maati took no joy in them. He lit a fresh candle and sat on the smooth-worn stone steps and considered the small wooden box that carried the only two irreplaceable things he owned. One was a painting he had done from memory of Nayiit Chokavi, the son he should have had, the child he had helped, however briefly, to raise, the boy whom Otah—Otah to whom no rules applied—had brought into the world in Saraykeht and taken out of it in Machi. The other was a book bound in black leather.

He opened the cover and considered the first page, squinting to bring the letters clear. He could not help but think of another book—that one brown—which had been his gift from Heshai-kvo and Seedless. Heshai's handwriting had been clearer than Maati's own, his gift for language more profound.

> I, Maati Vaupathai, am one of the two men remaining in the world who has wielded the power of the andat. As the references from which I myself learned are lost, I shall endeavor to record here what I know of grammar and of the forms of thought by which the andat may be bound and the abstract made physical. And, with that, my own profound error from which the world is still suffering.

Half-reading, he flipped through the pages, caught occasionally by a particular turn of phrase of which he was fond or tripped by a diagram or metaphor that was still not to his best liking. Though his eyes strained, he could still read what he'd written, and when the ink seemed to blur, he had the memory of what he had put there. He reached the blank pages sooner than he expected, and sat on his stairs, fingertips moving over the smooth paper with a sound like skin against skin. There was so much to say, so many things he'd thought and considered. Often, he would come back from a particularly good lecture to his students full of fire and intentions, prepared to write a fresh section. Sometimes his energy lasted long enough to do so. Sometimes not.

It will be a sad legacy to die with this half-finished, he thought as he let the cover close.

He needed a real school, the school needed a teacher, and he himself could manage only so much. There wasn't time to lecture all his students and write his manual and slink like a criminal through the dark corners of the Empire. If he'd been younger, perhaps—fifty, or better yet forty years old—he might have made the attempt, but not now. And with this mad scheme of Otah's, time had grown even dearer.

"Maati-cha?"

Maati blinked. Vanjit came toward him, her steps tentative. He tucked his book into its box and took a pose of welcome.

"The door wasn't bolted," she said. "I was afraid something had happened?"

"No," Maati said, rising and hoisting himself up the stairs. "I forgot it last night. An old man getting older is all."

The girl took a pose that was both an acceptance and a denial. She looked exhausted, and Maati suspected there were dark smudges under his own eyes to match hers. The scent of eggs and beef caught his attention. A small lacquer box hung at Vanjit's side.

"Ah," Maati said. "It that what I hope it is?"

She smiled at that. The girl did have a pleasant smile, when she used it. The eggs were fresh; whipped and steamed in bright orange blocks. The beef was rich and moist. Vanjit sat beside him in the echoing, empty space of the warehouse as the morning light pressed in at the high, narrow windows, blue then yellow then gold. They talked about nothing important: the wayhouse where she was staying, his annoyance with his failing eyes, the merits of their present warehouse as compared to the half-dozen other places where Maati had taken up his chalk. Vanjit asked him questions that built on what they'd discussed the night before: How did the different forms of being relate to time? How did a number exist differently than an apple or a man? Or a child?

Maati found himself holding forth on matters of the andat and the poets, his time with the Dai-kvo, and even before that at the school. Vanjit sat still, her gaze on him, and drank his words like water.

She had lost her family when she was barely six years old. Her mother, father, younger sister, and two older brothers cut down by the gale of Galtic blades. The pain of it had faded, perhaps. It had never gone. Maati felt, as they sat together, that perhaps she had begun, however imperfectly, to build a new family. Perhaps she would have sat at her true father's knee, listening to him with this same intensity. Perhaps Nayiit would have treated him with the same attention that Vanjit did now. Or perhaps their shared hunger belonged to people who had lost the first object of their love.

By the time Eiah and the others arrived in the late morning, Maati had reached the decision that he'd fought against the whole night. He took Eiah aside as soon as she came in.

"I have need of you," Maati said. "How much can you spirit away without our being noticed? We'll need food and clothing and tools. Lots of tools. And if there's a servant or slave you can trust . . ."

"There isn't," Eiah said. "But things are in disarray right now. Half the court in Nantani would chew their tongues out before offering hospitality to a Galt. The other half are whipped to a froth trying to get to Saraykeht before the rest. A few wagonloads here and there would be easy to overlook."

Maati nodded, more than half to himself. Eiah took a pose of query.

"You're going to build me a school. I know where there's one to be had, and with the others helping, it shouldn't take terribly long to have it in order. And we need a teacher."

"We have a teacher, Maati-kya," Eiah said.

Maati didn't answer, and after a moment, Eiah looked down.

"Cehmai?" she asked.

"He's the only other living poet. The only one who's truly held one of the andat. He could do more, I suspect, than I can manage."

"I thought you two had fallen out?"

"I don't like his wife," Maati said sourly. "But I have to try. The two of us agreed on a way to find one another, if the need arose. I can hope he's kept to it better than I have."

"I'll come with you."

"No," Maati said, putting a hand on Eiah's shoulder. "I need you to prepare things for us. There's a place—I'll draw you a map to it. The Galts attacked it in the war, killed everyone, but even if they dropped bodies down the well, the water'll be fresh again by now. It's off the high road between Pathai and Nantani. . . ."

"That school?" Eiah said. "The place they sent the boys to train as poets? That's where you want to go?"

"Yes," Maati said. "It's out of the way, it's built for itinerant poets, and there may be something there—some book or scroll or engravings on the walls—that the twice-damned Galts overlooked. Regardless, it's where it all began. It's where we are going to take it all back."

3

>+< The voyage returning Otah to the cities of the Khaiem took
     weeks to prepare, and if the ships that had left Saraykeht all those
months before had looked like an invading fleet, the ones returning
were a city built on the water. The high-masted Galtic ships with their
great billowing sails dyed red and blue and gold took to the sea by the
dozens. Every great family of Galt seemed bent on sending a ship greater
than the others. The ships of the utkhaiem—lacquered and delicate and
low to the water—seemed small and awkward beside these, their
newest seafaring cousins. Birds circled above them, screaming confusion
as if a part of the coast itself had set out for foreign lands. The trees and
hills of Otah's onetime enemies fell away behind them. That first night,
the torches and lanterns made the sea appear as full of stars as the sky.

One of the small gifts the gods had granted Otah was a fondness for
travel by ship. The shifting of the deck under his feet, the vast scent of
the ocean, the call of the gulls were like visiting a place he had once lived.
He stood at the prow of the great Galtic ship given him by the High
Council for his journey home and looked out at the rising sun.

He had spent years in the eastern islands as a boy. He'd been a middling fisherman, a better midwife's assistant, a good sailor. He had come
close to marrying an island woman, and still bore the first half of the marriage tattoo on his breast. The ink had faded and spread over the years as
if he were a parchment dropped in water. With the slap of waves against
wood, the salt-laden air, the morning light dancing gold and rose on the
water, he remembered those days.

This late in the morning, he would already have cast his nets. His fingers would have been numbed by the cold. He would have been eating
the traditional breakfast of fish paste and nuts from an earthenware jar.
The men he had known would be doing the same today, those who were
still alive. In another life, another world, he might be doing it still.

He had lived so many lives: half-starved street child; petty thief; seafront laborer; fisherman; assistant midwife; courier; Khai; husband; father; war leader; emperor. Put in a line that way, he could see how another person might imagine his life to be an unending upward spiral, but it didn't feel that way to him. He had done what he'd had to at the time. One thing had led to another. A man without particular ambition had been placed atop the world, and likewise the world had been placed atop him. And against all probability, he found himself here, wearing the richest robes in the cities, with a private cabin larger than some boats he'd worked, and thinking fondly of fish paste and nuts.

Lost in thought, he heard the little ship's boat hail—a booming voice speaking Galtic words—before he knew it was approaching. The watchman of his own vessel replied, and then the landsman's chair descended. Otah watched idly as a man in the colors of House Dasin was winched up, swung over, and lowered to the deck. A knot of Otah's own clerks and servants formed around the newcomer. Otah pulled his hands up into his sleeves and made his way back.

The boy was a servant of some sort—the Galts had a system of gradation that Otah hadn't bothered to memorize—with hair the color of beach sand and a greenish tint to his face. Seeing Otah, the servant took a pose of abject obeisance poorly.

"Most High," he said, his words heavily inflected, "Councilman Dasin sends his regards. He and his wife extend the invitation to a dinner and concert aboard the *Avenger* tomorrow evening."

The boy gulped and looked down. There had, no doubt, been a more formal and flowery speech planned. Nausea led to brevity. Otah glanced at his Master of Tides, a youngish woman with a face like a hatchet and a mind for detail that would have served her in any trade. She took a pose that deferred to Otah's judgment, gave permission, and offered to make excuse all with a single gesture. Dasin's servant wouldn't have seen a third of her meanings. Otah glanced over at the shining water. The sun's angle had already shifted, the light already changed its colors and the colors of the ocean that bore them. He allowed himself a small sigh.

Even here there would be no escape from it. Etiquette and court politics, parties and private audiences, favors asked and given. There was no end of it because of course there wasn't. No more than a farmer could stop planting fields, a fisherman stop casting nets, a tradesman close up warehouses and stalls and spend long days singing in teahouses or soaking in baths.

"I should be pleased," he said. "Please convey my gratitude to Farrer-cha and his family."

The boy bowed his thanks rather than make a formal pose, then, blushing, adopted a pose of gratitude and retreated back to the landsman's chair. With a great shouting and the creak of wood and leather, the chair rose, swung out over the water, and descended. Otah watched the boy vanish over the rail, but didn't see him safely to the boat. The invitation was a reminder of all that waited for him in his cabin below decks. Otah took a long, deep breath, feeling the salt and the sunlight in his lungs, and descended to the endless business of Empire.

Letters had arrived from Yalakeht outlining a conspiracy by three of the high families of the utkhaiem still bitter from the war to claim independence and name a Khai Yalakeht rather than acknowledge a Galtic empress. Chaburi-Tan had suffered another attack by pirates. Though the invaders had been driven off, it was becoming clear that the Westlands mercenary company hired to protect the city was also in negotiation with the raiders; the city's economy was on the edge of collapse.

There was some positive news from the palaces at Utani. Danat wrote that the low farms around Pathai, Utani, and Lachi were all showing a good crop, and the cattle plague they'd feared had come to nothing, so those three cities, at least, wouldn't be starving for at least the next year.

Otah read until the servants brought his midday meal, then again for two and a half hands. He slept after that in a suspended cot whose oiled chains shifted with the rocking ship but never let out so much as a whisper. He woke with the low sunlight of evening sloping in the cabin window and the dull thunder of feet above him announcing the change of watch as clearly as the drum and flute. He lay there for a moment, his mind pleasantly emptied by his rest, then swung his legs over, dropped to the deck, and composed two of the seven letters he would send ahead of the massive, celebratory fleet.

WHEN, THE NEXT EVENING, HIS MASTER OF TIDES SENT TO REMIND HIM OF the engagement he'd agreed to, Otah had indeed forgotten it. He allowed servants to dress him in robes of emerald silk and cloth of gold, his long, white hair to be bound back. His temples were anointed with oils smelling of lavender and sandalwood. Decades now he had been Emperor or else Khai Machi, and the exercise still struck him as ridiculous. He had been slow to understand the value of ceremony and tradition. He still wasn't entirely convinced.

The boat that bore him and his retinue across to the Dasins' ship, the *Avenger*, was festooned with flowers and torches. Blossoms fell into the water, floating there with the reflections of flame. Otah stood, watching as the oarsmen pulled him toward the great warship. His footing was as sure as a seaman's, and he was secretly proud of the fact. The high members of the utkhaiem who had joined him—Auna Tiyan, Piyat Saya, and old Adaut Kamau—all kept to their benches. The *Avenger* itself glowed with candlelight, the effect lessened by the last remnant of the glorious sunset behind it. When full darkness came, the ship would look like something from a children's story. Otah tried to appreciate it for what it would become.

The landsman's chair took each of them up in turn, Otah last out of respect for his rank. The deck of the *Avenger* was as perfect and controlled as any palace ballroom, any Khaiate garden, any high chamber of the Galts. Chairs that seemed made of silver filigree and breath were scattered over the fresh-scrubbed boards in patterns that looked both careless and perfect. Musicians played reed organ and harp, and a small chorus of singers sat in the rigging, as if the ship itself had joined the song. Swinging down in the landsman's chair, Otah saw half-a-dozen men he knew, including, his face upturned and amused, Balasar Gice.

Farrer Dasin stood with his wife Issandra and the young woman—the girl—Ana. Otah let himself be drawn up from the chair by his servants, and stepped forward to his hosts. Farrer stood stiff as cast iron, his smile never reaching his eyes. Issandra's eyes still had the reddened rims that Otah recalled, but there was also pleasure there. And her daughter . . .

Ana Dasin, the Galt who would one day be Empress of the Khaiem, reminded Otah of a rabbit. Her huge, brown eyes and small mouth looked perpetually startled. She wore a gown of blue as pale as a robin's egg that didn't fit her complexion and a necklace of raw gold that did. She would have seemed meek, except that there was something of her mother in the line of her jaw and the set of her shoulders.

All he knew of her had come from court gossip, Balasar Gice's comments, and the trade of formal documents that had flowed by the crate once the agreements were made. It was difficult to believe that this was the girl who had beaten her own tutor at numbers or written a private book of etiquette that had been the scandal of its season. She was said to have ridden horses from the age of four; she was said to have insulted the son of an ambassador from Eddensea to his face and gone on to make her case so clearly that the insulted boy had offered apology. She had climbed out windows on ropes made from stripped tapestry, had climbed the walls of the palaces of Acton dressed as an urchin boy, had broken the hearts of men twice her age. Or, again, perhaps she had not. He had heard a great deal about her, and knew nothing he could count as truth. It was to her he made his first greeting.

"Ana-cha," he said. "I hope I find you well."

"Thank you, Most High," she said, her voice so soft, Otah half-wondered whether he'd understood. "And you also."

"Emperor," Farrer Dasin said in his own language.

"Councilman Dasin," Otah said. "You are kind to invite me."

Farrer's nod made it clear that he would have preferred not to. The singers above them reached the end of one song, paused, and launched into another. Issandra stepped forward smiling and rested her hand on Otah's arm.

"Forgive my husband," she said. "He was never fond of shipboard life. And he spent seven years as a sailor."

"I hadn't known that," Otah said.

"Fighting Eymond," the councilman said. "Sank twelve of their ships. Burned their harbor at Cathir."

Otah smiled and nodded. He wondered how his own history as a fisherman would be received if he shared it now. He chose to leave the subject behind.

"The weather is treating us gently," Otah said. "We will be in Saraykeht before summer's end."

He could see in all their faces that it had been the wrong thing. The father's jaw tightened, his nostrils flared. The mother's smile lost its sharp corners and her eyes grew sad. Ana looked away.

"Come see what they've done with the kitchens, Most High," Issandra said. "It's really quite remarkable."

After a short tour of the ship, Issandra released him, and Otah made his way to the dais that was intended for him. Other guests arrived from Galtic ships and the utkhaiem, each new person greeting the councilman and his family, and then coming to Otah. He had expected to see a division among them: the Galts resentful and full of barely controlled rage much like Farrer Dasin, and Otah's own people pleased at the prospects that his treaty opened for them. Instead, he saw as the guests came and went, as the banquet was served, as priests of Galt intoned their celebratory rites, that opinions were more varied and more complex.

At the opening ceremony, the divisions were clear. Here, the robes of the Khaiem, there the tunics and gowns of the Galts. But very quickly, the people on the deck began to shift. Small groups fell into discussion, often no more than two or three people. Otah's practiced eye could pick out the testing smile and almost flirtatious laughter of men on the verge of negotiation. And as the evening progressed—candles burning down and being replaced, slow courses of wine and fish and meat and pastry making their way from the very cleverly built kitchens to the gently shifting deck—as many Galts as utkhaiem had the glint in their eyes that spoke of sensed opportunity. Larger groups formed and broke apart, the proportions of their two nations seeming almost even. Otah felt as if he'd stirred a muddy pool and was now seeing the first outlines of the new forms that it might take.

And yet, some groups were unmoved. Two clusters of Galts never budged or admitted in anyone wearing robes, but also a fair-sized clot of people of the cities of the Khaiem sat near the far rail, their backs to the celebration, their conversation almost pointedly relying on court poses too subtle for foreigners to follow.

Women, Otah noted. The people of his nation whose anger was clearest in their bodies and speech tended to be women. He thought of Eiah, and cool melancholy touched his heart. Trafficking in wombs, she would have called it. To her, this agreement would be the clearest and most nearly final statement that what mattered about the women of the cities—about his own daughter—was whether they could bear. He could hear her voice saying it, could see the pain in the way she held her chin. He murmured his counterarguments, as if she were there, as if she could hear him.

It wasn't a turning away, only an acknowledgment of what they all knew. The woman of the Khaiem were just as clever, just as strong, just as important as they had ever been. The brokering of marriage—and yes, specifically marriage bent on producing children—was no more an attack on Eiah and her generation than building city militias or hiring mercenary companies or any of the other things he had done to hold the cities safe had been.

It sounded patronizing, even to him.

There had to be some way, he thought, to honor and respect the pain and the loss that they had suffered without forfeiting the future. He remembered Kiyan warning him that some women—not all, but some— who could not bear children went mad from longing. She told stories of babies being stolen, and of pregnant women killed and the babes taken from their dying wombs.

Wanting could be a sickness, his wife had said. He remembered the night she'd said it, where the lantern had been, how the air had smelled of burning oil and pine boughs. He remembered his daughter's expression at hearing the phrase, like she'd found expression for something she'd always known, and his own sense of dread. Kiyan had tried to warn him of something, and it had to do with the backs of the people now at the rails, turned away from the Galts and the negotiated future forming behind them. Eiah had known. Otah felt he had still only half-grasped it. Farrer Dasin, he thought, might see it more clearly.

"It appears to be going quite well, wouldn't you say, Most High?"

Balasar Gice stood beside the dais, his hands in a pose of greeting. The cool night air or else the wine had touched his cheeks with red.

"Does it? I hope so," Otah said, smoothing away his darker thoughts. "I think there are more trade agreements than wars brewing tonight. It's hard to know."

"There's hope," Balasar said. And then, his voice growing reflective, "There's hope, and that's actually quite new. I hadn't realized it had become quite such a rare thing, these last few years."

"How nice," Otah said more sharply than he'd intended. Balasar looked at him more closely, and Otah waved the concern away. "I'm old and tired. And I've eaten more Galtic food than I could have wanted in a lifetime. It's astounding you people ever got up from your tables."

"You aren't expected to finish every dish," Balasar said. "Ah, I think the entertainment has begun."

Otah looked up. Servants and sailors were silently moving across the deck like a wind over the water. The glow of candles lessened and the scent of spent wicks filled the air as a stage appeared as if conjured across the deck from Otah's dais. The singers that had hung from the rigging had apparently made their way down, because they rose now, taking their places. Servants placed three more chairs on the dais at Otah's side, and Councilman Dasin and his family took their seats. Farrer smelled prodigiously of distilled wine and sat the farthest from him, his wife close at his side, leaving Ana nearest to Otah.

The singers bowed their heads for a moment, then the low sounds of their voices began to swell. Otah closed his eyes. It was a song he knew— a court dance from the Second Empire. The harmonies were perfect and rich, sorrowful and joyous. This, he understood, was a gift. Galtic voices raised in a song of an empire that was not their own. He let himself be carried by it, and when the voices fell again, the last throbbing notes fading to silence, he was among the first to applaud. Otah was surprised to find tears in his eyes.

Ana Dasin, at his side, was also weeping. When he met her eyes, she looked down, said something he couldn't hear, and walked briskly away. He watched her descend the stairs below decks as the singers began another, more boisterous song. Otah's gaze flickered to Issandra. In the dim light, the subtle signs of age were softened. He saw for a moment who she had been as a younger woman. She met his eyes with a profound weariness. Farrer had his hand on her arm, holding her gently to him, though the man's face remained turned away. Otah wondered, not for the first time, what brokering this agreement had cost Issandra Dasin.

He glanced at the stairs down which her daughter had vanished, and then back, his hands shifting into a pose that made an implicit offer. Issandra raised an eyebrow, a half-smile making a dimple in one cheek. Otah tugged at his robes, straightening the lines, and stepped carefully down from the dais. The girl Ana would be his daughter too, soon enough. If her true mother and father weren't placed to speak with her in her distress, perhaps it was time that Otah did.

Below decks, the Galtic ship was as cramped and close and ripe with the scent of tightly quartered humanity as any ship Otah had sailed with. Under normal circumstances, the deck now peopled with the guests of the Dasin family would have given room to a full watch of sailors. Instead, most were lurking in the tiny rooms, waiting for the songs to end and their own turn with fresh air to come. Still, Otah, Emperor of the Khaiem, found a way cleared for him, conversations stopping when he came in view. He made his way forward, squinting into the darkness for a glimpse of the rabbit-faced girl.

Galtic design divided the cargo hold in sections, and it was in one of these dark chambers that he heard the girl's voice. Crates and boxes loomed above him to either side, the binding ropes creaking gently with the rolling ship. Rats chattered and complained. And there, hunched over as if she were protecting something pressed to her belly, sat Ana Dasin.

"Excuse me," Otah said. "I don't mean to intrude, but . . . may I sit?"

Ana looked up at him. Her dark eyes shone in the dim light. Her nod was so faint it might almost have been the movement of the ship. Otah stepped carefully over the rough board, hitched his robes up to his shins, and sat at the girl's side. They were silent. Above them, the singers struck a complex rhythm, like jugglers tossing pins between them. Otah sighed.

"I know this isn't easy for you," he said.

"What isn't, Most High?"

"Otah. Please, my name is Otah. You can call me that. I mean all of this. Being uprooted, married off to a man you've never met in a city you've never been to."

"It's what's expected of me," she said.

"Yes, I know, but . . . it isn't really fair."

"No," she said, her voice suddenly hard. "It isn't."

Otah clasped his hands, fingers laced together.

"He isn't a bad man, my son," Otah said. "He's clever and he's strong, and he cares about people. He feels deeply. He's probably a better man than I was at his age."

"Forgive me, Most High," Ana Dasin said. "I don't know what you want me to say."

"Nothing. Nothing in particular. Only know that this life that we've forced on you . . . it might have some redeeming qualities. The gods all know the life I've had wasn't the one I expected, either. We do what we have to do. In my ways, I'm as constrained by it as you are."

She looked at him as if he were speaking a language she hadn't heard before. Otah shook his head.

"It's nothing, Ana-cha," he said. "Only know that I know how hard this time is, and it will get better. If you allow room for it, this new life might even surprise you."

The girl was quiet for a moment, her brow furrowed. She shook her head.

"Thank you?" she said.

Otah chuckled ruefully.

"I'm not doing a particularly good job of this, am I?" he said.

"I don't know," Ana Dasin said after a pause. Her tone carried the shielded contempt of an adolescent for her elders. "I don't know what you're doing."

Making his way back through the crowded belly of the ship, Otah wondered what he had thought he would say to a Galtic girl who had seen forty-five fewer summers than himself. He had expected to offer some kind of wisdom, some variety of comfort, and instead it had been like trying to hold a conversation with a cat. Who would have thought a man could be as old as he was, wield the power of empire, and still be so naïve as to think his heart would be explicable to an eighteen-year-old girl?

And, of course, as he reached the plank stairway that led up, he found what he wished he had said. He should have said that he knew what courage it took to face sacrifice. He should have said that he knew her suffering was real, and that it was in a noble cause. It made them alike, the Emperor and the Empress-to-be, that they compromised in order to make the lives of uncountable strangers better.

More than that, he should have encouraged her to speak, and he should have listened.

An approving roar came from the deck above him. A reed organ hummed and sang, flute and drum following a heartbeat later. Otah hesitated and turned back. He would try again. At worst, the girl would think he was ridiculous, and she likely already did that.

As he drew near the hold, he heard her weeping again, her voice straining at words he couldn't make out. A man's voice answered, not her father's. Otah hesitated, then quietly stepped forward.

In the gloom, Ana Dasin knelt, her arms around a young man. The boy, whoever he was, wore the work clothes of a sailor, but his arms were thin and his skin was as pale as the girl's. He returned her embrace, his arms finding their way around her as if through long acquaintance; his tear-streaked face nuzzled her hair. Ana Dasin stroked the boy's head, murmuring reassurances.

Ah, Otah thought as he stepped back, unnoticed. That's how it is.

Above deck, he smiled and nodded at Issandra and pretended to turn his attention back to the music. He wondered how many other sacrifices he had demanded in order to remake the world according to his vision, how many other lovers would be parted to further his little scheme to save two empires. He would likely never know the full price of it. As if in answer, the candles guttered in the breeze, the reed organ took a mournful turn, and the sea through which they sailed grew darker.

4

>+< The midday sun beat down on the lush green; gnats and flies filled the air. The river—not the Qiit proper but one of its tributaries—threaded its way south like a snake. Maati tied his mule under the wide leaves of a catalpa and squatted down on a likely-looking boulder. Pulling a pouch of raisins and seeds from his sleeve, he looked out over the summer. The wild trees, the rough wagon track he'd followed from the farmers' low town to the northwest, the cultivated fields to the south.

A cluster of small farms made a loose community here, raising goats and millet and, near the water, rice. The land between the cities was dotted with low communities like this one: the rural roots that fed the great, blossoming cities of the Khaiem. The accents were rougher here, the effete taint of a high court as foreign as another language. Men might be born, grow, love, marry, and die without ever traveling more than a day's walk, birthing bed and grave marker no more distant than a thrown pebble.

And one of those fields with its ripe green grasses had been plowed by the only other man in all the world who knew how to bind the andat. Maati took a mouthful of raisins and chewed slowly, thinking.

Leaving the warehouse outside Utani had proven harder than he had expected. For over a decade, he had been rootless, moving from one city or town to another, living in the shadows. One more journey—and this one heading south into the summer cities—hadn't seemed to signify anything more than a few weeks' time and, of course, the errand itself. But somewhere in the years since the Galtic invasion, Maati had grown accustomed to traveling with companions, and as he and his swaybacked pack mule had made their slow way down the tracks and low-town roads, he had felt their absence.

The world had changed in the years he had been walking through it. Having no one there to talk with forced his mind back in on itself, and the nature of the changes he saw were more disturbing than he'd thought they would be.

Many were things he had expected. The cities and towns had grown quieter, undisturbed by the laughter and games of children. The people were older, grayer. The streets felt too big, like the robes of a once-hale man who had grown thin with illness or age. And the scars of the war itself—the burned towns already half-reclaimed by foxes and saplings, the bright green swath from Utani all the way down to ruined Nantani on the southern coast where once an army had passed—had faded, but they had not disappeared.

The distrust of the foreign was driven deep into the flesh here. He had heard stories of Westlands women coming to marry among the low towns, thinking their wombs would make them of greater value here than in their own lands. Instead, they were recognized as a slower kind of invasion. Driven out with threats or stones. The men who had had the temerity to marry outside their own kind punished in ways to rival the prices paid by failed poets. Joints broken, drowned in night pots, necks snapped, and bodies thrown into creeks to drown in half a hand's depth of water.

And yet, the stories might only be stories. The more Maati traveled, the less certain he was.

Twice, great belching steam wagons had passed him on the trail. The men at the controls had been locals, but the machines themselves were Galtic, remnants of the war. Once he had seen plumes of smoke and steam rising from the river itself, a flat barge sitting low to the water and driven by the same chuffing, tarnished bulb as the wagons. Even the fields below him now were cultivated in a pattern he had never seen before the Galts came. Perhaps Otah's betrayal of the cities colored all of Maati's perceptions now, but it felt as if the Galts were invading again, only slowly this time, burrowing under the ground and changing all they touched in small, insidious ways.

Something tickled his arm. Maati plucked out the tick and cracked it between his thumbnails. He was wasting time. His feet ached from walking and his robe stuck to his back and legs, but the sooner this meeting happened, the sooner he would know where he stood. He emptied the last of the seeds into his hand, ate them, then put the pouch back in his sleeve and untied his mule.

Seven years before, he and Cehmai had parted for the last time at a wayhouse three days' walk northwest of the farms and the river and catalpa-shaded hill. It had not been an entirely friendly parting, but they had agreed to leave letters of their whereabouts at that house, should the need ever arise to find each other.

Maati had found the place easily. In the intervening years, the kitchens had burned, and the two huge trees in the courtyard. The boy who stabled the horses had grown to be a man. The bricks that had been brown and yellow had been painted white and blue. And the box they had paid the keeper to hold for them had a letter in it, sewn and sealed, with ciphered directions that would lead to the farmhouse Cehmai had taken under his new false name. Jadit Noygu.

Jadit Noygu, and his wife Sian.

Maati took the letter out again, consulting the deciphered text he'd marked in between the lines written in Cehmai's clean, clear hand. Forward down the track until he passed the ruin of an old mill, then the first east-turning pathway, and half a hand's walk to a low mud-and-straw farmhouse with a brick cistern in front. Maati clucked at the mule and resumed his walk.

He arrived in the heat of the afternoon; even the shade beneath the trees sweltered. Maati helped himself to a bowl of water from the cistern, and then another bowl for the mule. No one came out to greet him, but the shutters on the windows looked recently painted and the track that led around the side of the house was well-tended. There was no sense that the farm stood empty. Maati made his way toward the back.

A small herd of goats bleated at him from their pen, the disturbing, clever eyes considering him with as little joy as he had for them. The low sound of whistling came to him from a tall, narrow building set apart from both house and pen. A slaughterhouse.

He stepped into the doorway, blocking the light. The air was thick with smoke to drive the flies away. The body of the sacrificed goat hung from a hook, buckets of blood and entrails at the butcher's feet. The butcher turned. Her hands were crimson, her leather apron sodden with blood. A hooked knife flashed in her hand.

She was not the only reason that Maati and Cehmai had parted company, but she would have been sufficient. Idaan Machi, outcast sister to the Emperor. As a girl no older than Vanjit was now, Idaan had plotted the slaughter of her own family in a bloody-minded attempt to win Machi for herself and her husband. Otah had come near to being executed for her crimes, Cehmai had been seduced and used by her, and Maati still had a thick scar on his belly where her assassin had tried to gut him. Otah, for reasons that passed beyond Maati's understanding, had spared the murderess. Even less comprehensible, Cehmai had found her, and in their shared exile, they had once again become lovers. Only Maati still saw her for what she was.

Age had thickened her. Her hair, tied back in a ferocious knot, was more gray than black. Her long, northern face showed curiosity, then surprise, then for less than a heartbeat something like contempt.

"You'll want to see him, then," said Otah's exiled sister: the woman who had once set an assassin to kill Maati. Who had blamed Otah for the murders she and her ambitious lover had committed.

She sank the gory knife into the dead animal's side, setting the corpse swinging, and walked forward.

"Follow me," she said.

"Tell me where to find him," Maati said. "I can just as well . . ."

"The dogs don't know you," Idaan said. "*Follow* me."

Once Maati saw the dogs—five wide-jawed beasts as big as ponies, lazing in the rich dirt at the back of the house—he was glad she was there to guide him. She walked with a strong gait, leading him past the house, past a low barn where chickens scattered and complained, to a wide, low field of grass, its black soil under half an inch of water. At the far side of the field, a thin figure stood. He wore the canvas trousers of a workman and a rag the color of old blood around his head. By the time the man's face had ceased to be a leather-colored blur, they were almost upon him. There were the bright, boyish eyes, the serious mouth. The sun had coarsened his skin and complicated the corners of his eyes. He smiled and took a pose of greeting appropriate for one master of their arcane trade to another. Idaan snorted, turned, and walked back toward the slaughterhouse, leaving them alone.

"It's a dry year," Cehmai said. "You wouldn't know it, but it's a dry year. The last two crops, I was afraid that they'd mold in the field. This one, I'm out here every other week, opening the ditch gates."

"I need your help, Cehmai-cha," Maati said.

The man nodded, squinted out over the field as if judging something Maati couldn't see, and sighed.

"Of course you do," Cehmai said. "Come on, then. Walk with me."

The fields were not the largest Maati had seen, and reminded him of the gardens he'd worked as a child in the school. The dark soil of the river-fed lowlands was unlike the dry, pale soil of the high plains outside Pathai, but the scent of wet earth, the buzzing of small insects, the warmth of the high sun, and the subtle cool rising from the water all echoed moments of his childhood. Not all those memories were harsh. For a moment, he imagined slipping off his sandals and sinking his toes into the mud.

As they walked, he told Cehmai all he'd been doing in the years since they'd met. The idea of a women's grammar was one they had discussed before, so it required little more than to remind him of it. He outlined the progress he had made, the insights that had taken the project far enough to begin the experimental bindings. They paused under the broad shade of a catalpa and Cehmai shared a light meal of dried cherries and dense honey bread while Maati recounted his losses.

He did not mention Eiah or the school. Not yet. Not until he knew better which way his old colleague's opinions fell.

Cehmai listened, nodding on occasion. He asked few questions, but those he did were to the point and well-considered. Maati felt himself falling into familiar habits of conversation. When, three hands later, Cehmai rose and led the way back to the river gate, it was almost as if the years had not passed. They were the only two people in the world who shared the knowledge of the andat and the Dai-kvo. They had suffered through the long, painful nights of the war, working to fashion a binding that might save them. They had lived through the long, bitter winter of their failure in the caves north of Machi. If it had not made them friends, they were at least intimates. Maati found himself outlining the binding of Returning-to-Natural-Equilibrium as Cehmai turned the rough iron mechanism that would slow the water.

"That won't work," Cehmai said with a grunt. "Logic's wrong."

"I don't know about that," Maati said. "The girl's trained as a physician. She says that healing flesh is mostly a matter of letting it go back into the shape it tends toward anyway. The body actually helps the process that way, and—"

"But the logic, Maati-kvo," Cehmai said, using the honorific for a teacher as if by reflex. "It's a paradox. The natural balance of the andat is not to exist, and she wants to bind something whose essence is the return to its natural state? It's the same problem as Freedom-From-Bondage. She should reverse it."

"How do you mean?"

The river gates creaked as they closed. The flow thinned and then stopped. Cehmai squatted, elbows resting on his knees, and pointed toward the water with his chin.

"Water-Moving-Down didn't only make water move down. She also stopped it. She withdrew her influence, ne? So she could make rain fall or she could keep it in the sky. She could stop a river from flowing as easily as making it run fast. Your physician can't bind Returning-to-Balance or however she planned to phrase it. But if she bound something like

Wounded or Scarred-by-Illness, she could *withdraw* that from someone. She negates the opposite, achieves the same effect, and has something that isn't so slippery to hold."

Maati considered, then nodded.

"That's good," he said. "That's very good. And it's why I need you."

Cehmai smiled out at the waving green field, then glanced at the house and looked down.

"You'll stay the night?" Cehmai said.

Maati took a pose that accepted the invitation. He kept his trepidation at the thought of sleeping under Idaan's roof out of his stance and expression. It would have been too much to hope for that Cehmai would drop everything in his life and take to the road at once. And still, Maati had hoped for it. . . .

Inside the thick stone walls of the farmhouse, the air was cooler and rich with the scent of dog and old curry. The afternoon faded slowly, the sun lingering in the treetops to the west, its light thick and golden and softened by Maati's failing eyes. Cicadas set up a choir. He sat on a low stone porch, watching everything and nothing.

Maati had known quite well that Idaan and Cehmai had been lovers once, even while Idaan had been married to another man and arranging the deaths of her family. Cehmai's betrayal of her had been the key that brought her down, that lifted Otah into the role of Khai Machi, and from there to Emperor. Cehmai had, in his fashion, created the world as it was with the decision to expose his lover's crimes.

Maati had thought the man mad for still harboring feelings for the woman; she was a murderer and a traitor to her city and her family. He'd thought him mad twice over for wanting to find her again after the andat had vanished from the world and the poets had fallen from grace. She would, he had expected, kill Cehmai on sight.

And yet.

As a boy, Maati had taken another man's lover as his own, and Otah had forgiven it. In gratitude or something like it, Maati had devoted himself to proving Otah's innocence and helped to bring Idaan's crimes to light. Seedless, the first andat Maati had known, had betrayed both the poet Heshai who had bound him and the Galtic house that had backed the andat's cruel scheme. And the woman—what had her name been?—whose child died. Seedless had betrayed everyone, but had asked only Maati to forgive him.

The accrued weight of decades pressed upon him as the sun caught in the western branches. Dead children, war, betrayal, loss. And here, in this small nameless farm days' travel from even a low town of notable size, two lovers who had become enemies were lovers again. It made him angry, and his anger made him sad.

As the first stars appeared, pale ghost lights in the deepening blue before sunset, Idaan emerged from the house. With her leather gear gone, she looked less like a thing from a monster tale. She was a woman, only a woman. And growing old. It was only when she met his gaze that he felt a chill. He had seen her eyes set in a younger face, and the darkness in them had shifted, but it had not been unmade.

"There's food," she said.

The table was small and somehow more frail than Maati had expected. Three bowls were set out, each with rice and strips of browned meat. Cehmai was also pouring out small measures of rice wine from a bone carafe. It was, Maati supposed, an acknowledgment of the occasion and likely as much extravagance as Cehmai's resources would allow. Maati took a pose that offered thanks and requested permission to join the table. Cehmai responded with one of acceptance and welcome, but his movements were slow. Maati couldn't tell if it was from exhaustion or thought. Idaan added neither word nor pose to the conversation; her expression was unreadable.

"I've been thinking," Cehmai said. "Your plan. I have a few questions about it."

"Anything," Maati said.

"Would your scheme to undo what Sterile did include restoring the Galts?"

Maati took a strip of the meat from his bowl. The flesh was pleasantly rich and well-salted. He chewed slowly to give himself time to think, but his hesitation was answer enough.

"I don't think I can join you," Cehmai said. "This battle I've . . . I've lost my taste for it."

Maati felt his own frown like an ache.

"Reconsider," he said, but Cehmai shook his head.

"I've given too much of my life to the world already. I'd like to keep the rest of my years for myself. No more great struggles, no more cities or nations or worlds resting on what I do or don't do. What I have here is enough."

Maati wiped his fingers on his sleeve and took a pose of query that bordered on accusation. Cehmai's eyes narrowed.

"Enough for what?" Maati demanded. "Enough for the pair of you? It'll be more than enough before many years have passed. It'll be too much. How much do you work in a day? Raising your own food, tending your crop and your animals, making food and washing your robes and gathering wood for your fires? Does it give you any time at all to think? To rest?"

"It isn't as easy as living in the courts, that's truth," Cehmai said. His smile was the same as ever, even set in this worn face. "There are nights it would be good to leave the washing to a servant."

"It won't get easier," Maati said. "You'll get older. Both of you. The work will stay just as difficult, and you'll get tired faster. When you take sick, you'll recover slowly. One or the other of you will strain something or break an old bone or catch fever, and your children won't be there to care for you. The next farm over? His children won't be there for you either. Or the next. Or the next."

"He's not wrong, love," Idaan said. Maati blinked. Of all the people in the world, Idaan was the last he'd expected support from.

"I know all that," Cehmai said. "It doesn't mean that I should go back to being a poet."

"What else would you do?" Maati said. "Sell the land rights? Who is there to buy them? Take up some new trade? Who will there be to teach you? Binding the andat is the thing you've trained for. Your mind is built for the work. These girls . . . you should see them. The dedication, the engagement, the drive. If this thing can be done, they will do it. We can remake the world."

"We've done that once already," Cehmai said. "It didn't go well."

"We didn't have time. The Galts were at our door. We did what we had to do. And now we can correct our errors."

"Does my brother know about this?" Idaan asked.

"He refused me," Maati said.

"Is that why you hate him?"

The air around the table seemed to clench. Maati stared at the woman. Idaan met his gaze with a level calm.

"He is selling us," Maati said. "He is turning away from a generation of women whose injuries are as much his fault as ours."

"And is that why you hate him?" Idaan asked again. "You can't tell me that you don't, Maati-cha. I know quite a lot about hatred."

He let my son die to save his, Maati thought but did not say. There were a thousand arguments against the statement: Otah hadn't been there when Nayiit died; it wasn't Danat's fault that his protector failed to fend off the soldiers; Nayiit wasn't truly his son. He knew them all, and that none of them mattered. Nayiit had died, Maati had been sent into the wilderness, and Otah had risen like a star in the sky.

"What I feel toward your brother doesn't change what needs to be done," Maati said, "or the help I'll need to do it."

"Who's backing you?" Idaan said.

Maati felt a flash of surprise and even fear. An image of Eiah flickered in his mind and was banished.

"What do you mean?" he asked.

"Someone's feeding you," she said. "Someone's hiding you and your students. If the word got out that you'd been found, half the world would send armsmen to cut you down for fear you'd do exactly what you're doing now. And half of the rest would kick you to death for petty vengeance. If it's not Otah protecting you, who is it? One of the high families of the utkhaiem? A trading house? Who?"

"I have strong backing," Maati said. "But I won't tell you more than that."

"Every danger you face, my husband faces too," Idaan said. "If you want him to take your risks, you have to tell him what protection you can offer."

"I have an ear in the palaces anytime I need it. Otah won't be able to mount any kind of action against me without warning finding me. You can trust to that."

"You have to tell us more," Idaan said.

"He doesn't," Cehmai said, sharply. "He doesn't have to offer me protection because I'm not going to do the work. I'm done, love. I'm finished. I want a few more years with you and a quiet death, and I'll be quite pleased with that."

"The world needs you," Maati said.

"It doesn't," Cehmai said. "You've come a long way, Maati-kvo, and I've disappointed you. I'm sorry for that, but you have my answer. I used to be a poet, but I'm not anymore. I can reconsider as long as we both keep breathing, and we'll come to the same place."

"We can't stay on here," Idaan said. Her voice was soft. "I've loved it here too. This place, these years . . . we've been lucky to have them. But Maati-cha's right. This season, and perhaps five or ten after it, we'll make do. But eventually the work will pass us. We're not getting younger, and we can't hire on hands to help us. There aren't any."

"Then we'll leave," Cehmai said. "We'll do something else, only not that."

"Why not?" Maati asked.

"Because I don't want to kill any more people," Cehmai said. "Not the girls you're encouraging to try this, not the foreigners who would try to stop us, not whatever army came in the next autumn's war."

"It doesn't have to be like that," Maati said.

"It does," Cehmai said. "We held the power of gods, and the world envied us and turned against us, and they always will again. I can't say I think much of where we stand now, but I remember what happened to bring us here, and I don't see how making poets of women instead of men will make a world any different or better than the one we had then."

"It may not," Maati said, "but it will be better than the one we have now. If you won't help me, then I'll do without you, but I'd thought better of you, Cehmai. I'd thought you had more spine."

"Rice is getting cold," Idaan said. Her voice was controlled rage. "Perhaps we should eat it before it goes bad."

They finished the meal alternating between artificially polite conversation and strained silence. After, Cehmai took the bowls away to clean and didn't return. Idaan led Maati to a small room near the back with a straw pallet and a night candle already burning. Maati slept poorly and found himself still upset when he woke. He left in the dark of the morning without speaking again to either of his hosts, one from disappointment and shame and the other, though he would never have said it, from fear.

5

>+< Nantani was the nearest port to the lands of Galt, but the scars of war were too fresh there and too deep. Instead, the gods had conspired to return Otah to the city of his childhood: Saraykeht.

The fastest ships arrived several days before the great mass of the fleet. They stood out half a hand's travel from the seafront, and Otah took in the whole city. He could see the masts at the farthest end of the seafront, berthed in order to leave the greatest space for the incoming traffic. Bright cloth hung from every window Otah could see, starting with the dock master's offices nearest the water to the towers of the palaces, high and to the north where the vibrant colors were grayed by humidity.

Crowds filled the docks, and he heard a roar of voices and snatches of drum and flute carried by the breeze. The air itself smelled different: rank and green and familiar in a way he hadn't expected.

The Emperor of the Khaiem had been away from his cities for eight months, almost nine, and his return with the high families of Galt in tow was the kind of event seen once in history and never again. This was the day that every man and woman at the seafront or watching from the windows above the streets would recall until death's long fingers touched them. The day that the new empress, the Galtic empress, arrived for the first time.

There were stories Otah had read in books that had been ashes for almost as long as this new Empress had been alive, about an emperor's life mirroring the state of his empire. An emperor with many children meant rich, fertile land; one without heir spoke of poor crops and thin cattle. An emperor who drank himself to sleep meant an empire of libertines; one who studied and prayed, a somber land of great wisdom. He had half-believed the stories then. He had no faith in them now.

"You would think they would have made some allowance for our arrival," a man's peevish voice said from behind him. Otah looked back at

Balasar Gice, dressed in formal brocade armor and shining with sweat. Otah took a pose of powerlessness before the gods.

"The wind does what the wind does," he said. "We'll be on land by nightfall."

"We will," Balasar said. "But the others will be docking and unloading all night."

It was true. Saraykeht would likely add something near a tenth of its population in the next day, Galts filling the guest quarters and way-houses and likely half the beds in the soft quarter. It was the second time in Otah's life that a pale-skinned, round-eyed neighborhood without buildings had appeared in his city. Only now, it would happen without drawn blades and blood.

"They're sending tow galleys out for us," Otah said. "It will all be fine."

The galleys, with their flashing banks of white oars and ornamental ironwork rails, reached the great ship just after midday. With a great clamor of voices—protests, laughter, orders, counterorders—thick cables of hemp were made fast to the ship's deck. The sails were already down, and with the sound of a bell clanging like an alarm, Otah's ship lurched, shifted directly into the wind, and began the last, shortest leg of his journey home.

A welcoming platform had been erected especially for the occasion. The broad beams were white as snow, and a ceremonial guard waited by a litter while a somewhat less ceremonial one kept the press of the crowds at a distance. Balasar and six of the Galtic High Council had made their way to Otah's ship in order to disembark with him. The *Avenger* with Ana and her parents would likely come next, after which the roar of competing etiquette masters would likely drown out the ocean. Otah was more than willing to leave the fighting for position and status for the dock master to settle out.

The crowd's voice rose when the ship pulled in, and again when the walk bridged the shifting gap between ship and land. His servants preceded him in the proper array and sequence, and then Otah left the sea. The noise was something physical, a wind built of sound. The ceremonial guard adopted poses of obeisance, and Otah took his ritual reply. The first of the guard to stand, grinning, was Sinja.

"You've shaved your whiskers," Otah shouted.

"I was starting to look like an otter," Sinja agreed. His expression became opaque and he bowed to Otah's right. "Balasar-cha."

"Sinja," Balasar said.

The past intruded. Once Sinja had played the part of Balasar's man, expert on the cities of the Khaiem and mercenary leader of war. He had spied on the Galts, betrayed Balasar, and killed the man Balasar held dearest to his heart. It thickened the air between them, even now. Balasar's eyes shifted to the middle distance, a frown on his lips as if he were counting how many of his dead might have lived, had Sinja remained true. And then the moment was gone. Or if not gone, covered over for the sake of etiquette.

The others of the Galtic party lurched in from the ship, unsteady on planks that didn't move, and the assembled masses cheered each of them like a hero returned from war. Servants dressed in light cotton robes led each sweating Galt to a waiting litter, Otah's station of honor making him the last to leave.

"I suspect they'll be changing to local clothes before long," Sinja said. "They all look half-dead with the heat."

"I'm feeling it myself," Otah said.

"Should I interrupt protocol?" Sinja asked. "I could have you loaded and on your way up the hills in the time it takes to kill a chicken."

"No," Otah said with a sigh. "If we're doing this, let's do it well. But ride with me, eh? I want to hear what's going on."

"Yes," Sinja said. "Well. You've missed some dramatics, but I don't think there's anything particularly ominous waiting. Except the pirates. And the conspiracy. You did get the report about the conspiracy in Yalakeht? It's apparently got ties to Obar State."

"Well, that's just lovely," Otah said.

"No more plague than usual," Sinja offered gamely, and then it was time and servants stepped forward to escort Otah to his litter. The shifting gait of his bearers was similar to being aboard ship, but also wrong. Between that and the heat, Otah was beginning to feel nauseated, but the buildings that passed by his beaded window were comforting. Great blue and white walls topped with roof tiles of gray and red; banners hanging in the slow, thick air; men and women in poses of welcome or else waving small lengths of brightly colored cloth. If it had been autumn or winter, the old firekeepers' kilns would have been lit and strange flames would have accompanied him up the wide streets to the palaces.

"Any problems with the arrival?" he asked Sinja.

"A few. Angry women throwing stones, mostly. We've locked them away until the last ship comes in. Danat and I decided to put the girl and her family in the poet's house. It isn't the most impressive location, but it's comfortable, and it's far enough back from the other buildings that they might have some privacy. The gods all know they'll be gawked at like a three-headed calf the rest of the time."

"I think Ana has a lover," Otah said. "One of the sailors was built rather like a courtier."

"Ah," Sinja said. "I'll tell the guard to keep eyes out. I assume we'd rather he didn't come calling?"

"No, better that he not," Otah said.

"I don't suppose there's a chance the girl's still a virgin?"

Otah took a pose that dismissed the concern. Even if she weren't— and of course she wasn't—she wouldn't be bearing another man's child. Not if the boy he had glimpsed in the hold of the *Avenger* was a Galt. Otah felt a moment's unease.

"If the guard do find a boy sneaking in, have him held until I can speak with him. I'd rather that this whole situation not get more complex than it already is."

"Your word is law, Most High," Sinja said, his tone light. Otah chuckled.

He had missed the man's company. There were few people in the world who could see Otah beneath his titles, fewer still who dared mock him. It was a familiarity that had been forged by years. Together, they had acted against the plot which had first changed Otah from outcast to Khai Machi. They had loved the same woman and come near violence over it. Sinja had trained Otah's son in the arts of combat and strategy, had gotten drunk with the Emperor after Kiyan's funeral, had spoken his mind whether invited to or not. Otah had no other advisor or friend like him.

As they moved north, the crowd that lined the street changed its nature. Once they had passed out of the throng at the seafront, the robes and faces had been those of laborers and artisans. As they passed the compounds of the merchant houses, the robes and banners became more ornate. Rich and saturated colors were edged with embroidery of gold and worked in the symbols of the various houses. And then almost without a pause, the symbols and colors were not of merchants, but of the families of the utkhaiem, and the high walls and ornate shutters were not mercantile compounds, but palaces. Men and women in fine robes took poses of welcome and obeisance as servants and slaves fanned them. A hidden choir burst into song somewhere to his left, the voices in complex harmony. The litter stopped before the grand palace, the first palace, the Emperor's palace. Otah stepped out, sweeping his gaze over the ordered rows of servants and high officials until he saw the one man he'd longed for.

Danat was in his twentieth summer, his face a mixture of Otah's long, northern features and Kiyan's, thin and foxlike. The planes of his cheeks had sharpened since Otah had gone. He looked older, more handsome. He wore a robe of deep gray set off with a rich, red sash that suited him. And still, Otah could see all the boys that had made this man: the babe, the bumbling child new to his own feet, the long-ill boy kept in his bed, the awkward and sorrowful youth, and the young heir to the Empire. All of them stood before him, hands in a pose of formal welcome, a smile glittering in his eyes. Otah broke protocol, embracing his son. The boy's arms were strong.

"You've done well," Otah murmured.

"None of the cities actually burned down while you were gone," Danat replied softly. There was pride in his voice, pleasure at the compliment.

"But you sound too much like Sinja."

"You knew that was a risk."

Otah laughed and let the swarm of servants precede him to his chambers. There would be no end of ceremonies later. Welcomes would drag on for weeks, audiences, special pleadings, feasts, dances, negotiations, councils. It all lay before him like a life's work started late. But now, sitting in the cool breeze of his private apartments with Sinja across from him and Danat pouring chilled water into stone bowls, the world was perfect.

Except, of course, that it wasn't.

"Perhaps we can mend both breaks with the same nail," Sinja said. "A strong showing against the pirates protects Chaburi-Tan and warns Obar State to keep to its own house."

"And a weak showing against them?" Otah asked.

"Shows we're weak, after which things go poorly," Sinja said. "But if we're going to assume failure from the start, there's not going to be anything of use that I can offer."

Otah propped up his feet. The palaces still felt as if they were swaying: the ghost motion of weeks aboard ship. The feeling was oddly pleasant.

"On the other hand," he said, "if we plan to decimate the enemy with a flower and a pillow, it's not going to help us. How strong is our fleet? Do we have enough men to take the pirates in a fair fight?"

"If we don't have them now, we certainly won't next year when all the sailors are a year older," Sinja said. "Even if you magically transport every fertile girl in Galt straight to some poor bastard's bed, it will be ten years before they can deliver us anyone strong enough to coil rope, much less fight. If we're going to do anything, it has to be now. We're going to grow weaker before we're strong."

"If we manage to get strong," Otah said. "And I don't know that we can spare the ships. We have eleven cities and the gods alone know how many low towns. We're talking about moving half a million of our men to Galt and bringing back as many of their women."

"Well, yes, shipping out anyone we have of fighting age now won't help the matter," Sinja said.

"Galt could do it," Danat said. "They have experience with sea wars. They have fighting ships and the veterans."

Otah saw the considering expression on Sinja's face. He let the silence stretch.

"I don't like it," Sinja said at last. "I don't know why I don't like it, but I don't."

"We're still thinking of our problems as our own," Danat said. "Asking Galt to fight our battles might seem odd, but they'd be protecting their own land too. In a generation, Chaburi-Tan is going to be as much their city as ours."

Otah felt an odd pressure in his chest. It was true, of course. It was what he had spent years working to accomplish. And still, when Danat put it in bare terms like that, it was hard for him to hear it.

"It's more than that," Sinja said.

"Is it Balasar?" Otah asked.

Sinja leaned forward, his fingers laced on his knee, his mouth set in a scowl. At length, he spoke.

"Yes," he said. "Yes, it is."

"He's forgiven me," Otah said. "Perhaps the two of you—"

"All respect, Otah-cha," Sinja said. "You were his enemy. That's a fair position. I broke my oath, lied to him, and killed his best captain. He's a man who loves loyalty, and I was one of his men. It's not the same."

"Perhaps it isn't," Otah agreed.

"Balasar-cha doesn't have to be the one to lead it," Danat said. "Or, all respect, Sinja-cha, for that."

"No, of course we don't," Sinja said. "It's not my head that's struggling with the thought. It's just . . . The boy's right, Otah-cha. A mixed fleet, their ships and ours, sinking the pirates would be the best solution. I don't know if we can negotiate the thing, but it's worth considering."

Otah scratched his leg.

"Farrer-cha," he said. "Danat's new father. He has experience with sea fighting. I think he hates all of us together and individually for Ana-cha's upcoming marriage, but he would still be the man to approach."

Danat took a long drink of water and grinned. It made him look younger.

"After the ceremony's done with," Sinja said. "We'll get the man drunk and happy and see if we can't make him sign something binding before he sobers up."

"If it were only so simple," Otah said. "With the High Council and the Low Council and the Conclave, every step they take is like putting cats in a straight line. Watching it in action, it's amazing they ever put to-gether a war."

"You should talk to Balasar," Sinja said.

"I will," Otah replied.

They moved on to other topics. Some were more difficult: weavers and stonemasons on the coasts had started offering money to appren-tices, so the nearby farms were losing hands; the taxes from Amnat-Tan had been lower than expected; the raids in the northern passes were getting worse. Others were innocuous: court fashions had shifted toward robes with a more Galtic drape; the shipping traffic on the rivers was faster now that they'd figured out how to harness boilers to do the row-ing; and finally, Eiah had sent word that she was busy assisting a physi-cian in Pathai and would not attend her brother's wedding.

Otah paused over this letter, rereading his daughter's neat, clear hand. The words were all simple, the grammar formal and appropriate. She made no accusations, leveled no arguments against him. It might have been better if she had. Anger was, at least, not distance.

He considered the implications of her absence. On one hand, it could hardly go unnoticed that the imperial family was not all in attendance. On the other, Eiah had broken with him years ago, when his present plan had still been only a rough sketch. If she was there, it might have served only to remind the women of the cities that they had in a sense been discarded. The next generation would have no Khaiate mothers, and the solace that neither would they have Galtic fathers would be cold comfort at best. He folded his daughter's letter and tucked it into his sleeve, his heart heavy with the thought that not having her near was likely for the best.

After, Otah retired to his rooms, sent his servants away, and lay on his bed, watching the pale netting shift in a barely felt breeze. It was strange being home, hearing his own language in the streets, smelling the air he'd breathed as a youth.

Ana and her parents would be settled in by now, sitting, perhaps, on the porch that looked out over the koi pond and its bridge. Perhaps putting back the hinged walls to let in the air. Otah had spent some little time at the poet's house of Saraykeht once, back when he'd been Danat's age and the drinking companion and friend of Maati Vaupathai. Back in some other life. He closed his eyes and tried to picture the rooms as they'd been when Seedless and the poet Heshai had still been in the world. The confusion of scrolls and books, the ashes piled up in the grate, the smell of incense and old wine. He didn't realize that he was falling asleep until Seedless smirked and turned away, and Otah knew he was in dreams.

A human voice woke him. The angle of the sun had shifted, the day almost passed. Otah sat up, struggling to focus his eyes. The servant spoke again.

"Most High, the welcoming ceremonies are due in a hand and a half. Shall I tell the Master of Tides to postpone them?"

"No," Otah said. His voice sounded groggy. He wondered how long the servant had been trying to rouse him. "No, not at all. Send me clean robes. Or . . . no, send them to the baths. I'll be there."

The servant fell into a pose that accepted the command as law. It seemed a little overstated to Otah, but he'd grown accustomed to other people taking his role more seriously than he did himself. He refreshed himself, met with the representatives of two high families and a trading house with connections in Obar State and Bakta, and allowed himself to be swept along to the grand celebration. They would welcome their onetime invaders with music and gifts and intrigue and, he suspected, the equivalent weight of the palaces in wine and food.

The grandest hall of his palaces stood open on a wide garden of night-blooming plants. A network of whisperers stood on platforms, ready to repeat the ceremonial greetings and ritual out to the farthest ear. Otah didn't doubt that runners were waiting at the edge of the gardens to carry reports of the event even farther. The press of bodies was intense, the sound of voices so riotous that the musicians and singers set to wander the garden in serenade had all been sent home.

Otah sat on the black lacquer chair of the Khai Saraykeht, his spine straight and his hands folded as gracefully as he could manage. Cushions for Danat and Sinja and all of Otah's highest officers were arrayed behind him, perhaps two-thirds filled. The others were, doubtless, in the throng of silk and gems. There was nowhere else to be tonight. Not in Saraykeht. Perhaps not in the world.

Danat brought him a bowl of cold wine, but it was too loud to have any conversation beyond the trading of thanks and welcome. Danat took his place on the cushion at Otah's side. Farrer Dasin, Otah saw, had been given not a chair but a rosewood bench. Issandra and Ana were on cushions at his feet. All three looked overwhelmed about the eyes. Otah caught Issandra's gaze and adopted a pose of welcome, which she returned admirably.

He turned his attention to her husband. Farrer Dasin, stern and gray. Otah found himself wondering how best to approach the man about this new proposal. Though he knew better, he could not help thinking of Galt and his own cities as separate, as two empires in alliance. Farrer Dasin—indeed, most of the High Council—were sure to be thinking in the same ways. They were all wrong, of course, Otah included. They were marrying two families together, but more than that they were binding two cultures, two governments, two histories. His own grandchildren would live and die in a world unrecognizably different from the one Otah had known; he would be as foreign to them as Galt had been to him.

And here, on this clear, crowded night, the cycle of ages was turning. He found himself irrationally certain that Farrer Dasin could be persuaded to lead, or at least to sponsor, a campaign against the pirates at Chaburi-Tan. They had done this. They could do anything.

The signal came: flutes and drums in fanfare as the cloth lanterns rose to the dais. Otah stood up and the crowd before him went silent. Only the sound of a thousand breaths competed with the songbirds and crickets.

Otah gave his address in the tones appropriate to his place, practiced over the course of years. He found himself changing the words he had practiced. Instead of speaking only of the future, he also wanted to honor the past. He wanted every person there to know that in addition to the world they were making, there was a world—in some ways good, in others evil—that they were leaving behind.

They listened to him as if he were a singer, their eyes fastened to him, the silence complete apart from his own words in the hundred throats of the whisperers echoing out into the summer night. When he took the pose that would end his recitation, he saw tears on more than one face, and on the faces of more than one nation. He made his way to Farrer Dasin and formally invited the man to speak. The Galt stood, bowed to Otah as a gesture between equals, and moved forward. Otah returned to his seat with only the lightest twinge of trepidation.

"Are you sure you should let him speak?" Sinja murmured.

"There's no avoiding it," Otah replied, still smiling. "It will be fine."

The councilman cleared his throat, stood in the odd, awkward style of Galtic orators—one foot before the other, one hand in the air, the other clasping his jacket—and spoke. All of Otah's worst fears were put at once to rest. It was as if Issandra had written the words and spoke them now through her husband's mouth. The joy that was children, the dark years that the war had brought, the emptiness of a world without the laughter of babes. And now, the darkness ended.

Otah felt himself begin to weep slightly. He wished deeply that Kiyan had lived to see this night. He hoped that whatever gods were more than stories and metaphors took word of it to her. The old Galt bowed his head to the crowd. The applause was like an earthquake or a flood. Otah rose and held his hand out to Danat as Farrer Dasin did the same with his daughter. The Emperor-to-be and his Empress meeting here for the first time. There would be songs sung of this night, Otah knew.

Ana was beautiful. Someone had seen to it that the gown she wore flattered her. Her face was painted in perfect harmony with her hair and the gold of her necklace. Danat wore a black robe embroidered with gold and cut to please the Galtic eye. Farrer and Otah stepped back, leaving their children to the center of the dais. Danat tried a smile. The girl's eyes fluttered; her cheeks were flushed under the paint, her breath fast.

"Danat Machi?" she said.

"Ana Dasin," he replied.

The girl took a deep breath. Her pretty, rodentlike face shone. When she spoke, her voice was strong and certain.

"I will never consent to lay down with you, and if you rape me, I will see the world knows it. My lover is Hanchat Dor, and I will have no other."

Otah felt his face go white. In the corner of his eye, he saw Farrer Dasin rock back like a man struck by a stone and then raise a hand to his face. Danat's mouth opened and closed like a fish's. The whisperers paused, and then a heartbeat later, the words went out where they could never be called back. The voice of the crowd rose up like the waters of chaos come to drown them all.

6

>+< Maati relived his conversation with Cehmai a thousand times in the weeks that followed. He rose in the morning from whatever rough camp or wayhouse bed he'd fallen into the night before, and he muttered his arguments to Cehmai. He rode his weary mule along overgrown tracks thick with heat and heavy with humidity, and he spoke aloud, gesturing. He ate his evening meals with the late sunset of summer, and in his mind, Cehmai sat across from him, dumbfounded and ashamed, persuaded at last by the force of Maati's argument. And when Maati's imagination returned him to the world as it was, his failure and shame poured in on him afresh.

Every low town he passed through, the mud streets empty of the sound of children, was a rebuke. Every woman he met, an accusation. He had failed. He had gone to the one man in the world who might have lightened his burden, and he had been refused. The better part of the season was lost to him now. It was time he should have spent with the girls, preparing the grammar and writing his book. They were days he would never win back. If he had stayed, perhaps they would have had a breakthrough. Perhaps there would already be an andat in the world, and Otah's plans ruined.

And what if by going after Cehmai, Maati had somehow lost that chance? With every day, it seemed more likely. As the trees and deer of the river valleys gave way to the high, dry plains between Pathai and ruined Nantani, Maati became more and more sure that his error had been catastrophic. Irretrievable. And so it was also another mark against Otah Machi. Otah, the Emperor, to whom no rules applied.

Maati found the high road, and then the turning that would lead, given half a day's ride, to the school. To his students. To Eiah. He camped at the crossroads.

He was too old to be living on muleback. Lying in the thin folds of his bedroll, he ached as if he'd been beaten. His back had been suffering spasms for days; they had grown painful enough that he hadn't slept deeply. And his exhaustion seemed to make his muscles worse. The high plains grew cool at night, almost cold, and the air smelled of dust. He heard the skittering of lizards or mice and the low call of owls. The stars shone down on him, each point of light smeared by his aging eyes until the whole sky seemed possessed by a single luminous cloud.

There had been a time he'd lain under stars and picked out constellations. There was a time his body could have taken rest on cobblestone, had the need arisen. There was a time Cehmai, poet of Machi and master of Stone-Made-Soft, had looked up to him.

It was going to be hard to tell Eiah that he'd failed. The others as well, but Eiah knew Cehmai. She had seen them work together. The others might be disappointed, but Eiah alone would understand what he had lost.

His dread slowed him. At this, his last camp, he ate his breakfast and watched the slow sunrise. He packed his mule slowly, then walked westward, his shadow stretching out ahead and growing slowly smaller. The shapes of the hills grew familiar, and the pauses he took grew longer. Here was the dry streambed where he and the other black-robed boys had sat in the evenings and told one another stories of the families they had already half-forgotten. There, a grouping of stumps showed where the stand of trees they had climbed had been felled by Galtic axes and burned. A cave under an outcropping of rock where they'd made the younger boys slither into the darkness to hunt snakes. The air was as rich with memory as the scent of dust and wildflowers. His life had been simpler then, or if not simpler, at least a thing that held promise.

He managed to postpone his arrival at the school itself until the sun was lowering before him. The grand stone buildings looked smaller than he remembered them, but the great bronze door that had once been reserved for the Dai-kvo was just as grand. The high, narrow windows were marked black at the tops, the remnants of some long-dead fire. The wall of one of the sleeping chambers had fallen, stones strewn on the ground. The gardens were gone, marked only by low mounds where stones had once formed their borders. Time and violence had changed the place, but not yet beyond recognition. Another decade of rain washing mortar from between the stones, another fire, and perhaps the roofs would collapse. The ground would reclaim its own.

Maati tied his mule to a low, half-rotten post and made his way in. The grand room where he and the other boys had stood in rows each morning before marching off to their duties and classes. The wide corri-

dors beyond it, lit only by the reddish rays of the evening sun. Where
were the bodies of the boys who had been here on the day the armies
of Galt arrived? Where had those bones been buried? And where, now,
were Maati's own students? Had something gone awry?

When he reached the inner courtyard, his concerns eased. The flagstone paths were clear of dirt and dust, the weeds and grass had been
pulled from between the stones. And there, in the third window that had
once been the teachers' quarters, a lantern glowed already against the
falling night.

The door that opened to the wide central hall had been fitted with a
new leather hinge. The walls and floors, freshly washed, shone in the
light of a hundred candles. The scent of curry and the sound of women's
voices raised in conversation came through the air as if the one were part
of the other. Maati found himself disoriented for a moment, as if he'd
walked down a familiar street only to find it opening upon some unknown city. He walked forward slowly, drawn in by the voices as if
they were music. There was Ashti Beg's dry voice, Large Kae's laughter.
As he drew nearer, the pauses between the louder voices were filled
with the softer voices of Vanjit and Irit. The first words he made out
were Eiah's.

"Yes," she said, "but how would you fit that into a grammatic structure that doesn't already include it? Or am I talking in a circle?"

"I think you may be," Small Kae replied. "Maati-kvo said that binding an andat involves all kinds of inclusions. I don't see why this one
would be any different."

There was a pause, a sound that might have been the ghost of a sigh.

"Add it to the list," Eiah said as Maati turned through a well-lit doorway and into the room.

"What list?" he asked.

There was a moment's silence, and then uproar. The circle of chairs
was abandoned, and Maati found himself the subject of a half-dozen
embraces. The dread and anger and despair that had dogged his steps
lightened if it didn't vanish. He let Vanjit lead him to an empty chair,
and the others gathered around him, their eyes bright, their smiles genuine. It was like coming home. When Eiah returned to his question, he
had forgotten it. It took a moment to understand what she was saying.

"It's a list of questions for you," she said. "After we came and put the
place more or less to rights, we started . . . well, we started holding class
without you."

"It wasn't really the same," Small Kae said with an apologetic pose.

"We only didn't want to forget what we'd learned. We were only talking about it."

"After a few nights it became clear we were going to need some way to keep track of the parts that needed clarifying. It's become rather a long list. And some of the questions . . ."

Maati took a pose that dismissed her concerns, somewhat hampered by the bowl of curried rice in his hand.

"It's a good thought," he said. "I would have recommended it myself, if I'd been thinking clearly. Bring me the list tonight, and perhaps we can start going over it in the morning. If you are all prepared to begin working in earnest?"

The roar of agreement drowned out his laughter. Only Eiah didn't join in. Her smile was soft, almost sad, and she took no pose to explain it. Instead, she poured a bowl of water for him.

"Is Cehmai-kvo here?" Large Kae asked.

Maati took a bite of the rice, chewing slowly, letting the spices burn his tongue a little before answering.

"I didn't find him," Maati said. "There was a message, but it was out-of-date. I searched as long as there seemed some chance of finding him, but there was no sign. I left word where I could, and it may very well reach him. He might join us at any time. My job is to have you all prepared in case he does."

It was kinder than the truth. If Maati's failure had been only that he hadn't found help, it left them the hope that help might still arrive. It was no great lie to give them an image of the future in which something good might come. And it was easier for him if he didn't have to say he'd been refused. Only Eiah knew; he could hear it in her silence. She would follow his lead.

Maati's mule was seen to, his things hauled into the room they had prepared for him, and a bath drawn in a wide copper tub set before a fire grate. It reminded him of nothing so much as his days living in court, servants available at any moment to cater to his needs. It was strange to recall that he had lived that way once. It seemed both very recent and very long ago. And also, the slaves and servants that had driven the life in the palaces of Machi hadn't been women he knew and cared for. Slipping into the warm water, feeling his travel-abused joints ache just a degree less, letting his eyes rest, Maati wondered what it would have been like to receive so much female attention when he'd been younger. There would have been a time when the simple sensual pleasures of food and a warm bath might have suggested something more sexual. It might still, if bone-deep weariness hadn't held him.

But no, that wasn't true. He wasn't dead to lust, but it had been years since it had carried the urgency that he remembered from his youth. He wondered if that wasn't part of why women had been barred from the school and the village of the Dai-kvo. Would any poet have been able to focus on a binding if half his mind was on a woman his body was aching for? Or perhaps there was something in that mind-set itself that would affect the binding. So much of the andat was a reflection of the poet who bound it, it would be easy to imagine andat fashioned by younger poets in the forms of wantons and whores. Apart from the profoundly undignified nature of such a binding, it might actually make holding the andat more difficult as decades passed and a man's fires burned less brightly. He wondered if there was an analogy with women.

The scratch at the door brought him back. He'd half fallen asleep there in the water. He rose awkwardly, reaching for his robe and trying not to spill so much water that it flowed into the fire grate and killed the flames.

"Yes, yes," he called as he fastened the robe's ties. "I'm not drowned yet. Come in."

Eiah stepped through the doorway. There was something in her arms, held close to her. Between the unsteady light of the fire and his own age-blunted sight, he couldn't tell more than it looked like a book. Maati took a pose of welcome, his sleeves water-stuck to his arms.

"Should I come back later?" she asked.

"No, of course not," Maati said, pulling a chair toward the fire for her. "I was only washing the road off of me. Is this the famed list?"

"Part of it is," she said as she sat. She was wearing a physician's robe of deep green and gold. "Part of it's something else."

Maati settled himself on the tub's wide lip and took a pose that expressed curiosity and surprise. Eiah handed him a scroll, and he unfurled it. The questions were all written in a large hand, clearly, and each with a small passage to give some context. He read three of them. Two were simple enough, but the third was more interesting. It touched on the difficulties of generating new directionals, and the possibility of encasing absolute structures within relative ones. It gave the grammar an odd feeling, as if it were suggesting that fire was hot rather than asserting it.

It was interesting.

"Are they all like this?" he asked.

"The questions? Some of them, yes," Eiah said. "Vanjit's especially were beyond anything we could find a plausible answer for."

Maati pursed his lips and nodded. An absolute made relative. What would that do? He found himself smiling without knowing at first what he was smiling about.

"I think," he said, "leaving you to your own company may have been the best thing I've done."

The firelight caught Eiah's answering smile.

"I wasn't going to say so," she said. "It's been fascinating. At first, it was as if we were sneaking pies from the kitchens. Everyone wanted to do the thing, but it seemed . . . wrong? I don't know if that's the word. It seemed like something we shouldn't do, and more tempting because of it. And then once we started talking with each other, it was like being on a loose cart. We couldn't stop or even slow down. Half the time I didn't know if we were going down the wrong road, but . . ."

She shrugged, nodding at the scroll in his hands.

"Well, even if you were, some of this may be quite useful."

"I'd hoped so," Eiah said. "And that brings me to something else. I found some books at court. I brought them."

Maati blinked, the scroll forgotten in his hands.

"Books? They weren't all burned?" he said.

"Not that sort. These aren't ours," she said. "They're Westlands'. Books from physicians. Here."

She took back the scroll and put a small, cloth-bound book in his hand. One of the sticks in the fire grate broke, sending out embers like fireflies. Maati leaned forward.

The script was small and cramped, the ink pale. It would have been difficult in sunlight; by fire and candle, it might as well not have been written. Frustrated, Maati turned the pages and an eye stared back at him from the paper. He turned back and went more slowly. All the diagrams were of eyes, some ripped from their sockets, some pierced by careful blades. Comments accompanied each orb, laying, he assumed, its secrets open.

"Sight," Eiah said. "The author is called Arran, but it was more likely written by dozens of people who all used the same name. The wardens in the north had a period four or five generations ago when there was some brilliant work done. We ignored it, of course, because it wasn't by us. But these are very, very good. Arran was brilliant."

"Whether he existed or not," Maati said. He meant it as a joke.

"Whether he existed or not," Eiah agreed with perfect seriousness. "I've been working with these. And with Vanjit. We have a draft. You should look at it."

Maati handed her back the book and she pulled a sheaf of papers from her sleeve. Maati found himself almost hesitant to accept them. Vanjit, and her dreamed baby. Vanjit, who had lost so much in the war. He didn't want to see any of his students pay the price of a failed binding, but especially not her.

He took the papers. Eiah waited. He opened them.

The binding was an outline, but it was well-considered. The sections and relationships sketched in with commentary detailing what would go in each, often with two or three notes of possible approaches. The andat would be Clarity-of-Sight, and it would be based in the medical knowledge of Westlands physicians and the women's grammar that Maati and Eiah had been creating. Even if some Second Empire poet had managed to hold the andat before, this approach, these descriptions and sensibilities, was likely to be wholly different. Wholly new.

"Why Vanjit?" he asked. "Why not Ashti Beg or Small Kae?"

"You think she isn't ready?"

"I . . . I wouldn't go so far as that," Maati said. "It's only that she's young, and she's had a harder life than some. I wonder whether . . ."

"None of us are perfect, Maati-kya," Eiah said. "We have to work with the people we have. Vanjit is clever and determined."

"You think she can manage it? Bind this andat?"

"I think she has the best hope of any of us. Except possibly me."

Maati sighed, nodding as much to himself as to her. Dread thickened his throat.

"Let me look at this," he said. "Let me think about it."

Eiah took a pose that accepted his command. Maati looked down again.

"Why didn't he come?" Eiah asked.

"Because," Maati began, and then found he wasn't able to answer as easily as he'd thought. He folded the papers and began to tuck them into his sleeve, remembered how wet the cloth was, and tossed them instead onto his low, wood-framed bed. "Because he didn't want to," he said at last.

"And my aunt?"

"I don't know," Maati said. "I thought for a time that she might take my side. She didn't seem pleased with how they were living. Or, no. That's not right. She seemed to care more than he did about how they would live in the future. But he wouldn't have any of it."

"He's given up," Eiah said.

Maati recalled the man's face, the lines and weariness. The authenticity of his smile. When they'd first met, Cehmai had been little more than a boy, younger than Eiah was now. This was what the world had done to that boy. What it had done to them all.

"He has," Maati said.

"Then we'll do without him," Eiah said.

"Yes," Maati said, hoisting himself up. "Yes we will, but if you'll forgive me, Eiah-kya, I think the day's worn me thin. A little rest, and we'll begin fresh tomorrow. And where's that list of questions? Ah, thank you. I'll look over all of this, and we'll decide where best to go from here, eh?"

She took his hand, squeezing his knuckles gently.

"It's good to have you back," she said.

"I'm pleased to be here," he said.

"Did you have any news of my father?"

"No," he said. "I didn't ask. It's the first rule of running a race, isn't it? Not to look back at who's behind you?"

Eiah chuckled, but didn't respond otherwise. Once she'd left and Maati had banked the fire, he sat on the bed. The night candle stood straight in its glass case, the burning wick marking the hours before dawn. It wasn't to its first-quarter mark and he felt exhausted. He moved the papers and the scroll safely off the bed, pulled the blanket up over himself, and slept better than he had in weeks, waking to the sound of morning birds and pale light before dawn.

He read over the list of questions on the scroll, only surveying them and not bothering to think of answers just yet, and then turned to the proposed binding. When he went out, following the smells of wood smoke and warmed honey, his mind was turning at twice its usual speed.

They had made a small common room from what had once been the teachers' cells, and Irit and Large Kae were sitting at the window that Maati remembered looking out when he had been a child called before Tahi-kvo. Bald, mean-spirited Tahi-kvo, who would not have recognized the world as it had become; women studying the andat in his own rooms, the poets almost vanished from the world, Galts on the way to becoming the nobles of this new, rattling, sad, stumble-footed Empire. Nothing was the same as it had been. Everything was different.

Vanjit, sitting with her legs crossed by the fire grate, smiled up at him.

Maati took a pose of greeting and lowered himself carefully to her side. Irit and Large Kae both glanced at him, their eyes rich with curiosity and perhaps even envy, but they kept to their window and their conversation. Vanjit held out her bowl of cooked wheat and raisins, but Maati took a pose that both thanked and refused, then changed his mind and scooped two fingers into his mouth. The grain was rich and salted, sweetened with fruit and honey both. Vanjit smiled at him; the expression failed to reach her eyes.

"I looked over your work. Yours and Eiah-cha's," he said. "It's interesting."

Vanjit looked down, setting the bowl on the stone floor at her side. After a moment's hesitation, her hands took a pose that invited his judgment.

"I . . ." Maati began, then coughed, looked out past Large Kae and Irit to the bright and featureless blue of the western sky. "I don't want to hurry this. And I would rather not see any more of you pay the price of falling short."

Her mouth tightened, and her eyebrows rose as if she were asking a question. She said nothing.

"You're sure you want this?" he asked. "You have seen all the women we've lost. You know the dangers."

"I want this, Maati-kvo. I want to try this. And . . . and I don't know how much longer I can wait," she said. Her gaze rose to meet his. "It's time for me. I have to try soon, or I think I never will."

"If you have doubts about—"

"Not doubts. Only a little despair now and then. You can take that from me. If you let me try." Maati started to speak, but the girl went on, raising her voice and speaking faster, as if she feared what he would say next. "I've seen death. I won't say I'm not afraid of it, but I'm not so taken by the fear that I can't risk anything. If it's called for."

"I didn't think you were," he said.

"And I helped bury Umnit. I know what the price can look like. But I buried my mother and my brother and his daughter too, and they didn't die for a reason. They were only on the streets when Udun fell," she said, and shrugged. "We all die sometime, Maati-kvo. Risking it sooner and for a reason is better than being safe and meaningless. Isn't it?"

Brave girl. She was such a brave girl. To have lost so much, so young, and still be strong enough to risk the binding. Maati felt tears in his eyes and forced himself to smile.

"We chose it for *you*. Clarity-of-Sight," she said. "I saw how hard it is for you to read some days, and Eiah and I thought . . . if we could help . . ."

Maati laid his hand on hers, his heart aching with something equally joy and fear. Vanjit was weeping a bit as well now. He heard voices coming down the hallway—Eiah and Ashti Beg—but Irit and Large Kae were silent. He was certain they were watching them. He didn't care.

"We'll be careful," he said. "We'll make it work."

Her smile outshone the sun. Maati nodded; yes, they would attempt the binding. Yes, Vanjit would be the first woman in history to hold an andat or else the next of his students to die.

7

>+< "No, I will not forbid her a goddamned thing. The girl's got more
       spine than all the rest of us put together. We could learn some-
thing from her," Farrer Dasin said, his arms folded before him, his chin
high and proud. And when he said *the rest of us,* Otah was clear that he
meant the Galts. The courts of the Khaiem, the cities and people of
Otah's empire were not part of Farrer Dasin's *us*; they were still apart
and the enemy.

Six members of the High Council sat at the wide marble table along
with Balasar Gice and Issandra Dasin. Otah, Danat, and representatives
of four of the highest families of the utkhaiem sat across from them. Otah
wished he'd been able to scatter each side among the other instead of
dividing the table like a battlefield. Or else keep the group smaller. If it
had been only himself, Farrer, and Issandra, there might have been a
chance.

Ana, the girl who had taken a stick to this political beehive, was not
present, nor was she welcome.

"There are agreements in place," Balasar said. "We can't unmake
them on a whim."

"Yes, Dasin-cha. Contracts have been signed," one of the utkhaiem
said. "Is it Galt's intention that any contract can be invalidated if the
signer's daughter objects?"

"That isn't what happened," the councilman at Farrer's right hand
said. "We have our hands full enough without exaggerating."

And so it started off again, voices raised each over the other with the effect that nothing but babble could be heard. Otah didn't add to the clamor,
but sat forward in his chair and watched. He considered the architecture—
vaulted ceiling of blue and gold tiles, the sliding wooden shutters. He
found a scent in the air: sugared almonds. He struggled to hear a sound
beyond the table: the wind in the treetops. Then, slowly, he pulled his
awareness back to the people before him. It was an old trick he'd learned

during his days as a courier, a way of withdrawing half a step from the place where he was and considering the ways that people moved and held themselves, the expressions they wore when they were silent and when they spoke. It often said more than the words. And now, he saw three things.

First, he was not the only silent one at the table. Issandra Dasin was rocked a degree back in her chair, her eyes fixed on the middle distance. Her expression spoke of exhaustion and a barely hidden sorrow, the complement to her husband's self-destructive pleasure. Danat was also withdrawn, but with his body canted forward, as if he was trying to hear every phrase that fluttered through the heavy air. He might as easily drink a river.

Second, Otah saw that neither side was united. The Galts across from him ran the gamut from defiant to conciliatory, the utkhaiem from outraged to fearful. It was the same outside. The palaces, the teahouses, the baths, the street corners—all of Saraykeht was filled with agreements and negotiations that were suddenly, violently uncertain. He recalled something his daughter had said once about the reopened wound being the one most plagued by scars.

Third, and perhaps least interesting, it became clear that he was wasting his time.

"Friends," Otah said. Then again, louder, "Friends!"

Slowly, the table grew quiet around him.

"The morning has been difficult," he said. "We should retire and reflect on what has been said."

Whatever it was, he didn't add.

There was a rumble of assent, if not precisely agreement. Otah took a pose of gratitude to each man and woman as they left, even to Farrer Dasin, for whom he felt very little warmth. Otah dismissed the servants as well, and soon only he and Danat remained. Without the pandemonium of voices, the meeting room seemed larger and oddly forlorn.

"Well," his son said, leaning against the table. He was wearing the same robe as he had at the botched ceremony the day before. The cloth itself looked weary. "What do you make of it?"

Otah scratched idly at his arm and tried to focus his mind. His back ached, and there was an uneasy, bright feeling in his gut that presaged a sleepless and uncomfortable night. He sighed.

"Primarily, I think I'm an idiot," Otah said. "I should have written to the daughters. I forget how different their world is. Your world, too."

Danat took a pose that asked elaboration. Otah rose, stretching. His back didn't improve.

"Political marriage isn't a new thing," Otah said. "We've always suffered it. They've always suffered it. But, once the rules changed, it stopped meaning so much, didn't it? As long as Ana-cha has been alive, she hasn't seen political marriages take place. If Radaani married his son to Saya's daughter, they wouldn't be joining bloodlines. No children, no lasting connection between the houses. Likewise in Galt. I doubt it's stopped the practice entirely, but it's changed things. I should have thought of it."

"And she could take lovers," Danat said.

"People took lovers before," Otah said.

"Not without fear," Danat said. "There's no chance of a child. It changes how willing a girl would be."

"And how exactly do you know that?" Otah asked.

Danat blushed. Otah walked to the window. Below, the gardens were in motion. Wind shifted the boughs of the trees and set the flowers nodding. The scent of impending rain cooled the air. There would be a storm by nightfall.

"Papa-kya?" Danat said.

Otah looked over his shoulder. Danat was sitting on the table, his feet on the seat of a cushioned chair. It was the pose of a casual boy in a cheap teahouse. Danat's face, however, was troubled.

"Don't bother it," Otah said. "It might be a new world for sex, but there was an old world for it too. And I'm sure there are any number of other men who've made the same discoveries you have."

"That wasn't the matter. It's the wedding. I don't think I can . . . I don't think I can do it. When it was just thinking of it, I hadn't seen what it would be to be married to someone who hated me. I have now."

His voice was thick with distress. A gust of stronger wind came, rattling the shutters in their frames. Otah slid the wood closed, and the meeting room dimmed, gold tiles turning bronze, blue tiles black.

"It will be fine," Otah said. "At worst, there are other councillors with other daughters. It won't be a pleasant transition, but—"

"A different girl won't fix this. At best we'd find a girl less willing to struggle. At worst, we'd find someone who hated me just as much, but better versed in deceit."

Otah took his seat again. He could feel his brow furrow. If he hadn't been so tired to begin with, it wouldn't have taken him as long to think through Danat's words.

"Are you . . ." Otah said, then stopped and began again. "You're saying you won't have *Ana*?"

"I thought I could. I would have, if she hadn't done what she did. But I've spent all night looking at it, and I don't see a way."

"I do. I see it perfectly clearly. High families have been arranging marriages for as long as there have been high families. It binds them together. It shows trust."

"You didn't. You were Khai Machi. You could have had dozens of wives, but you didn't. Even after the fever took Mother, you didn't. You could have," Danat said. And then, "You could now. You could make one of these girls your wife. Marry Ana-cha."

"You know quite well that I couldn't. A man of my years bedding a girl? They wouldn't see a marriage so much as a debauch."

"Yes," Danat said. "And putting me in your place would only change how it looked, not what it was. I'll do whatever I can to help. You know that. I could marry a stranger and make the best of it. But I won't father a child on an unwilling girl."

"Don't be an idiot," Otah said, and knew immediately that it was the wrong thing. His son's smile was a mask now, cold and bright and hard as stone. Otah raised his hands in a pose that took the words back, but Danat ignored it.

"I won't do something I know in my bones is wrong," Danat said. "If it's the only way to save us, then we aren't worth saving."

Otah watched the boy leave. There were a thousand arguments to make, a thousand ways to rephrase the issue, to make something different of these same circumstances. None of them would matter. He let his head sink to his hands.

There had been a time when Otah had been young and the world had been, if not simple, at least certain. Decades and experience had made him sure that his sense of right and wrong were not the only ones. Before he'd had that beaten out of him by the gods, he might well have taken the same stand Danat had just now. Do what he believed to be right and endure the consequences, no matter how terrible.

If only his children were less like him.

There had to be a way. The whole half-dead mess of it had to be salvageable. He had only to see how.

Voices and argument filled the halls as he made his way through the palaces. Columns wrapped in celebratory cloth mocked him. Uncertain, falsely bright gazes met his own and were ignored. The thick air of the summer cities left sweat running down Otah's spine and the sense of a damp cloth pressed against his face. There was a way to salvage this. He had only to find it.

Letters and requests for audiences waited for him, stacks of paper as long as his forearm. He ignored them for now and sent his servants scurrying for fresh paper and chilled tea. He sat at his desk, the pen's bright bronze nib in the air just above the brick of ink, and gave himself a moment before he began.

Kiyan-kya—

Well, love, it's all gone as well as a wicker fish boat. Ana won't have Danat. Danat won't have Ana. I find myself host to the worst gathering in history not actually struck by plague. I think the only thing I've done well was that I didn't wrestle our son to the ground when he walked away from me. I feel like everyone is wrapped up in what happened before, and I'm alone in fearing what will come after. We won't survive, love. The Khaiem and the Galts both are sinking, and we're so short-sighted and mean of spirit we're willing to die if it means the other bastard goes down too.

I don't mean Ana or Danat. They're only young and brave and stupid the way young, brave people are. I mean her father. Farrer Dasin is happy to see this fail. I imagine there are a fair number in my court who feel the same way.

There are two sides to this, love. But they aren't the two sides we think of—not the Khaiem and the Galts. It's the people in love with the past and the ones who fear for the future. And, though the gods alone know how I'm going to do it, I have to win Danat and Ana over from the one camp to the other.

Otah paused, something shifting in the back of his mind. It felt the way it had when Kiyan was alive and speaking to him from the next room, her voice too low to make out the words. He put down the pen and closed his eyes.

Win Ana over. He had to win Ana over.

"Oh," he said.

"ISSANDRA-CHA. THANK YOU FOR COMING. YOU KNOW MY SON, I THINK," OTAH said.

The sun touched the hills to the west of Saraykeht. Ruddy air rich with the scent of evening roses came through the unshuttered windows.

A small meal of cheese and dried apple and plum wine waited for their pleasure on a low lacquered table. Issandra Dasin rose from her divan to greet Danat as he came forward.

"Issandra-cha," Danat said and returned her welcome.

"Danat needs your help," Otah said. Danat glanced over at him, surprise in his gaze. "You see, your daughter has convinced him that it would be wrong to marry an unwilling woman. I can argue it to be the lesser evil, but if we two work together, I think the issue might be avoided altogether."

Issandra returned to her seat, sighing. She looked older than when Otah had first met her.

"It won't be simple," Issandra said.

"What won't be simple?" Danat asked.

"Wooing my daughter," Issandra said. "What did you think we were talking about?"

Otah took a bit of dried apple in his mouth while Danat blinked. Words stumbled over the boy's tongue without finding a sentence.

"You won't have a different girl for fear she'll hate you and lie about it," Otah said in the tone of a man explaining the solution of a simple mechanical problem. "Ana, we are all quite aware, isn't going to hide her feelings on the matter. So if she chooses you, you can believe her. Yes?"

"We have a small advantage in that her present lover is something of a cow," Issandra said. "I suspect that, had the circumstances been otherwise, she would already have grown tired of him. But he's a point of pride now." She fixed Danat with her eyes. "You have a hard road before you, son."

"You want me to seduce your daughter?" Danat asked, his voice breaking slightly at *seduce*.

"Yes," Issandra said.

Danat sank to a cushion. His face flushed almost the color of sunset.

"I thought he might deliver an apology," Otah said. "It would give him a reason to speak with Ana-cha in private, separate him from the political aspect of the arrangement, and place him in her camp."

"Apologize for what?" Danat said.

"Well, for me," Otah said. "Express your shame that I would treat her so poorly."

"She'll smell that in a heartbeat," Issandra said. "And if you begin by giving her the upper hand, you'll never have it back. Ask an apology *from* her. Respect her objections, but tell her she was wrong in humiliating you. You are as much a pawn in this as she is. And do you have a lover?"

"I . . . I was . . ."

"Well, find one," Issandra said. "Preferably someone prettier than my daughter. You needn't look shocked, my boy. I've lived my life in court. While you poor dears are out swinging knives at each other, there are wars just as bloody at every grand ball."

A scratching came at the door, followed by a servant woman. She took a pose of abject apology.

"Most High, there's a courier for you."

"It can wait," Otah said. "Or if it can't, send for Sinja-cha."

"The courier's come from Chaburi-Tan," the servant said. "The letter is sealed and signed for you alone. He says the issue is urgent."

Otah cursed under his breath, but he rose. As he stepped out to the antechamber, he heard Danat and Issandra resume the conversation without him. The antechamber felt as close as a grave, heavy tapestries killing any sound from within the greater meeting room. The courier was a young man, hardly more than Danat's age. Otah saw the calm, professional eyes sum him up. If the boy had been longer in the gentleman's trade, Otah would never have noticed it. He accepted the letter and ripped it open there, not waiting for a blade to cut the silk-sewn edging.

The cipher was familiar to him, but it made for slower reading than plain text. It was from the Kajiit Miyan, servant to the Emperor Otah Machi who had founded the Third Empire. Otah skipped down past the honorifics and empty form, decoding words and phrases in his mind until he reached something of actual importance. Then he read more slowly. And then he went back and read it again.

The mercenaries hired to protect Chaburi-Tan were ending their contract and leaving. Within a month, the city would be reduced to its citizen militia. The pirates who had been harrying the city would find them only token resistance. Their options, his agent said, were to surrender and pray for mercy or else flee the city. There would be no defense.

Otah took the servant girl by the elbow.

"Find Balasar. And Sinja. Bring them . . ." Otah looked over his shoulder. "Bring them to the winter garden of the second palace. Do it now. You. Courier. You'll wait until I have word to take back."

The twilight world lost its color like a face going pale. Otah paced the lush green and blossomless garden, wrenching his mind from one crisis to the next. A different servant led Balasar into the space between the willows.

"Find us some light," Otah said. "And Sinja-cha. Get Sinja-cha."

The servant, caught between two needs, hesitated, then hurried off. Otah led Balasar to a low stone bench. The general wore a lighter jacket, silk over cotton. His breath smelled of wine, but he gave no sign of being drunk. Otah looked out at the gray sky, the dark, looming palaces with windows glimmering like stars and cursed Sinja for his absence.

"Balasar-cha, I need you. The Galtic fleet has to travel to Chaburi-Tan," Otah said.

He outlined the letter he'd had, the history of increasing raids and attacks, and his half-imagined scheme to show the unity of Galt and the Khaiem. With every word, Balasar seemed to become stiller, until at the end, it was like speaking to stone.

"We can only show unity where it exists," Balasar said. His voice was low, and in the rising darkness it seemed to come from no direction at all. "After what happened yesterday, the fleet's as likely to turn on the city as the raiders."

"I don't have the ships and men to protect Chaburi-Tan," Otah said. "Not without you. The city will fall, and thousands will be killed. If the Galtic fleet came in, the pirates would turn back without so much as an arrow flown. And it would halfway unmake yesterday's mess."

"It can't happen," Balasar said.

"Then tell me what can," Otah said.

The general was silent. A moth took wing, fluttering between them like a clot of shadows and dust before it vanished.

"There is . . . something. It will make things here more difficult," Balasar said. "There are families who have committed to your scheme. That have already been brokering contracts and arranging alliances. I can gather them. It won't be anything like the full force of war, but if they sent their private ships and soldiers along with whatever you can muster up, it might serve."

"At the cost of sending away what allies I have," Otah said.

"That would be the price of it," Balasar said. "Send away your friends, and you're left eating with your enemies. It could poison the court against us."

Us. At least the man had said *us*.

"Get them," Otah said. "Get whoever you can quickly, and then send for me. I can't let another city die."

It only occurred to him as he stalked back through the wide stone halls and softly glowing lanterns of the first palace that he had been speaking to the man that had killed Udun and the village of the Dai-kvo, the man who had maimed Nantani and Yalakeht.

The meeting chamber was empty when he reached it; Danat and Issandra had gone. The cheese and apples and wine had been cleared away. The lanterns had blown out. Otah called for a servant to fetch him food and light. He sat, his annoyance and unease rising in his breast like the tide climbing a sea cliff.

Ana Dasin and her petulant, self-important father were well on their way to seeing both empires chewed away one bit at a time by pirates and foreign conspiracies. And failing crops. And time. Childless years growing one upon another like a winter with no promise of spring. There were so many things to fix, so uncountably many things that had gone wrong. He was the Emperor, the most powerful man in the cities of the Khaiem, and he was tired to his heart.

When the food arrived—pork in black sauce, spiced rice, sugared apple, wine and herbs—Otah was hardly hungry any longer. Moments after that, Sinja finally arrived.

"Where have you been?" Sinja demanded. "I've been wandering around the winter garden for half a hand looking for you."

"I should ask the same. I must have had half the servants in the palace looking for you."

"I know. Six of them found me. It got inconvenient telling them all I was busy. You need to come with me."

"You were busy?"

"Otah-cha, you need to come with me."

He breathed deeply and took a pose that commanded obedience. Sinja's eyebrows rose and he adopted an answering pose that held nuances of both query and affront.

"I have no intention of going anywhere until I have finished eating," Otah said. It embarrassed him to hear the peevishness in his voice, but not so much as to unsay it. Sinja tilted his head, stepped forward, and lifted one end of the table. The plates and bowl spun to the floor. One shattered. Otah was on his feet with no memory of standing. His face felt as warm as if he were looking into a fire. His ears filled with a buzzing of rage.

Sinja took a step back.

"I can have you killed," Otah said. "You know I can have you killed."

"You're right," Sinja said. "That passed the mark. I apologize, Most High. But you have to come with me. Now."

Servants came in, their eyes wide as little moons, their hands fluttering over the carnage of his dinner.

"What is it?" Otah said.

"Not here. Not where someone might hear us."

Sinja turned and walked from the room. Otah hesitated, mumbled an obscenity that made the servants turn their faces away, and followed. As his own anger faded, he saw the tension in Sinja's shoulders and through his neck. They were the sorts of signs he should have picked up on at once. He was tired. He was slipping.

Sinja was quartered in apartments of the third palace, where the Khai Saraykeht's second son would have lived, had there been a Khai Saraykeht or any sons. The walls were black marble polished until the darkness itself shone in the torchlight. Doors of worked silver still showed where gems had been wrenched from them by Galtic hands. They were beautiful all the same. Perhaps more beautiful than when they had been intact; scars created character.

Without speaking, Sinja went to each window in turn, poking his head out into the night, then closing outer shutters and inner. Otah stood, arms in his sleeves, unease growing in his heart.

"What is this?" Otah said, but the man only took a pose that asked patience and continued in his errand. At the last, he looked out into the corridor, sent the servant there away, then closed and bolted the main door.

"We have a problem, Otah-cha," Sinja said. He was breathing hard, like a man who'd run up stairs.

"We have a hundred of them," Otah said.

"The others may not matter," a woman's voice said from the shadows of the bedchamber. Otah turned.

Idaan was shorter than he remembered her, wider through the shoulders and the hips. Her hair was gray, her robe a cheaply dyed green and travel-stained. Otah took a step back without meaning to. His sister's appearance chilled his heart like an omen of death, but he wouldn't let it show.

"Why are you here?" he said.

His exiled sister pursed her lips and shrugged.

"Gratitude," she said. "You did away with my lover and his family. You took everything I had, including my true name, and sent me out into the world to survive as best I could."

"I'm not sorry," Otah said.

"And I am? It's the kindest thing anyone's ever done for me," Idaan said. "I mean that. And I'm here to repay the debt. You're in trouble, brother mine, and I'm the only one who can warn you. The andat are coming back to the world. And this time, the poets won't be answering to you."

8

>+< Autumn came early on the high plains. Even though the leaves were as green, the grasses as thick, Maati felt the change. It wasn't a chill, but the presentiment of one: a sharpness to air that had been soft and torpid with summer heat. Another few weeks and the trees would turn to red and gold, the mornings would come late, the sunsets early. The endless change would change again. For the first time in years, Maati found himself pleased by the thought.

The days following his return had fallen into a rhythm. In the mornings, he and his students worked on the simple tasks of maintenance that the school demanded: mending the coops for the chickens they'd brought from Utani, weeding the paths, washing the webs and dust from the corners of the rooms. At midday, they stopped, made food, and rested in the shade of the gardens or on the long, sloping hills where he had taken lessons as a boy. Afterward, he would retire for the afternoon, preparing his lectures and writing in his book until his eyes ached and then taking a short nap to revive before the evening lecture. And always, whatever the day brought, the subject drew itself back to Vanjit and Clarity-of-Sight.

"What about when you see things that aren't there?" Small Kae said.

"Dreams, you mean?" Eiah asked.

Maati leaned forward on the podium. The classroom was larger than they required, all six of his students sitting in the first row. The high, narrow windows that had never known glass let the evening breeze disturb their lanterns. He had ended his remarks early. He found there was less need to fill the time with his knowledge than there had once been. Now a few remarks and comments would spur conversation and analysis that often led far from where he had intended. But it was rarely unproductive and never dull.

"Dreams," Small Kae said. "Or when you mistake things for other things."

"My brother had a fever once," Ashti Beg said. "Saw rats coming through the walls for three days."

"I don't think that applies," Eiah said. "The definitions we've based the draft on are all physicians' texts. They have to do with the actual function of the eye."

"But if you see a thing without your eyes," Small Kae began.

"Then you're imagining them," Vanjit said, her voice calm and certain. "And the passages on clarity would prevent the contradiction."

"What contradiction?" Large Kae asked.

"Who can answer that?" Maati said, leaping into the fray. "It's a good question, but any of you should be able to think it through. Ashti-cha? Would you care to?"

The older woman sucked her teeth for a moment. A sparrow flew in through one window, its wings fluttering like a pennant in the wind, and then out again.

"Clarity," Ashti Beg said slowly. "The sense of clarity implies that it's reflecting the world as it is, ne? And if you see something that's not there to be seen, it's not the world as it is. Even if imagining something is like sight, it isn't like clarity."

"Very good," Maati said, and the woman smiled. Maati smiled back.

The binding had progressed more quickly than Maati had thought possible. For the greatest part, the advances had been made in moments like these. Seven minds prodding at the same thought, debating the nuances and structures, challenging one another to understand the issues at hand more deeply. Someone—anyone—would find a phrase or a thought that struck sparks, and Vanjit would pull pages from her sleeve and mark down whatever had pushed her one step nearer the edge.

It was happening less and less often. The binding, Maati knew, was coming near its final form. The certainty in Vanjit's voice and the angle of her shoulders told him as much about her chances of success as looking over the details of her binding.

As they ended the evening's session, reluctant despite yawns and heavy-lidded eyes, Maati realized that the work they were doing was less like his own training before the Dai-kvo and more like the long, arduous hours he had spent with Cehmai. Somehow, during his absence, they had all become equals. Not in knowledge—he was still far and away the best informed—but in status. Where he had once had a body of students, he was working now with a group of novice poets. A lizard scampered along before him and then up the rough wall and into the darkness. A nightingale sang.

He was exhausted, his body heavy, his mind beginning to spark and slip. And he was also elated. The wide night sky above him seemed rich with promise, the ground he walked upon eager to bear him up.

His bed, however, didn't invite sleep. Small pains in his knees and spine prodded him, and his mind failed to calm. The light of the half-moon cast shadows on the walls that seemed to move of their own accord. The restlessness of age, as opposed, he thought with weary amusement, to the restlessness of youth. As he lay there, small doubts began to arise, gnawing at him. Perhaps Vanjit wasn't ready yet to take on the role of poet. Perhaps he and Eiah in their need and optimism were sending the girl to her death.

There was no way to know another person's heart. No way to judge. It might be that Vanjit herself was as afraid of this as he was, but held by her despair and anger and sense of obligation to the others to move forward as if she weren't.

Every poet that bound an andat came face-to-face with their own flaws, their own failures. Maati's first master, Heshai-kvo, had made Seedless the embodiment of his own self-hatred, but that was only one extreme example. Kiai Jut three generations earlier had bound Flatness only to find the andat bent on destroying the family the poet secretly hated. Magar Inarit had famously bound Unwoven only to discover his own shameful desires made manifest in his creation. The work of binding the andat was of such depth and complexity, the poet's true self was difficult if not impossible to hide within it. And what, he wondered, would Vanjit discover about herself if she succeeded? With all the hours they had spent on the mechanics of the binding, was it not also his responsibility to prepare the girl to face her imperfections?

His mind worried at the questions like a dog at a bone. As the moon vanished from his window and left him with only the night candle, Maati rose. A walk might work the kinks from his muscles.

The school was a different place at night. The ravages of war and time were less obvious, the shapes of the looming walls and hallways familiar and prone to stir the ancient memories of the boy Maati had been. Here, for instance, was the rough stone floor of the main hall. He had cleaned these very stones when his hands had been smooth and strong and free from the dark, liver-colored spots. He stood at the place where Milah-kvo had first offered him the black robes. He remembered both the pride of the moment and the sense, hardly noticed at the time, that it was an honor he didn't wholly deserve.

"Would you have done it differently, Milah-kvo?" he asked the dead man and the empty air. "If you had known what I was going to do, would you still have made the offer?"

The air said nothing. Maati felt himself smile without knowing precisely why.

"Maati-kvo?"

He turned. In the dim light of his candle, Eiah seemed like a ghost. Something conjured from his memory. He took a pose of greeting.

"You're awake," she said, falling into step beside him.

"Sometimes sleep abandons old men," he said with a chuckle. "It's the way of things. And you? I can't think you make a practice of wandering the halls in the middle of the night."

"I've just left Vanjit. She sits up after the lecture is done and goes over everything we said. Everything anyone said. I agreed to sit with her and compare my memory to hers."

"She's a good girl," Maati said.

"Her dreams are getting worse," Eiah said. "If the situation were different, I'd be giving her a sleeping powder. I'm afraid it will dull her, though."

"They're bad then?" Maati said.

Eiah shrugged. In the dim light, her face seemed older.

"They're no worse than anyone who watched her family die before her eyes. She has told you, hasn't she?"

"She was a child," Maati said. "The only one to live."

"She said no more than that?"

"No," Maati said. They passed through a stone archway and into the courtyard. Eiah looked up at the stars.

"It's as much as I know too," Eiah said. "I try to coax her. To get her to speak about it. But she won't."

"Why try?" Maati said. "Talking won't undo it. Let her be who and where she is now. It's better that way."

Eiah took a pose that accepted his advice, but her face didn't entirely match it. He put a hand on her shoulder.

"It will be fine," he said.

"Will it?" Eiah said. "I tell myself the same thing, but I don't always believe it."

Maati stopped at a stone bench, flicked a snail from the seat, and rested. Eiah sat at his side, hunched over, her elbows on her knees.

"You think we should stop this?" he asked. "Call off the binding?"

"What reason could we give?"

"That Vanjit isn't ready."

"It isn't true, though. Her mind is as good as any of ours will ever be. If I called this to a halt, I'd be saying I didn't trust her to be a poet. Because of what she's been through. That the Galts had taken that from her too. And if I say that of her, who won't it be true of? Ashti Beg lost her husband. Irit's father burned with his farm. Large Kae only had her womb turned sick and saw the Khai Utani slaughtered with his family. If we're looking for a woman who's never known pain, we may as well pack up our things now, because there isn't one."

Maati let the silence stretch, in part to leave Eiah room to think. In part because he didn't know what wisdom he could offer.

"No, Uncle Maati, I don't want to stop. I only . . . I only hope this brings her some peace," Eiah said.

"It won't," Maati said, gently. "It may heal some part of her. It may bring good to the world, but the andat have never brought peace to poets."

"No. I suppose not," Eiah said. Then, a moment later, "I'm going into Pathai. I'll just need a cart and one of the horses."

"Is there need?"

"We aren't starving, if that's what you mean. But buying at the markets there attracts less notice than going straight to the low towns. It would be better if no one knows there are people living out here. And there might be news."

"And if there's news, there will be some idea of how soon Vanjit-cha will need to make her attempt."

"I was thinking more of how much time I have," Eiah said. She turned to look at him. The warm light of the candle and the cool glow of the moon made her seem like two different women at once. "This doesn't rest on Vanjit. It doesn't rest on any of them. Binding an andat isn't enough to . . . fix things. It has to be the right one."

"And Clarity-of-Sight isn't the right one?" he asked.

"It won't give any of these women babies. It won't put them back in the arms of the men who used to be their husbands or stop men like my father from trading in women's flesh like we were sheep. None of it. All the binding will do is prove that it can be done. That a solution exists. It doesn't even mean I'll be strong enough when my turn comes."

Maati took her hand. He had known her for so many years. Her hand had been so small that first time he had seen her. He remembered her deep brown eyes, and the way she had gurgled and burrowed into her mother's cradling arms. He could still see the shape of that young face in the shape of her cheeks and the set of her jaw. He leaned over and kissed her hair. She looked up at him, amused to see him so easily moved.

"I was only thinking," he said, "how many of us there are carrying this whole burden alone."

"I know I'm not alone, Maati-kya. It only feels like it some nights."

"It does. It certainly does," he said. Then, "Do you think she'll manage it?"

Eiah rose silently, took a pose that marked parting with nuances as intimate as family, and walked back into the buildings of the school. Maati sighed and lay back on the stone, looking up into the night sky. A shooting star blazed from the eastern sky toward the north and vanished like an ember gone cold.

He wondered if Otah-kvo still looked at the sky, or if he had grown too busy being the Emperor. The days and nights of power and feasting and admiration might rob him of simple beauties like a night sky or a fear grown less by being shared. Might, in fact, cut Otah-kvo off from all the things that gave meaning to people lower than himself. He was, after all, planning his new empire by denying all the women injured by the last war any hope of those simple, human pleasures. A babe. A family. Tens of thousands of women, cut free from the lives they were entitled to, now to be forgotten.

He wondered if a man who could do that still had enough humanity left to enjoy a falling star or the song of a nightingale.

He hoped not.

Eiah left the next morning. The high road was still in good repair, and travel along it was an order of magnitude faster than the tracking Maati had done between the low towns. When Maati and the others saw her off, she was wearing simple robes and the leather satchel hung at her side. She could have been mistaken for any traveling physician. Maati might have imagined it, but he thought that Vanjit held her parting stance longer than the others, that her eyes followed Eiah more hungrily.

When the horse and cart had gone far enough that even the dust from the hooves and wheels was invisible, they turned back to the business at hand. Until midday, they scraped soot and a decade's fallen leaves out from the shell of one of the gutted buildings. Irit found the bones of some forgotten boy who had been caught in that long-cooled fire, and they held a brief ceremony in remembrance of the slaughtered poets and student boys in whose path they all traveled. Vanjit especially was sober and pale as Maati finished his words and committed the bones to a fresh-made, hotter blaze that would, he hoped, return the old bones to their proper ash.

As they made their way back from the pyre, he made a point to walk at her side. Her olive skin and well-deep eyes reminded him of his first lover, Liat. The mother of the child who should have been his own. Even before she spoke, his breast ached like a once-broken arm presaging a shift of weather.

"I was thinking of my brother," Vanjit said. "He was near that boy's age. Not highborn, of course. They didn't take normal people here then, did they?"

"No," Maati said. "Nor women, for that."

"It's a strange thought. It already seems like home to me. Like I've always been here," the girl said, then shifted her weight, her shoulders turning a degree toward Maati even as they walked side by side. "You've always known Eiah-cha, haven't you?"

"As long as she's known anything," Maati said with a chuckle. "Possibly a bit longer. I was living in Machi for years and years before the war."

"She must be very important to you."

"She's been my salvation, in her way. Without her, none of us would be here."

"You would have found a way," Vanjit said. Her voice was odd, a degree harder than Maati had expected. Or perhaps he had imagined it, because when she went on, there was no particular bite to the words. "You're clever and wise enough, and I'm sure there are more people in places of influence that would have given you aid, if you'd asked."

"Perhaps," Maati said. "But I knew from the first I could trust Eiah. That carries quite a bit of weight. Without trust, I don't know if I would have hit on the idea of coming here. Before, I always kept to places I could leave easily."

"She said that you wouldn't let her bind the first andat," Vanjit said. "One of us has to succeed before you'll let her make the attempt."

"That's so," Maati agreed, a moment's discomfort passing through him. He didn't want to explain the thinking behind that decision. When Vanjit went on, it was happily not in that direction.

"She's shown me some of the work she's done. She's working from the same books that I am, you know."

"Yes," Maati said. "That was a good thought, using sources from the Westlands. The more things we can use that weren't part of how the old poets thought, the better off we are."

Maati described Cehmai's suggestion of making an andat and with-drawing its influence as a strategy of Eiah, pleased to have steered the conversation to safe waters. Vanjit listened, her full attention upon him. Ashti Beg and Irit, walking before them, paused. If Vanjit hadn't hesitated, Maati thought he might not have noticed until he bumped into them.

"Small Kae is making soup for dinner," Irit said. "If you have time to help her . . ."

"Maati-kvo's much too busy for that," Vanjit said.

When Ashti Beg spoke, her voice was dry as sand.

"Irit-cha might not have been speaking to him."

Vanjit's spine stiffened, and then, with a laugh, relaxed. She smiled at all of them as she took a contrite pose, accepting the correction. Irit reached out and placed her hand on Vanjit's shoulder as a sister might.

"I'm so proud of you," Irit said, grinning. "I'm just so happy and proud."

"So are we all," Ashti Beg said. Maati smiled, but the sense that something had happened sat at the back of his mind. As the four of them walked to the kitchens—the air growing rich with the salt-and-fat scent of pork and the dark, earthy scent of boiled lentils—Maati reviewed what each of them had said, the tones of voice, the angles at which they had held themselves. Small Kae assigned tasks to all of them except Maati, and he waited for a time, listening to the simple banter and the crack of knives against wood. When he took his leave, he was troubled.

He was not so far removed from his boyhood that he had forgotten what jealousy felt like. He'd suffered it himself in these same halls and rooms. One boy or another was always in favor, and the others wishing that they were. Walking through the bare gardens, Maati wondered whether he had allowed the same thing to happen. Vanjit was certainly the center of all their work and activity. Had Ashti Beg and Irit interrupted their conversation from an urge to take his attention, or at least deny it to her?

And then there was some question of Vanjit's heart.

The truth was that Eiah had been right. For all the hope and attention placed upon her, the project of the school was not truly Vanjit and Clarity-of-Sight. It would be Eiah and Wounded. Vanjit had seen it. It couldn't be pleasant, knowing she was taking the lead not for her own sake but to blaze the trail for another. He would speak to her. He would have to speak with her. Reassure her.

After the last of the lentil soup had been sopped up by the final crust of bread, Maati took Vanjit aside. It didn't go as he had expected.

"It isn't that Eiah-cha's work is more important," Maati said, his hands in a pose meant to convey a gentle authority. "You are taking the greater risk, and the role of the first of the poets of a new age. It's only that there are certain benefits that Eiah-cha brings because of her position at court. Once those aren't needed any longer, you see—"

Vanjit kissed him. Maati sat back. The girl's smile was broad, genuine, and oddly pitying. Her hands took a pose that offered correction.

"Ah, Maati-kvo. You think it matters that Eiah is more important than I am?"

"I didn't . . . I wouldn't put it that way."

"Let me. Eiah is more important than I am. I'm first because I'm the scout. That's all. But if I do well, if I can make this binding work, then she will have your permission. And then we can do anything. That's all I want."

Maati ran a hand through his hair. He found that none of the words he had practiced fit the moment. Vanjit seemed to understand his silence. When she went on, her voice was low and gentle.

"There's a difference between why you came to this place and why we have," she said. "Your father sent you here in hopes of glory. He hoped that you would rise through the ranks of all the boys and be sent to the Dai-kvo and become a poet. It isn't like that for me. I don't want to be a poet. Did you understand that?"

Maati took a pose that expressed both an acceptance of correction and a query. Vanjit responded with one appropriate to thanking someone of higher status.

"I had the dream again," Vanjit said. "I've been having it every night, almost. He's in me. And he's shifting and moving and I can hear his heart beating."

"I'm sorry," Maati said.

"No, Maati-kvo, that's just it. I wake up, and I'm not sad any longer. It was only hard when I thought it would never come. Now, I wake up, and I'm happy all day long. I can feel him getting close. He'll be here. What is being a poet beside that?"

Nayiit, he thought.

Maati didn't expect the tears, they simply welled up in his eyes. The pain in his breast was so sudden and sharp, he almost mistook the sorrow for illness. She put her hand on his, her expression anxious. He forced himself to smile.

"You're quite right," he said. "Quite right. Come along now. The bowls are all washed, and it's time we got to work."

He made his way to the hall they had set aside for classes. His heart was both heavy and light: heavy with the renewed sorrow of his boy's death, light at Vanjit's reaction to him. She had known Eiah's work to be of greater importance, and had already made her peace with her own lesser role. He wondered whether, in her place and at her age, he would have been able to do the same. He doubted it.

That evening, his lecture was particularly short, and the conversation after it was lively and pointed and thoughtful. In the days that followed, Maati abandoned his formal teaching entirely, instead leading discussion after discussion, analysis after analysis. Together, they tore Vanjit's binding of Clarity-of-Sight apart, and together they rebuilt it. Each time, Maati thought it was stronger, the images and resonances of it more appropriate to one another, the grammar that formed it more precise.

It was difficult to call the process to a halt, but in the end, it was Vanjit and Vanjit alone who would make the attempt. They might help her and advise her, but he allocated two full weeks in which the binding was hers and hers alone.

Low clouds came in the morning Eiah returned. They scudded in from the north on a wind cold as winter. Maati knew it wouldn't take. There were weeks of heat and sun to come before the seasons changed. And yet, there was a part of Maati's mind that couldn't help seeing the shift as an omen. And a positive one, he told himself. Change, the movement of the seasons, the proper order of the world: those were what he tried to see in the low, gray roof of the sky. Not the presentiment of barren winter.

"The news is strange," Eiah said as they unloaded her cart. Boxes of salt pork and raw flour, canisters of spice and hard cheese. "The Galts have fallen on Saraykeht like they owned it, but something didn't go well. I can't tell if my brother thought the girl was too ugly or she fell into a fit when she was presented, but something went badly. What I heard was early and muddled. I'll know better next time I go."

"Anything that hurts him helps us," Maati said. "So whatever it was, it's good."

"That was my thought," Eiah said, but her voice was somber. When he took a pose of query, she didn't answer it.

"How have things progressed here?" she asked instead.

"Well. Very well. I think Vanjit is ready."

Eiah stopped, wiping her sleeve across her forehead. She looked old. How many summers had she seen? Thirty? Thirty-one? Her eyes were deeper than thirty summers.

"When?" she asked.

"We were only waiting for you to come back," he said. Then, trying for levity, "You've brought the wine and food for a celebration. So tomorrow, we'll do something worth celebrating."

Or else something to mourn, he thought but did not say.

9

">+<" "By everything holy, don't tell Balasar," Sinja said. "He can't know about this."

"Why?" Idaan asked, sitting on the edge of the soldier's bed. "What would he do?"

"I don't know," Sinja said. "Something bloody and extreme. And effective."

"Stop," Otah said. "Just stop. I have to think."

But sitting there, head resting in his hands, clarity of mind wasn't coming to him easily. Idaan's story—her travels in the north after her exile, Cehmai's appearance on her doorstep, their rekindled love, and Maati's break with his fellow poet and then his return—had the feel of an old poem, if not the careful structure. If he hadn't had the pirates or Ana or her father or his own son or the conspiracy between Yalakeht and Obar State, or the incursions from the Westlands, he might have enjoyed the tale for its own sake.

But she hadn't brought it to him as a story. It was a threat.

"What role has Cehmai taken in this?" he asked.

"None. He wanted nothing to do with it. Or with my coming here, for that. I've left him to look after things until I've paid my debt to you. Then I'll be going home."

"Is it working?" Otah said at length. "Idaan-cha, did Maati say anything to suggest it was working?"

His sister took a pose of negation that held a sense of uncertainty.

"He came to Cehmai for help," Sinja said. "That means at least that he thinks he needs help."

"And Cehmai didn't agree to it," Idaan said. "He isn't helping. But he also doesn't want to see Maati hung. He cut Maati off before he told me who was backing him."

"What makes you think he has backing?"

"He said as much. Strong backing and an ear in the palaces whenever he wanted one," Idaan said. "Even if that overstates the truth, he isn't out hunting rabbits or wading through a rice field. Someone's feeding him. And how many people are there who might want the andat back in the world?"

"No end of them," Otah said. "But how many would think the thing was possible?"

Sinja opened a small wooden cabinet and took out a fluted bottle of carved bone. When he lifted out the stopper, the scent of wine filled the room. He asked with a gesture. Otah and Idaan accepted simultaneously, and with the same pose.

"The books are all burned," Otah said. "The histories are gone, the grammars are gone. I didn't think he could do this when he wrote to me before, I don't see that he could manage it now."

Sinja, stunned, overfilled one of the wine bowls, the red pooling on his table like spilled blood. Idaan hoisted a single eyebrow.

"He wrote to you before?" she said.

"It was years ago," Otah said. "I had a letter. A single letter. Maati said he was looking for a way to recapture the andat. He wanted my help. I sent a message back refusing."

"All apologies, Most High," Sinja said. He hadn't bothered to wipe up the spilled wine. "Why is this the first I'm hearing of it?"

"It came at a bad time," Otah said. "Kiyan was dying. It was hopeless. The andat are gone, and there's no force in the world that can bring them safely back."

"You're sure of that?" Idaan asked. "Because Maati-cha didn't think it was hopeless. The man is many things, but he isn't dim."

"It hardly matters," Sinja said. "Just the word that this is happening, and that—may all the gods keep it from happening—you knew he was thinking of it. That you've known for *years* . . ."

"It's a dream!" Otah shouted. "Maati was dreaming, that's all. He wants something back that's gone beyond his reach. Well, so do I. Anyone who has lived as long as we have knows that longing, and we know how useless it is. What's gone is gone, and we can't have it back. So what would you have had me do? Send the message back with an assassin? Announce to the world that Maati Vaupathai was out, trying to bind the andat, so they should all send invading armies at their first convenience?"

"Why didn't you?" Idaan asked. "Send the assassin, I mean. The invading armies, I understand. For that, why did you let them go at the end of the war?"

"I am not in the mood, Idaan-cha, to be questioned by a woman who killed my father, schemed to place the blame on me, and is only breathing air now because I chose to let her. I understand that you would have happily opened their throats."

"Not Cehmai's," she said softly. "But then I know why I wouldn't have done it. It doesn't follow that I should know why you didn't. The two aren't the same."

Otah rocked back in his chair. His face was hot. Their gazes locked, and he saw her nod. Idaan took a pose that expressed both understanding and contrition while unmasking the question.

"That isn't true," she said. "Thinking for a moment, I suppose they are."

Otah took the bowl Sinja held out to him. The wine was unwatered, rich and astringent. He drank it dry. Sinja looked nervous.

"There's nothing I can do about any of this tonight," Otah said. "I'm tired. I'm going to bed. If I decide it needs talking of further, it'll be another time."

He rose, taking a pose that ended an audience, then feeling a moment's shame, shifted to one that was merely a farewell.

"Otah-cha," Sinja said. "One last thing. I'm sorry, but you left standing orders. If she came back, I was supposed to kill her."

"For plotting to take my chair and conspiring with the Galts," Otah said. "Well. Idaan-cha? Are you hoping to become Emperor?"

"I wouldn't take your place as a favor," she said.

Otah nodded.

"Find apartments for her," he said. "Lift the death order. The girl we sent out in the snow might as well have died. And the man who sent her, for that. We are, all of us, different people now."

Otah walked back to his rooms alone. The palace wasn't quiet or still. Perhaps it never wholly was. But the buzzing fury of the day had given way to a slower pace. Fewer servants made their way down the halls. The members of the high families who had business here had largely gone back to their own palaces, walking stone paths chipped by the spurs and boot nails of Galtic soldiers, passing through arches whose gold and silver adornments had been hacked off by Galtic axes. They went to palaces where the highest men and women of Galt had come as guests, eating beef soup and white bread and fruit tarts. Sipping tea and wine and water and working, some of them at least, to build a common future.

And Idaan had come to warn him against Maati.

He slept poorly and woke tired. The Master of Tides attended him as he was bathed and dressed. The day was full from dawn to nightfall. Sixteen audiences had been requested, falling almost equally between members of the utkhaiem and the Galts. Three of the Galtic houses had left letters strongly implying that they had daughters who might be pressed to serve should Ana Dasin refuse. One of the priests at the temple had left a request to preach against the recalcitrance of women who failed to offer up sex. Two of the trading houses had made it clear that they wished to be released from shipping contracts to Chaburi-Tan. The Master of Tides droned and listed and laid out the form of another painful, endless, wasted day. When the stars came out again, Otah knew he would feel like a wrung towel and all the great problems he faced would still be unsolved.

He instructed that the priest be forbidden, the trading houses be referred to Sinja-cha and the Master of Chains, who could renegotiate terms but not break the contract, and then dictated a common response to the three letters offering up new wives for Danat that neither encouraged nor refused them. All this before the breakfast of fresh-brewed tea, spiced apples, and seared pork had appeared.

He had hardly begun to eat when the Master of Tides returned with a sour expression and took a pose that asked forgiveness, but pointedly did not suggest that the offending party was the Master of Tides herself.

"Most High, Balasar Gice is requesting to join you. I have suggested that he apply for an audience just as anyone else, but he seems to forget that his conquest of Saraykeht was temporary."

"You'll treat Balasar-cha with respect," Otah said, though he couldn't quite keep from smiling. And then a breath later, his chest tightened. *Something bloody and extreme. And effective.* What if the general had heard Idaan's news? "See him in. And bring another bowl for tea."

The Master of Tides took a pose that accepted the command.

"A clean bowl," Otah added to the woman's back.

Balasar followed all the appropriate forms when the servants escorted him back. Otah matched him, and then gestured for all the others to leave. When they were alone, Balasar lowered himself to the cushion on the floor, took the bowl of tea and the bit of pork that Otah offered him, and stretched out. Otah watched the man's face and body, but there was no sign there that he'd heard of Idaan's arrival or of her news.

"I've had a couple of discreet conversations," Balasar said.

"Yes?"

"About taking a fleet to Chaburi-Tan?"

Otah nodded. Of course. Of course that was what they were meeting about.

"And what have you found?" Otah asked.

"It can be done, but there are two ways to go about it. We have enough men to make a small, effective fighting force. Eight ships, perhaps, fully armed and provisioned. I wouldn't go to war on it, but it would outman most raiding parties."

Otah sipped his tea. The water wasn't quite hot enough to scald.

"The other way?"

"We can use the same number to man twenty ships. A mixed force, ours and your own. Throw on as many men as we can find who are well enough to stand upright. It would actually be easier to defeat in a battle. The men who knew what they were about would be spread thin, and amateurs are worse than nothing in a sea fight. But weigh it against the sight of twenty ships. The pirates would be mad to come against us in force."

"Unless they know we're all lights and empty show," Otah said. "There are suggestions that the mercenaries we have at Chaburi-Tan are working both sides."

Balasar sucked his teeth.

"That makes it harder," he agreed.

"How long would you need?" Otah asked.

"A week for the smaller force. Twice that for the larger."

"How many of our allies would we lose in the court here?"

"Hard to say. Knowing who your friends are is a tricky business right now. You'll have fewer than if they stayed."

Otah took a slice of apple, chewing the soft flesh slowly to give himself time. Balasar was silent, his expression unreadable. It occurred to Otah that the man would have made a decent courier.

"Give me the day," he said. "I'll have an answer for you tonight. Tomorrow at the latest."

"Thank you, Most High," Balasar said.

"I know how much I've asked of you," Otah said.

"It's something I owe you. Or that we owe each other. Whatever I can do, I will."

Otah smiled and took a pose of gratitude, but he was wondering what limits that debt would find if Idaan spoke to the old general. He was dancing around too many blades. He couldn't keep them all clear in his mind, and if he stumbled, there would be blood.

Otah finished his meal, allowed the servants to change his outer robe to a formal black with threads of gold throughout, and led his ritual procession to the audience chamber. The members of his court flowed into their places in the appropriate order, with the custom-driven signs of loyalty and obeisance. Otah restrained himself from shouting at them all to hurry. The time he spent in empty form was time stolen. He didn't have it to spare.

The audiences began, each a balancing between the justice of the issue, the politics behind those involved, and the massive complex webwork that made up the relationships of the court, of the cities, of the world. When he'd been young, the Khai Saraykeht had held audiences for things as simple as land disputes and broken contracts. Those days were gone, and nothing reached so high as the Emperor of the Khaiem unless no one lower dared rule on the matter. Nothing was trivial, everything fraught with implication.

Midday came and went, and the sun began its slow fall to the west. Storm clouds rose, white and soft and taller than mountains, but the rain stayed out over the sea. The daylight moon hung in the blue sky to the north. Otah didn't think of Balasar or Idaan, Chaburi-Tan or the andat. When at last he paused to eat, he felt worn thin enough to see through. He tried to consider Balasar's analysis, but ended by staring at the plate of lemon fish and rice as if it were enthralling.

Because he had been hoping for a moment's peace, he'd chosen to eat his little meal in one of the low halls at the back of the palace. The stone floor and simple, unadorned plaster walls made it seem more like the common room of a small wayhouse than the center of empire. That was part of its appeal. The shutters were open on the garden behind it: crawling lavender, starfall rose, mint, and, without warning, Danat, in a formally cut robe of deep blue hot with yellow, blood running from his nose to cover his mouth and chin. Otah put down the bowl.

Danat stalked into the hall and halfway across it before he noticed that a table was occupied. He hesitated, then took a pose of greeting. The fingers of his right hand were scarlet where he had tried to stanch the flow and failed. Otah didn't recall having stood. His expression must have been alarmed, because Danat smiled and shook his head.

"It's not bad," he said. "Just messy. I didn't want to come through the larger halls."

"What happened?"

"I have met my rival," Danat said. "Hanchat Dor."

"There's blood? There's blood between you?"

"No," Danat said. "Well, technically yes, I suppose. But no."

He lowered himself to sit at the table where Otah's food lay abandoned. There was a carafe of water and a porcelain bowl. As Otah sat, his boy wet one of his sleeves and set about wiping the blood from around his grin. Otah's first violent impulses to protect his son and punish his assailant were disarmed by that smile. Not conquered, but disarmed.

"He and Ana-cha were haunting the path between the palaces and the poet's house, just before the pond," Danat said. "We had words. He took some exception to our demand that Ana-cha apologize. He suggested that I should feel honored to have breathed the same air as his darling chipmunk. Seriously, Papa. 'Darling chipmunk.'"

"It might be a Galtic endearment," he said, trying to match his son's light tone.

Danat waved the thought away. It would be no more dignified, Otah admitted to himself, because a whole culture said it. Danat went on.

"I said that my business wasn't with him, but with Ana-cha. He began declaiming something in rhymed verse about him and his love being one flesh. Ana-cha told him to stop, but he only started bellowing it."

"How did Ana-cha react?"

Danat's grin widened. Blood had pinked his teeth.

"She seemed a bit embarrassed. I began speaking to her as if he weren't there. And . . ."

Danat shrugged.

"He hit you?"

"I may have goaded him," Danat said. "A little."

Otah sat back, stunned. Danat raised his hands to a pose appropriate to the announcement of victory in a game. Otah let himself smile too, but there was a touch of melancholy behind it. His son was no longer the ill, fragile child he'd known. That boy was gone. In his place was a young man with the same instinct to rough-and-tumble as any number of young men. The same as Otah had suffered once himself. It was so easy to forget.

"I had the palace armsmen throw him in a cell," Danat said. "I've set a guard on him in case anyone decides to defend my abused dignity by killing him."

"Yes, that would complicate things," Otah agreed.

"Ana followed the whole way shrieking, but she was as angry at Hanchat-cha as at me. Once I get to looking a bit less like an apprentice showfighter's first night, I'm sending an invitation to Ana-cha for a formal dinner at which we can further discuss her poor treatment of our hospitality. And then I'm going to meet my new lover."

"Your new lover?"

"Shija Radaani has offered to play the role. I think she was flattered to be asked. Issandra-cha is adamant that nothing makes a man worth having like another woman smiling at him."

"Issandra-cha is a dangerous woman," Otah said.

"She is," Danat agreed.

They laughed together for a moment. Otah was the first to sober.

"Will it work, do you think?" he asked. "Can it be done?"

"Can I win Ana's heart and make her want what she's professed before everyone of power in two empires that she hates?" Danat said. Saying it that way, he sounded like his mother. "I don't know. And I can't say what I feel about the way it's happening. I'm plotting against her. Her own mother is plotting against her. I feel that I ought to disapprove. That it isn't honest. And yet . . ."

Danat shook his head. Otah took a querying pose.

"I'm enjoying myself," Danat said. "Whatever it says of me, I've been struck bloody by a Galt boy, and I feel I've scored a point in some game."

"It's an important game."

Danat rose. He took a pose that promised his best effort, appropriate to a junior competitor to his teacher, and left.

There had to be some way that he could aid in Danat's task, but for the moment, he couldn't think what it might be. Perhaps if there was a way to arrange some sort of isolation for the two. A journey, perhaps, to Yalakeht. Or, no, there was the conspiracy with Obar State there that still hadn't been rooted out. Well, Cetani, then. Something long and arduous and cold by the time they got there. And without the bastard who'd struck his son . . .

Otah finished his fish and rice, lingering over a last bowl of wine and looking out at the small garden. It was, he thought, the size of the walled yard at the wayhouse Kiyan had owned before she became his first and only wife and he became the Khai Machi. That little space of green and white, of finches in the branches and voles scuttling in the low grass, might have been the size of his life.

Until the Galts came and slaughtered them all with the rest of Udun.

And instead, he had the world, or most of it. And a son. And, however little she liked it, a daughter. And Kiyan's ashes and his memory of her. But it had been a pretty little garden.

Otah returned to the waiting supplicants with his mind moving in ten different directions at once. He did his best to focus on the work before him, but everything seemed trivial. No matter that men's fortunes lay in his decision. No matter that he was the final appeal for justice, or if not that, at least peace. Or mercy. Justice and peace and mercy all seemed insignificant when held next to duty. His duty to Chaburi-Tan and all the other cities, to Danat and Eiah and the shape of the future. By the time the sun sank in the western hills, he had almost forgotten Idaan.

His sister waited for him in the apartments Sinja had found for her. She looked out of place among the sweeping arches and intricately carved stonework. Her hands were thick and calloused, her face roughened by sun. Some servant had arranged a robe for her, well-cut silk of green and cream. He considered her dark eyes and calm, weighing expression. He could not forget that she had killed men coldly, with calculation. But then so had he.

"Idaan-cha," he said as she rose. Her hands took a pose of greeting formal as court, but made awkward by decades without practice. Otah returned it.

"You've made a decision," she said.

"Actually, no. I haven't. I hope to by this time tomorrow. I'd like you to stay until then."

Idaan's eyes narrowed, her lips pressed thin. Otah fought the urge to step back.

"Forgive me if it isn't my place to ask, Most High. But is there something more important going on than Maati bringing back the andat?"

"There are a hundred things that are more certain," Otah said. "He may manage it, but the chances are that he won't. Meantime, I know for certain of three . . . four other things that are happening that could unmake the cities of the Khaiem. I don't have time to play in *might be*."

He'd meant to turn at the end of his pronouncement and walk from the rooms. Her voice was cutting.

"So instead, you'll wait until *is*?" Idaan said. "Or is it only that you have too many apples in the air, and you're only a middling juggler?"

"I'm not in the mood to be—"

"Dressed down by a woman who's only breathing because you've chosen to let her? Listen to yourself. You sound like the villain from some children's bedtime story."

"Idaan-cha," he said, and then found that he had nothing to follow it.

"I've come to tell you that your old friend and enemy is harnessing gods, and not for your benefit. It's the most threatening thing I can imagine happening. And what's your response? You knew. You've known for years. What's more, knowing now that he's redoubling his efforts, you can't be bothered even to consider the question until you've cleared your sheet of audiences? I've held a thousand opinions of you over the years, brother, but I never thought you were stupid."

Otah felt rage bloom in his chest, rising like a fiery wave, only to die with the woman's next words.

"It's the guilt, isn't it?" she said. When he didn't answer at once, she nodded to herself. "You aren't the only one that's done this, you know."

"Been Emperor? Are there others?"

"Betrayed the people you loved," she said. "Come. Sit down. I still have a little tea."

Almost to his surprise, Otah walked forward, sitting on a divan while the former exile poured pale green tea into two carved bone bowls.

"After you set me free, I spent years without sleeping through a full night. I'd dream of the people I'd . . . the people I was responsible for. Our father. Adrah. Danat. You never knew Danat, did you?"

"I named my son for him," Otah said. Idaan smiled, but there was a sorrow in her eyes.

"He'd have liked that, I think. Here. Choose a bowl. I'll drink first if you'd like. I don't mind."

Otah drank. It was overbrewed and sweetened with honey; sweet and bitter. Idaan sipped at hers.

"After you sent me away, there was a time I went about the business of living with what I'd done by working myself like a war slave," she said. "Sunrise to dark, I did whatever it was I was doing until I could fall down at the end half-dead and too tired to dream."

"It doesn't sound pleasant," Otah said.

"I did a lot of good," Idaan said. "You wouldn't guess it, but I organized a constabulary through half of the low towns in the north. I was actually a judge for a few years, if you'll picture that. I found that meting out justice wasn't something I felt suited for, but I kept a few murderers and rapists from making a habit of it. I made a few places safer. I wasn't utterly ineffective, even though half the time I was too tired to focus my eyes."

"And you think I'm doing the same thing?" Otah said. "You don't understand what it is to be an emperor. All respect for whatever you did after Machi, but I have hundreds of thousands of people relying upon me. The politics of empire aren't like a few low towns organizing to keep the local thugs in line."

"You also have a thousand servants," she said. "Dozens of high families who would do your bidding just for the status that comes from being asked. Tell me, why did you go to Galt yourself? You have men and women who'd have been ambassador for you."

"It needed me," Otah said. "If it had been someone lower, it wouldn't have carried the weight."

"Ah, I see," she said. She sounded less than persuaded.

"Besides which, I don't have anything to feel guilt over."

"You broke the world," she said. "You ordered Maati and Cehmai to bind that andat, and when it went feral on them and shredded every womb in the cities, my own included, you threw your poets into the wind. Men who trusted you and sacrificed for you. You became the heroic figure that bound the cities together, and they became outcasts."

"Is that how you see it?"

Idaan put her bowl down softly on the stone table. Her black eyes held his. She had a long face. Northern, like his own. He remembered that of all the children of the old Khai Machi, he and Idaan had shared a mother.

"It doesn't matter how I see it," she said. "My opinion doesn't make the world. Or unmake it. All that matters is what it actually is. So, tell me, Most High, am I right?"

Otah shook his head and rose, leaving his tea bowl beside hers.

"You don't know me, Idaan-cha. We've spoken to each other fewer times than I have fingers. I don't think you're in a position to judge my motives."

"Yours, no," she said. "But I've made the mistakes you're making now. And I know why I did."

"We aren't the same person."

She smiled now, her gaze cast down and her hands in a pose that accepted correction and apologized for her transgression without making it clear what transgression she meant.

"Of course not," she said. "I'll stay through tomorrow, Most High. In case you come to a decision that I might be able to aid you with."

Otah left with the uncomfortable impression that his sister pitied him. He made his way back to his apartments, ate half of the meal the servants brought him, and refused the singers and musicians whose only function in the world was to wait upon his whim. Instead, he took a chair out to his balcony and sat in the starlight, looking south to the sea.

Thin clouds streaked the high air, and the ocean was a vast darkness. The city that spilled down the hills before him glittered brighter than the stars; torches and lanterns, candles and firekeepers' kilns. The breeze smelled of smoke and salt and the lush flowers of early autumn. He closed his eyes.

He could feel the palaces behind him, looming like a weight he'd shifted off his back for a moment and would need to shoulder again. His mind ran free without him, bouncing from one crisis to another without ever pausing long enough to make sense of any one of them. And, intruding upon all of it, he found himself replaying his conversation with Idaan, searching for the cutting replies that hadn't occurred to him at the time.

Who was she to pity him? She'd made a low-town judge of herself, and now a farmer. It was an improvement from traitor and murderer, but it didn't give her moral authority over him. And to instruct him on the nature of his feelings about Maati and Cehmai was ridiculous. She hardly knew him. Coming to court in the first place had been a kind of madness on her part. He could have had her killed outright rather than sit like a dog while she heaped her abuse on him.

She thought he'd broken the world, did she? Well, what about the old way had been worth saving? It hadn't brought justice. The peace it offered had been purchased at the cost of lives of misery and struggle. And from that first moment, more than forty summers earlier, when the Dai-kvo had told him that they could not offer Saraykeht a replacement should Seedless slip its leash, Otah had known it was doomed.

The genius of the Galts—of all the rest of the world, for that—was that they had built their power on ideas that could grow one on another. A better forge led to better metalwork led to stronger tools and so on to the end of their abilities. By contrast, the Empire, the Second Empire, the cities of the Khaiem: all of them had wielded unthinkable power and fashioned wonders. And when the first poet had bound the first andat, anything had been possible. Anything a mind could fathom could be harnessed; anything that could be thought could be done.

But when the first andat had escaped and been harder to recapture, that potential had dropped a degree. Once a binding failed, each one that followed had to be different, and there were only so many ways to describe a thing fully enough to hold it as a slave. It was the central truth of the long, slow, dwindling of power that had brought them all here.

It was like a man's life. For a time in his youth, Otah had been capable of anything. His body had been strong, his judgment so certain he'd been willing to kill a man. And every day and every decision had narrowed him. Every year had weakened his back and his knees, eaten at his sight and wrinkled his skin. Time had taken Kiyan from him. His judgment had lost him his daughter.

He could have done anything, and he had chosen this. Or had it chosen for him.

And he wasn't yet dead, so there were other choices still to be made. Other days and years to live through. Other duties and failures and disappointments he would be responsible for not making right. His anger with Idaan was perfectly comprehensible. He was enraged by her because she had seen to the heart of something he hadn't wanted to understand.

He tried to imagine Kiyan sitting on the stone rail, smiling down at him the way she had. It was very, very easy.

What should I do? he asked the ghost his mind had conjured.

You can do anything, love, she said, *it's just that you can't do everything.*

Otah, Emperor of the Khaiem, wept, and he couldn't say how much was from sorrow and how much from relief.

In the morning, he had the Master of Tides clear his schedule. He met with Balasar and Sinja first. The meeting room was blond stone, ornately carved. Otah had heard that the carvings illustrated some ancient epic, but he'd never bothered to consider it. They were only figures in stone, unmoving and incapable of change. Unlike the men.

Balasar and Sinja sat across from each other, their spines straight and their expressions polite. They were divided by blood and broken faith. Otah poured the tea himself.

"I am placing you in joint control of the fleets and what armsmen we have," Otah said. "Between the two of you, you will protect Chaburi-Tan from the raiders and bring the mercenary forces into compliance with their contracts. I've written an edict that officially grants you my unrestricted permissions."

"Most High," Balasar said. His voice was careful and precise. "Forgive me, but is this wise? I am not one of your countrymen."

"Of course you are," Otah said. "Once Danat and Ana marry, we will be a united empire. Are you refusing the command?"

Sinja replied in the general's place.

"We're an odd pairing, Most High," he said. "It might be better if—"

"You've been my right hand for decades. You know our resources and our strengths. You're known and you're trusted," Otah said. "Balasar-cha's the best commander in Galt. You're both grown men."

"What exactly do you want from us?" Balasar asked.

"I want you to take this problem from me and fix it," Otah said. "I'm only one man, and I'm tired and overcommitted. Besides which, I'm a third-rate war leader, as I think we are all aware."

Sinja coughed to cover laughter. Balasar leaned forward, stroking his chin and looking down as if he'd discovered something fascinating in the grain of the table before him. Slowly, he nodded. After that, it was only a matter of working out the wording of the edict to the satisfaction of Sinja and Balasar both.

There would be trouble between them. That couldn't be avoided. But, Otah told himself, that was theirs to work. Not his. Not his any longer. He left the meeting room feeling oddly giddy.

He had scheduled a similar meeting with Danat and Issandra Dasin concerning the politics of the court and the intermarriage of Galt and the Khaiem. And then he thought Ashua Radaani was the man to address the issues of the conspiracy between Yalakeht and Obar State. He wasn't certain of that yet. Panjit Dun might also do well with it.

And once all that was done, all the best minds he could choose given their autonomy, he would closet himself with his sister and begin the work that couldn't be safely trusted to others: tracking Maati and whatever enemy among the courts of the utkhaiem had been supporting him.

10

⟩+⟨ Dawn crept over the school. The dark walls gained detail; the fragile lacing of frost burned away almost before it was visible. Birdsong that had begun in darkness grew in volume and complexity. The countless stars faded into the pale blue and rose of the east. Maati Vaupathai walked the perimeter of the school, his memory jogged with every new corner he turned. Here was the classroom where he'd first heard of the andat. There, the walkway where an older boy had beaten him for not taking the proper stance. The stables, empty now but for the few animals Eiah had brought, which Maati had made the younger boys clean with their bare hands after he had been elevated to the black robes of the older boys.

Ever since his return, Maati had suffered moments when his mind would spiral back through time, unearthing memories as fresh as yesterday. This morning in particular, the past seemed present. He walked past the long-dead echoes of boys crying in their cots, the vanished scent of the caustic soap they'd used to wash the stone floors, the almost-forgotten smell of young bodies and old food and misery. And then, just as memory threatened to sweep him away, he heard one of the girls. Large Kae singing, Irit's laughter, anything. The walls themselves shifted. The school became something new again, never seen in the world. Women poets, working together as the risen sun washed the haze from the air.

When he stepped into the kitchen, the warmth of the fire and the damp of the steam made him feel like he was walking into summer. Eiah and Ashti Beg sat at the wide table, carving apples into slivers. An iron pot of rough-ground wheat, rice, and millet burped to itself over the fire. The gruel was soft and rich with buttercream and honey.

"Maati-kvo!" Small Kae called, and he took a pose of welcome that the others matched. "There's fresh tea in the green pot. And that bowl there is clean. The blue one."

"Eiah was just telling us about the news from Pathai," Ashti Beg said.

"Little that there was of it," Eiah said. "Nothing to compare with what you were all doing here."

"Nothing we did while you were away is going to compare with what we'll do next," Small Kae said. Her face was bright, her smile taut. She covered her fear with an unwillingness to conceive of defeat. Maati poured himself the tea. It smelled like fresh-picked leaves.

"Have we seen Vanjit?" he asked and lowered himself to a cushion beside the fire. He grunted only a little bit.

"Not yet," Eiah said. "Large Kae went to wake her."

"Perhaps it would be better to let her sleep," Small Kae said. "It is her day, after all. It seems rude to make demands on her just because we all want to share it with her."

Eiah smiled, but her gaze was on Maati. A private conversation passed between them, no longer than three heartbeats together. More would be decided today than Vanjit and Clarity-of-Sight. Likely they all knew as much, but no one would say the words. Maati filled a fresh bowl with the sweet grain, holding it out for Ashti Beg to cover with apple. He didn't answer Eiah's unspoken question: *What will we do if she fails?*

Vanjit arrived before he had finished half the bowl. She wore a robe of deep blue shot with red, and her hair was woven with glass beads and carved shells. Her face was painted, her lips widened and red, her eyes touched by kohl. Maati hadn't even known she'd brought paints and baubles to the school. She had never worn them before, but this morning, she looked like the daughter of a Khai. When no one was looking, he took a pose of congratulation to Eiah. She replied with an inclination of the head and a tiny smile that admitted the change was her doing.

"How did you sleep, Vanjit-cha?" Maati asked as she swept the hem of her robe aside and sat next to him.

She took his hand and squeezed it, but didn't answer his question. Large Kae brought her a bowl of tea, Irit a helping of the grain and butter already covered with apple. Vanjit took a pose of thanks somewhat hampered by the food and drink.

While they all ate, the conversation looped around the one concern they all shared. The Galts, the Emperor, the weather, the supplies Eiah had brought from Pathai, the species of insect peculiar to the dry lands around the school. Anything was a fit topic except Vanjit's binding and the fear that lay beneath all their merriment and pleasure.

Vanjit alone seemed untouched by care. She was beautiful and, for the first time since Maati had met her, comfortable in her beauty. Her laughter seemed genuine and her movements relaxed. Maati thought he was seeing confidence in her, the assurance of a woman who was about to do a thing she had no thought might be beyond her. His opinion didn't change until after all the bowls had been gathered and rinsed, the cored apples and spilled grain swept up and carried away to the pit in the back of the school, when she took him by the hand and led him gently aside.

"I wanted to thank you," she said as they reached the bend of the wide hallway.

"I can't see I've done anything worth it," he said. "If anything, I should be offering you . . ."

There were tears brimming in her eyes, the shining water threatening her kohl. Maati took the end of his sleeve and dabbed her eyes gently. The brown cloth came away stained black.

"After Udun," Vanjit began, then paused. "After what the Galts did to my brothers . . . my parents. I thought I would never have a family again. It was better that there not be anyone in my life that I cared for enough that it would hurt me to lose them."

"Ah, now. Vanjit-kya. You don't need to think of that now."

"But I do. I do. You are the closest thing I've had to a father. You are the most dedicated man I have ever known, and it has been an honor to be allowed a place in your work. And I've broken the promise I made myself. I will miss you."

Maati took a pose that both disagreed and asked for clarification. Vanjit smiled and shook her head, the beads and shells in her braids clicking like claws on stone. He waited.

"We both know that the chances are poor that I'll see the sunset," she said. Her voice was solemn and composed. "This grammar we've made is a guess. The forces at play are deadlier than fires or floods. If I were someone else, I wouldn't wager a length of copper on my chances if you offered me odds."

"That isn't true," Maati said. He hadn't meant to shout, and lowered his voice when he spoke again. "That isn't true. We've done good work here. The equal of anything I learned from the Dai-kvo. Your chances are equal to the best any poet has faced. I'll swear to that if you'd like."

"There's no call," she said. From down the hall, he heard voices in bright conversation. He heard laughter. Vanjit took his hand. He had never noticed how small her hands were. How small she was, hardly more than a child herself.

"Thank you," she said. "Whatever happens, thank you. If I die today, thank you. Do you understand?"

"No."

"You've made living bearable," she said. "It's more than I can ever repay."

"You can. You can repay all of it and more. Don't die. Succeed."

Vanjit smiled and took a pose that accepted instruction, then moved forward, wrapping her arms around Maati in a bear hug. He cradled her head on his breast, his eyes pressed closed, his heart sick and anxious.

The chamber they had set aside for the binding had once been the sleeping room for one of the younger cohorts. The lines of cots were gone now. The windows shone with the light of middle morning. Vanjit took a round of chalk and began writing out her binding on the wide south wall, ancient words and recent blending together in the new grammar they had all created. From Maati's cushion at the back of the room, the letters were blurry and indistinct, but from their shape alone, he could see that the binding had shifted since the last time he'd seen it.

Eiah sat at his side, her hand on his arm, her gaze fixed on the opposite wall. She looked half-ill.

"It's going to be all right," Maati murmured.

Eiah nodded once, her eyes never leaving the pale words taking over the far wall like a bright shadow. When Vanjit was finished, she walked to the beginning again, paced slowly down the wall reading all she'd written, and then, satisfied, put the chalk on the ground. A single cushion had been placed in the middle of the room for her. She stopped at it, her binding behind her, her face turned toward the small assembly at the back. She took a silent pose of gratitude, turned, and sat.

Maati had a powerful urge to stand, to call out. He could wash the wall clean, talk through the binding again, check it for errors one last time. Vanjit began to chant, the cadences unlike anything he had heard before. Her voice was soft, coaxing, gentle; she was singing her andat into the world. He clenched his fists and stayed quiet. Eiah seemed to have stopped breathing.

The sound of Vanjit's voice filled the air, reverberating as if the building had grown huge. The chant began to echo, and Vanjit's actual voice receded. Words and phrases combined, voice against echo, making new sentences and meanings. The lilt of the girl's voice fell into harmony with itself, and Maati heard a third voice, neither Vanjit nor her echo, but something deep and sonorous as a bell. It was reciting syllables borrowed from the words of the binding, creating another layer of sound and intention. The air thickened, and Vanjit's back—her shoulders hunched, her head bowed—seemed very far away. Maati smelled hot iron, or perhaps blood. His heart began to race with a fear he couldn't express.

Something's wrong. We have to stop her, he said to Eiah, but though he could feel the words vibrate in his throat, he couldn't hear them. Vanjit's circling voice had made a kind of silence that Maati was powerless to break. Another layer of echoes came, the words seeming to come before Vanjit spoke them, echoing from the other direction in time. Beside him, Eiah's face had gone white.

Vanjit's voice spoke a single word—the last of the binding—at the same time as all the layered echoes, a dozen voices speaking as one. The world itself chimed, pandemonium resolving into a single harmonious chord. The room was only a room again. When Maati stood, he could hear the hem of his robe whispering against the stone. Vanjit sat where she had been, her head bowed. No new form stood before her. It should have been there.

She's failed, Maati thought. It hasn't worked, and she's paid the price of it.

The others were on their feet, but he took a pose that commanded them to remain where they were. This was his. However bad it was, it was his. His belly twisted as he walked toward her corpse. He had seen the price a failed binding exacted: always different, always fatal. And yet Vanjit's ribs rose and fell, still breathing.

"Vanjit-kya?" he said, his voice no more than a murmur.

The girl shifted, turned her head, and looked up at him. Her eyes were bright with joy. In her lap, something squirmed. Maati saw the round, soft flesh, the tubby, half-formed hands and feet, a toothless mouth, and black eyes full of empty rage. Except for the eyes, it could have been a human baby.

"He's come," Vanjit said. "Look, Maati-kvo. We've done it. He's here."

As if freed from silence by the poet's words, Clarity-of-Sight opened its tiny throat and wailed.

11

Kiyan-kya—

>+<   *I look at how long I carried the world, or thought I did, and I won-*
der how many times we have to learn the same lessons. Until we remember
them, I suppose. It isn't that I've stopped worrying. The gods all know I
crawl into my bed at night half-tempted to call for reports from Sinja and
Danat and Ashua. Even if I had them dragged into my chambers to re-
count everything they'd seen and done, how would it change things? Would
I need less sleep? Would I be able to remake the world through raw will like
a poet? I'm only a man, however fancy the robes they put me in. I'm not
more suited to lead a war fleet or root out a conspiracy or win a young
girl's love than any of them.

Why is it so hard for me to believe that someone besides myself might be
competent? Or did I fear that letting go of any one part would mean every-
thing would fall away?

No, love. Idaan was right. I have been punishing myself all this time for
not saving the people I cared for most. I think some nights that I will never
stop mourning you.

Otah's pen hung in the cool night air, the brass nib just above the paper. The night breeze smelled of the sea and the city, rich and heavy as
an overripe grape whose skin has only just split. In Machi, they would
already be moving down to the tunnels beneath the city. In Utani, where
his central palace stood wrapped in cloth, awaiting his return, the leaves
would have turned to red and yellow and gold. In Pathai, where Eiah
worked with her latest pet physician and pointedly ignored all matters
of politics and power, there might be frost in the mornings.

Here in Saraykeht, the change of seasons was only a difference of
scent and the surprise that the sun, which had so plagued them at summer's height, could grow tired so early. He wrote a few more sentences,
the pen sounding like bird's feet against the paper, and then blew on the

ink to cure it, folded the letter, and put it in with all the others he had written to her.

His eyes ached. His back ached. The joints of his hands were stiff, and his spine felt carved from wood. For days, he had been poring over records and agendas, letters and accountancy reports, searching for some connection that would uncover Maati's suspected patron. There were patterns to be looked for—people who had traveled extensively in the past few years who might be moving with the poet, supplies that had vanished with no clear destination, opposition to the planned alliance with Galt. And, with that, Maati's boast of an ear in the palaces. And the gods all knew there were patterns to be found. The courts of the Khaiem were thick with petty intrigue. Flushing out any one particular scheme was like plucking a particular thread from a tapestry.

To make matters worse, the servants and high families that Idaan had chided him for not making better use of had no place here. Even if Maati didn't have the well-placed spy he'd claimed, Otah still couldn't afford the usual gossip. Maati had to be found and the situation resolved before he managed to bind some new andat, and no one—Galt, Westlander, no one—could hear of it for fear of the reaction it would bring.

That meant that the records and reports were brought to Otah's private chambers. Crate after crate until they piled near the ceiling. And the only eyes that he could trust to the task were his own and, through the twisted humor that gods seemed to enjoy, Idaan's.

She was stretched out on a long silk divan now, half a month's lading records from the harbor master's office arrayed about her. Her closed eyes shifted beneath their lids, but her breath was as steady as the tide. Otah found a thin wool blanket and draped it over her.

It had not particularly been his intention to embrace his exiled sister and make her a part of the hunt for Maati, but the work was more than he could manage on his own. The only other person who knew of the problem was Sinja, and he was busy with Balasar and the creation of the unlikely fleet whose mission was to save Chaburi-Tan. Idaan knew the workings of the poets as well as any woman alive; she had been the enemy of one, the lover of another. She knew a great deal about court intrigue and also the mechanics of living an unobtrusive life. There was no one better equipped for the investigation.

He did not trust her, but had resolved to behave as if he did. At least for the present. The future was as unpredictable as it had always been, and he'd given up hope of anticipating its changes.

He knew from long experience that he wouldn't sleep if he went to bed now. His mind might be in a deep fog, but his body was punishing him for sitting too long. As it would have punished him for working too hard. The range allowed to him was so much narrower than when he'd been young. A walk to loosen his joints, and he might be able to rest.

The armsmen at the door of his apartments took poses of obeisance as he stepped out. He only nodded and made his way south. He wore a simple robe of cotton. The cloth was of the first quality, but the cut was simple and the red and gray less than gaudy. Someone who didn't know him by sight might have mistaken him for a member of the utkhaiem, or even a particularly powerful servant. He made a game of walking with his head down, trying to pass as a functionary in his own house.

The halls of the palaces were immense and ornate. Many small items—statues, paintings, jeweled decoration—had vanished during the brief occupation by Galt, but the huge copper-sheathed columns and the high, clear glass of the unshuttered windows spoke of greater days. The wood floors shone with lacquer even where they were scraped and pitted.

Incense burned in unobtrusive brass bowls, filling the air with the scent of sandalwood and desert sage. Even this late at night, singing slaves carried their harmonies in empty chambers. Crickets, Otah thought, would have been as beautiful.

His back had begun to relax and his feet to complain when the illusion of traveling the palaces unnoticed was broken. A servant in a gold robe appeared at the far end of the hall, walking purposefully toward him. Otah stopped. The man took a pose of obeisance and apology as he drew near.

"Most High, I am sorry to interrupt. Ana Dasin has come to request an audience. I would have turned her away, but under the circumstances . . ."

"You did well," he said. "Take her to the autumn garden."

The servant took a pose that accepted the command, but then hesitated.

"Should I send for an outer robe, Most High?"

Otah looked down at the wrinkled fabric and wondered what Ana would see if he met her like this: a man of great power and consequence at the end of a long day's work, or an old slob in a cotton robe.

"Yes," he said with a sigh. "An outer robe would be welcome. And tea. Bring us fresh tea. She might not care for it, but I want some."

The man scurried away. They had known where he was, and that he didn't wish to be disturbed. And they had known when to disturb him.

To be the Emperor of the Khaiem was above all else to be known by people he did not know. He had discovered that truth a thousand times before, and likely would do so a thousand times again, and each one discomforted him.

The autumn garden was nestled within the palaces. Trees and vines hid the stone walls, and paper lanterns gave the flagstone path a soft light. Near the center, a small brass fountain, long given to verdigris, chuckled to itself and a small wooden pavilion rested in the darkness. Otah walked down the path, still tugging the black and silver outer robe into place. Ana Dasin sat in the pavilion, her gaze on the water sluicing over bronze. The tea, set on a lacquered tray, had preceded him as if the servants had anticipated that he would ask for it as well and had had it ready.

Otah gathered himself. He was almost certain that Danat had already had his second meeting with the girl. Hanchat Dor, Danat's rival, was set to be freed in the morning. Otah found himself curious to see who Ana Dasin was in these circumstances.

"Ana," he said in her language. "I had not expected your company."

The girl stood. The soft light made her face rounder than it was, her eyes darker. She was wearing a dress of Galtic cut with pearls embroidered down the sleeves. Her hair, which had been pulled back into a severe formality, was escaping. Locks hung at the side of her face like silken banners draped from towers' windows.

"Emperor Machi. I have to thank you for seeing me so late," she said. Her voice was hard, but not accusatory. Otah caught the faint scent of distilled wine. The girl was fortified with drink, but not yet dulled by it.

"I am an old man," Otah said as he poured pale tea into two porcelain bowls. "I need less sleep than I once did. Here, take one."

His little act of kindness seemed to make her stiffer and less pleased, but she accepted the bowl. Otah sat, blowing across the tea's steaming surface.

"I've come . . ."

He waited.

"I've come to apologize," she said. She spoke the words as if she were vomiting.

Otah sipped his tea. It was perfectly brewed, the leaves infusing the water with a taste like summer sun and cut grass. It made the moment even more pleasant, and he wondered if he was being unkind by taking pleasure in Ana's predicament.

"May I ask what precisely you wish to apologize for," Otah said. "I would hate to have any further misunderstandings between us."

Ana sat, putting the bowl on the bench at her side. The porcelain clicked against the stone.

"I presented myself poorly," she said. "I . . . set out to humiliate you and Danat. That was uncalled for. I could have made my feelings known in private."

"I see," Otah said. "And is that all?"

"I would like to thank you for the mercy you've shown to Hanchat."

"It's Danat you should thank for that," Otah said. "I only respected his wishes."

"Not every parent respects her child," Ana said, then looked away, lips pressed thin. *Her* child, meaning Issandra. Ana was right. The mother was indeed scheming against her own daughter, and Otah had made himself a party to the plot. He would not have done it to his own child. He took another sip of his tea. It wasn't quite as pleasant as the first.

The fountain muttered to itself, the wind sighed. Here was the moment that chance had given him, and he wasn't sure how to use it. Ana, on whom all his plans rested, had come to him. There was something here, some word or phrase, some thought, that would narrow the distance between them. And in the space of a few more breaths, she would have collected herself again and gone.

"I should apologize to you as well," Otah said. "I forget sometimes that my view on the world isn't the only one. Or even the only correct one. I doubt you would have been driven to humiliate me if I hadn't done the same to you."

Her gaze shifted back to him. Whatever she had expected of him, it hadn't been this.

"I went to the wives of the councillors. There was very little time, and I thought they would have greater sway than the children. Perhaps they did. But I traded you as a trinket and didn't even think to ask you your thoughts and feelings. That should have been beneath me."

"I'm a woman," Ana said, her tone managing to be both dismissive and a challenge. *I'm a woman, and we've always been traded, married off, shifted as the tokens of power and alliance.* Otah smiled, surprised to find himself possessed by genuine sorrow.

"Yes," he said. "You are. And with my sister, my wife, my daughter . . . of all the men in the world, I should have known what that meant, and I forgot. I was in such a hurry to fix all the things I've done poorly that I did this poorly too."

She was frowning at him again as she had once before, on the journey to Saraykeht. He might have begun speaking in the language of birds or belching stones, to judge by her expression. He chuckled.

"It was not my intention to treat you with disrespect, Ana-cha. That I did so shames me. I accept your apology, and I hope that you will accept mine."

"I won't marry him," she said.

Otah drank the rest of his tea and set the empty bowl mouth-down on the lacquer tray.

"My son, you mean," Otah said. "You'll stay with this other man. Hanchat? No matter what the price or who's called on to pay it, no man deserves even your consideration? If it destroys your country and mine both, it would still be just."

"I . . . I don't . . ." the girl said. "That isn't . . ."

"I know. I understand. I'll say this. Danat is a good man. Better than I was at his age. But what you choose is entirely yours," Otah said. "If we've established anything, you and I, it's that."

"Not his?"

"Danat's decision is whether he'll marry you," Otah said with a smile. "Not the same thing at all."

He meant to leave her there. It seemed the right moment, and there was nothing more he could think to say. As he bent forward, preparing to rise, Ana spoke again.

"Your wife was a wayhouse keeper. You didn't put her aside. You never took a second wife. It was an insult to the whole body of the utkhaiem."

"It was," Otah said and stood with a grunt. There had been a time he could sit or stand in silence. "But I didn't marry her for the effect it had on other people. I did it because she was Kiyan, and there wasn't anyone else like her in the world."

"How can you ask Danat to obey tradition when you've broken it?" she demanded.

Otah considered her. She seemed angry again, but it seemed as much on Danat's behalf as her own.

"By asking," Otah said. "It's the best I can manage. I've damaged the world badly. The reasons I had for doing it seemed good at the time. I would like to be part of putting it back together again. With his help. With yours."

"I didn't break all this," Ana said, her chin stubborn. "Danat didn't either, for that matter. It's not fair that we should have to sacrifice whatever we want to unmake your mistakes."

"It isn't. But I can't repair this."

"Why do you think I can?"

"I have some faith in you both," he said.

By the time he made his way back to his rooms, Idaan had departed, leaving only a brief note saying that she intended to return in the morning and had some questions for him. Otah sat on a low couch by the fire grate, his eyes focused on nothing. He wondered what Eiah would have made of his conversation with the Galtic girl, and of whom he was truly asking forgiveness. His mind wandered, and he did not realize he had lain back until he woke to the cool light of dawn.

He was sitting in his private bath, the hot water easing the knots that sleeping away from his bed had tied in his back, when the servant announced Sinja's arrival. Otah considered the effort that rising, drying himself, and being dressed would require and had the man brought to him. Sinja, dressed in the simple canvas and leather of a soldier, looked more like a mercenary captain than the nearest advisor to an emperor. He squatted at the edge of the bath, looking down at Otah. The servant poured tea for the newcomer, took a ritual pose appropriate to a withdrawal from which he would have to be specifically summoned to return, and left. The door slid closed behind him, the waxed wooden runners as silent as breath.

"What's happened?" Otah asked, dreading the answer.

"I was going to ask the same thing. You spoke to Ana Dasin last night?"

"I did," Otah said.

Sinja sipped his tea before he spoke again.

"Well, I don't know what you said to her, but this morning, I had a runner from Farrer Dasin offering his ships and his men for Balasar's fleet. The general's meeting with him now to arrange the details."

Otah sat forward, the water swirling around him.

"Farrer-cha . . ."

Sinja put down the bowl of tea.

"The man himself. Not Issandra, not one of his servants. The handwriting was his own. There weren't details, only the offer. And since he's been reticent and dismissive every time Balasar asked, it seemed that something had changed. If it's what it looks like, it will mean putting off departure for a few days, but when we get there, it will be a real fighting force."

"That's . . ." Otah began. "I don't know how that happened."

"I've been swimming through palace gossip ever since, trying to find what made the change, and the only thing half-plausible I've heard is that Ana Dasin met with Danat-cha, after which she went to a second-rate teahouse, drank more than was considered healthy, and came here. After talking with you, she went back to the old poet's house; the lanterns were all lit and they didn't stop burning until the sun rose."

"We didn't talk about the fleet," Otah said. "The subject never came up."

Sinja unstrung his sandals and slid his feet into the warm water of the bath.

"Why don't you tell me what was said," Sinja asked. "Because somehow, in the middle of it, you seem to have done something right."

Otah recounted the meeting, rising from his bath and drying himself as he did. Sinja listened for the most part, interrupting only to laugh when Otah told of apologizing to the girl.

"That likely had as much to do with it as anything," Sinja said. "A high councillor's daughter with the Emperor of the Khaiem calling himself down for disrespecting her. Gods, Otah-kya, with that low an opinion of your own dignity, I don't know how you managed to hold power all these years."

Otah paused, his hands shifting to a pose of query.

"You apologized to a Galtic girl."

"I'd treated her poorly," Otah said.

Sinja raised his hands. It wasn't a formal pose, but it carried the sense of surrender. Whatever it was Sinja didn't understand about the act, he clearly despaired of ever learning.

"Tell me the rest," Sinja said.

There wasn't a great deal more, but Otah told it. He pulled on his robes by himself. The servants could adjust them when the meeting ended. Sinja drank another bowl of tea. The water in the bath grew still and as clear as air.

"Well," Sinja said when he had finished, "that's unexpected all around."

"You think Ana-cha interceded for us."

"I can't think anything else," Sinja said. "She's an interesting girl, that one. Quick to anger and about as tough as boiled leather if confronted, but I think you made her feel for you. It was clever."

"I didn't mean it as a ploy," Otah said.

"That's likely what made the ploy work," Sinja said. "Issandra and Danat should hear more of it. You know that little conspiracy is beginning to slip its stitches?"

"What do you mean?"

"Danat's false lover. Shija Radaani? It seems your boy is starting to fall in love with her. Or if not love, at least bed. That was the other gossip this morning. Shija went to Danat's rooms last night and hasn't yet come out."

Otah tugged at the sleeves, his eyebrows trying to crawl up his forehead. Sinja nodded.

"Perhaps it's part of Issandra's plan?" Otah said.

"If it is, she's more of a gambler than I am."

"I'll look into it," Otah said.

"Don't bother. I've already sent word to all the parties who need to know."

"Meaning Issandra."

"And nobody else," Sinja said. "You worry about finding Maati and his poet girls. And your sister. Whatever you're doing, keep one eye toward her."

Otah was halfway to objecting, but Sinja only tilted his head. Idaan had killed Otah's brothers. His father. She was capable of casual slaughter, and everyone knew it. There was no point in pretending the world was something it wasn't. Otah took a pose that accepted the advice and promised his best effort.

In point of fact, Idaan was waiting in his rooms when he returned from his breakfast and the morning of audiences that he could not postpone. She wore a borrowed robe of blue silk as dark as a twilight sky. Her arms and shoulders were thicker than the robe allowed, the fabric straining. Her hair was pulled back in a gray tail as thick as a mane. She did not smile.

"Idaan-cha," he said.

"Brother," she replied.

He sat across from her. Her long face was cool and unreadable. She touched the papers and scrolls on the low table between them. The scents of cedar and apples should have made the room more comfortable.

"I'm not done," she said. "But I doubt a year and ten clerks would be enough to do a truly thorough job. With just the pair of us, and you off half the time at court, we can't really hope for more than a weighted guess."

"Then we should get to work," he said. "I'll have them bring us food and—"

"Before that," Idaan said. "Before that, there's something we should discuss. Alone."

Otah considered her eyes. They were the same black-brown as his own. Her jaw was softer, her mouth pale and lined. He could still see the girl she had been, whom he had drawn up from the deepest cells beneath Machi and given freedom where she'd expected slavery or death.

"I'll send the servants away," he said. She took a pose that offered thanks.

When he returned, she was pacing before the windows, her hands clasped behind her. The soft leather soles of her boots whispered against the wood. The city spread below them, and then the sea.

"I never thought about them," she said. "The andat? I never gave them half a thought when I was young. Stone-Made-Soft was something halfway between a trained hunting cat and another courtier in a world full of them. But they could destroy everything, couldn't they? If a poet bound something like Steam or Fog, all that ocean could vanish in a moment, couldn't it?"

"I suppose," Otah agreed.

"I would have controlled it. Stone-Made-Soft, I mean. And Cehmai. If all the things I'd planned had happened as I planned them, I would have had the command of that power."

"Your husband would have," he said. Otah had ordered her husband executed. Adrah Vaunyogi's body had hung from the ruins of his family's palace, food for the crows. Idaan smiled.

"My husband," she said, her voice warm and amused. "Even worse."

She shook herself and turned back to the table. Her thick fingers plucked out a clerk's writing tablet. Otah could see letters carved into the wax.

"I've made a list of those people who seem most likely," she said. "I have a dozen, and I could give you a dozen more if you'd like it. They've all traveled extensively in the past four years. They've all had expenditures that look suspicious to one degree or another. And as far as I can see, all of them oppose your treaty with the Galts or are closely related to someone who does. And they all have the close connections to the palace that Maati boasted of."

Otah held out his hand. Idaan didn't pass the tablet to him.

"I think about what would have happened if I had been given that kind of power," she said. "I think of the girl I was back then. And the things I did. Can you imagine what I might have done?"

"It wouldn't have happened," Otah said. "Cehmai only answered to you so long as the Dai-kvo told him to. If you had started draining oceans or melting cities, he would have forbidden it."

"The Dai-kvo is dead, though. Years dead, and almost forgotten."

"What are you saying, Idaan-cha?"

She smiled, but her eyes made it sorrow.

"All the restraints we had to keep the poets from doing as they saw fit? They're gone now. I'm saying you should remember that when you see this list. Remember the stakes we're playing for."

The tablet was heavy in his hand, the dark wax scored with white where she had written on it. He frowned as his finger traced down the names. Then he stopped, and the blood left his face. He understood what Idaan had been saying. She was telling him to be ruthless, to be cold. She meant to steel him against the pain of what he might have to sacrifice.

"My daughter's name is on this list," he said, keeping his voice low and matter-of-fact.

His sister replied with silence.

12

>+< "There," Vanjit said, her finger pointing up into a featureless blue sky. "Right there."

On her hip, the andat squirmed and waved its tiny hands. She shifted her weight, drawing the small body closer to her own, her outstretched finger still indicating nothing.

"I don't see it," Maati said.

Vanjit smiled, her attention focusing on the babe. Clarity-of-Sight mewled, shook its head weakly, and then stilled. Vanjit's lips pressed thin, and the sky above Maati seemed to sharpen. Even where there was nothing to see, the blue itself seemed legible. And then he caught sight of it. Little more than a dot at first, and then a moment later, he made out the shape of the outstretched wings. A hawk, soaring high above the ground. Its beak was hooked and sharp as a knife. Its feathers, brown and gold, trembled in the high air. A smear of old blood darkened its talons. There were mites in its feathers.

Maati closed his eyes and looked away, shaken by vertigo.

"Gods!" he said. He heard Vanjit's delighted chuckle.

The spirit of elation filled the stone halls, the ruined gardens, the spare meadows. All the days since the binding, it had felt to Maati as if the world itself had taken a deep breath and then laughed aloud. Whenever the chores and classes had allowed it, the girls had crowded around Vanjit and Clarity-of-Sight, and himself along with them.

The andat itself was beautiful and fascinating. Its form was identical to a true human child, but small things in its behavior showed Vanjit's inexperience. She had not held a babe or seen one since she herself had been no more than a child. The strength of its neck and the sureness of its gaze were subtly wrong. Its cry, while wordless, expressed a richness and variety of emotion that in Maati's experience children rarely developed before they could walk. Small errors of imagination that affected only the form that the andat took. Its function, as Vanjit delighting in showing, was perfect and precise.

"I've seen other things too," Vanjit said. "The greater the change, the more difficult it is at first."

Maati nodded. He could see the individual hairs on her head. The crags where tiny flakes of dead skin peeled from the living tissue beneath. An insect the shape of a tick but a thousand times smaller clung to the root of her eyelash. He closed his eyes.

"Forgive me," he said. "Could I put upon you to undo some part of that? It's distracting. . . ."

He heard her robe rustle and go silent. When he opened his eyes again, his vision was clear but no longer inhumanly so. He smiled.

"Once I've made the change, I forget that it doesn't fall back on its own," she said.

"Stone-Made-Soft was much the same," Maati said. "Once it had changed the nature of a rock, it remained weakened until Cehmai-kvo put an effort into changing it back. Then there was Water-Moving-Down, who might stop a river only so long as its poet gave the matter strict attention. The question rests on the innate capacity for change within the object affected. Stone by nature resists change, water embraces it. I suspect that whatever eyes you improve will still suffer the normal effects of age."

"The change may be permanent, but we aren't," she said.

"Well put," Maati said.

The courtyard in which they sat showed only small signs of the decade of ruin it had suffered. The weeds had all been pulled or cut, the broken stones reset. Songbirds flitted between the trees, lizards scurried through the low grass, and far above, invisible to him now, a hawk circled in the high, distant air.

Maati could imagine that it wasn't the school that he had suffered in his boyhood: it had so little in common with the half-prison he recalled. A handful of women instead of a shifting cadre of boys. A cooperative struggle to achieve the impossible instead of cruelty and judgment. Joy instead of fear. The space itself seemed remade, and perhaps the whole of the world along with it. Vanjit seemed to guess his thoughts. She smiled. The thing at her hip grumbled, fixing its black eyes on Maati, but did not cry.

"It's unlike anything I expected," Vanjit said. "I can feel him. All the time, he's in the back of my mind."

"How burdensome is it?" Maati asked, sitting forward.

Vanjit shook her head.

"No worse than any baby, I'd imagine," she said. "He tires me some-times, but not so much I lose myself. And the others have all been kind. I don't think I've cooked a meal for myself since the binding."

"That's good," Maati said. "That's excellent."

"And you? Your eyes?"

"Perfect. I've been able to write every evening. I may actually man-age to complete this before I die."

He'd meant it as a joke, but Vanjit's reply was grim, almost scolding.

"Don't say that. Don't talk about death lightly. It isn't something to laugh at."

Maati took an apologetic pose, and a moment later the darkness seemed to leave the girl's eyes. She shifted the andat again, freeing one hand to take an apologetic pose.

"No," Maati said. "You're right. You're quite right."

He steered the conversation to safer waters—meals, weather, recon-structing the finer points of Vanjit's successful binding. Contentment seemed to come from the girl like heat from a fire. He regretted leaving her there, and yet, walking down the wide stone corridors, he was also pleased.

The years he had spent scrabbling in the shadows like a rat had been so long and so thick with anger and despair, Maati had forgotten what it was to feel simple happiness. Now, with the women's grammar proved and the andat returned to the world, his flesh itself felt different. His shoulders had grown straighter, his heart lighter, his joints looser and stronger and sure. He had managed to ignore his burden so long he had mistaken it for normalcy. The lifting of it felt like youth.

Eiah sat cross-legged on the floor of one of the old lecture halls, un-tied codices, opened books, unfurled scrolls laid out around her like ripples on the surface of a pond. He glanced at the pages—diagrams of flayed arms, the muscles and joints laid bare as if by the most meticulous butcher in history; Westlands script with its whorls and dots like a child's angry scribble; notations in Eiah's own hand, outlining the definitions and limitations and structure of violence done upon flesh. Wounded. The andat at its origin. And all of it, he could make out from where he stood without squinting or bending close.

Eiah looked up at him with a pose equal parts welcome and despair. Maati lowered himself to the floor beside her.

"You look tired," he said.

Eiah gestured to the careful mess before her, and then sighed.

"This was simpler when I wasn't allowed to do it," she said. "Now that my own turn has come, I'm starting to think I was a fool to think it possible."

Maati touched one of the books with his outstretched fingers. The paper felt thick as skin.

"There is a danger to it," Maati said. "Even if your binding is perfectly built, there might have been another done that was too much like it. These books, they were written by men. Your training was done by men. The poets before Vanjit were all men. Your thinking could be too little like a man's."

Eiah smiled, chuckling. Maati took a pose of query.

"Physicians in the Westlands tend to be women," she said. "I don't think I have more than half-a-dozen texts that I could say for certain were written by men. The problem isn't that."

"No?"

"No, it's that no matter what's between your thighs, a cut is a cut, a burn is a burn, and a bruise is a bruise. Break a bone now, and it snaps much the way it did in the Second Empire. Vanjit's binding was based on a study of eyes and light that didn't exist back then. Nothing I'm working from is *new*."

There was frustration in her voice. Perhaps fear.

"There is another way," Maati said. Eiah shifted, her gaze on his. Maati scratched his arm.

"We have Clarity-of-Sight," he said. "It proves that we can do this thing, and that alone gives us a certain power. If we send word to Otah-kvo, tell him what we've done and that he must turn away from his scheme with the Galts, he would do it. He would have to. We could take as much time as you care to take, consult as many scholars as we can unearth. Even Cehmai would have to come. He couldn't refuse the Emperor."

It wasn't something he'd spoken aloud before. It was hardly something he'd allowed himself to think. Before Vanjit and Clarity-of-Sight, the idea of returning to the courts of the Khaiem—to Otah—in triumph would have been only a sort of torture of the soul. It would have been like wishing for his son to be alive, or Liat at his side, or any of the thousand regrets of his past to be unmade.

Now it was not only possible but perhaps even wise. Another letter, sent by fast courier, announcing that Maati had succeeded and made himself the new Dai-kvo, and Otah would have no choice but to honor him. He could almost hear the apology now, sweeter for coming from the lips of an emperor.

"It's a kind thought, but no," Eiah said. "It's too big a risk."

"I don't see how," Maati said, frowning.

"Vanjit's one woman, and binding an andat doesn't mean that a good man and a sharp knife can't end you," Eiah said. "And she may slip, at which point half the world will want our heads on sticks, just to be sure it doesn't happen again. Once we've managed a few more, it will be safe. And Wounded can't wait."

"If you heal all the women of the cities, they'll know we've bound an andat," Maati said. "It will be just as clear a message as sending a letter. And by your argument, just as dangerous."

"If they wait until after I've given back the chance of bearing children, the Galts can kill me," Eiah said. "It will be too late to matter."

"You don't believe that," Maati said, aghast. Eiah smiled and shrugged.

"Perhaps not," she agreed. "Say rather, if I'm going to die, I'd rather it was after I'd finished this."

Maati put a hand on her shoulder, then let his arm fall to his side. Eiah described the issues of the binding that troubled her most. To pull a thought from abstraction into concrete form required a deep understanding of the idea's limits and consequences. To bind Wounded, Eiah needed to find the common features of a cut finger and a burned foot, the difference between a tattooing quill and a rose thorn, the definitions that kept the thought small enough for a single mind to encompass.

"Take Vanjit's work," Eiah said. "Your eyes were never burned. No one cut them or bruised them. But they didn't see as well as when you were young. So there must have been some damage to them. So are the changes of age wounds? White hair? Baldness? When a woman loses her monthly flow, is it because she's broken?"

"You can't consider age," Maati said. "For one thing, it muddies the water, and for another, I will swear to you that more than one poet has reached for Youth-Regained or some such."

"But how can I make that fit?" Eiah said. "What makes an old man's failing hip different from a young girl's bruised one? The speed of the injury?"

"The intention," Maati said, and touched a line of symbols. His finger traced the strokes of ink, pausing from time to time. He could feel Eiah's attention on him. "Here. Change *ki* to *toyaki*. Wounds are either intentional or accident. *Toyaki* includes both senses."

"I don't see what difference it makes," Eiah said.

"*Ki* also includes a nuance of proper function. Behavior that isn't misadventure or conscious intention, but a product of design," Maati said. "If you remove that . . ."

He licked his lips, his fingers closing in the air above the page. Once, many years before, he had been asked to explain why the poets were called poets. He remembered his answer vaguely. That the bindings were the careful shaping of meaning and intention, that makers or thought-weavers were just as apt. It had been a true answer for as far as it went.

And also, sometimes, the grammar of a binding would say something unexpected. Something half-known, or half-acknowledged. A profound melancholy touched him.

"You see, Eiah-cha," he said, softly, "time is meant to pass. The world is meant to change. When people fade and die, it isn't a deviation. It's the way the world is made."

He tapped the symbol *ki*.

"And that," he said, "is where you make that distinction."

Eiah was silent for a moment, then drew a pen from her sleeve and a small silver ink box. With a soft pressure, gentler than rain on leaves, she added the strokes that remade the binding.

"You accept my argument, then?" Maati asked.

"I have to," Eiah said. "It's why we're here, isn't it? Sterile didn't add anything to the world, it only broke the way humanity renews itself. I've seen enough decline and death to recognize its proper place. I'm not here to stop time or death. Just to put back the balance so that new generations can come up fresh."

Maati nodded. When Eiah spoke, her voice sounded tired.

"I miss him," she said. He knew that she meant her father. "The last time I saw him, he looked so old. I still picture him with dark hair. It hasn't been like that in years, but it's what's in my mind."

"We're doing the right thing," Maati said. His voice was little more than a whisper.

"I don't doubt it," Eiah said. "He's turned his back on a generation of women as if their suffering were insignificant. Sexual indenture used to be restricted to bed slaves, and he would make an industry of it if he could. He would haul women across like bales of cotton. I hate everything about the scheme, but I miss him."

"I do too," Maati said.

"You also hate him," she said. There was no place in this room for half-truths.

"That too," Maati agreed.

Dinner that night was a brace of quail Large Kae had trapped. The flesh was soft and rich. Maati sat at the head of the long table, Vanjit and

Clarity-of-Sight at the far end, and plucked the delicate bones. The bright chattering voices of Small Kae and Irit seemed distant, the dry wit of Ashti Beg grim. Eiah also seemed subdued, but it might only have been that she was thinking of the binding. The meal seemed to last forever, and yet he found himself surprised when Ashti Beg gathered up the bowls and the talk shifted to cleanup chores.

"I don't think I can," Vanjit said, her voice apologetic. "I assumed that we had changed the rotation."

"We skipped you last time, if that's what you mean," Ashti Beg said. "I don't know if that's the same as agreeing to wait on you."

There was laughter in the older woman's voice, but it had teeth. Small Kae was smiling a fixed smile and staring at the table. If he hadn't been so distracted, Maati would have seen this coming before it arrived.

"I don't think I can, though," Vanjit said, still firmly in her seat. The thing on her lap shifted its gaze from the poet to Ashti Beg and back as if fascinated.

"I seem to recall my mother keeping the house even when she had a babe on her hip," Ashti Beg said. "But she always was unusually talented."

"I have the andat. That's more work than washing dishes," Vanjit said. "At court, poets are forgiven other duties, aren't they, Maati-kvo?"

"The smallest brat of the utkhaiem is forgiven their duties," Ashti Beg said before Maati could frame a reply. "That's why it's court. Because some people set themselves above others."

The air was suddenly heavy. Maati stood, unsure what he was about to say. Irit's sudden chirp saved him.

"Oh, it isn't much. No need to fuss about it. I'll be happy to do the thing. No, Vanjit-cha, don't get up. If you don't feel up to doing it, you ought not strain yourself."

The last words rose at the end as if they were a question. Maati nodded as if something had been decided, then walked out of the hall. Vanjit followed without speaking, and took herself and her small burden down a side hall and out to the gardens. Maati could hear the voices of the others as they cleaned away the remnants of the small, fallen birds.

They met as they always did, sitting in a rough circle and discussing the fine points of binding the andat. There was no sign of the earlier conflict; Vanjit and Ashti Beg treated each other with their customary kindness and respect. Eiah explained the difference between accident, intention, and consequence of design to Irit and Small Kae and, Maati thought, learned by the experience. By the warm, soft light of the lanterns, they might have been talking of anything. By the end, there was even real laughter.

It should have been a good evening, but as he went back toward his bed, Maati was troubled and couldn't quite say why. It had to do with Otah-kvo and Eiah, Vanjit and Clarity-of-Sight. The Galts and his own unsettling if unsurprising insight into the nature of time and decay.

He opened his book, reading his own handwriting by the light of the night candle. Even the quality of his script had changed since Vanjit had sharpened his vision. The older entries had been . . . not sloppy, never that. But not so crisp as he was capable of now. It had been an old man's handwriting. Now it was something different. He picked up his pen, touched nib to ink, but found nothing coherent to say.

He wiped the pen clean and put the book aside. Somewhere far to the south, Otah was dining with the men who had destroyed the Khaiem. He was sleeping on a bed of silk and drinking wine from bowls of beaten gold, while here in the dry plains his own daughter prepared to risk her life to make right what he had done.

What they had done together. Otah, Cehmai, and Maati himself. One was crawling into bed with the enemy, another turning away and hiding his face. Only Maati had even tried to make things whole again. Vanjit's success meant it had not been wasted effort. Eiah's fear reminded him that it was not yet finished.

He made his way down the corridors in the near darkness. Only candles and a half-moon lit his way. He was unsurprised to see Vanjit sitting alone in the gardens. Unlike the courtyard where they had spoken before, the gardens were bleak and bare. They had come too late to plant this season. Eiah's occasional journeys to Pathai provided food enough, and they didn't have the surplus of spare hands that had once held up the school. The wilderness encroached on the high stone walls here, young trees growing green and bold in plots where Maati had sown peas and harvested pods.

She heard him approaching and glanced back over her shoulder. She shifted, adjusting her robes, and Maati saw the small, black eyes of the andat appear from among the folds of cotton. She had been nursing it. It shocked him for a moment, though on reflection it shouldn't have. The andat had no need of milk, of course, but it was a product of Vanjit's conceptions. Stone-Made-Soft had been involved with the game of stones. Three-Bound-as-One had been fascinated by knots. The relationship of poet and andat was modeled on mother and child as it had never been before in all of history. The nursing was, Maati supposed, the physical emblem of it.

"Maati-kvo," she said. "I didn't expect anyone to be here."

He took a pose of apology, and she waved it away. In the cold light, she looked ghostly. The andat's eyes and mouth seemed to eat the light, its skin to glow. Maati came nearer.

"I was worried, I suppose," he said. "It seemed . . . uncomfortable at dinner this evening."

"I'd been thinking about that," Vanjit said. "It's hard for them. Ashti Beg and the others. I think it must be very hard for them."

"How do you mean?"

She shrugged. The andat in her lap gurgled to itself, considering its own short, pale fingers with fascination.

"They have all put in so much time, so much work. Then to see an-other woman complete a binding and gain a child, all at once. I imagine it must gnaw at her. It isn't that she intends to be rude or cruel. Ashti is in pain, and she lashes out. I knew a dog like that once. A cart had rolled over it. Snapped its spine. It whined and howled all night. You would have thought it was begging aid, except that it tried to bite anyone who came near. Ashti-cha is much the same."

"You think so?"

"I do," she said. "You shouldn't think ill of her, Maati-kvo. I doubt she even knows what she's doing."

He folded his arms.

"I can't think it's simple for you either," he said. He had the sense of testing her, though he couldn't have said quite how. Vanjit's face was as clear and cloudless as the sky.

"It's perfect," she said. "Nowhere near as difficult as I'd thought. Only he makes me tired. No more than any mother with a new babe, though. I've been thinking of names. My cousin was named Ciiat, and he was about this old when the Galts came."

"It has a name already," Maati said. "Clarity-of-Sight."

"I meant a private name," Vanjit said. "One for just between the two of us. And you, I suppose. You are as near to a father as he has."

Maati opened his mouth, then closed it. Vanjit's hand slipped into his own, her fingers twined around his. Her smile seemed so genuine, so in-nocent, that Maati only shook his head and laughed. They remained there for the space of ten long breaths together, Vanjit sitting, Maati standing at her side, and the andat, shifting impatiently in her lap.

"Once Eiah's bound Wounded," Maati said, "we can all go back."

Vanjit made a small sound, neither cough nor gasp nor chuckle, and released Maati's hand. He glanced down. Vanjit smiled up at him.

"That will be good," she said. "This must all be hard for her as well. I wish there was something we could do to ease things."

"We'll do what can be done," Maati said. "It will have to be enough."

Vanjit didn't reply, and then raised her arm, pointing to the horizon.

"The brightest star," she said. "The one just coming up over the trees there? You see it?"

"I do," Maati said. It was one of the traveling stars that made their slow way through the night skies.

"It has moons around it. Three of them."

He laughed and shook his head, but Vanjit didn't join him. Her face was still and cool. Maati's laughter died.

"A star with . . . *moons*?"

Vanjit nodded. Maati looked up again at the bright golden glimmer above the trees. He frowned first and then smiled.

"Show me," he said.

13

>+< The fleet left Saraykeht on the first truly cool morning of autumn. A dozen ships with bright sails, and the marks of the Empire and Galt flying together from their masts. From the shore, Otah could no longer make out the shapes of the individual sailors and soldiers that crowded the distant decks, much less Sinja himself, dressed though the man was in gaudy commander's array. Farrer Dasin's ships still stood at anchor, and the other Galtic ships which had been promised but were not yet prepared to sail.

Sinja had met with him for the last time less than a hand and a half before he'd stepped onto the small boat to make his last inspection. Otah had made himself comfortable in a teahouse near the seafront, waiting for the ceremony that would send off the fleet. The walls of the place were stained with decades of lantern smoke, the floorboards spotted with the memory of spilled wine. Sitting at the back table, Otah had felt like a peacock in a hen coop. Sinja, breezing through the open doors in a robe of bright green and hung with silk scarves and golden pendants, had made him feel less ridiculous only by comparison.

"Well, this is your last chance to call the whole thing quits," Sinja said, dropping into the chair across from Otah as casually as a drinking companion. Otah fumbled in his sleeve for a moment and drew out the letters intended for the utkhaiem of Chaburi-Tan. Sinja took them, considered the bright thread that sewed each of them closed, and sighed.

"I'd feel better if Balasar was leading the first command," Sinja said.

"I thought you'd decided that he'd be better staying to arrange your reinforcements."

"Agreed. I agreed. He decided. And it does make sense. Farrer-cha and the others who've followed his example will be able to swallow all this better if they're answering to a Galtic general."

"And waiting for them to be ready . . ." Otah said.

"Madness," Sinja said, slipping the letters into his own sleeve. "We've been too long already. I'm not saying that it's a bad plan. I only wish that there was a brilliant, well-crafted scheme that had Balasar-cha going out and me following behind to see whether the raiders sank everyone. Any word from Chaburi-Tan?"

"Nothing new," Otah said.

"Fair enough. We'll send word once we get there."

A silence followed, the unasked questions as heavy in the air as smoke. Otah leaned forward. Sinja knew about Idaan's list; Otah had told him in a fit of candor and regretted it since. Sinja knew better than to raise the issue where they might be overheard, but disapproval haunted his expression.

"There is some movement on the question of Obar State," Otah said. "Ashua Radaani bribed their ambassador. He has a list of men who have been in negotiation to break the eastern cities from the Empire with backing from Obar State. Two dozen men in four families."

"That's good work," Sinja said.

"He's asking permission to kill them."

"Sounds very tidy, assuming it's true and Radaani isn't involved in the conspiracy himself."

"Very tidy then too," Otah said. "I'm ordering the men brought to Utani. I can speak with them there."

"And if Radaani refuses?"

"Then I'll invite just him," Otah said. Sinja took an approving pose. Otah thought for a moment that they might be done.

"The other matter?"

"Being addressed," Otah said.

Four of the members of Idaan's list had been quietly looked into, the irregularities of their behavior clarified. One had been hiding half-a-dozen mistresses from a wife with a notoriously short temper. Two others had been conspiring to undercut the glass trades in the north, setting up workshops nearer the alum mines of Eddensea. The fourth had also appeared on Ashua Radaani's list, and had no clear connection to Maati.

Sinja had made it perfectly clear that he thought examining Eiah's actions was the wisest course. If she was Maati's backer, better to find it quickly and put a stop to the whole affair. If she wasn't, best to know that and stop losing sleep. There was a cold logic to his argument, and Otah knew what his own reluctance meant. His daughter had turned to her Uncle Maati. Turned against her father. And the pain of that loss was almost more than he could bear.

"Well," Sinja said. "I suppose I'd better go before the sailors all get too drunk to know sunrise from sunset and land us all in Eymond. If I don't come back, make sure they put up statues of me."

"You'll come back," Otah said.

"You only say that because I always have before," Sinja replied, smiling. He sobered. "See that Balasar comes quickly, though. These ships will make a grand spectacle, but it would be a short fight."

"I'll see to it," Otah said.

Sinja rose and took a pose of leave-taking. It might be the last time Otah ever saw the man. It was a fact he'd known, but something in the set of Sinja's body or the studied blankness of his face drove the point home. For the space of a breath, Otah felt the loss as if the worst had already happened.

"I would have been lost without you, these last years," Otah said. "You know that."

"I know you think it," Sinja said, matching Otah's quiet tone. "Take care, Most High. Do what needs doing."

Sitting now on his dais, watching the ships recede and vanish, Otah thought the phrase had been intended as last words. Do what needs doing. Meaning, more specifically, find Eiah. The sun rose from its morning home in the east; the seafront surged with a hundred languages, creoles, pidgins. Where the armsmen of the palace ended, merchants set up their tall, thin stalls and proclaimed their wares. When Otah took his leave, they would do the same in the space he now inhabited. Returning to the palaces would be like taking his finger out of water. It wouldn't leave a hole. He wondered, sometimes, if the whole world wasn't the same.

Back at the palaces, Otah suffered through the ritual change of robes, the closing ceremony that followed seeing off the fleet. He dearly hoped that when Balasar's reinforcements departed, he could avoid repeating the entire pointless exercise. He hoped, but doubted it. Once the last cymbal had chimed, the last priest intoned the final passage, and Otah had done his duty as Emperor, he went back to his rooms. Danat and Issandra were waiting there.

Otah greeted them both with a single pose appropriate to near family. If it was still an optimism, the Galtic woman didn't comment on it. She put down a bowl of tea she'd been drinking from, and Danat rose to his feet.

"Thank you for joining me," Otah said. "I wanted to know the . . . the status of your work."

The pair exchanged glances. Issandra spoke.

"In one respect, I think you could say we're doing quite well. Ana's request that her father add himself to your naval adventure has caused something of a strain between her and Hanchat. He seems to think she's being disloyal to Galt in general and therefore him in particular."

"I can understand that," Otah said, lowering himself to a cushion. "The gods all know she surprised me with it."

"The problem is that she feels she's cleared all accounts by the gesture," Issandra said. "Any sense of obligation she might have felt toward Danat-cha from her misbehavior or his clemency toward Hanchat is done."

"I see," Otah said.

"There's something else," Danat said. "I think Shija-cha has . . ."

"The imitation lover has developed ambitions," Issandra said. "Apparently you've entrusted her uncle with some particularly delicate task?"

Shija Radaani. Ashua's niece.

"I have," Otah said.

"She's taken that fact and the request that she act as Danat's escort, and drawn the most remarkable conclusion," Issandra said. "She thinks that Danat-cha is in love with her, and intends to sabotage his connection to Ana on her behalf."

"It's not only that," Danat said. "This is my fault. I . . . I lost my perspective. It was . . ."

"You bedded her," Otah said.

Danat's blush could have lit houses. It was as Otah had feared. Issandra sighed.

"This Radaani woman," she said. "Can you safely offend her family?"

"At the moment, it would be awkward," Otah said.

"Then I can't see that the girl is that far wrong," Issandra said. "Danat *has* sabotaged things."

"I'm very sorry," he said. "It wasn't . . . gods."

Danat sat again, his head in his hands.

"What is Ana's opinion of the matter of Shija and Danat?" Otah asked.

"I don't know," Issandra said. Her voice went softer, sorrow creeping in at the seams. "I believe she's avoiding me."

Otah pressed his fingers against his eyelids until colors swam in the darkness. No one spoke, and the silence pressed on his shoulder like a hand.

"Well," he said at last, "how do the two of you intend to move forward from here?"

"She wants to put them together," Danat said. His voice was equal parts plea and outrage. "She wants Shija and Ana to be seated beside each other at every dance, every meal . . ."

"You can't envy what you don't see," Issandra said. "It's more difficult if this other girl can't be easily removed, but if Ana's run with her present lover is nearing an end, and Shija makes it clear that she considers Ana a threat . . ."

Danat yelped and began to spout objections, Issandra pressing on against him. Otah kept his eyes closed, the paired voices draining each other of meaning. Instead he imagined the girl to be before him as she had been the night she came to speak with him. Half-drunk. Too proud to be ruled by pride.

He took a pose that commanded silence. Danat's words ended at once. Issandra's took a moment longer to trail off.

"Between the two of you, you'll have to devise something," he said. "I don't have the time or the resources to fix this for you. But consider that you might be treating Ana with less respect than she deserves. Danat-cha, do you intend to build a life with Shija Radaani?"

Danat sobered. He took no pose, spoke no word. Otah nodded.

"Then it would be disrespectful to behave as if you did," Otah said. "Be honest with her, and if it damages relations with House Radaani, then it does."

"Yes, Father," Danat said, hesitated, and then took a pose that asked forgiveness before walking from the room.

Otah's spine ached. His eyes felt gritty with the efforts of the day. It was all far from over.

"Issandra-cha," he said. "I don't know Ana well, but I lost my own daughter by treating her as the girl I remembered instead of the woman she'd become. Don't repeat my mistake. Ana may not be subject to the manipulations that work on younger girls."

Issandra Dasin's face hardened. For a moment, Otah saw the resemblance between mother and daughter. She took a pose of acknowledgment. It was awkward, but her form was correct.

"There is, perhaps, another approach," she said. "I wouldn't have considered it before, but I've spent a certain number of hours with your son. He might be able to manage it."

Otah nodded her on.

"He could choose to fall in love with her. Cultivate the feeling within himself, and then . . ." She shrugged. "Let the world take its course. I haven't known many women who failed to be charmed by an attractive man's genuine admiration."

"You think he could simply decide to feel what we want him to feel?"

"I've done it every day for nearly thirty years," Issandra said.

"That is either the most romantic thing I've heard or the saddest,"

Otah said. And then, "Ana-cha did me a great favor. I'm sorry that Danat repaid it with an indiscretion."

Issandra waved the apology away.

"I doubt she took offense. I'm sure she assumed Danat and this Radaani creature were sharing whatever flat surfaces came available. I remember what it was like at their age. We were all heat and dramatic gestures. We thought we were the first generation to truly discover love or sex or betrayal." Her voice softened.

Otah recalled a girl named Liat with skin the brown of eggshell and the night his one true friend had confessed his affair with her. The night Maati had confessed. He hadn't seen or spoken to either of them for years afterward. He had killed a man, in part as a blessing upon them, Liat and Maati, and the freedom that together they had given him.

All heat and dramatic gestures, he thought. Amusement mixed with sorrow, the way it always did.

"Still, it is a pity," Issandra said. "The Radaani girl is beautiful, and vanity is a powerful lever, no matter how sophisticated you take my daughter to be."

"We may hope for the best," Otah said. "Perhaps Shija-cha will take Danat's apology in stride and return to only acting the role."

Issandra's gaze told him exactly how likely she thought that was, but she only shook her head.

"It would be pleasant," she said.

He ate alone that night, though there were scores of men, Galtic and utkhaiem both, who would have been pleased to share his table. The pavilion sat atop a high tower, the air smelling of lavender and the sea. Otah sat on a cushion by a low table and watched the sunset; orange and red and gold spread out upon a wide canvas of clouds and sky. There were no singing slaves here, but soft chimes danced in the breeze with a sound like bells made from wood. An iron brazier sat close to keep him warm. The evening was beautiful and rich with sadness.

He had known that his daughter was angry with him. He had encouraged the high families to import wives for their sons. They had come from Bakta, Eymond, Eddensea. Women of middling birth commanded huge dowries. The coffers of the utkhaiem had dropped, but a handful of children had been born. A few dozen, perhaps, in every city. It hadn't been enough. And so he'd conceived the plan to join with Galt, old enemies made one people. Yes, it left behind a generation of Khaiate women. And Galtic men, for that. No doubt they would feel angered, lost, discarded. It was a small price to pay for a future.

The Comfort House Empire, she'd called it the last time they'd spoken. And her father, *her* father, the Procurer King. She said it, and she spat. Thinking of it stung.

A flock of gulls wheeled below him and to the south. Lemon rice and river trout rested warm on his fingers and in his mouth. When he was alone, he still ate like a laborer.

He wondered if he had been wrong. Perhaps in the approach he had taken, trying to find women capable of bearing children for the cities. Perhaps in speaking to Eiah about it in the terms he'd used. Perhaps in failing to accept her criticism, in speaking harshly. Eiah had accused him of turning his back on the women whom Sterile had wounded because they were inconvenient. Eiah was one of those women, and the injury she'd suffered was as deep as any of his own. Deeper.

It might, he supposed, have been enough to turn her against him. She had always been close to Maati. She had spent long evenings at the library of Machi, where Maati had made his home. She had known Nayiit, the man that Otah had fathered and Maati had called son. In the many years that he had struggled with being merely the Khai Machi, Eiah had made a friend and an uncle of Maati Vaupathai. There was little reason to believe that she would withhold her loyalty from Maati now.

The wheeling gulls landed, leaving the sky to itself. The fleet had long passed the horizon, and Otah wished he had some magical glass that would let him see it still. It was a short enough voyage to Chaburi-Tan. Shorter if the pirates and raiders came out to confront them. He wished Sinja had stayed behind. In the failing light, the gaudy sunset turning to gray, he wanted his old friend back and was only half-startled to realize he meant Maati as much as Sinja.

A servant emerged from the darkened arches at the pavilion's edge and came forward. Otah knew the news he carried before he spoke. Idaan Machi had answered his summons and awaited at his pleasure. Otah ordered that she be brought to him. Her and more food.

Do what needs doing, Sinja said from his memory.

He heard her soft footsteps and didn't turn around. His belly was knotted, and the fish before him smelled suddenly unpleasant. Idaan walked past him and stood at the edge of the pavilion, looking down the height of the tower. Her outer robe was dark, the hem fluttering as if she were about to fall or take flight. When she turned back to him, her expression was mild.

"Lovely view," she said. "But still nothing beside Machi. Do you miss the towers?"

"No," Otah said. "Not really. They're too cold to use in the winter, too hot in the summer, and the tracks they use to haul things up the side have to be replaced every fifth year. They're the best example I know of doing a thing just to show it's possible."

Idaan lowered herself to a cushion opposite him. The fading glow of western clouds silhouetted her.

"True enough," she said. "Still. I miss them."

She considered the bowls of food before them, then took a scoop of rice and fish on two curled fingers. Otah smiled. His sister chewed apprecia-tively and took a pose that opened a negotiation.

"Yes," he agreed. "There's something I want from you."

Idaan nodded, but didn't speak. Otah squinted out into the wide air above Saraykeht.

"There's too much," he said. "Even turning everything I can manage over to Sinja and Danat and Ashua Radaani, there's too much."

"Too much to allow for what?" She knew, he thought, what was com-ing.

"Too much for me to leave," he said. "Being Emperor is like being the most honored slave in the world. I can do anything, except that I can't. I can go anywhere, except that I mustn't."

"It sounds awful."

"Don't laugh. I'm not saying I'd rather be lifting crates at the seafront, but senior overseer of a courier service? Something with a few dozen chests of silver lengths and a favorite teahouse."

"Fewer meetings like this one," Idaan suggested.

"That," Otah said. "Gods yes, that."

Idaan scooped up another mouthful of rice, chewed slowly, and let her dark eyes play across his face. He didn't know what she saw there. After a swallow of water and a small sigh, she spoke.

"You want me to find Eiah," she said.

"You know what Maati looks like," he said. "You have the experience of living among low towns and hiding who you are. You understand poets as well as anyone alive, I'd guess."

"And I know what I'm looking for," she said, her voice light and con-versational. "Anyone else, and you'd have to bring them into your confi-dence. Explain what you wanted to know and why. Well, Sinja-cha perhaps, but you've sent him off the other direction."

This is madness, Otah thought but didn't say. She is a killer. She was born without a conscience. However she may seem now, she slaughtered her brothers and the father she loved. She's got the eyes of a pit hound and the heart of a butcher.

"Will you do it?" he said aloud.

Idaan didn't answer at once. A gust of wind pushed at her sleeve and drew a lock of gray hair out behind her like a banner from the mast of a fighting ship. Otah's hands ached, and he forced his fists to open by an act of will.

"Maati hunted me once," she said, hardly louder than the wind. "It only seems fair to return the favor."

Otah closed his eyes. Perhaps it was an empty task. Eiah might very well have nothing to do with Maati's schemes. She might truly be working with some low-town physician, hoping through her own hard work to atone for her father's misdeeds. For his misdeeds. When he looked up, his sister was considering him with hooded eyes.

"I will have a cart and driver ready for you in the morning," he said. "You'll be able to take whatever fresh horses or food you need along the way. I've written the orders up already."

"All the horses and food we need along the way?" Idaan said. "You're right. Being Emperor must be raw hell."

He didn't answer her. She finished the rice and fish. The clouds behind her had gone dark, and since neither had called for candles or torches, the only light was the cold blue moon and the fiery embers in the brazier. Idaan took a pose that accepted his charge.

"You don't want to negotiate payment?" he said.

"I'm just pleased you've decided to do the thing. I was afraid you'd put it off until it was too late," Idaan said. "One question, though. If I find her, and she is the one, what action should I take?"

Meaning should Idaan kill her, kill Maati and as many of the other fledgling poets as she could to prevent them from accomplishing their aims.

Do what needs doing.

"Nothing," Otah said, nerve failing. "Do nothing. There will be couriers in Pathai. You can send the fastest of them back. I'll give you a cipher."

"You're sure?" Idaan said. "It's a lot of time on the road, sending me out and then someone else back. And then waiting while you make your way to Pathai or wherever the trail leads."

"If you find her, send word," Otah said. "You aren't to act against her."

Idaan's smile was crooked with meanings he couldn't quite follow. Otah felt anger growing in his spine, only it wasn't rage so much as dread.

"I'll do as you say, Most High," Idaan said. "I'll go at first light."

"Thank you," he said.

Idaan rose and walked back toward the arches. He heard her pause for a moment and then go on. The stars had come out, glimmering in the darkness like gems thrown on black stone. Otah sat in silence until he was sure he could walk, and then went down to his rooms. The servants had left him a bowl of candied fruit, but he couldn't stand the prospect.

A fire burned in the grate, protecting the air from even the slightest chill and tainting it with tendrils of pine smoke. The summer cities had always been overly vigilant of cold. Thin blood. Everything south of Udun was plagued by thinness of the blood. Otah came from the winter cities, and he threw open the shutters, letting in what cold there was. He didn't notice that Danat was there until the boy spoke.

"Father."

Otah turned. Danat stood in the doorway that led to the inner chambers. He wore the same robe that he had before, but the cloth sagged like an unmade bed. Danat's eyes were rimmed with red.

"Danat-kya," Otah said. "What's happened?"

"I've done as you said. Shija and I went to the rose pavilion. Just the two of us. I . . . spoke with her. I broke things off."

"Ah," Otah said. He walked back from the open windows and sat on a couch before the fire. Danat came forward, his eyes glittering with unfallen tears.

"This is my fault, Papa-kya. In a different world, I might have . . . I have been careless with her. I've *hurt* her."

Was I ever as young as this? Otah thought, and immediately pressed it away. Even if the question was fair, it was unkind. He held out his hand, and his son—his tall, thick-shouldered son—sat beside him, curled into Otah's shoulder the way he had as a boy. Danat sobbed once.

"I only . . . I know you and Issandra-cha were relying on me and . . ."

Otah hushed the boy.

"You've taken a willing girl to bed," Otah said. "You aren't who she hoped you might be, and so she's disappointed. Yes?"

Danat nodded.

"There are worse things." Otah saw again the darkness of Idaan's eyes. He was sending the woman behind those eyes after his Eiah, his little girl. The ghost of nausea touched him and he stroked Danat's hair. "People have done worse."

14

>+< Maati frowned at the papers before him. A small fire crackled in the brazier on his desk, and he was more than half-tempted to drop the pages onto the flames. Eiah, sitting across from him, looked no more pleased.

"You're right," he said. "We're moving backward."

"What's happened?" Eiah asked, though she knew as well as he did.

The few weeks that had passed since Vanjit's successful binding had only grown more difficult. To start, the other students excepting Eiah were more distracted. The mewling and cries of the andat disrupted any conversation. Its awkward crawling seemed capable of entrancing them for a full morning. Perhaps he had known too much of the andat, but he held the growing impression that it was perfectly aware of the effect its toothless smile could have. And that it was especially cultivating the admiration of Ashti Beg.

Added to that, Vanjit herself had come almost disconnected from the rest. She would sit for whole days, the andat in her lap or at her breast, staring at water or empty air. Maati had some sympathy for that. She had shown him the most compelling of the wonders her new powers had uncovered, and he had been as delighted as she was. But her little raptures meant that she wasn't engaged in the work at hand: Eiah, and the binding of Wounded.

"There is something we can do," Eiah said. "If we set the classes in the mornings, just after the first meal, we won't have had a full day behind us. We could come at it fresh each time."

Maati nodded more to show he'd heard her than from any real agreement. His fingertips traced the lines of the binding again, tapping the page each time some little infelicity struck him. He had seen bindings falter this way before. In those first years when Maati had been a new poet, the Dai-kvo had spoken of the dangers of muddying thoughts by too much work. One sure way to fail was to build something sufficient and then not stop. With every small improvement, the larger structure became less tenable, until eventually the thing collapsed under the weight of too much history.

He wondered if they had gone too far, corrected one too many things which were not truly problems so much as differences of taste.

Eiah took a pose that challenged him. He looked at her directly for perhaps the first time since she'd come to his study.

"You think I'm wrong," she said. "You can say it. I've heard worse."

It took Maati the space of several heartbeats to recall what her proposal had been.

"I think it can't hurt. But I also think it isn't our essential problem. We were all quite capable of designing Clarity-of-Sight with meetings in the evening. This"—he rattled the papers in his hand—"is something different. Half-measures won't suffice."

"What then?" she said.

He put the papers down.

"We stop," he said. "For a few days, we don't touch it at all. Instead we can send someone to a low town for meat and candles, or clear the gardens. Anything."

"Do we have time for that?" Eiah asked. "Anything could have happened. My brother may be married. His wife may be carrying a child. All of Galt may be loading their daughters in ships, and the men of the cities may be scuttling off to Kirinton and Acton and Marsh. We are out here where there's no one to talk to, no couriers on the roads, and I know it feels that time has stopped. It hasn't. We've been weeks at this. Months. We can't spend time we don't have."

"You'd recommend what, then? Move faster than we can move? Think more clearly than we can think? It isn't as if we can sit down with a serious expression and demand that the work be better than it is. Have you never seen a man ill with something that needed quiet and time? This is no different."

"I've also watched ill men die," Eiah said. "Time passes, and once you've waited too long for something, there's no getting it back."

Her mouth bent in a deep frown. There were dark circles under her eyes. She bit her lower lip and shook her head as if conducting some conversation within her mind and disagreeing with herself. The coal burning in the brazier settled and gave off a dozen small sparks as bright as fireflies. One landed on the paper, already cold and gray. Ash.

"You're reconsidering," Maati said.

"No. I'm not. We can't tell my father," she said. "Not yet."

"We could send to others, then," Maati said. "There are high families in every city that would rise up against Otah's every plan if they knew the andat were back in the world. You've lived your whole life in the courts. Two or three people whose discretion you trust would be all it took. A rumor spoken in the right ears. We needn't even say where we are or what's been bound."

Eiah combed her fingers through her hair. Every breath that she didn't answer, Maati felt his hopes rise. She would, if he only gave her a little more time and silence to convince herself. She would announce their success, and everyone in the cities of the Khaiem would know that Maati Vaupathai had remained true to them. He had never given up, never turned away.

"It would mean going to a city," Eiah said. "I can't send half-a-dozen ciphered letters under my own seal out from a low town without every courier in the south finding out where we are."

"Then Pathai," Maati said, his hands opening. "We need to step back from the binding. The letters will win us time to make things right."

Eiah turned, looking out the window. In the courtyard, the maple trees were losing their leaves. A storm, a strong wind, and the branches would be bare. A sparrow, brown and gray, hopped from one twig to another. Maati could see the fine markings on its wings, the blackness of its eyes. It had been years since sparrows had been more than dull smears. He glanced at Eiah, surprised to see the tears on her cheek.

His hand touched her shoulder. She didn't look back, but he felt her lean into him a degree.

"I don't know," she said as if to the sparrow, the trees, the thousand fallen leaves. "I don't know why it should matter. It's no secret what he's done or what I think of it. I don't have any doubts that what we're doing is the right choice."

"And yet," Maati said.

"And yet," she agreed. "My father will be disappointed in me. I would have thought I was old enough that his opinion wouldn't matter."

He searched for a response—something gentle and kind and that would strengthen her resolve. Before he found the words, he felt her tense. He took back his hand, adopting a querying pose.

"I thought I heard something," she said. "Someone was yelling."

A long, high shriek rang in the air. It was a woman's voice, but he couldn't guess whose. Eiah leaped from her stool and vanished into the dark hallways before Maati recovered himself. He followed, his heart pounding, his breath short. The shrieking didn't stop, and as he came nearer the kitchen, he heard other sounds—clattering, banging, high voices urging calm or making demands that he couldn't decipher, the andat's infantile wail. And then Eiah's commanding voice, with the single word *stop*.

He rounded the last corner, his fist pressed to his chest, his heart hammering. The cooking areas were raw chaos come to earth. An earthenware jar of wheat flour had been overturned and cracked. The thin stone block Irit used for chopping plants lay in shards on the floor. Ashti Beg stood in the middle of the room, a knife in her hand, her chin held high like a statue of abstract vengeance. In the corner, Vanjit held the still-mewling andat close to her breast. Large Kae, Small Kae, and Irit were all cowering against the walls, their eyes wide and mouths hanging open. Eiah's expression was calm and commanding at the same time, like a mother calling back her children from a cliff edge.

"It's done, Ashti-cha," Eiah said, walking slowly toward the woman. "I'll have the knife."

"Not until I find that bitch and put it in her heart," Ashti Beg spat, turning toward Eiah's voice. Maati saw for the first time that the woman's eyes were as gray as storm clouds.

"I'll have the knife," Eiah said again. "Or I will beat you down and take it. You know you're more likely to hurt the others than Vanjit."

The andat whimpered and Ashti Beg whirled toward it. Eiah stepped forward smoothly, took Ashti Beg's elbow and wrist in her hands, and twisted. Ashti Beg yelped, the blade clattering to the floor.

"What . . ." Maati gasped. "What is happening?"

Four voices answered at once, words tripping over each other. Only Eiah and Vanjit remained silent, the two poets considering each other silently in the center of the storm. Maati raised his hands in a pose that commanded silence, and all of them stopped except Ashti Beg.

". . . power over us. It isn't right, it isn't fair, and I will not simper and smile and lick her ass because she happened to be the one to go first!"

"Enough!" Maati said. "Enough, all of you. Gods. *Gods*. Vanjit. Come with me."

The girl looked over as if noticing him for the first time. The rage in her expression faltered. Her hands were shaking. Eiah stepped forward, keeping herself between Ashti Beg and her prey as Vanjit walked across the room.

"Eiah, see to Ashti-cha," Maati said, taking Vanjit's wrist. "The rest of you, clean this mess. I'd rather not eat food prepared in a child's playpen."

He turned away, pulling Vanjit and Clarity-of-Sight after him. The andat was silent now. Maati crossed the hallway and started down a flight of stone stairs that led to the sleeping rooms for the younger cohorts. The voices of the others rose behind them and faded. He wasn't certain where he was taking her until he reached the branching hall that led to the slate-paved rooms where the teachers had once disciplined boys with the cutting slash of a lacquered rod. He stopped in the hallway instead, putting the reflexive impulse to violence aside. Vanjit bowed her head.

"I would like an explanation of that," he said, his voice shaking with anger.

"It was Ashti Beg," Vanjit said. "She can't contain her jealousy any longer, Maati-kvo. I have tried to give her the time and consideration, but she won't understand. I am a poet now. I have an andat to care for. I can't be expected to work and toil like a servant."

The andat twisted in her grasp, looking up at Maati with tears in its black eyes. The tiny, toothless mouth gaped in what would have been distress if it had been a baby.

"Tell me," Maati said. "Tell me what happened."

"Ashti Beg said that I had to clean the pots from breakfast. Irit offered to, but Ashti wouldn't even let her finish her sentences. I explained that I couldn't. I was very calm. I am patient with her, Maati-kvo. I'm always very patient."

"What happened?" Maati insisted.

"She tried to take him," Vanjit said. Her voice had changed. The pleading tone was gone. Her words could have been shaved from ice. "She said that she could look after him as well as anyone, and that I was more than welcome to have him back once the kitchen had been cleaned."

Maati closed his eyes.

"She put her *hands* on him," Vanjit said. In her voice, it sounded like a violation. Perhaps it was.

"And what did you do," Maati asked, though he knew the answer.

"What you told me," Vanjit said. "What you said about Wounded."

"Which was?" he said. Clarity-of-Sight gurgled and swung its thick arms at Vanjit's ears, its dumb show of fear and distress forgotten.

"You said that Eiah-cha couldn't make an andat based on things being as they're meant to, because the andat aren't meant to be bound. It's not their nature. You said she had to bind Wounded and then withdraw it from all the women who still can't bear babes. And so we withdrew from Ashti Beg."

The andat cooed. It might have been Maati's imagination, but the thing seemed proud. Clarity-of-Sight. And so also Blindness.

The warmth that bloomed in his breast, the tightening of his jaw, the near-unconscious shaking of his head. They were not anger so much as a bone-deep impatience.

"It is manipulating you," he said. "We've talked about this from the beginning. The andat wants its freedom. Whatever else it is, it will always struggle to be free. It has been courting Ashti Beg and the others for days to precipitate exactly this. You have to know yourself better than it does. You have to behave like a grown woman, not a self-righteous child."

"But she—"

Maati put two fingers against the girl's lips. The andat was silent now, staring at him with silent anger.

"You have been entrusted with a power beyond any living person," Maati said, his tone harsher than he'd intended. "You are responsible for that power. You understand me? Responsible. I have tried to make you see that, but now I think I've failed. Poets aren't simply men . . . or women . . . who have a particular profession. We aren't like sailors or cabinetmakers or armsmen. Holding the andat is like holding small gods, and there is a price you pay for that. Do you understand what I'm saying?"

"Yes, Maati-kvo," Vanjit whispered.

"I doubt that," he said. "After what I've seen today, I very much doubt it."

She was weeping silently. Maati opened his mouth, some cutting comment ready to humiliate her further, and stopped. For a moment, he was a boy again, in this same hallway. He could feel the thin robes and the winter cold, and the tears on his own cheeks as the older boys mocked him or Tahi-kvo—bald, cruel Tahi-kvo, who had later become the Dai-kvo—beat him. He wondered if this fear and rage had been what drove his teachers back then, or if it had been something colder.

"Fix it," Maati said. "Put Ashti Beg back as she was, and never, never use the andat for petty infighting again."

"No, Maati-kvo."

"And wash the pots when your turn comes."

Vanjit took a pose that was a promise and an expression of gratitude. The quiet sobs as she walked away made Maati feel smaller. If they had been in a city, he would have gone to a bathhouse or some public square, listened to beggars singing on the corners and bought food from the carts. He would have tried to lose himself for a while, perhaps in wine, perhaps in music, rarely in gambling, and never in sex. At the school, there was no escape. He walked out, leaving the stone walls and memories behind him. Then the gardens. The low hills that haunted the land west of the buildings.

He sat on the wind-paved hillside, marking the passage of the sun across the afternoon sky, his mind tugged a hundred different ways. He had been too harsh with Vanjit, or not harsh enough. The binding of Wounded was overworked or not deeply enough considered, doomed or on the edge of being perfected. Ashti Beg had been in the wrong or justified or both. He closed his eyes and let the sunlight beat down on them, turning the world to red.

In time, the turmoil in his heart calmed. A small, blue-tailed lizard scrambled past him. He had chased lizards like it when he'd been a boy. He hadn't recalled that in years.

It was folly to think of poets as different from other men. Other women, now that Vanjit had proved their grammar effective. It was that mistake which had made the school what it was, which had deformed the lives of so many people, his own included. Of course Vanjit was still subject to petty jealousy and pride. Of course she would need to learn wisdom, just the same as anyone else. The andat had never changed who someone was, only what they could do.

He should have taught them that along with all the rest. Every now and again, he could have spent an evening talking about what power was, and what responsibility it carried. He'd never thought to do it, he now realized, because when he imagined a woman wielding the power of the andat, that woman was always Eiah.

Maati made his way back as the cold afternoon breeze set the trees and bushes rustling. He found the kitchen empty but immaculate. The broken cutting stone had been replaced with a length of polished wood, but otherwise everything was as it had been. His students, he found under Eiah's command in the courtyard. They were raking the fallen leaves into a pit for burning and resetting a half-dozen flagstones that had broken from years of frost, tree roots, and neglect. Vanjit knelt with Large Kae, lifting the stones from the ground. Clarity-of-Sight nestled in Irit's lap, its eyes closed and its mouth a perfect O. Ashti Beg, her vision clearly restored, was by Small Kae's side, a deep pile of russet leaves before them.

"Maati-kvo," Eiah said, taking a pose of greeting, which he returned. The others acknowledged him with a smile or simple pose. Vanjit turned away quickly, as if afraid to see anger still in his expression.

He trundled to a rough boulder, resting against it to catch his breath. Irit joined him and, without a word, passed the andat to him. It stirred, groaned once, and then turned to nestle its face into his robes. The andat had no need of breath. Maati had known that since he had first met Seedless over half a century earlier. Clarity-of-Sight's deep, regular sighs were manipulations, but Maati welcomed them. To hold something so much like a child but as still as the dead would have unnerved him.

Irit especially talked in light tones, but no one seeing them would have guessed that one of the group had been swinging a knife at another earlier in the day. Apart from a mutually respected distance between Ashti Beg and Vanjit, there was no sign of unease.

Large Kae and Small Kae left to prepare a simple meal just as Eiah put the torch to the pit of leaves. The flames rose, dancing. Pale smoke filled the air with the scent of autumn, then floated into the sky while the rest of them watched: Vanjit and Eiah, Ashti Beg, Irit, Maati and Clarity-of-Sight, who was also Blindness. The andat seemed captivated by the flames. Maati stretched his palm out to the fire and felt the heat pushing gently back.

They ate roasted chicken and drank watered wine. By the end of the meal, Vanjit was smiling again. When the last wine bowl was empty, the last thin, blood-darkened bone set bare on its plate, she was the first to rise and gather the washing. Maati felt a relief that surprised him. The trouble had passed; whether it had been Vanjit's pride or Ashti Beg's jealousy, it didn't matter.

To show his approval, Maati joined in the cleaning himself, sweeping the kitchen and building up the fire. In place of the usual lecture, they discussed the difficulties of looking too long at a binding. It came out that all of them had felt some disquiet at the state of Eiah's work. Even that was reassuring.

He and Eiah sat together after the session ended. A small kettle smelled equally of hot iron and fresh tea. The wind was picking up outside, cold and fragrant with the threat of rain or snow. By the warm light of the fire grate, Eiah looked tired.

"I'll leave in the morning," Eiah said. "I want to beat the worst of the weather, if I can."

"That seems wise," Maati said and sipped his tea. It was still scalding hot, but its taste was comforting.

"Ashti Beg wants to come with me," she said. "I don't know what to do about that."

He put down his bowl.

"What are you thinking?" he asked.

"That she might leave. After today, I'm afraid she's been soured on the work."

Maati snorted and waved the concern away.

"She'll move past it," Maati said. "It's finished. Vanjit overstepped, and she's seen it. I don't think Ashti's so petty as to hold things past that."

"Perhaps," Eiah said. "You think I should take her with me, then?"

"Certainly. There's no reason not to, and it will give you another pair of hands on the road. And besides, we're a school, not a prison. If she truly wants to leave, she should be able to."

"Even now?" Eiah asked.

"What option do we have?" Maati asked. "Chain her to a tree? Kill her? No, Eiah-kya. Ashti Beg won't abandon the work, but if she does, we have no choice but to let her."

Eiah was silent for five slow breaths together. When she looked up, he was surprised by her grim expression.

"I still can't quite bring myself to believe Vanjit did that."

"Why not?"

Eiah frowned, her hands clasped together. Some distant shutter's ties had slipped; wood clapping against stone. A soft wind pushed at the windows and unsettled the fire in the grate.

"She's a poet," Eiah said. "She's *the* poet."

"Poets are human," Maati said. "We err. We can be petty on occasion. Vindictive. Small. Her world has been turned on its head, and she hasn't come yet to understand all that means. Well, of course she hasn't. I'd have been more surprised if she'd never made a misstep."

"You don't think we have a problem then?" Eiah said.

"She's a reasonable girl. Given power, she's misbehaved once. Once." Maati shook his head. "Once is as good as never."

"And if it becomes twice?" Eiah asked. "If it becomes every time?"

"It won't," Maati said. "That isn't who she is."

"But she's changed. You said it just now. The binding gave her power, and power changes people."

"It changes their situation," Maati said. "It changes the calculations of what things they choose to do. What they forbear. It doesn't change their souls."

"I've cut through a hundred bodies, Uncle. I've never weighed out a soul. I've never judged one. When I picked Vanjit, I hope I did the right thing."

"Don't kill yourself with worry," Maati said. "Not yet, at any rate."

Eiah nodded slowly. "I've been thinking about who to send letters to. I've picked half-a-dozen names. I'll hire a courier when we reach Pathai. I won't be there long enough to bring back replies."

"That's fine," Maati said. "All we need is enough time to perfect Wounded."

Eiah took a pose that agreed and also ended the conversation. She walked away into the darkened hall, her shoulders bent, her head bowed. Maati felt a pang of guilt. Eiah was tired and sorrowful and more fearful than she let on. He was sending her to announce to the world that she had betrayed her father. He could have been gentler about her concerns over Vanjit and Clarity-of-Sight. He didn't know why he'd been so harsh.

He made his evening ablutions and prepared himself to write a few pages in his book, scratching words onto paper by the light of the fluttering night candle, thanks in no small part to Vanjit. He was less than surprised when a soft scratching came at his door.

Vanjit looked small and young. The andat held in the crook of her arm looked around the dim room, gurgling to itself almost like a baby. Maati gestured for her to sit.

"I heard Eiah-cha speaking to Ashti Beg," Vanjit said. "They're leaving?"

"Eiah is taking the cart to Pathai for supplies and to send off some letters for me. Ashti Beg is going to help. That's all," he said.

"It's not because of me?"

"No, Vanjit-kya," Maati said warmly. "No. It was planned before anything happened between you and Ashti-cha. It's only . . . we need time. Eiah needs time away from her binding to clear her mind. And we need to be sure that the Emperor and his son can't make a half-Galtic heir before we've done what needs doing. So we're asking help. Eiah is the daughter of the Empire. Her word carries weight. If she tells a few people well-placed in the utkhaiem what we've done and what we intend to do, they can use their influence to stop the Galts. And then . . ."

He gestured to Vanjit, to the school, to the wide plain of possibilities that lay before them, if only they could gain the time. The andat cooed and threw its own arms wide, in joy or possibly mockery.

"Why is he doing it?" Vanjit asked. "Why would he trade with those people? Is he so in love with Galt?"

Maati took a long breath, letting the question turn itself in his mind.

It was the habit of years to lay any number of sins at Otah's feet. But, reluctantly, not this.

"No," Maati said. "Otah-kvo isn't evil. Petty, perhaps. Misguided, certainly. He sees that the Galts are strong, and we need strength. He sees that their women can bear babes with our men, and he believes it's the only hope of a new generation. He doesn't understand that what we've broken, we can also repair."

"Given time," Vanjit said.

"Yes," Maati said with a sigh. "Given time to rebuild. Remake."

For a moment, he was in the cold warehouse in Machi, the andat Sterile looking at him with her terrible, beautiful smile.

"It takes so long to build the world," he said softly, "and so very little to break it. I still remember what it felt like. Between one breath and the next, Vanjit-kya. I ruined the world in less than a heartbeat."

Vanjit blinked, as if surprised, and then a half-smile plucked her lips. Clarity-of-Sight quieted, looking at her as if she'd spoken. The andat was as still as stone; even the pretense of breath had gone.

Maati felt unease stir in his belly.

"Vanjit? Are you well?" and when she didn't reply, *"Vanjit?"*

She started, as if she'd forgotten where she was and that he was there. He caught her gaze, and she smiled.

"Fine. Yes, I'm fine," she said. There was a strange tone in her voice. Something low and languid and relaxed. It reminded Maati of the aftermath of sex. He took a pose that asked whether he had failed to understand something.

"No, nothing," Vanjit said; and then not quite in answer to his question, "Nothing's wrong."

15

>+< Shortly after midday, Otah walked along the winding path that led from the palaces themselves to the building that had once been the poet's house. Since the first time he had come this way, little more than a boy, many things had changed. The pathway itself was the white of crushed marble with borders of oiled wood. The bridge that rose over the pond had blackened with time; the grain of the wood seemed coarser. One of the stands of trees which gave the poet's house its sense of separation from the palaces had burned. White-oak seedlings had been planted to replace them. The trees looked thin, awkward, and adolescent. One day, decades ahead, they would tower over the path.

He paused at the top of the bridge's arch, looking down into the dark water. Koi swam lazily under the surface, orange and white and gold appearing from beneath lily pads and vanishing again. The man reflected in the pond's surface looked old and tired. White hair, gray skin. Time had thinned his shoulders and taken the roundness from his cheeks. Otah put out his hand, and the reflection did as well, as if they were old friends greeting each other.

When he reached the house itself, it seemed less changed than the landscape. The lower floor still had walls that were hinged like shutters which could be pulled back to open the place like a pavilion. The polished wood seemed to glow softly in the autumn light. He could almost imagine Maati sitting on the steps as he had been then. Sixteen summers old, and wearing the brown robes of a poet like a mark of honor. Or frog-mouthed Heshai, the poet whom Otah had killed to prevent the slaughter of innocents. Or Seedless, Heshai's beautiful, unfathomable slave.

Instead, Farrer Dasin sat on a silk-upholstered couch, a book in one hand, a pipe in the other. Otah approached the house casually as if they were merchants or workers, men whose dignity was less of a burden. The Galt closed his book as Otah reached the first stair up.

"Most High," he said in the Khaiate tongue.

"Farrer-cha," Otah replied.

"None of them are here. There's apparently a gathering at one of the lesser palaces. I believe one of the high-prestige wives of your court is showing her wealth in the guise of judging silks."

"It isn't uncommon. Especially if there is someone particularly worth impressing," Otah said. "I am surprised that Ana-cha chose to attend."

"To be honest, so am I. But I am on the verge of despairing that I will ever understand women."

It was hard to say whether the light, informal tone that the Galt adopted was intended as an offering of peace or as an insult. Likely it was both. The smoke rising from the pipe was thin and gray as fog, and smelled of cherries and bark.

"I don't mean to intrude," Otah said.

"No," Farrer Dasin said, "I imagine you don't. I've sent the servant away. You can take that seat there, if you like."

Otah, Emperor of the cities of the Khaiem, pulled a wood-backed chair to face the Galt, sat in it, and leaned back.

"I was a bit surprised you wanted to speak with me," Farrer said. "I thought we did all of our communication through my family."

A mosquito whined through the air as Otah considered this. Farrer Dasin waited, his mild expression a challenge.

"We have met and spoken many times over the past year, Farrer-cha. I don't believe I've ever turned you away. And as to your family, the first time I had no other option," Otah said. "The council was poised to refuse me, and there was a chance that your wives might be my allies. The second time, it was Ana who came to me. I didn't seek her out."

Farrer looked at Otah, his green-gray eyes as enigmatic as the sea.

"What brings you, Most High?" Farrer asked.

"I had heard rumors the decision to lend me your ships had perhaps weakened your position in the council. I had hoped I could offer some assistance."

Farrer drew on his pipe, then gestured out at the pond, the palaces, the world. When he spoke, the pipe smoke made the words seem solid and gray.

"I've failed. I know that. I was bullied into agreeing to this union between our houses, but so were half of the councillors. They can't think less of me for that, except for the few who genuinely backed your plan. They never thought much of me. And then I let myself be wheedled into helping you, so those whose love Ana won in her little speech think I'm ruled by the whims of a girl who hasn't seen twenty summers. The damning thing is, I can't say they're wrong."

"You love her," Otah said.

"I love her too much," Farrer said. His expression was grim. "It keeps me from knowing my own mind."

Otah's thoughts flickered for a moment, roving west to Idaan and her hunt. He brought himself back with a conscious effort.

"The city you're helping to protect is precious," Otah said. "The people whose lives you save won't think less of you for hearing wisdom from your daughter."

"Yes," Farrer said with a chuckle, "but they aren't on the council, are they."

"No," Otah said. "I understand that you are invested in sugar? There are cane fields east of Saraykeht, but most of what we have comes from Bakta. Much better land for it there. If Chaburi-Tan failed, we would feel the effect here and all through the Westlands."

Farrer grunted noncommittally.

"It's surprising how much Baktan trade flows through Chaburi-Tan. Not so much as through Saraykeht, but still a great deal. The island is easier to approach. And it's a good site for any trade in the south. Obar State, Eymond. Far Galt, for that. Did you know that nearly all the ore from Far Galt passes through the port at Chaburi-Tan?"

"Less since you've raised the taxes."

"I don't set those taxes," Otah said. "I appoint the port's administration. Usually they agree to pay a certain amount for the privilege and then try to make back what they've spent before their term ends."

"And how long are their terms?"

"As long as the Emperor is pleased to have them in that place," Otah said. "So long as I think they've done a good job with maintaining the seafront and keeping the flow of ships through, they may hold power for years. Or, if they've mismanaged things, perhaps even required a fleet to come out and save the city, they might be replaced."

The frown on Farrer's face was the most pleasant thing Otah had seen all morning. The truth of the matter was that Otah no more liked the Galt than he was liked by him. Their nations were old enemies, and however much Otah and Issandra plotted, there was a way in which their generation would die as enemies.

But what he did now, as little as Otah liked it personally, was intended for people as yet unborn, unconceived. It was a long game he was playing, and it got longer, it seemed, the less time he had to live.

Farrer coughed, sucked his teeth, and leaned forward.

"Forgive me, Most High," he said, formality returning to his diction. "What is the conversation we're having?"

"I would appoint you or your agent to oversee Chaburi-Tan's seafront," Otah said. "It would, I think, demonstrate that my commitment to joining our nations isn't only that you should send us your daughters."

"And have the council believe that I'm not only controlled by my wife and child, but also the tool of the Emperor, bought and paid for?" His tone was more amused than aggressive.

Otah pulled a small book from his sleeve and held it out.

"The accounting of the Chaburi-Tan seafront," Otah said. "We are an empire of fallen cities, Farrer-cha. But we were very high before, and falling for years hasn't yet brought us down to be even with most of the world."

The Galt clamped his pipe between his teeth and accepted the proffered book. Otah waited as he flipped through the thin pages. He saw Farrer's eyebrows rise when he reached the quarter's sums, and then again at the half-year's.

"You would want something from me," Farrer said.

"You have already lent me your boats," Otah said. "Your sailors. Let the others on the council see what effect that has."

"You can afford to give away this much gold to make them jealous?"

"I know that Ana-cha has objected to marrying Danat. I hope there may yet be some shift of her position. Then I would be giving the gold to my grandson's grandfather," Otah said.

"And if she doesn't?" Farrer asked, scowling. His eyes had narrowed like a seafront merchant distrustful of too good a bargain.

"If she doesn't, then I've made a poor wager," Otah said. "We are gamblers, Farrer-cha, just by getting up from bed in the morning."

Farrer Dasin didn't answer except to relax his gaze, laugh, and tuck the book into his belt. Otah took a pose that ended a meeting. It had a positive nuance that Dasin was unlikely to notice, but Otah didn't mind. It was as much for himself as the Galt.

The walk back to the palaces seemed shorter, less haunted by nostalgia. He returned to his rooms, allowed himself to be changed into formal robes, and began the long, slow work of another day. The court was its customary buzz of rituals and requirements. The constant speculation on the Galtic treaty's fate made every other facet of the economic and political life of the Empire swing like a ship's mast in high seas. Otah did what he could to pour oil on the waters. For the most part, he succeeded.

Before the early sunset of middle autumn, Otah had seen the heads of both Galtic and Khaiate stone masons disputing a contract upon which the Galtic Council had already ruled. He had taken audiences with two other members of the High Council and three of the highest families of the utkhaiem. And, in the brightest moment of his day, a visibly unnerved representative of Obar State had arrived with gifts and assurances of the good relations between his small nation and the cities of the Khaiem.

No courier came from Idaan or Eiah. Likely his sister was still on the roads between Saraykeht and Pathai. There was no reason to expect word back so soon, and yet every time a servant entered his chambers with a folded paper, his belly went tight until he broke the seal.

The night began with a banquet held in the honor of Balasar Gice and the preparation of what the Galtic Council called the second fleet and the utkhaiem, dismissively and in private, the other ships. The great hall fluttered with fine robes and silk banners. Musicians and singing slaves hidden behind screens filled the air with soft music of Galtic composition. Lanterns of colored glass gave the light a feeling of belonging to some other, gentler world. Otah sat on his high dais, Balasar at his side. He caught a glimpse of Danat dressed in formal robes of black and gold, sitting among his peers of the high utkhaiem. The group included Shija Radaani. Though Farrer and Issandra Dasin were among the Galts present, Otah did not see Ana. He tried not to find her absence unnerving.

The food and drink had been prepared by the best cooks Otah could find: classic Galtic dishes made if not light at least less heavy; foods designed to represent each of the cities of the Khaiem; all of it served with bowls of the best wines the world could offer.

Peace, Otah meant the celebration to say. *As we send our armsmen and sailors away to fight and die together, let there be peace between us. If there cannot be peace in the world, at least let it be welcome here.* It pleased him to see the youth of both countries sitting together and talking, even as it disturbed him that so many places set aside for the utkhaiem remained empty.

He did not notice that Issandra had taken her leave until the note arrived. The servant was very young, having seen no more than sixteen summers, and he approached Balasar with a small message box of worked gold. Balasar plucked the folded paper from it, read the message, then nodded and waved the boy away. The musicians nearest them shifted to a light, contemplative song. Balasar leaned toward Otah, as if to whisper some comment upon the music.

"This is for you," the general murmured.

General Gice, please pass this to the Emperor with all haste discretion allows. I would prefer that it not be immediately obvious that I am communicating with him, but time may be short.

Emperor. Please forgive my note, but I believe something is going to happen in the moon garden of the third palace at the beginning of the entertainments that you would be pleased to see. Consider claiming a moment's necessity and joining me.

It was signed with Issandra Dasin's chop.

Balasar was considering him silently. Otah slipped the paper into his sleeve. It was less than half a hand before the acrobats and dancers, trained dogs and fire-eaters were to take to the floor. It wasn't much time.

"I don't like this," Otah said, leaning toward Balasar so that no one could overhear.

"You think it's a plot to assassinate you," Balasar said.

"Might it be?"

Balasar smiled out into the hall, his eyes flickering as if looking for concealed archers.

"She sent the message through me. That provides a witness. It isn't the sort of thing I would do if I intended to kill you," Balasar said. "Still, if you go, take a guard."

Otah felt the weight of the note in his sleeve, feather-light and yet enough to command all his attention. He had almost decided to ignore it when, as the trumpets blared the first of the entertainments to the floor, he noticed that Danat had also gone. He slipped down from the back of the dais, chose two of the guards that he recognized, and made his way out to the third palace.

The moon garden had been built as a theater; great half-circles of carved stone set into a slope were covered with moss and snow ivy. At the deepest recess, three old wooden doors led to hallways where players or musicians could crouch, awaiting their entrance. The gardens were dark when he arrived, not even a lantern glowing to mark the paths. Behind him, the guards were as silent as shadows.

"Otah-cha," a woman whispered. "Here. Quickly."

Issandra huddled in the darkness under an ivy-choked willow. Otah walked forward, his hands in a pose of query. Issandra didn't reply, her eyes on the guards at his back. Her expression went from disapproval to acceptance barely seen in the dim light. She motioned all of them close to her.

"What is this?" Otah asked as he crouched in the darkness.

"Hush," Issandra said. "They should almost be here. There now. Be quiet, all of you."

One of the wooden doors at the base of the garden was opening, the light of a lantern spilling out onto the green of the grass, the black of the soil. Otah squinted. Ana Dasin stepped out. She wore a rough cloak over what appeared to be simple peasant robes, but her face and hair would have proclaimed her in the darkest teahouse. She looked like a girl who wanted to travel unnoticed but didn't know the trick of it. As Otah watched, she raised her lantern, scanning the wide stone curve, and then sat down.

"What is—" he whispered.

Issandra pressed her hand to his mouth. One of the guards shifted, but Otah gestured him back. It wasn't everyone who could gag the Emperor of the Khaiem, but he was too curious to disrupt things over a point of etiquette. Besides which, he didn't truly care.

Another of the doors shifted and creaked open. Danat stepped out. Being discovered crouched in the ivy, eavesdropping on their own children might be the least dignified thing possible, so Otah tried to be very, very still. When Danat spoke, the sound carried perfectly.

"I received your message. I'm here."

"And I received your poem," Ana said.

It was too dark to actually see how deeply Danat blushed, but Otah recognized the discomfort in his son's body.

"Ah. That," he said.

Otah tapped Issandra on the shoulder and mouthed the word *poem?* Issandra pointed back down to their children.

"I am not a toy," Ana said. "If this is another scheme of your father's or my mother's, you can carry word back to them that it didn't work. I know better than to trust you."

"You think I've lied?" Danat said. "What have I said to you that wasn't true?"

"As if you'd let yourself be caught out," Ana said.

Danat sat, one leg tucked under him, the other bent. He looked up at her like a player in some ancient epic. In the dim light, his expression seemed bemused.

"Ask anything," he said. "Do it now. I won't lie to you."

Ana crossed her arms, looking down on Danat like a low-town judge. Her brows were furrowed.

"Are you trying to seduce me?"

"Yes," Danat said. His voice was calm and solid as stone.

"Why?"

"Because I think you are worth seducing," Danat said.

"Only that? Not to please your father or my mother?"

Danat chuckled. One of the guards at Otah's side shifted his weight, the leaves beneath him crackling. Neither of the children below had ears for it.

"It began that way, I suppose," Danat said. "A political alliance. A world to remake. All of that has its appeal, but it didn't write that poem."

Ana fumbled at her belt for a moment and drew out a folded sheet of paper. Danat hesitated, then reached up and accepted it from her. They were quiet. Otah sensed the tension in Issandra's crouched body. Ana was refusing the token. And then the girl spoke, and her mother relaxed.

"Read it," Ana said. "Read it to me."

Otah closed his eyes and prayed to all the gods there were that neither he nor Issandra nor either of the guards would sneeze or cough. He had never lived through a more excruciatingly awkward scene. Below, Danat cleared his throat and began to declaim.

It wasn't good. Danat's command of Galtic didn't extend to the subtlety of rhyme. The images were simple and puerile, the sexuality just under the surface of the words ham-fisted and uncertain, and worst of all of it, Danat's tone as he spoke was as sincere as a priest at temple. His voice shook at the end of the last stanza. Silence fell in the garden. One of the guards shook once with suppressed laughter and went still.

Danat folded the paper slowly, then offered it up to Ana. It hesitated there for a moment before the girl took it.

"I see," she said. Against all reason, her voice had softened. Otah could hardly believe it, but Ana appeared genuinely moved. Danat rose to stand a hand's breadth nearer to her than before. The lanterns flickered. The two children gazed at each other with perfect seriousness. Ana looked away.

"I have a lover," she said.

"You've made that quite clear," Danat replied, amusement in his voice.

Ana shook her head. The shadows hid her expression.

"I can't," she said. "You are a fine man, Danat. More an emperor than your father. But I've sworn. I've sworn before everyone . . ."

"I don't believe that," Danat said. "I've hardly known you, Ana-kya, and I don't believe the gods themselves could stop you from something if it was truly what you wanted. Say you won't have me, but don't tell me you're refusing me out of fear."

Ana began to speak, stumbled on the words, and went silent. Danat rose, and the girl took a step toward him.

And a moment later, "Does Hanchat know you're here?"

Ana was still, and then almost imperceptibly she shook her head. Danat put a hand on her shoulder and gently turned her to face him. Otah might have been imagining it, but he thought the girl's head inclined a degree toward that hand. Danat kissed Ana's forehead and then her mouth. Her hand, palm against Danat's chest, seemed too weak to push him away. It was Danat who stepped back.

He murmured something too low to hear, then bowed in the Galtic style, took his lantern, and left her. Ana slowly lowered herself to the ground. They waited, one girl alone in the night and four hidden spies with legs and backs slowly beginning to cramp. Without word or warning, Ana sobbed twice, rose, scooped up her own lantern, and vanished through the door she'd first come from. Otah let out a pained sigh and made his uncomfortable way out from beneath the willow. There were green streaks on his robe where his knees had ground into the ivy. The armsmen had the grace to move away a few paces, expressionless.

"We're doing well," Issandra said.

"I didn't hear a declaration of marriage," Otah said. He felt disagreeable despite the evidence of Ana's changing heart. He felt dishonest, and it made him sour.

"So long as nothing comes to throw her off, it will come. In time. I know my daughter. I've seen this all before."

"Really? How odd," Otah said. "I know my son, and I never have."

"Then perhaps Ana is a lucky woman," Issandra said. He was surprised to hear something wistful in the woman's voice. The moon passed behind a high cloud, deepening the darkness around them, and then was gone. Issandra stood before him, her head high and proud, her mouth in a half-smile. She was, he thought, an interesting woman. Not beautiful in the traditional sense, and all the more attractive for that.

"A marriage is what you make of it," she said.

Otah considered the words, then took a pose that both agreed and expressed a gentle sorrow. He did not know how much of his meaning she understood. She nodded and strode off, leaving him with his armsmen.

Otah suffered through the rest of the banquet and returned to his apartments, sure he would not sleep. The night air had cooled. The fire in the grate warmed his feet. The fear that had dogged him all these last months didn't vanish, but its hold upon him faded. Somewhere under the stars just then, Danat and Ana were playing out their drama in touches and whispers; Issandra and Farrer Dasin in silences and the knowledge of long association. Idaan was hunting, Ashua Radaani was hunting, Sinja was hunting. And he was alone and sleepless with nothing to do.

He closed his eyes and tried to feel Kiyan's presence, tried to bring some sense of her out of the scent of smoke and the sound of distant singing. He tricked himself into thinking that she was here, but not so well that he could forget it was a trick.

Tomorrow, there would be another wide array of men and women requesting his time. Another schedule of ritual and audience and meeting. Perhaps it would all go as well as today had, and he would end the day in his rooms, feeling old and maudlin despite his success. There were so many men and women in the court—in the world—who wanted nothing more than power. Otah, who had it, had always known how little it changed.

He slept deeply and without dreams. When he woke, every man and woman of Galt had gone blind.

16

>+< It had been raining for two full days. Occasionally the water changed to sleet or hail, and small accumulations of rotten ice had begun to form in the sheltered corners of the courtyard. Maati closed his shutters against the low clouds and sat close to the fire, the weather tapping on wood like fingers on a table. It might almost have been pleasant if it hadn't made his spine stiffen and ache.

The cold coupled with Eiah's absence had turned life quiet and slow, like a bear preparing to sleep through the winter. Maati went down to the kitchen in the morning and ate with the others. Large Kae and Irit had started rehearsing old songs together to pass the time. They sang while they cooked, and the harmonies were prettier than Maati would have imagined. When Vanjit and Clarity-of-Sight were there, the andat would grow restive, its eyes shifting from one singer to the next and back again until Vanjit started to fidget and took her charge away. Small Kae had no ear for music, so instead spent her time reading the old texts that Clarity-of-Sight had been built from and asking questions about the finer points of their newly re-created grammar.

Most of the day, Maati spent alone in his rooms, or dressed in several thick robes, walking through the halls. He would not say it, but the space had begun to feel close and restricting. Likely it was only the sense of winter moving in.

With the journey to Pathai and back, along with the trading and provisioning, he couldn't expect Eiah's return for another ten days. He hadn't expected to feel that burden so heavily upon him, and so both delight and dread touched him when Small Kae interrupted his half-doze.

"She's come back. Vanjit's been watching from the classroom, and she says Eiah's come back. She's already turned from the high road, and if the path's not too muddy, she'll be here by nightfall."

Maati rose and opened the shutters, as if by squinting at the gray he could match Vanjit's sight. A gust of cold and damp pulled at the shutter in his hand. He was half-tempted to find a cloak of oiled silk and go out to meet her. It would be folly, of course, and gain him nothing. He ran a hand through the thin remnants of his hair, wondering how many days it had been since he'd bathed and shaved himself, and then realized that Small Kae was still there, waiting for him to speak.

"Well," he said, "whatever we have that's best, let's cook it up. Eiah-cha's going to have fresh supplies, so there's no point in saving it."

Small Kae grinned, took a pose that accepted his instruction, and bustled out. Maati turned back to the open window. Ice and mud and gloom. And set in it, invisible to him, Eiah and news.

There was no sunset; Eiah arrived shortly after the clouds had faded into darkness. In the light of hissing torches, the cart's wheels were beige with mud and clay. The horse trembled with exhaustion, driven too hard through the wet. Large Kae, clucking her tongue in disapproval, took the poor beast off to be rubbed down and warmed while the rest of them crowded around Eiah. She wrung the water from her hair with pale fingers, answering the first question before it was asked.

"Ashti Beg's left. She said she didn't want to come back. We were in a low town just south of here off the high road. She said we could talk about it, but when I got up in the morning, she'd already gone." She looked at Maati when she finished. "I'm sorry."

He took a pose that forgave and also diminished the scale of the thing, then waved her in. Vanjit followed, and then Irit and Small Kae. The meal was laid out and waiting. Barley soup with lemon and quail. Rice and sausage. Watered wine. Eiah sat near the brazier and ate like a woman starved, talking between mouthfuls.

"We never reached Pathai. There was a trade fair halfway to the city. Tents, carts, the wayhouse so full they were renting out space on the kitchen floor. There was a courier there gathering messages from all the low towns."

"So the letters were sent?" Irit asked. Eiah nodded and scooped up another mouthful of rice.

"Ashti Beg," Maati said. "Tell me more about her. Did she say why she left?"

Eiah frowned. Color was coming back to her cheeks, but her lips were still pale, her hair clinging to her neck like ivy.

"It was me," Vanjit said, the andat squirming in her lap. "It's my doing."

"Perhaps, but it wasn't what she said," Eiah replied. "She said she was tired, and that she felt we'd all gone past her. She didn't see that she would ever complete a binding of her own, or that her insights were particularly helping us. I tried to tell her otherwise, give her some perspective. If she'd stayed on until the morning, perhaps I could have."

Maati sipped his wine, wondering how much of what Eiah said was true, how much of it was being softened because Vanjit and Clarity-of-Sight were in the room. It seemed more likely to him that Ashti Beg had taken offense at Vanjit's misstep and been unable to forgive it. He recalled the woman's dry tone, her cutting humor. She had not been an easy woman or a particularly apt pupil, but he believed he would miss her.

"Was there other news? Anything of the Galts?" Vanjit asked. There was something odd about her voice, but it might only have been that Clarity-of-Sight had started its wordless, wailing complaint. Eiah appeared to notice nothing strange in the question.

"There would have been if I'd reached Pathai, I'd expect," she said. "But since there would have been nothing to do about it and our business was done early, I wanted to come back quickly."

"Ah," Vanjit said. "Of course."

Maati tugged at his fingers. There was something near disappointment in the girl's tone. As if she had expected someone that had not arrived.

"You're ready to work again?" Small Kae said. Irit flapped a cloth at her, and Small Kae took a pose that unasked the question. Eiah smiled.

"I've had a few thoughts," she said. "Let me look them over tonight after we unload the cart, and we can talk in the morning."

"Oh, there's no more work for you tonight," Irit said. "You've been on the road all this time. We can hand a few things down from a cart."

"Of course," Vanjit said. "You should rest, Eiah-kya. We'll be happy to help."

Eiah put down her soup and took a pose that offered gratitude. Something in the cant of her wrists caught Maati's attention, but the pose was gone as quickly as it had come and Eiah was sitting back, drinking wine and leaning her still-wet hair toward the fire. Large Kae rejoined them, smelling of wet horse, and Eiah told the whole story again for her benefit and then left for her rooms. Maati felt the impulse to follow her, to speak in private, but Vanjit took him by the hand and led him out to the cart with the others.

The supplies were something less than Maati had expected. Two chests of salted pork, a few jars of lard and flour and sweet oil. Bags of rice. It wasn't inconsiderable—certainly there was enough to keep them all well-fed for weeks, but likely not months. There were few spices, and no wine. Large Kae made a few small remarks about the failures of low-town trade fairs, and the others chuckled their agreement. The rain slackened, and then, as Vanjit balanced the last bag of rice on one hip and Clarity-of-Sight on the other, snow began to fall. Maati went back to his rooms, heated a kettle over his fire, and debated whether to try to boil enough water for a bath. Immersion was the one way he was sure he could chase the cold from his joints, but the effort required seemed worse than enduring the chill. And there was an errand he preferred to complete.

Light glowed through the cracks around Eiah's door. Dim and flickering, it was still more than a single night candle would have made. Maati scratched at the door. For a moment, nothing happened. Perhaps Eiah had taken to her cot. Perhaps she was elsewhere in the school. A soft sound, no more than a whisper, drew him back to the door.

"Eiah-kya?" he said, his voice low. "It's me."

Her door opened. Eiah had changed into a simple robe of thick wool, her hair tied back with a length of twine. She looked powerfully like her mother. The room she brought Maati into had once been a storage pantry. Her cot and brazier and a low table were all the furnishings. There was no window, and the air was thick with the heat and smoke from the coals.

Papers and scrolls lay on the table beside a wax tablet half-whitened by fresh notes. Medical texts in the languages of the Westlands, Eiah's own earlier drafts of the binding of Wounded. And also, he saw, the completed binding they had all devised for Clarity-of-Sight. Eiah sat on the cot, the frail structure creaking under her. She didn't look up at him.

"Why did she leave?" Maati asked. "Truth, now."

"I told her to," Eiah said. "She was frightened to come back. I told her that I understood. What happens if two poets come into conflict? If one poet has something like Floats-in-Air and the other has something like Sinking?"

"Or one poet can blind, and the other heal injury?"

"As an example," Eiah said.

Maati sighed and lowered himself to sit beside her. The cot complained. He laced his fingers together, looking at the words and diagrams without seeing them.

"I don't entirely know. It hasn't happened in my lifetime. It hasn't happened in generations."

"But it has happened," Eiah said.

"There was the war. The one that ended the Second Empire. That was . . . what, ten generations ago? The andat are flesh because we've translated them into flesh, but they are also concepts. Abstractions. It might simply be that the poets' wills are set against each other's. A kind of wrestling match mediated through the andat. Whoever has the greater strength of mind and the andat more suited to the struggle gains the upper hand. Or it could be that the concepts of the two andat don't coincide, and any struggle would have to be expressed physically. In the world we inhabit. Or . . ."

"Or?"

"Or something else could happen. The grammar and meaning in one binding could relate to some structure or nuance in another. Imagine two singers in competition. What if they chose songs that harmonized? What if the words of one song blended with the words of the other, and something new came from it? Songs are a poor metaphor. What are the odds that the words of any two given songs would speak to each other? If the bindings are related in concept, if the *ideas* are near, it's much more likely that sort of resonance could happen. By chance."

"And what would that do?"

"I don't know," Maati said. "Nobody does. I can say that what was once a land of palm trees and rivers and palaces of sapphire is a killing desert. I can say that people who travel in the ruins of the Old Empire tend to die there. It might be from physical expressions of that old struggle. It might be from some interaction of bindings. There is no way to be sure."

Eiah was silent. She turned the pages of her medical books until she reached diagrams Maati recognized. Eyes cut through the center, eyes sliced through the back. He had seen them all thousands of times when Vanjit was preparing herself, and they had seemed like the keepers of great secrets. He hadn't considered at the time that each image was the result of some actual, physical orb meeting with an investigative blade, or that all the eyes pictured there were sightless.

He felt Eiah's sigh as much as heard it.

"What happened out there?" he asked. "The truth, not what you said in front of the others."

Eiah leaned forward. For a moment, Maati thought she was weeping, but she straightened again. Her eyes were dry, her jaw set. She had pulled a small box of carved oak from under the cot, and she handed it to him now. He opened it, the leather hinge loose and soft. Six folded pages lay inside, sewn at the edges and sealed with Eiah's personal sigil.

"You didn't send them?"

"It was true about the trade fair. We did find one. It wasn't very good, but it was there, so we stopped. There are Galts everywhere now. They came to Saraykeht at the start, and apparently the councillors and the court are all still there. There are others who have fanned out. The ones who believe that my father's plan is going to work."

"The ones who see a profit in it. Slavers?"

"Marriage brokers," Eiah said as if the terms were the same. "They've been traveling the low towns making lists of men in want of Galtic peasant girls to act as brood mares for their farms. Apparently eight lengths of copper will put a man's name on the list to travel to Galt. Two of silver for the list to haul a girl here."

Maati felt his belly twist. It had gone further than he had dared think.

"Most of them are lying, of course," Eiah said. "Taking money from the desperate and moving on. I don't know how many of them there are out there. Hundreds, I would guess. But, Maati-cha, the night I left? All of the Galts lost their sight. All of them, and at once. No one cares any longer what's happened with my brother and the girl he was supposed to marry. No one talks about the Emperor. All anyone cares about is the andat. They know that some poet somewhere has bound Blindness or something like it and loosed it against the Galts."

It was as if the air had gone from the room, as if Maati were suddenly on a mountaintop. His breath was fast, his heart pounding. It might have been joy or fear or something of each.

"I see," Maati said.

"Uncle, they hate us. All those farmers and traders and shepherds? All those men who thought that they would have wives and children? All those women who thought that even if it hadn't come from their body, at least there would be a baby nearby to care for? They think we've taken it from them. And I have never seen so much rage."

Maati felt as if he'd been struck, caught in the moment between the blow and the bloom of pain. He said something, words stringing together without sense and trailing to silence. He put his face in his hands.

"You didn't know," Eiah said. "She didn't tell you."

"Vanjit's done this," Maati said. "She can undo it. I can . . ." He stopped, catching his breath. He felt as if he'd been running. His hands trembled. When Eiah spoke, her voice was as level and calm as a physician's announcing a death.

"Twice."

Maati turned to her, his hands taking a pose of query. Eiah put her hand on the table, papers shifting under her fingers with a sound like sand against glass.

"This is twice, Maati-cha. First with Ashti Beg, and now . . . Gods. Now with all of Galt."

"Is this why Ashti Beg left?" Maati asked. "The true reason?"

"The true reason is that she was afraid of Vanjit," Eiah said. "And I couldn't reassure her."

"Children," Maati said. The pain in his chest was easing, the shock of the news fading away. "I'll speak with Vanjit. She did this all. She can undo it as well. And . . . and it does speak to the purpose. We wanted to announce that the andat had returned to the world. She's done that in no small voice."

"Maati-cha," Eiah began, but he kept talking, fast and loud.

"This is why they did it, you know. All those tests and lies and opportunities to prove ourselves. Or fail to prove ourselves. They broke us to the lead first, and gave us power when they knew we could be controlled."

"It looked like a wiser strategy, if this is the alternative," Eiah said. "Do you think she'll listen to you?"

"Listen, yes. Do as I command? I don't know. And I don't know that I'd want her to. She's learning responsibility. She's learning her own limits. Even if I could tell her what they are, she couldn't learn by having it said. She's . . . exploring."

"She's killed thousands of people, at the least."

"Galts," Maati said. "She's killed Galts. We were never here to save them. Yes, Eiah-kya. Vanjit went too far, and because she's holding an andat, there are consequences. When you slaughter a city? When you send your army to kill a little girl's family in front of her? There are consequences to that too. Or by all the gods there should be."

"You're saying this is justice?" Eiah asked.

"We made peace with Galt," Maati said. "None of Vanjit's family were avenged. There was no justice for them because it was simpler for Otah to ignore their deaths. Just as it's simpler for him to ignore all the women of the cities. Vanjit has an andat, and so her will is now more important than your father's. I don't see that makes it any more or less just."

Eiah took a pose that respectfully disagreed, then dropped her hands to her sides.

"I don't argue that she's gone too far," Maati said. "She's killing a horsefly with a hammer. Only that it's not as bad as it first seems. She's still young. She's still new to her powers."

"And that forgives everything?" Eiah said.

"Don't," Maati said more sharply than he'd intended. "Don't be so quick to judge her. You'll be in her position soon enough. If all goes well."

"I wonder what I'll forget. How I'll go too far," Eiah said, and sighed. "How did we ever think we could do good with these as our tools?"

Maati was silent for a moment. His memory turned on Heshai and Seedless, Cehmai and Stone-Made-Soft. The sickening twist that was Sterile, moving through his own mind like an eel through muddy water.

"Is there another way to fix it?" Maati asked. "After Sterile, is there a way other than this to make the world whole? All those women who will never bear a child. All those men whose money is going to charming Galtic liars. Is there a way to make the world well again besides what we're doing?"

"We could wait," Eiah said, her voice gray and toneless. "Given enough time, we'll all die and be forgotten."

Maati was silent. Eiah closed her eyes. The flame of the night candle fluttered in a draft that smelled of fresh snow and wet cloth. Eiah's gaze focused inward, on some landscape of her own mind. He didn't think she liked what she saw there. She opened her mouth as if to speak, closed it again, and looked away.

"You're right, though," Maati said. "This is twice."

They found Vanjit in her room, the andat wailing disconsolately as she rocked it in her arms. Maati entered the room first to Vanjit's gentle smile, but her expression went blank when Eiah came in after him and slid the door shut behind her. The andat's black eyes went from Vanjit to Eiah and back, then it squealed in delight and held its thick, short arms up to Eiah as if it was asking to be held.

"You know, then," Vanjit said. "It was inevitable."

"You should have told me what you intended," Maati said. "It was a dangerous, rash thing to do. And it's going to have consequences."

Vanjit put Clarity-of-Sight on the floor at her feet. The thing shrieked complaint, and she bent toward it, her jaw clenched. Maati recognized the push and pull of wills between andat and poet. Even before the andat whimpered and went silent, he had no doubt of the outcome.

"You were going to tell the world of what we'd done anyway," Vanjit said. "But you couldn't be sure they would have stopped the Emperor, could you? This way they can't go forward."

"Why didn't you tell Maati-kvo what you were doing?" Eiah asked.

"Because he would have told me not to," Vanjit said, anger in her voice.

"I would have," Maati said. "Yes."

"It isn't fair, Maati-kya," Vanjit said. "It isn't right that they should come here, take our places. They were the killers, not us. They were the ones who brought blades to our cities. Any of the poets could have destroyed Galt at any time, and we never, ever did."

"And that makes it right to crush them now?" Eiah demanded.

"Yes," Vanjit said. There were tears in her eyes.

Eiah tilted her head. Long familiarity told Maati the thoughts that occupied Eiah's mind. This girl, sitting before them both, had been granted the power of a small god by their work. Maati's and Eiah's. The others had helped, but the three of them together in that room carried the decision. And so the weight of its consequences.

"It was ill advised," Maati said. "The low towns should have been our allies and support. Now they've been angered."

"Why?" Vanjit asked.

"They don't know what our plan is," Maati said. "They don't know about Eiah and Wounded. All they see is that there was a glimmer of hope. Yes, I know it was a thin, false hope, but it was all that they had."

"That's stupid," Vanjit said.

"It only seems that way because we know more than they," Eiah said.

"We can tell them," Vanjit said.

"If we can calm them long enough to listen," Maati said. "But that isn't what I've come here for. I am your teacher, Vanjit-cha. I need two things of you. Do you understand?"

The girl looked at the ground, her hands rising in a pose of acceptance appropriate for a student to her master.

"First, you must never take this kind of action with the andat without telling me. We have too many plans and they are too delicate for any of us to act without the others knowing it."

"Eiah sent Ashti Beg away," Vanjit said.

"And we discussed that possibility before they left," Maati said. "The second thing . . . What you've done to the Galts, only you can undo."

The girl looked up now. Anger flashed in her eyes. The andat gurgled and clapped its tiny hands. Maati held up a finger, insisting that she wait until he had finished.

"If you hold to this," he said, "thousands of people will die. Women and children who are innocent of any crime."

"It's what they did to us," she said. *What they did to me.* Maati reached forward and took her hand.

"I understand," he said. "I won't tell you to undo this thing. But for me, think carefully about how the burden of those deaths will weigh on you. You're angry now, and anger gives you strength. But when it's faded, you will still be responsible for what you've done."

"I will, Maati-kvo," Vanjit said.

Eiah made a sound in the back of her throat, its meaning unguessable. Maati smiled and put a hand on Vanjit's shoulder.

"Well. That's settled. Now, I suppose it's time to get back to work. Give these people in the low towns something to celebrate."

"You've done it, then, Eiah-kya?" Vanjit asked. "You've found the insight you needed? You understand Wounded?"

Eiah was quiet for a moment, looking down at Vanjit and Clarity-of-Sight. Her lips twitched into a thin, joyless smile.

"Closer," Eiah said. "I've come closer."

17

>+< Seeing Balasar Gice shook Otah more than he had expected. He had always known that the general was not a large-framed man, but his presence had always filled the room. Seeing him seated at a table by the window with his eyes the gray of old pearls, Otah felt he was watching the man die. The robes seemed too large on him, or his shoulders suddenly grown small.

Outside the window, the morning sun lit the sea. Gulls called and complained to one another. A small plate had the remnants of fresh cheese and cut apple; the cheese flowed in the day's heat, the pale flesh of the apple had gone brown. Otah cleared his throat. Balasar smiled, but didn't bother turning his head toward the sound.

"Most High?" Balasar asked.

"Yes," Otah said. "I came . . . I came when I heard."

"I am afraid Sinja will have to do without my aid," Balasar said, his voice ironic and bleak. "It seems I'll be in no condition to sail."

Otah leaned against the window's ledge, his shadow falling over Balasar. The general turned toward him. His voice was banked rage, his expression impotence.

"Did you know, Otah? Did you know what they were doing?"

"This wasn't my doing," Otah said. "I swear that."

"My life was taking your god-ghosts out of the world. I thought we'd done it. Even after what you bastards did to me, to all of us, I was content trying to make peace. I lost my men to it, and I lived with that because the loss meant something. However desperate the cost, at least we'd be rid of the fucking andat. And now . . ."

Balasar struck the table with an open palm, the report like stone breaking. Otah lifted his hands toward a pose that offered comfort, and then stopped and let his arms fall to his sides.

"I'm sorry," Otah said. "I will send my best agents to find the new poet and resolve this. Until then, all of you will be cared for and—"

Balasar's laughter was a bark.

"Where do I begin, Most High? We will all be cared for? Do you really think this has only happened to the Galts who came to your filthy city? I will wager any odds you like that everyone back home is suffering the same things we are. How many fishermen were on their boats when it happened? How many people were traveling the roads? You could no more care for all of us than pluck the moon out of the sky."

"I'm sorry for that," Otah said. "Once we've found the poet and talked to . . ." He stumbled on his words, caught between the expected *him* and the more likely *her.*

Balasar gestured to him, palms up as if displaying something small and obvious.

"If it wasn't your pet andat that did this, then what hope do you have of resolving anything?" Balasar asked. "They may have left you your sight for the moment, but there's nothing you can do. It's the andat. There's no defense. There's no counterattack that means anything. Gather your armsmen. Take to the field. Then come back and die beside us. You can do *nothing.*"

This is my daughter's work, Otah thought but didn't say. I can hope that she still loves me enough to listen.

"You've never felt this," Balasar said. "The rest of us? The rest of the world? We know what it is to be faced with the andat. You can't end this. You can't even negotiate. You have no standing now. The best you can do is beg."

"Then I will beg," Otah said.

"Enjoy that," Balasar said, sitting back in his chair. It was like watching a showfighter collapse at the end of a match. The vitality, the anger, the violence snuffed out, and the general was only a small Galtic man with crippled eyes, waiting for some kind soul to take away the remains of his uneaten meal. Otah rose and walked quietly from the room.

All through the city, the scenes were playing out. Men and women who had been well the night before were in states of rage and despair. They blundered into the unfamiliar streets, screaming, swinging whatever weapon came to hand at anyone who tried to help them. Or else they wept. Or, like Balasar, folded in upon themselves. The last was the most terrible.

Balasar had been only the first stop in Otah's long, painful morning journey. He'd meant to call on each of the high councillors, to promise his efforts at restoration and the best of care until then. The general had spoiled the plan. Otah did see two more men, made the same declarations.

Neither of the others scoffed, but Otah could see that his words rang as hollow as a gourd.

Instead of the third councillor, Otah went back to his palaces. He prayed as he walked, that some message would have come from Idaan. None had. Instead, his audience chambers were filled with the utkhaiem, some in fine robes hastily thrown on, others still in whatever finery they had slept in. The sound of their voices competing one over another was louder than surf and as incomprehensible. Everywhere he walked, their eyes turned toward him. Otah walked with a grave countenance, his spine as straight as he could keep it. He greeted the shock and the fear with the same equanimity as the expressions of joy.

There was more joy than he had expected. More than he had hoped. The andat had come back to the world, and the Galts made to suffer, and that was somehow a cause to celebrate. Otah didn't respond to those calls, but he did begin a mental catalog of who precisely was laughing, who weeping. Someday, he told himself, someday the best of these men and women would be rewarded, the worst left behind. Only he didn't know how.

In his private rooms, the servants fluttered like moths. No schedules were right, no plans were made. Orders from the Master of Tides contradicted the instructions from the Master of Keys, and neither allowed for what the guards and armsmen said they needed to do. Otah built his own fire in the grate, lighting it from the stub of a candle, and let raw chaos reign about him.

Danat found him there, looking into the fire. His son's eyes were wide, but his shoulders hadn't yet sagged. Otah took a pose of welcome and Danat crouched before him.

"What are you doing, Papa-kya," Danat said. "You're just sitting here?"

"I'm thinking," Otah said, aware as he did so how weak the words sounded.

"They need you. You have to gather the high utkhaiem. You have to tell them what's going on."

He looked at his son. The strong face, the sincere eyes the same rich brown as Kiyan's had been. He would have made a good emperor. Better than Otah had. He took his boy's hand.

"The fleet is doomed," Otah said. "Galt is broken. These new poets, wherever they are, no longer answer to the Empire. What would you have me say?"

"That," Danat said. "If nothing else, say that. Say what everyone knows is true. How can that be wrong?"

"Because I have nothing to say after it," Otah said. "I don't know what to do. I don't have an answer."

"Then tell them that we're thinking of one," Danat said.

Otah sat silent, his hands on his knees, and let the fire in the grate fill his eyes. Danat shook his shoulder with a sound that was part frustration and part plea. When Otah couldn't find a response, Danat stood, took a pose that ended an audience, and strode out. The young man's impatience lingered in the air like incense.

There had been a time when Otah had been possessed of the certainty of youth. He had held the fate of nations in his hands, and done what needed doing. He had killed. Somewhere the years had pressed it out of him. Danat would see the same complexity, futility, and sorrow, given time. He was young. He wasn't tired yet. His world was still simple.

Servants came, and Otah turned them away. He considered going to his desk, writing another of his letters to Kiyan, but the effort of it was too much. He thought of Sinja, riding the swift autumn waves outside Chaburi-Tan and waiting for aid that would never come. Would he know? Were there Galts enough among his crew to guess what had happened?

The world was so large and so complex, it was almost impossible to believe that it could collapse so quickly. Idaan had been right again. All the problems that had plagued him were meaningless in the face of this.

Eiah. Maati. The people he had failed. They had taken the world from him. Well, perhaps they'd have a better idea what to do with it. And if a few hundred or a few thousand Galts died, there was nothing Otah could do to save them. He was no poet. He could have been. One angry, rootless boy's decision differently made, and everything would have been different.

A servant woman came and took away a tray of untouched food that Otah hadn't known was there. The pine branches in the grate were all ashes now. The sun was almost at the height of its day's arc. Otah rubbed his eyes and only then recognized the sound that had drawn him from his reverie. Trumpets and bells. Callers' voices ringing out over the palaces, over the city, over sea and sky and everything in it. A pronouncement was to be made, and all men and women of the utkhaiem were called to hear it.

He made his way through the back halls, set like stagecraft, that allowed him to appear at the appropriate ritual moment. What few servants there were bent themselves almost double in poses of obeisance as he passed. Otah ignored them.

A side hall, almost too narrow for a man to walk down, took him to a hidden seat. Years before, it had been a place where the Khai Saraykeht could watch entertainments without being seen. Now it was Otah's own. He looked down upon the hall. It was packed so thickly there was no room to sit. The cushions meant to allow people to take their rest were all being trampled underfoot. Whisperers had to fight to hold their positions. And among the bright robes and jeweled headdresses of the utkhaiem, there were also the tunics and gray, empty eyes of Galts come to hear what was said. He saw them and thought of an old dream he'd had of Heshai, the poet he had once killed, attending a dinner though still very much dead. Corpses walked among the utkhaiem. Balasar was not among them.

Silence took the hall as if someone had cupped his hands over Otah's ears, and he turned toward the dais. His son stood there, his robe the pale of mourning.

"My friends," Danat said. "There is little I can say which you do not already know. Our brothers and sisters of Galt have been struck. The only plausible cause is this: a new poet has been trained, a new andat has been bound, and, against all wisdom, it has been used first as a weapon."

Danat paused as the whisperers repeated his words out through the wide galleries and, no doubt, into the streets.

"The fleet is in peril," Danat continued. "Chaburi-Tan placed at risk. We do not know who the poet is that has done this thing. We cannot trust that they will be as quick to blind our enemies as they have our friends. We cannot trust that they will undo the damage they have caused to our new allies. Our new families. And so my father has asked me to find this new poet and kill him."

Otah's fingers pressed against the carved stone until his joints ached. His chest ached with dread. *He doesn't know,* Otah wanted to shout. *His sister is part of this, and he does not know it.* He shook and kept silent. There was only the swelling roar of the people, the whisperers shouting above it, and his son standing proud and still, shoulders set.

"There are some among us who look upon what has happened today as a moment of hope. They believe that the andat returned to the world marks the end of our hard times. With all respect, it marks their beginning, and neither I nor . . ."

Otah turned away, pushing his way down the narrow hall, afraid to let his hands leave the stone for fear he should lose his balance. In the dim hallways, he gathered himself. He had expected shame. Seeing Danat speaking as he himself could not, he thought that he would feel shame. He didn't. There was only anger.

The first servant he found, he grabbed by the sleeve and spun halfway around. The woman started to shout at him, then saw who he was, saw his face, and went pale.

"Whatever you were doing, stop it," Otah said. "Find me the Master of Tides. Bring her to my rooms. Do it now."

She might have taken a pose that accepted the command or one of obeisance or any other of the hundred thousand things the physical grammar of the Khaiem might express. Otah didn't stop long enough to see, and didn't care.

In his rooms, he called for a traveler's basket. The thin wicker shifted and creaked as he pulled the simplest robes from his wardrobes and stuffed them in, one atop the other like they were canvas trousers. The dressing servants made small pawing movements, and Otah didn't bother to find out whether they were meant to help or slow him before he sent them all away. He found eight identical pairs of strapped leather boots, put three pairs into his basket, then snarled and took the extra ones back out. He only had two feet, he didn't need more boots than that. He didn't notice the Master of Tides until the woman made a small sound, like someone stepping on a mouse.

"Good," Otah said. "You have something to write with?"

She fumbled with her sleeve and pulled out a small ledger and a finger charcoal. Otah reeled off half-a-dozen names, all the heads of high families of the utkhaiem. He paused, then named Balasar Gice as well. The Master of Tides scribbled, the charcoal graying her fingers.

"That is *my* High Council," Otah said. "Here with you as witness, I invest them with the power to administrate the Empire until Danat or I return. Is that clear enough?"

"Most High," the Master of Tides said, her face pale and bloodless, "there has never . . . the authority of the Emperor can't be . . . and Gice-cha isn't even . . ."

Otah strode across the room toward her, blood rushing in his ears. The Master of Tides fell back a step, anticipating a blow, but Otah only plucked the ledger from her hands. The charcoal had fallen to the floor, and Otah scooped it up, turned to a fresh page, and wrote out the investment he'd just spoken. When he handed it back, the Master of Tides opened and closed her mouth like a fish on sand, then said, "The court. The utkhaiem. A council with explicit imperial authority? This . . . can't be done."

"It can," Otah said.

"Most High, forgive me, but what you've suggested here changes everything! It throws aside all *tradition*!"

"I do that sometimes," Otah said. "Get me a horse."

Danat's force was small—a dozen armsmen with swords and bows, two steamcarts with rough shedlike structures on the flats, and Danat in a wool huntsman's robes. Otah's own robe was leather dyed the red of roses; his horse was taller at the shoulder than the top of his own head. The wicker traveler's basket jounced against the animal's flank as he cantered to Danat's side.

"Father," Danat said. He took no pose, but his body was stiff and defiant.

"I heard your speech. It was rash," Otah said. "What was your plan, now that I've sent you off to find and kill this new poet?"

"We're going north to Utani," Danat said. "It's central, and we can move in any direction once we've gotten word where he is."

"She," Otah said. "Wherever *she* is."

Danat blinked, his spine relaxing in his surprise.

"And you can't announce a plan like this, Danat-kya," Otah said. "No matter how fast you ride, word will move faster. And you'll know when the news has reached her, because you'll be just as crippled as the Galts."

"You knew about this?" Danat murmured.

"I know some things. I'd had reports," Otah said. His mount whickered uneasily. "I had taken some action. I didn't know it had gone so far. Utani is the wrong way. We need to ride west. Toward Pathai. And whichever rider is fastest goes ahead and stops any couriers heading back toward Saraykeht. I'm expecting a letter, but we can meet it on the road."

"You can't go," Danat said. "The cities need you. They need to see that there's someone in control."

"They do see that. They see it's the poet," Otah said.

Danat glanced at the steamcarts with their covered burdens. He looked nervous and lost. Otah felt the impulse to tell him, there on the open street, what he was facing: Maati's plan, his own reluctance to act, the specter of Eiah's involvement, Idaan's mission. He restrained himself. There would be time later, and fewer people who might overhear.

"Papa-kya," Danat said. "I think you should stay here. They need . . ."

"They need the poets ended," Otah said, knowing as he said it that he also meant his daughter. For a moment, he saw her. In his imagination, she was always younger than the real woman. He saw her dark eyes and furrowed brow as she studied with the court physicians. He felt the warmth and weight of her, still small enough to rest in his arms. He smelled the sour-milk breath she'd had before the soft place in her skull had grown closed. It might not come to that, he told himself.

He also knew that it might.

"We'll do this together," Otah said. "The two of us."

"Papa . . ."

"You can't stop me from this, Danat-kya," Otah said gently. "I'm the Emperor."

Danat tried to speak, first confusion in his eyes, then distress, and then amused resignation. Otah looked out at the armsmen, their eyes averted. The steamcarts chuffed and shuddered, the sheds on them larger than some homes Otah had kept as a child. The anger rose in him again. Not with Danat or Eiah, Maati or Idaan. His anger was with the gods themselves and the fate that had brought him here, and it burned in him.

"West," Otah called. "West. All of us. Now."

They passed the arch that marked the edge of the city at three hands past midday. Men and women had come out, lining the streets as they passed. Some cheered them, others merely watched. Few, Otah thought, were likely to believe that the old man at the front was truly the Emperor.

The buildings west of the city proper grew lower and squat. Instead of roof tiles, they had layers of water-grayed wood or cane thatching. The division between the last of Saraykeht and the nearest low town was invisible. Traders pulled aside to let them pass. Feral dogs yipped at them from the high grass and followed along just out of bowshot. The sun slipped down in its arc, blinding Otah and drawing tears.

A thousand small memories flooded Otah's mind like raindrops in an evening storm. A night he'd spent years before, sleeping in a hut made from grass and mud. The first horse he'd been given when he took the colors of House Siyanti and joined the gentleman's trade. He had traveled these very roads, back then. When his hair had still been dark and his back still strong and Kiyan still the loveliest wayhouse keeper in all the cities he had seen.

They rode until full dark came, stopping at a pond. Otah stood for a moment, looking into the dark water. It wasn't quite cold enough for ice to have formed on its surface. His spine and legs ached so badly he wondered whether he would be able to sleep. The muscles of his belly protested when he tried to bend. It had been years since he'd taken to the road in anything faster or more demanding than a carried litter. He remembered the pleasant near-exhaustion at the end of a long day's ride, and his present pain had little in common with it. He thought about sitting on the cool, wet grass. He was more than half afraid that once he sat down, he wouldn't be able to stand.

Behind him, the kilns of the steamcarts had been opened, and the armsmen were cooking birds over the coals. The smaller of the two sheds perched atop the steamcarts had been opened to reveal tightly rolled blankets, crates of soft fuel coal, and earthenware jars inscribed with symbols for seeds, raisins, and salted fish. As Otah watched, Danat emerged from the second shed, standing alone in the shadows at the end of the cart. One of the armsmen struck up a song, and the others joined in. It was the kind of thing Otah himself would have done, back when he had been a different man.

"Danat-kya," he said when he'd walked close enough to be heard over the good cheer of their companions. His son squatted at the edge of the cart, and then sat. In the light from the kilns, Danat seemed little more than a deeper shadow, his face hidden. "There are some things we should discuss."

"There are," Danat said, and his voice pulled Otah back.

Otah shifted to sit at his son's side. Something in his left knee clicked, but there was no particular pain, so he ignored it. Danat laced his fingers.

"You're angry that I've come?" Otah said.

"No," Danat said. "It's not . . . not that, quite. But I hadn't thought that you would be here, or that we'd be going west. I made arrangements with my own plan set, and you've changed it."

"I can apologize. But this is the right thing. I can't swear that Pathai is—"

"That's not what I'm trying . . . Gods," Danat said. He turned to his father, his eyes catching the kiln light and flashing with it. "Come on. You might as well know."

Danat shifted, rose, and walked across the wide, wooden back of the steamcart. The shed's door was shut fast. As Otah pulled himself up, grunting, Danat worked a thick iron latch. The armsmen's singing faltered. Otah was aware of eyes fixed upon them, though he couldn't see the men as more than silhouettes.

Otah made his way to the shed's open door. Inside was pure darkness. Danat stood, latch in his hand, silent. Otah was about to speak when another voice came from the black.

"Danat?" Ana Dasin asked. "Is it you?"

"It is," Danat said. "And my father."

Gray-eyed, the Galtic girl emerged from the darkness. She wore a blouse of simple cotton, a skirt like a peasant worker's. Her hands moved before her, testing the air until they found the wood frame of the shed's door. Otah must have made a sound, because she turned as if to look at him, her gaze going past him and into nothing. He almost took a pose of formal greeting but stopped himself.

"Ana-cha," he said.

"Most High," she replied, her chin high, her brows raised.

"I didn't expect to see you here," he said.

"I went to her as soon as I heard what had happened," Danat said. "I swore it was nothing that we'd done. We hadn't been trying to recapture the andat. She didn't believe me. When I decided to go, I asked her to come. As a witness. We've left word for Farrer-cha. Even if he disapproves, it doesn't seem he'd be able to do much about it before we returned."

"You know this is madness," Otah said softly.

Ana Dasin frowned, hard lines marking her face. But then she nodded.

"It makes very little difference whether I die in the city or on the road," she said. "If this isn't treachery on the part of the Khaiem, then I don't see that I have anything to fear."

"We are on an improvised campaign against powers we cannot match. I can name half-a-dozen things to fear without stopping to think," Otah said. He sighed, and the Galtic girl's expression hardened. Otah went on, letting a hint of bleak amusement into his voice. "But I suppose if you've come, you've come. Welcome to our hunt, Ana-cha."

He nodded to his son and stepped back. Her voice recalled him.

"Most High," she said. "I want to believe Danat. I want to think that he had nothing to do with this."

"He didn't," Otah said. The girl weighed his words, and then seemed to accept them.

"And you?" she said. "Was any of this yours?"

Otah smiled. The girl couldn't see him, but Danat did.

"Only my inattention," Otah said. "It's a failure I've come to correct."

"So the andat can blind you as easily as he has us," Ana said, stepping out of the shed and onto the steamcart. "You aren't protected any more than I am."

"That's true," Otah said.

Ana went silent, then smiled. In the dim light of the fire, he could see her mother in the shape of her cheek.

"And yet you take our side rather than ally with the poets," she said. "So which of us is mad?"

18

>+< The snow fell and stayed, as deep as Maati's three fingers together. The winds of autumn whistled through the high, narrow windows that had never known glass. The women—Eiah, Irit, and the two Kaes— were in a small room, clustered around a brazier and talking with hushed fervor about grammar and form, the distinctions between age and wounds and madness. Vanjit, wrapped in thick woolen robes and a cloak of waxed silk, was sitting on a high wall, her gaze to the east. She sang lullabies to Clarity-of-Sight, and her voice would have been beautiful if she'd been cradling a real babe. Maati considered interrupting her or else returning to the work with the others, but both options were worse than remaining alone. He turned away from the great bronze door and retreated into the darkness.

It would be only weeks until winter was upon them. Not the killing storms of the north, but enough that even the short journey to Pathai would become difficult. He tried to imagine the long nights and cold that waited for him, for all of them, and he wondered how they would manage it.

A darkness had taken Eiah since her return. He saw it in her eyes and heard the rasp of it in her voice, but there was no lethargy about it. She was awake before him every morning and took to her bed long after sunset. Her attention was bent to the work of her binding, and her ferocity seemed to pull the others in her wake. Only Vanjit held herself apart, attending only some of Eiah's discussions. It was as if there were a set amount of attention, and as Eiah bore down, Vanjit floated up like a kite. Maati, caught between the pair, only felt tired and sick and old.

It had been years since he had lived in one place, and then it had been as the permanent guest of the Khai Machi. He had had a library, servants who brought him wine and food. Eiah had been no more than a girl, then. Bright, engaged, curious. But more than that, she had been joyful. And he remembered himself as being a part of that joy, that comfort.

He lumbered into one of the wide, bare rooms where rows and columns of cots had once held boys no older than ten summers, wrapped in all the robes they owned to keep off the cold. He leaned against the wall, feeling the rough stone against his back.

Another winter in this place. There was a time when he'd thought it wise.

Footsteps came from behind him. Vanjit's. He knew them from the sound. He didn't turn to greet her. When she stepped into the room, waxed silk shining like leather, she didn't at first look at him. She had grown beautiful in an odd way. The andat held against her hip clung to her, and there was a peace in her expression that lent her an air of serenity. He wanted to trust her, to take her success as the first of a thousand ways in which he would be able to set the world right, to unmake his mistakes.

"Maati-kvo," Vanjit said. Her voice was low and soft as a woman newly woken.

"Vanjit," he said, taking a pose of greeting.

She and the andat came to sit at his side. The tiny thing balled its hands in the folds of Maati's robe, tugging as if to draw his attention. Vanjit appeared not to notice.

"Eiah-cha is doing well, isn't she?" Vanjit asked.

"I think so," Maati said. "She's taken a wide concept, and that's always difficult. She's very serious, though. There are a few flaws. Structures that work against each other instead of in concert."

"How long?" Vanjit asked. Maati rubbed his eyes with the palms of his hands.

"Until she's ready? If she finds a form that resolves the conflict, I suppose she could start the last phase tomorrow. Two weeks. Three at the earliest. Or months more. I don't know."

Vanjit nodded to herself, not looking up at him. The andat tugged at his robe again. Maati looked down into the black, eager eyes. The andat gave its wide, toothless grin.

"We've been talking," Vanjit said. "Clarity-of-Sight and I have been talking about Eiah and what she's doing. He pointed something out that I hadn't considered."

That was possible, but only in a fashion. The andat was a part of her, as all of them reflected the poets who had bound them. Whatever thought it had presented in the deep, intimate battle it waged with Vanjit, it had to have originated with her. Still, she was as capable of surprising herself as any of them. Maati took a pose that invited her to continue.

"We can't know how Eiah-cha's binding will go," Vanjit said. "I know that we were first as a test of the grammar. That Clarity-of-Sight exists is proof that the bindings can work. It isn't proof that Eiah-cha . . . Don't misunderstand, Maati-kvo. I know as well as anyone that Eiah-cha is brilliant. Without her, I would never have managed my binding. But until she makes the attempt, we can't be sure that she's the right sort of mind to be a poet. Even with all our work, she might still fail."

"That's true," Maati said, trying to turn away from the thought even as he spoke.

"It would all end, wouldn't it? What I can do, what we can do. It wouldn't mean anything without Eiah-cha. She's the one who can undo what Sterile did, and unless she can do that . . ."

"She's our best hope," Maati said.

"Yes," Vanjit said, and turned to look up at Maati. Her face was bright. "Yes, our best hope. But not the only one."

The andat at her hip clucked and giggled to itself, clapping tiny hands. Maati took a pose of query.

"We know for certain that we have one person who could bind an andat, because I already have. I want Eiah-cha to win through as badly as anyone, but if her binding does fail, I could take it up."

Maati smiled because he could think of nothing else to do. Dread knotted in his chest. His breath had grown suddenly short, and the warehouse-wide walls of the sleeping quarters had narrowed. Vanjit stood, her hand on his sleeve. Maati took a moment, shook his head.

"Are you well, Maati-kvo?" Vanjit asked.

"I'm old," he said. "It's nothing. Vanjit-kya, you can't hold another andat. You of all of us know how much of your attention Clarity-of-Sight requires."

"I would have to release him for a time," Vanjit said. "I understand that. But what makes him him comes from me, doesn't it? All the things that aren't innate to the idea of sight made clear. So when I bind Wounded, it would be almost like having him back. It would be, because it would come from me, just as he does."

"It . . . it might," Maati said. His head still felt light. A chill sweat touched his back. "I suppose it might. But the risk of it would also be huge. Once the andat was let go, you wouldn't be able to recall it. Even if you were to bind another, Clarity-of-Sight would be gone. We have the power now . . ."

"But my power doesn't mean anything," Vanjit said. Her voice was taking on a strained tone, as if some banked anger was rising in her. "Eiah matters. Wounded matters."

He thought of the Galts, blinded. Had Vanjit held Wounded, they would doubtless all have died. A nation felled—every woman, every man—by invisible swords, axes, stones. It was a terrible power, but they weren't here for the benefit of the Galts. He put his hand over Vanjit's.

"Let us hope it never comes to that," he said. "It would be far, far better to have two poets. But if it does, I'm glad you'll be here."

The girl's face brightened and she darted forward, kissing Maati's lips as brief and light as a butterfly. The andat on her hip gurgled and flailed. Vanjit nodded as if it had spoken.

"We should go," Vanjit said. "We've spent so much time talking about how to approach you, I've neglected the classes. Thank you, Maati-kvo. I can't tell you how much it means to know that I can still help."

Maati nodded, waited until girl and andat had vanished, then lowered himself to the floor. Slowly, the knot in his chest relaxed, and his breath returned to its normal depth and rhythm. In the snow-gray sunlight, he considered the backs of his hands, the nature of the andat, and what he had just agreed to. The cold of the stone and the sky seemed to take his energy. By the time he rose, his fingers had gone white and his feet were numb.

He found the others in the kitchen. Chalk marks on the walls sketched out three or four grammatical scenarios, each using different vocabulary and structures. Eiah, considering the notes, took a brief pose of welcome when he appeared, then turned to stare at him. Irit fluttered about, chattering merrily until he was seated by the fire with a bowl of warm tea in his hand. Large Kae and Small Kae were in the middle of a conversation about the difference between cutting and crushing, which in other circumstances would have been disturbing to hear. Vanjit sat with a beatific smile, Clarity-of-Sight perched on her lap. Maati motioned at Eiah that she should carry on, and with a reluctance he didn't understand, she did.

The tea was warm and smelled like spring. Coals glowed in the brazier. The voices around him seemed hopeful and bright. But then he saw the andat's black eyes and was reminded of his unease.

The session came to its end and the women scattered, each to her own task, leaving only Vanjit sitting by the fire, nursing the andat from a breast swollen with milk. Maati made his way back to his rooms. He was tired past all reason and unsteady on his feet. As he had hoped, Eiah was waiting outside his door.

"That seemed to go well," Maati said. "I think Irit's solution was fairly elegant."

"It has promise," Eiah agreed as she followed him into the room. He sat in a leather chair, sighing. Eiah blew life into the coals in the fire grate, added a handful of small tinder and a twisted length of oak to the fire, then took a stool and pulled it up before him.

"How do you feel about the binding's progress?" he asked.

"Well enough," she said, taking both his forearms in her hands. Her gaze was locked somewhere over his left shoulder, her fingers pressing hard into the flesh between the bones of his wrists. A moment later, she dropped his right hand and began squeezing his fingertips.

"Eiah-kya?"

"Don't mind me," she said. "It's habit. The binding's coming closer. There are one or two more things I'd like to try, but I think we've come as near as we're going to."

She went on for half a hand, recounting the fine issues of definition, duration, and intent that haunted the form of her present binding. Maati listened, submitting himself to her professional examination as she went on. Outside the window, the snow was falling again, small flakes gray against the pure white sky. Before Vanjit, he wouldn't have been able to make them out.

"I agree," Maati said as she ended, then plucked his sleeves back into their proper place. "Do you think . . ."

"Before Candles Night, certainly," Eiah said. "But there is going to be a complication. We have to leave the school. Utani would be best, but Pathai would do if that's impossible. You and I can leave in the morning, and the others can join us."

Maati chuckled.

"Eiah-kya," he said. "You've apologized for letting Ashti Beg go. I understand why you did it, but there's nothing to be concerned about. Even if she did tell someone that we're out here, Vanjit could turn Clarity-of-Sight against them, and we could all walk quietly away. The power of the andat—"

"Your heart is failing," Eiah said. "I don't have the herbs or the baths to care for you here."

She said it simply, her voice flat with exhaustion. Maati felt the smile fading from his lips. He saw tears beginning to glimmer in her eyes, the drops unfallen but threatening. He took a pose that denied her.

"Your color is bad," she said. "Your pulses aren't symmetric. Your blood is thick and dark. This is what I do, Uncle. I find people who are sick, and I look at the signs, and I think about them and their bodies. I look at you, here, now, and I see a man whose blood is slow and growing slower."

"You're imagining things," Maati said. "I'm fine. I only haven't slept well. I would never have guessed that you of all people would mistake a little lost rest for a weak heart."

"I'm not—"

"I am fine!" Maati shouted, pounding the arm of the chair. "And we cannot afford to run off into the teeth of winter. You aren't a physician any longer. That's behind you. You are a poet. You are the poet who's going to save the cities."

She took his hand in both of hers. For a moment, there was no sound but the low murmur of the fire and the nearly inaudible sound of her palm stroking the back of his hand. One of the threatened tears fell, streaking her cheek black. He hadn't realized she wore kohl.

"You," he said softly, "are the most important poet there is. The most important one there ever was."

"I'm just one woman," Eiah said. "I'm doing the best I can, but I'm tired. And the world keeps getting darker around me. If I can't take care of everything, at least let me take care of you."

"I will be fine," Maati said. "I'm not young anymore, but I'm a long way from death. We'll finish your binding, and then if you want to haul me to half the baths in the Empire, I'll submit."

Another tear marked her face. Maati took his sleeve and wiped her cheek dry.

"I'll be fine," he said. "I'll rest more if you like. I'll pretend my bones are made of mud brick and glass. But you can't stop now to concern yourself with me. Those people out there. They're the ones who need your care. Not me."

"Let me go to Pathai," she said. "I can get teas there."

"No," Maati said. "I won't do that."

"Let me send Large Kae, then. I can't stand by and do nothing."

"All right," Maati said, holding up a placating hand. "All right. Let's wait until morning, and we can talk to Large Kae. And perhaps you'll see that I'm only tired and we can move past this."

She left in the end without being convinced. As darkness fell, Maati found himself slipping into a soft despair. The world was quiet and still and utterly unaware of him.

His son was dead. The people he had counted as his friends had become his enemies, and he was among the most despised men in the world. Eiah was wrong, of course. His health was fine. But someday, it would fail. All men died, and most were forgotten. The few that the world remembered were not always celebrated.

He lit the night candle by holding it to the fire, the wax hissing where it dripped on the coals. He found his book and settled close to the fire grate before opening the cover and considering the words.

I, Maati Vaupathai, am one of the two men remaining in the world who has wielded the power of the andat.

Already, it was not true. There were three living poets now, and one of them a woman. Between the time he had touched a pen to this page and this moment, reading it in the early night, the world had moved on. He wondered how much of the rest was already old, already the property of a past that could never be regained. He read slowly, tracing the path his own mind had taken. The candle lent the pages an orange glow, the ink seeming to retreat into the pages, as if they were much larger and much farther away. The fire warmed his ankles and turned strong, solid wood into ashes softer than snow.

He was surprised to see the anger and bitterness in the book. There was a thread, he thought, of hatred in these words. He didn't think he'd meant it to be there, and yet sitting alone with his slowing blood, it could not be denied. Hatred of Otah and the Galts, of course, but also of Cehmai. Of Liat, whom he mentioned more frequently than he remembered and in terms that he knew she didn't deserve. Hatred toward the gods and the world. And thus, he had to think, toward himself. Before he reached the last page, Maati was weeping quietly.

He found an ink brick and a fresh pen, lit all the lanterns and candles he could find, and sat at his desk. He drew a line across the middle of the last page, marking a change in the book and in himself that he could not yet describe. He freshened the ink and did not know precisely what he intended to write until the nib touched the page, tracing out letters with a sound as dry and quiet as a lizard on stones.

If it were within my power, I would begin again. I would begin as a boy again, and live my life a different way. I have been told tonight that my heart is growing weak. Looking back upon the man I have been until now, I think it always has been. I think it was shattered one time too many and put back without all the shards in place.

And, though I think this is the cry of a coward, I do not want to die. I want to see the world made right. I want to live that long, at least.

He paused, looking at the words where they grew fainter, the ink running thin.

He found Eiah asleep on her cot, still wearing the robes she'd worn all day. Her door stood ajar, and his scratch woke her.

"Uncle," she said, yawning. "What's happened? Is something wrong?"

"You're certain. What you said about my blood. You're sure."

"Yes," she said. There was no hesitation in her.

"Perhaps," he said, then coughed. "Perhaps we should go to Utani."

Tears came to her eyes again, but with them a smile. The first true smile he'd seen from her since her journey to the low town. Since Vanjit's blinding of the Galts.

"Thank you, Uncle," she said.

In the morning, the others were shocked, and yet before the sun broke through the midday clouds, the cart was loaded with food and books, wax tables and wineskins. The horses were fitted with their leads and burdens, and all six of the travelers, seven if he counted Clarity-of-Sight, were wrapped in warm robes and ready for the road. The only delay was Irit scrambling back at the last moment to find some small, forgotten token.

Maati pulled himself deep into the enfolding wool as the cart shifted under him, and the low buildings with snow on the roofs and the cracks between stones receded. His breath plumed before him, rubbing out the division between sky and snow.

Vanjit sat beside him, the andat wrapped in her cloak. Her expression was blank. Dark smudges of fatigue marked her eyes, and the andat squirmed and fussed. The wide wheels tossed bits of hard-packed snow up into the cart, and Maati brushed them away idly. It would be an hour or more to the high road, and then perhaps a day before they turned into the network of tracks and roads that connected the low towns that would take them to the grand palaces of Utani, center of the Empire. Maati found himself wondering whether Otah-kvo would have returned there, to sit on the gold-worked seat. Or perhaps he would still be in Saraykeht, scheming to haul countless thousands of blinded women from Kirinton, Acton, and Marsh.

He tried to picture his old friend and enemy, but he could conjure only a sense of his presence. Otah's face escaped him, but it had been a decade and a half since they had seen each other. All memory faded, he supposed. Everything, eventually, passed into the white veil and was forgotten.

The snow made roadway and meadow identical, so the first bend in the road was marked by a stand of thin trees and a low ridge of stone. Maati watched the dark buildings vanish behind the hillside. It was unlikely that he would ever see them again. But he would carry his memories of the warmth of the kitchens, the laughter of women, the first binding done by a woman, and the proof that his new grammar would function. Better that than the death house it had been when the Galts had come down this same road, murder in their minds. Or the mourning chambers for boys without families before that.

Vanjit shuddered. Her face was paler. Maati freed his hands and took a pose that expressed concern and offered comfort. Vanjit shook her head.

"He's never been away," she said. "He's leaving home for the first time."

"It can be frightening," Maati said. "It will pass."

"No. Worse, really. He's happy. He's very happy to be leaving," Vanjit said. Her voice was low and exhausted. "All the things we said about the struggle to hold them. It's all truth. I can feel him in the back of my mind. He never stops pushing."

"It's the nature of the andat," Maati said. "If you'd like, we can talk about ways to make bearing the burden easier."

Vanjit looked away. Her lips were pale.

"No," she said. "We'll be fine. It's only a harder day than usual. We'll find another place, and see you cared for, and then all will be well. But when the time comes to bind Wounded, there are things I'll do differently."

"We can hope it never comes to that," Maati said.

Vanjit shifted, her eyes widening for a moment, and the soft, almost flirting smile came to her lips.

"Of course not," she said. "Of course it won't. Eiah-cha will be fine. I was only thinking aloud. It was nothing."

Maati nodded and lay back. His thick robes cushioned the bare wood of the cart's side. Crates and chests groaned and shifted against their ropes. Small Kae and Irit began singing, and the others slowly joined them. All of them except Vanjit and himself. He let his eyes close to slits, watching Vanjit from between the distorting bars of his eyelashes.

The andat squirmed again, howled out once, and her face went hard and still. She glanced over at Maati, but he feigned sleep. The others, involved in their song and the road, didn't see it when she pulled Clarity-of-Sight from her cloak, staring at it. The tiny arms flailed, the soft legs whirled. The andat made a low, angry sound, and Vanjit's expression hardened.

She shook the thing once, hard enough to make the oversized head snap back. The tiny mouth set itself into a shocked grimace and it began to wail. Vanjit looked about, but no one had seen the small violence between them. She pulled the andat back to her, cooing and rocking slowly back and forth while it whimpered and fought. Desolate tears tracked her cheeks. And were wiped away with a sleeve.

Maati wondered how often scenes like this one had passed without comment or notice. Many years before, he had cared for an infant himself, and the frustration of it was something he understood. This was something different. He thought of what it would have been to have a child that hated him, that wanted nothing more than to be free. Clarity-of-Sight was all the longing that haunted Vanjit and all the anger that sustained her put into a being that would do whatever was needed to escape. Vanjit had been betrayed by the cruelty of the world, and now also her own desire made flesh.

At last she had the baby that had haunted her dreams. And it wanted to die.

Eiah spoke in his memory. *What makes us imagine we can do good with these as our tools?*

19

>+< Low towns clustered around the great cities of the Khaiem, small centers of commerce and farming, justice and healing. Men and women could live out their lives under the nominal control of the Khaiem or now of the Emperor and never pass into the cities themselves. They had low courts, road taxes, smiths and stablers, wayhouses and comfort houses and common meadows for anyone's use. He had seen them all, years before, when he had only been a courier. They were the cities of the Khaiem writ small, and as he passed through them with his arms-men, his son, and the Galtic half-stowaway, Otah saw all his fears made real.

Silences lay where children should have been playing street games. Great swings made from rope and plank hung from ancient branches that shadowed the common fields, no boys daring each other higher. As a child who had seen no more than twelve summers, Otah had set out on his own, competing with low-town boys for small work. With every low town he entered, his eyes caught the sorts of things he had done: roofs with thatch that wanted care, fences and stone walls in need of mend-ing, cisterns grown thick and black with weeds that required only a strong back and the energy of youth to repair. But there were no boys, no girls; only men and women whose smiles carried a bewildered, per-manent sorrow. The leaves on the trees had turned brown and yellow and fallen. The nights were long, and the dawns touched by frost.

The land was dead. He had known it. Being reminded brought him no joy.

They stopped for the night in a wayhouse nestled in a wooded valley. The walls were kiln-fired brick with a thick covering of ivy that the au-tumn chill had turned brown and brittle. News of his identity and errand had spread before him like a wave on water, making quiet investigation impossible. The keeper had cleared all his rooms before they knew where they meant to stop, had his best calf killed and hot baths drawn on the chance that Otah might stop to rest. Sitting now in the alcove of a room large enough to fit a dozen men, Otah felt his muscles slowly and incompletely unknotting. With the supplies carried on the steam wagons and the men shifting between tending the kilns and riding, Pathai was less than two days away. Without the Galtic machines, it would have been four, perhaps five.

Low clouds obscured moon and stars. When Otah closed the shutters against the cold night air, the room grew no darker. The great copper tub the keeper had prepared glowed in the light of the fire grate. The earthenware jar of soap beside it was half-empty, but at least Otah felt like his skin was his own again and not hidden under layers of dust and sweat. His traveling robes had vanished and he'd picked a simple garment of combed wool lined with silk. The voices of the armsmen rose through the floorboards. The song was patriotic and bawdy, and the drum that accompanied them kept missing the right time. Otah rose on bare feet and walked out to the stairs. No servants scuttled out of his way, and he noticed the absence.

Danat was not among the armsmen or out with the horses. It was only when Otah approached the room set aside for Ana Dasin that he heard his son's voice. The room was on the lower floor, near the kitchens. The floor there was stone. Otah's steps made no sound as he walked forward. Ana said something he couldn't make out, but when Danat answered, he'd come near enough to hear.

"Of course there are, it's only Papa-kya isn't one of them. When I was a boy, he told me stories from the First Empire about a half-Bakta boy. And he nearly married a girl from the eastern islands."

"When was that?" Ana asked. Otah heard a sound of shifting cloth, like a blanket being pulled or a robe being adjusted.

"A long time ago," Danat said. "Just after Saraykeht. He lived in the eastern islands for years after that. They build their marriages in stages there. He's got the first half of the marriage tattoo."

"Why didn't he finish it?" Ana asked.

Otah remembered Maj as he hadn't in years. Her wide, pale lips. Her eyes that could go from blue the color of the sky at dawn to slate gray. The stretch marks on her belly, a constant reminder of the child that had been taken from her. In his mind, she was linked with the scent of the ocean.

"I don't know," Danat said. "But it wasn't that he was trying to keep his bloodline pure. Really, there's a strong case that my lineage isn't particularly high. My mother didn't come from the utkhaiem, and for some people that's as much an insult as marrying a Westlander."

"Or a Galt," Ana said, tartly.

"Exactly," Danat said. "So, yes. Of course there are people in the court who want some kind of purity, but they've gotten used to disappointment over the last few decades."

"They would never accept me."

"You?" Danat said.

"Anyone like me."

"If they won't, then they won't accept anyone. So it hardly matters what they think, because they won't have any sons or daughters at court. The world's changed, and the families that can't change with it won't survive."

"I suppose," Ana said. They were silent for a moment. Otah debated whether he should scratch on her door or back quietly away, and then Ana spoke again. Her voice had changed. It was lower now, and dark as rain on stone. "It doesn't really matter, though, does it. There isn't going to be a Galt."

"That's not true," Danat said.

"Every day that we're like . . . like this, more of us are dying. It's harvest time. How are they going to harvest the grain if they can't see it? How do you raise sheep and cattle by sound?"

"I knew a blind man who worked leather in Lachi," Danat said. "His work was just as good as a man's with eyes."

"One man doesn't signify," Ana said. "He wasn't baking his own bread or catching his own fish. If he needed to know what a thing looked like, there was someone he could ask. If everyone's sightless, it's different. It's all falling apart."

"You can't know that," Danat said.

"I know how crippled I am," Ana said. "It gives me room to guess. I know how little I can do to stop it."

There was a soft sound, and Danat hushing her. Otah took a careful step back, away from the door. When Ana's voice came again, it was thick with tears.

"Tell me," she said. "Tell me one of those stories. The ones where a child with two races could still win out."

"In the sixteenth year of the reign of the Emperor Adani Beh," Danat said, his voice bright and soft, "there came to court a boy whose blood was half-Bakta, his skin the color of soot, and his mind as clever as any man who had ever lived. When the Emperor saw him . . ."

Otah backed away, his son's voice becoming a murmur of sound, inflected like words but too faint to mean anything. Their whole journey, it had been like this. Each time Otah thought they might have a moment alone, Ana was near, or one of the armsmen, or Otah had brought himself to the edge of speech and then failed. Every courier they stopped along the road was another reminder to Otah that his son had to know, had to be told. But no word had come from Idaan, and Danat still didn't know that Eiah was involved in the slow death of Galt and, with it, the future Otah had fought for.

Before Pathai, Otah had told himself when they were on the road. During the journey itself, it hardly mattered whether Danat knew, but once they reached their destination, his son couldn't be set out without knowing what it was they were searching for and why. Otah had no faith that another, better chance would come the next day. He made his way back upstairs, found a servant woman, and had cheese, fresh bread, and a carafe of rice wine taken to Danat's room. Otah waited there until the Galtic clock, clicking to itself in a corner, marked the night as almost half-gone. Otah didn't notice that he was dozing until the opening door roused him.

Otah broke the news as gently as he could, outlining his own half-knowledge of Maati's intentions, Idaan's appearance in Saraykeht, Eiah's appearance on the list of possible backers, and his own decision to set his sister to hunt down his daughter. Danat listened carefully, as if picking through the words for clues to some deeper mystery. When, at length, Otah went silent, Danat looked into the fire in its grate, wove his fingers together, and thought. The flames made his eyes glitter like jewels.

"It isn't her," he said at last. "She wouldn't do this."

"I know you love her, Danat-kya. I love her too, and I don't want to think this of her either, but—"

"I don't mean she didn't back Maati," Danat said. "We don't know that she did, but at least that part's plausible. I'm only saying that this blindness isn't her work."

His voice wasn't loud or strident. He seemed less like a man fighting an unpalatable truth than a builder pointing out a weakness in an archway's design. Otah took a pose that invited him to elaborate.

"Eiah hates your plan," Danat said. "She even came to me a few times to argue that I should refuse it."

"I didn't know that."

"I didn't tell you," Danat said, his hands taking a pose that apologized, though his voice held no regret. "I couldn't see that it would make things between the two of you any better. But my point is that her arguments were never against Galts. She couldn't stand to see a generation of our own women ignored. Their pain was what she lived in. When you started allowing the import of bed slaves as . . . well . . ."

"Brood mares," Otah said. "I do remember her saying that."

"Well, that," Danat agreed. "Eiah took that as saying that none of the women here mattered. That *she* didn't matter. If the problems of the Empire could be solved by hauling in wombs that would bear, then all that was important to you about women was the children they could yield."

"But if there's no children, there can't be—"

Danat shifted forward in his seat, putting his palm over Otah's mouth. The boy's eyes were dark, his mouth set in the half-smile Kiyan had often worn.

"You need to listen to me, Papa-kya. I'm not telling you that she's right. I'm not telling you she's wrong, for that. I'm telling you Eiah loves people and she hates pain. If she's been backing Uncle Maati, it's to take away the pain, not to . . ."

Danat gestured at the shutters, and by implication at the world on the other side of them. The logs in the grate popped and the song of a single cricket, perhaps the last one alive before the coming winter, sang counterpoint to the ticking clock. Otah rubbed his chin, his mind turning his son's words over like a jeweler considering a gem.

"She may be part of this," Danat said. "I think you're right to find her. But the poet we want? It isn't her."

"I wish I could be certain of that," Otah said.

"Well, start with not being certain that she is," Danat said. "The world will carry you the rest of the way, if I'm right."

Otah smiled and put his hand on his son's head.

"When did you become wise?" Otah asked.

"It's only what you'd have said, if you weren't busy feeling responsible for all of it," Danat said. "You're a good man, Papa-kya. And we're doing what we can in unprecedented times."

Otah let his hand fall to his side. Danat smiled. The cricket, wherever it was, went silent.

"Go," Danat said. "Sleep. We've got a long ride tomorrow, and I'm exhausted."

Otah rose, his hands taking a pose that accepted the command. Danat chuckled; then as Otah reached the door, he sobered.

"Thank you, by the way, for what you said about Ana," Danat said. "You were right. We weren't treating her with the respect she deserved."

"It's a mistake we all make, one time and another," Otah said. "I'm glad it was an error we could correct."

Perhaps mine also will be, he thought. It terrified him in some fundamental and joyous way to think that possibly, *possibly*, this might still end without a sacrifice that was too great for him to bear. He hadn't realized how much he had tried to harden himself against the prospect of killing his own daughter, or how poorly he had managed it.

He crawled into his bed. Danat's certainty lightened the weight that bore him down. The poet wasn't Eiah. This blindness wasn't in her, wasn't who she was. The andat might have been bound by Maati or some other girl. Some girl whom he could bring himself to kill. He closed his eyes, considering how he might avoid having the power of the andat turned on him. The fear would return, he was sure of that. But now, for a moment, he could afford himself the luxury of being more frightened of loss than of the price of victory.

They left before sunrise with the steamcarts' supplies of wood, coal, and water refreshed, the horses replaced with well-rested animals, and the scent of snow heavy in the air. They moved faster than Otah had expected, not pausing to eat or rest. He himself took a turn at the kiln of the larger steamcart, keeping the fire hot and well-fueled. If the armsmen were surprised to see the Emperor working like a commoner, they didn't say anything. Two couriers passed them riding east, but neither bore a message from Idaan. Three came up behind them bearing letters for the Emperor from what seemed like half the court at Saraykeht and Utani.

Nightfall caught them at the top of the last high, broad pass that opened onto the western plains. On the horizon, Pathai glittered like a congress of stars. The armsmen assembled the sleeping tents, unrolling layers of leather and fur to drape over the canvas. Otah squatted by the kiln, reading through letter after letter. The silk threads that had once sewn the paper closed rested in knots and tangles by his feet. The snow that lay about them was fresh though the sky had cleared, and the cold combined with the day's work to tire him. The joints of his hands ached, and his eyes were tired and difficult to focus. He dreaded the close, airless sleeping tents and the ache-interrupted night that lay before him almost as much as he was annoyed by the petty politics of court.

Letter after letter praised or castigated him for his decision to leave. The Khaiate Council, as it had been deemed in his absence, was either a terrible mistake or an act of surpassing wisdom, and whichever it was, the author of the letter would be better placed on it than someone Otah had named.

Balasar Gice, the only Galt on the council, was pressing for relief ships to sail for Galt with as much food as could be spared and men to help guide and oversee the blinded. The rest of the council was divided, and a third of them had written to Otah for his opinion. Otah put those letters directly into the fire. If he'd meant to answer every difficult question from the road, he wouldn't have created the council.

There was no word from Sinja or Chaburi-Tan. Balasar, writing with a secretary to help him, feared the worst. This letter, Otah tucked into his sleeve. There was no reason to keep it. He could do nothing to affect its news. But he couldn't bring himself to destroy something to do with Sinja when his old friend's fate already seemed so tentative.

Uncertain footsteps sounded behind him. Ana Dasin was walking the wide boards toward the kiln. Her hair was loose and her robe blue shot with gold. Her grayed eyes seemed to search the darkness.

"Ana-cha," he said, both a greeting and a warning that he was there. The girl started a little, but then smiled uncertainly.

"Most High," she said, nodding very nearly toward him. "Is . . . I was wondering if Danat-cha was with you?"

"He's gone to fetch water with the others," Otah said, nodding uselessly toward a path that led to a shepherd's well. "He will be back in half a hand, I'd think."

"Oh," Ana said, her face falling.

"Is there something I can do?"

Watching the struggle in the girl's expression seemed almost more an intrusion than his previous eavesdropping. After a moment, she drew something from her sleeve. Cream-colored paper sewn with yellow thread. She held it out.

"The courier said it was from my father," she said. "I can't read it."

Otah cleared his throat against an unexpected tightness. He felt unworthy of the girl's trust, and something like gratitude brought tears to his eyes.

"I would be honored, Ana-cha, to read it for you," he said.

Otah rose, took the letter, and drew Ana to a stool near enough the kiln to warm her, but not so close as to put her in danger of touching the still-scorching metal. He ripped out the thread, unfolded the single page, and leaned in toward the light.

It was written in Galtic though the script betrayed more familiarity with the alphabet of the Khaiem. He knew before he began to read that there would be nothing in it too personal to say to a secretary, and the fact relieved him. He skimmed the words once, then again more slowly.

"Most High?" Ana said.

"It is addressed to you," Otah said. "It says this: *I understand that you've seen fit to run off without telling me or your mother. You should know better than that.* Then there are a few more lines that restate all that."

Ana sat straight, her hands on her knees, her face expressionless. Otah coughed, cleared his throat, and went on.

"There is a second section," he said. "He says . . . well."

Otah smoothed the page with his fingers, tracing the words as he spoke.

"*Still, I was your age once too. If good judgment were part of being young, there would be no reason to grow old. In God's name write back to tell us you're well. Your mother's sick that you'll fall off the trail and get eaten by dogs, and I'm half-sick that you'll come back wed and pregnant,*" Otah said. "He goes on to offer a brief analysis of my own intelligence. I'll skip that."

Ana chuckled and wiped away a tear. Otah grinned and kept the smile in his voice when he went on.

"He ends by saying that he loves you. And that he trusts you to do what's right."

"You're lying," Ana said.

Otah took a pose that denied an unjust accusation, then flapped his hands in annoyance. The physical language of the Khaiem was a difficult habit to put aside.

"Why would I lie?" he asked.

"To be polite? I don't know. But my father? Farrer Dasin putting on paper that he trusts his little girl's judgment? The stars would dance on treetops first. The wed-and-pregnant part sounded like him, though."

"Well," Otah said, placing the folded page into her fingers. "He might surprise you. Keep this, and you can read it for yourself once we've fixed all this mess."

Ana took a pose that offered thanks. It wasn't particularly well done.

"You are always welcome," Otah said.

They sat in silence until Danat and the other water bearers returned. Then Otah left his seat to Danat and crawled into the sleeping tent, where, true to expectations, he shifted from discomfort to discomfort until the sun rose again.

They reached Pathai at midday. Silk banners streamed from the towers and the throng that met them at the western arch cheered and sang and played flutes and drums. Men and women hung from lattices of wood and rope to get a better view of Otah and Danat, their armsmen, the steamcarts. The air was thick with the scents of honeyed almonds and mulled wine and bodies. The armsmen of Pathai met them, made an elaborate ritual obeisance, and then cleared a path for them until they reached the palaces.

A feast had been prepared, and baths. Servants descended on the group like moths, and Otah submitted to being only emperor once again.

The celebration of his arrival was as annoying as it was pointless. Dish after dish of savory meat and sweet bread, hot curry and chilled fish, all accompanied by the best acrobats and musicians that could be scraped together with little notice. And Ana Dasin sitting at his table, her empty eyes a constant, unintentional reproach. Finding Maati and this new poet was going to be like hunting quail with a circus. He would have to do something to let them move discreetly. He didn't yet know what that would be.

The rooms he'd been given were blond stone, the ceiling vaulted and set with tiles of indigo and silver. A thousand candles set the air glowing and filled his senses with the scent of hot wax and perfume. It was, he thought, the sort of space that was almost impossible to keep warm. Danat, Ana, and the armsmen were all being seen to elsewhere. He sat on a long, low couch and hoped that Danat, at least, would be able to get out into the city and make a few inquiries.

When a servant came and announced Sian Noygu, Otah almost refused the audience before he recognized it as the name Idaan traveled under. His heart racing, he let himself be led to a smaller chamber of carved granite and worked gold. His sister sat between a small fountain and a shadowed alcove. She wore a gray robe under a colorless cloak, and her boots were soft with wear. A long scratch across the back of her hand was the dark red of scabs and old blood.

The servant made his obeisance and retreated. Otah took a pose of greeting appropriate to close family, and Idaan tilted her head like a dog hearing an unfamiliar sound.

"I had intended to meet you when you came into the city. I didn't know you were planning a festival."

"I wasn't," Otah said, sitting beside her. The fountain clucked and burbled. "Traveling quietly seems beyond me these days."

"It was all as subtle as a rockslide," Idaan agreed. "But there's some good in it. The louder you are, the less people are looking at me."

"You've found something then?" Otah asked.

"I have," Idaan said.

"What have you learned?"

A different voice answered from the darkness of the alcove at Idaan's side. A woman's voice.

"Everything," it said.

Otah rose to his feet. The woman who emerged was young: not more than forty summers and the white in her hair still barely more than an accent. She wore robes as simple as Idaan's but held herself with a mixture of angry pride and uncertainty that Otah had become familiar with. Her pupils were gray and sightless, but her eyes were the almond shape that marked her as a citizen of the Empire. This was a victim of the new poet, but she was no Galt.

"Idaan-cha knows everything," the blind woman said again, "because I told it to her."

Idaan took the woman's hand and stood. When she spoke, it was to her companion.

"This is my brother, the Emperor," Idaan said, then turned to him. "Otah-cha, this is Ashti Beg."

20

>+< When before Maati had considered death, it had been in terms of what needed to be done. Before he died, he had to master the grammars of the Dai-kvo, or find his son again, or most recently see his errors with Sterile made right. It was never the end itself that drew his attention. He had reduced his mortality to the finish line of a race. This and this and this done, and afterward, dying would be like rest at the end of a long day.

With Eiah's pronouncement, his view shifted. No list of accomplishments could forgive the prospect of his own extinction. Maati found himself looking at the backs of his hands, the cracked skin, the dark blotches of age. He was becoming aware of time in a way he never had. There was some number of days he would see, some number of nights, and then nothing. It had always been true. He was no more or less a mortal being because his blood was slowing. Everything born, dies. He had known that. He only hadn't quite understood. It changed everything.

It also changed nothing. They traveled slowly, keeping to lesser-known roads and away from the larger low towns. Often Eiah would call the day's halt with the sun still five hands above the horizon because they had found a convenient wayhouse or a farm willing to board them for the night. The prospect of letting Maati sleep in cold air was apparently too much for her to consider.

On the third day, Eiah had parted with the company, rejoining them on the fifth with a cloth sack of genuinely unpleasant herbs. Maati suffered a cup of the bitter tea twice daily. He let his pulses be measured against one another, his breath smelled, his fingertips squeezed, the color of his eyes considered and noted. It embarrassed him.

The curious thing was that, despite all his fears and Eiah's attentions, he felt fine. If his breath was short, it was no shorter than it had been for years. He tired just when he'd always tired, but now six sets of eyes shifted to him every time he grunted. He dismissed the anxiety when he saw it in the others, however closely he felt it himself.

He would have expected the two feelings to balance each other: the dismissive self-consciousness at any concern over him and the presentiment of his death. He did not understand how he could be possessed by both of them at the same time, and yet he was. It was like there were two minds within him, two Maati Vaupathais, each with his own thoughts and concerns, and no compromise between them was required.

For the most part, Maati could ignore this small failure to be at one with himself. Each morning, he rose with the others, ate whatever rubbery eggs or day-old meat the waykeeper had to offer, choked down Eiah's tea, and went on as usual. The autumn through which they passed was crisp and fragrant of new earth and rotting leaves. The snow that had plagued the school had also visited the foothills and shallow passes that divided the western plains of Pathai from the river valleys of the east, but it was rarely more than three fingers deep. In many places, the sun was still strong enough to banish the pale mourning colors to the shadows.

With rumors that Otah himself had taken up the hunt, they kept a balance between the smaller, less-traveled roads and those that were wider and better maintained. So far from the great cities, the ports and trading posts, there were no foreign faces to be seen. None of the handful of adventurous Westlands women had made their way here to try for a Khaiate husband and a better life. There was no better life to be had here. The lack of children, of babies, gave the towns a sense of tolerating a slow plague. It was only the world. It no longer troubled Maati. This was another journey in a life that seemed to be woven of distance. Apart from the overattentiveness of his traveling companions, there was no reason to reflect on his mortality; he had no cause to consider that these small chores and pleasantries of the road might be among his last.

It was only days later, at the halfway point between the school and the river Qiit, that without intending it, Eiah called the question.

They had stopped at a wayhouse at the side of a broad lake. A wide wooden deck stood out over the water, the wind pulling small waves to lap at its pilings. A flock of cranes floated and called to one another at the far shore. Maati sat on a three-legged stool, his traveling cloak still wrapping his shoulders. He looked out on the shifting water, the gray-green trees, the hazy white sky. He heard Eiah behind him, her voice coming from the main building as if it were coming from a different world. When she came out, he heard her footsteps and the leather physician's satchel bumping against her hip. She stopped just behind him.

"They're beautiful," he said, nodding at the cranes.

"I suppose," Eiah said.

"Vanjit? The others?"

"In their rooms," Eiah said, a trace of satisfaction in her voice. "Three rooms, and all of them private. Meals this evening and before we go. One length of silver and two copper."

"You could have paid them the normal price," Maati said.

"My pride won't allow it," Eiah said. She stepped forward and knelt. "There was something. If you're not tired."

"I'm an old man. I'm always tired."

Her eyes held some objection, but she didn't give it voice. Instead she unbuckled her satchel, rooted in it for a moment, and drew out a paper. Maati took it, frowning. The characters were familiar, a part of Eiah's proposed binding, but the structure of them was different. Awkward.

"It isn't perfect," Eiah said. "But I thought we could consider it. I've mentioned the idea to Large Kae, and she has some ideas about how to make it consonant with the grammar."

Maati lifted his hand, palm out, and stopped the flow of words. The cranes called, their harsh voices crossing the water swifter than arrows. He sounded out each phrase, thinking through the logic as he did.

"I don't understand," he said. "This is the strongest part of the binding. Why would you change . . ."

And then he saw her intentions. Each change she had made broadened the concept of wounds. Of harm. Of damage. And there, in the corner of the page, was a play on the definitions of blood. He folded the page, slipping it into his sleeve.

"No," he said.

"I think it can—"

"No," Maati said again. "What we're doing is hard enough. Making it fit the things that Sterile has done is enough. If you try to make everything fit into it, you'll end with more than you can hold."

Eiah sighed and looked out across the water. The wind plucked a lock of hair, the black threads dancing on her cheek. He could see in her expression that she'd anticipated all he would say. And more, that she agreed. He put a hand on her shoulder. For a moment, neither spoke.

"Once we reach the river, things will move faster," Eiah said. "With the Galts' paddle boats, we should reach Utani before the worst cold comes." To their left, a fish leaped from the water and splashed back down. "Once I have you someplace with real physicians, I'm going to try the binding."

Maati drew in a deep breath and let it out slowly. A sick dread uncurled in his belly.

"You're sure?" he said.

Eiah took a pose that confirmed her resolve and also chided him. When he replied with one that expressed mild affront, she spoke.

"You sit here like something from a philosopher's daydream, refusing to let me even try to mend your heart," she said, "and then you start quaking like an old woman when I'm the one at risk."

"'Quaking like an old woman'?" Maati said. "I think we haven't known the same old women. And of course I'm concerned for you, Eiah-kya. How could I not be? You're like a daughter to me. You always have been."

"I might not fail," she said. And a moment later, rose, kissed his hair, and walked in, leaving him alone with the world. Maati sank deeper into his cloak, determined to watch the birds until his mind calmed. Half a hand later, he went inside the building, muttering to himself.

The evening meal was a soup of ground lentils, rice, and a sweet, hot spice that made Maati's eyes water. He paid an extra length of copper for a second bowl. The commons with its low ceilings and soot-stained walls also served as a teahouse for the nearby low towns. By the time he'd finished eating, local men and women had begun to appear. They took little notice of the travelers, which suited Maati quite well.

In less interesting times, the table talk would have turned on matters of weather, of crop yields and taxes and the small jealousies and dramas that humanity drew about itself in all places and times. Instead, they spoke of the Emperor, his small caravan on its way to Pathai or else Lachi or else some unknown destination in the Westlands. He was going to broker a new contract for women, now that the Galts had been destroyed, or else retrieve the new poet and march back in triumph. He had been secretly harboring the poets all this time, or had become one himself. Nothing that approached the truth. Small Kae, listening to two of the local men debate, looked on the edge of laughter the whole evening.

As the last of the sunset faded, a pair of the older men took up drums, and the tables nearest the fire grate were pulled aside to clear space for dancers. Maati was prevented from excusing himself from the proceedings only by Vanjit's appearance at his side.

"Maati-kvo," she murmured, her hand slipping around his arm, "I spoke to Eiah-kya. I know it was wrong of me to interfere, but please, please, will you reconsider?"

The older of the two men set up a low throbbing beat on his drum. The second drummer closed his eyes and bobbed his head almost in time with the first. Maati suspected that both were drunk.

"This isn't the place to discuss it," Maati said. "Later, we can . . ."

"Please," Vanjit said. Her breath wasn't free from the scent of distilled wine. Her cheeks were flushed. "Without you, none of us matter. You know that. You're our teacher. We need you. And if Eiah . . . she pays its price, you know that I'll be there. I can do the thing. I've already managed once, and I *know* that I could do it again."

The second drum began, dry and light and not quite on its mark. No one seemed to be paying attention to the old man in the corner or the young woman attached to his arm. Maati leaned close to Vanjit, speaking low.

"What is it, Vanjit-kya?" he asked. "This is the second time you've offered to bind Wounded. Why do you want that?"

She blinked and released his arm. Her eyes were wider, her mouth thin. It was his turn to take her arm, and he did, leaning close enough to speak almost into her ear.

"I have known more poets than I can count," he said. "Only a few held the andat, and none of them took joy in it. My own first master, Heshai of Saraykeht, planned out a second binding of Seedless. It could never have worked. It was too near what he'd done before, and part of Sterile's failure was that I borrowed too much from his design."

"I don't know what you mean, Maati-kvo," Vanjit said. Three women had stepped into the dancing space and were thumping in a simple pattern, keeping time with one drum or the other.

"I mean that everyone wants a second chance," Maati said. "Clarity-of-Sight . . ."

Maati bit down, glancing to see if anyone had heard him. The music and the dance were the focus of the room.

"The little one," Maati said, more quietly, "isn't what you'd hoped. But neither would the next one be."

He might just as well have slapped her. Vanjit's face went white, and she stood so quickly the bench scraped out from under her. By the time Maati rose, she was halfway to the door leading out to the stables and courtyard, and when he reached her, they were outside in the chill. A thin fog blurred the lantern hanging above the wayhouse door.

"Vanjit!" Maati called, and she turned back, her face a mask of pain.

"How could you say that? How could you say those things to me?" she demanded. "You had as much to do with that binding as I did. You are just as much responsible for him. I offered to take Eiah's place because someone would have to, not because it's something that I want. I love him. He's my boy, and I love him. He is everything I'd hoped. *Everything!*"

"Vanjit—"

She was weeping openly now, her voice high, thin, and wailing.

"And he loves me. No matter what you say, I know he does. He's my boy, and he loves me. How could you think that I'd want a second chance? I offered this for *you!*"

He took her sleeve in his fist, and she pulled back, yelping. She tried to turn away, but he would not let her.

"Listen to me," he said sternly. "You don't need to tell me how deeply you—"

Vanjit snarled, her lips pulled back from her teeth like a pit dog's. She pulled away sharply, and Maati stumbled, falling to his knees. When he rose, he could hear her running footsteps fading into the dark, but the fog had thickened so badly that he couldn't see his own hand in front of his face.

Except that, of course, it hadn't.

He stood still, heart racing, hands trembling. The raucous sounds of the dance came from behind him and to the left. The poorly played drums became his polestar. He turned and made his slow, careful way back toward the wayhouse. The ground was rough under his feet, gravel and weeds taking him at slightly different angles with every step.

He shouldn't have tried to hold her. She was upset. He should have let her go. He cursed himself for his stubbornness and her for her lack of control. The drums had given way to a flute and a low, warbling singer. Maati's outstretched fingers found the rough planks of the wall. He leaned against it, unsure what to do next. If he went back to the main room, his sudden infirmity would call attention to him, to the others, to Vanjit. But if he didn't, what would he do? He couldn't navigate his way back to his room, couldn't reach shelter. His robes were damp with the fog, the wood under his palm slick. He could stay here, pressing against the wayhouse like he was holding it up, or he could move. If there was only some way to find Eiah . . .

He began inching away from the door. He could follow the walls around the building, and find the deck. If he waited long enough, Eiah would come looking for him, and that might well be one of the first places she'd look. He tried to recall where the deck's railing began and ended.

He had been there for hours earlier, but now he found the details escaped him.

He stumbled over a log and bruised his knee, but he didn't cry out. The cold was beginning to numb him. He reached the corner and a set of stairs he didn't remember. The prospect of sitting in the cold at the edge of the unseen lake was becoming less and less sustainable. He started devising stories that would cover his blindness. He could go near the common room, cry out, and collapse. If he kept his eyes closed, he could feign unconsciousness. They would bring Eiah to him.

He stepped in something wet and soft, like mud but with a sudden, billowing smell of rotting plants. Maati lifted his foot slowly to keep the muck from pulling off his boot. It occurred to him for the first time that they had done this—precisely this—to a nation.

His boot was heavy and made a wet sound when he put weight on it, but it didn't slip. He started making his way back toward where he'd been. He thought he'd made it halfway there when the world suddenly clicked back into place. His hands pink and gray against the damp, black wood. The thin fog hardly worth noticing. He turned and found Vanjit sitting cross-legged on the stones of the courtyard. Her dark eyes were considering. He wondered how long she'd been watching.

"What you said before? It was uncalled for," she said. Her voice was steady as stone, and as unforgiving.

Maati took a pose that offered apology but also pointedly did not end the conversation. Vanjit considered him.

"I love Eiah-cha," she said, frowning. "I would never, *never* wish her ill. Suggesting that I want her to fail just so I could remain the only poet . . . it's madness. It hurts me that you would say it."

"I never did," Maati said. "I never said anything like it. If that's what you heard, then something else is happening here."

Vanjit shifted back, surprise and dismay in her expression. Her hands moved toward some formal pose, but never reached it. The shriek came from within the wayhouse. The music stopped. Vanjit stood up muttering something violent and obscene, but Maati was already moving to the door.

The large room was silent, drums and flute abandoned where they had fallen. The woman who'd screamed was sitting on a stool, her hands still pressed to her mouth, her face bloodless, and her gaze fixed on the archway that led to the private rooms. No one spoke. Clarity-of-Sight stood in the archway, its hands on the wall, its tiny hips swaying crazily as it lost and regained and lost its balance. It saw Vanjit, let out a high squeal, and waved its tiny arms before sitting down hard and suddenly. The delight never left its face.

"It is," someone said in a voice woven from awe and tears. "It's a baby."

And as if the word had broken a dam, chaos flowed through the wayhouse. Vanjit dashed forward, her hands low to scoop up the andat, and the crowd surged with her. The chorus of questions and shouts rose, filling the air. Maati started forward, then stopped. The older of the drummers appeared from amid the throng and embraced him, tears of joy in the man's eyes.

Through the press of the crowd, Maati saw Eiah standing alone. Her expression was cold. Maati pulled back from his grinning companion and struggled toward her. He heard Vanjit talking high and fast behind him, but couldn't make out the words. There were too many voices layered over it.

"Apparently we've decided not to travel quietly," Eiah said in tone of cold acid.

"Get the others," he said. "I'll prepare the cart. We can leave in the night."

"You think anyone here is going to sleep tonight?" Eiah said. "There's a baby. A full-blooded child of the cities, and Vanjit the mother. If the gods themselves walked in the door right now, they'd have to wait for a room. They'll think it's to do with me. The physician who has found a way to make women bear. They'll hound me like I've stolen their teeth."

"I'm sorry," Maati said.

"Word of this is going to spread. Father's going to hear of it, and when he does, he'll be on our heels."

"Why would he think it was you?"

"Galt went blind, and he headed west. For Pathai. For me," Eiah said.

"He can't know you're part of this," Maati said.

"Of course he can," Eiah said. "I am, and he isn't dim. I didn't think it was a problem when no one knew who or where we were."

A round of cheering broke out, and the wayhouse keeper appeared as if from nowhere, two bottles of wine in each hand. Vanjit had been ushered to a seat by the fire grate. Clarity-of-Sight was in her arms, beaming at everyone who came close. Vanjit's cheeks were flushed, but she seemed pleased. Proud. Happy.

"This was my mistake," Maati said. "My failure as much as anything.

I distracted her from the thing. It has more freedom when her mind is elsewhere."

Eiah turned her head to look at him. There was nothing soft in her eyes. Maati drew himself up, frowning. Anger bloomed in his breast, but he couldn't say why or with whom.

"Why is it so important to you," Eiah asked, "that nothing she does be wrong?"

And with a sensation that was almost physical, Maati knew what he had been trying for months to ignore. A wave of vertigo shook him, but he forced himself to speak.

"Because she should never have become a poet," he said. "She's too young and too angry and more than half mad. And that beast on her lap? We gave it to her."

Eiah's startled expression lasted only a moment before something both resignation and weariness took its place. She kissed Maati's cheek. They stood together, a silence within the storm. He had said what she had already known, and she too had wished it was not truth.

Large Kae and Small Kae quietly prepared the cart and horses. While the wayhouse and every man and woman within running distance came to pay homage to child, mother, and physician, Irit and Maati packed their things. Eiah saw to it that the wine flowed freely, that—near the end—the celebratory drinks were all laced with certain herbs.

It was still four hands before dawn when they made their escape. Maati and Eiah drove the cart. Large Kae rode ahead, leading the spare horses. The others slept in the cart, exhausted bodies fitted in among the crates and sacks. The moon had already set, and the road before them was black and featureless apart from Large Kae's guiding torch. The fog had cleared, but a deep cold kept Maati's cloak wrapped tight. His eyes wanted nothing more than to close.

"We can make the river in seven days if we go through the night. Large Kae will fight against it for the horses' sake," Maati said.

"I'll fight against it for yours," Eiah said. "There was a reason I was trying to make this journey restful."

"I'm fine. I'll last to Utani and years past it, you watch." He sighed. His flesh seemed about to drip off his bones from simple exhaustion. "You watch."

"Crawl back," Eiah said. "Rest. I can do this alone."

"You'd fall asleep," Maati said.

"And use you for a pillow, Uncle. I'm fine. Go."

He looked back. There was a place for him. Irit had made it up with two thick wool blankets. He couldn't see it in the night, but he knew it was there. He wanted nothing more than to turn to it and let the whole broken world fade for a while. He couldn't. Not yet.

"Eiah-kya," he said softly. "About your binding. About Wounded . . ."

She turned to him, a shadow within a shadow. He bent close to her, his voice as low as he could make it and still be heard over the clatter of hooves on stone.

"You know the grammar well? You have it all in mind?"

"Of course," she said.

"Could you do it without it being written? It's usual to write it all out, the way Vanjit-cha did. And it helps to have that there to follow, but you could do the thing without. Couldn't you?"

"I don't know," Eiah said. "Perhaps. It isn't something I'd thought about particularly. But why . . . ?"

"We should postpone your binding," Maati said. "Until you are certain you could do it without the reference text."

Eiah was silent. Something fluttered by, the sound of wings against air.

"What are you saying?" Eiah said, her words low, clipped, and precise. Maati squeezed his hands together. The joints had started aching sometime earlier in the night. The ancient dagger scar in his belly itched the way it did when he'd grown too tired.

"If you were performing the binding, and something happened so that you couldn't see," Maati said. "If you were to go blind when you'd already started . . . you should know the words and the thoughts well enough to keep to it. Not to slip."

"Not pay its price," Eiah said. Meaning, they both knew, die. A moment later, "She'd do that?"

"I don't know," Maati said. "I don't know anything anymore. But be ready if she does."

Eiah shifted the reins, the pattern of the horses' stride altered, and the cart rocked gently. She didn't speak again, and Maati imagined the silence to be thoughtful. He shifted his weight carefully, turned, and let himself slip down to the bed of the cart. The wool blankets were where he'd remembered them. Feeling his way through the darkness reminded him of his brush with blindness. He told himself that the shudder was only the cold of the morning.

The shifting of the cart became like the rocking of a ship or a cradle. Maati's mind softened, slipped. He felt his body sinking into the planks below him, heard the creak and clatter of the wheels. His heart, low and steady, was like the throbbing drum at the wayhouse. It didn't sound at all unwell.

On the shifting edge of sleep, he imagined himself capable of moving between spaces, folding the world so that the distance between himself and Otah-kvo was only a step. He pictured Otah's awe and rage and impotence. It was a fantasy Maati had cultivated before this, and it went through its phases like a habit. Maati's presentation of the poets, the women's grammar, the andat. Otah's abasement and apologies and humble amazement at the world made right. For years, Maati had driven himself toward that moment. He had brought on the sacrifice of ten women, each of them paying the price of a binding that wasn't quite correct.

He watched now as if someone else were dreaming it. Dispassionate, cold, thoughtful. He felt nothing—not disappointment or regret or hope. It was like being a boy again and coming across some iridescent and pincered insect, fascinating and beautiful and dangerous.

More than half asleep, he didn't feel the tiny body inching its way to him until it lay almost within his arms. With the reflex of a man who has cared for a baby, instincts long unused but never forgotten, he gathered the child close.

"You have to kill her," it whispered.

21

⟩+⟨ Otah stood in the ruins of the school's west garden. Half a century before, he'd been in this same spot, screaming at boys not ten summers old. Humiliating them. This was where, in a fit of childish rage, he had forced a little boy to eat clods of dirt. He'd been twelve summers old at the time, but he recalled it with a vividness like a cut. Maati's young eyes and blistered hands, tears and apologies. The incident had begun Maati's career as a poet and ended his own.

The stone walls of the school were lower than he remembered them. The crows that perched in the stark, leafless trees, on the other hand, were as familiar as childhood enemies. As a boy, he had hated this place. With all its changes and his own, he still did.

Ashti Beg had told them of Maati's clandestine school. Of Eiah's involvement, and the others'. Two women named Kae, another—Ashti Beg's particular confidante—named Irit. And the new poet, Vanjit. Ashti Beg had escaped the school and the increasingly dangerous poet and her false baby, the andat Blindness. Or Clarity-of-Sight.

Three days after Eiah had left her in one of the low towns, she had lost her sight without warning. The poet girl Vanjit taking revenge for whatever slight she imagined. In a spirit of vengeance, Ashti Beg had offered to lead Otah to them all. Under cover of night, if he wished.

There was no need. Otah knew the way.

The armsmen had gone first, scouting from what little cover there was. No sign of life had greeted them, and they had arrived to find the school cleaned, repaired, cared for, and empty. They had come too late, and the wind and snow had erased any clue to where Maati and Eiah and the other women had gone. Including the new poet.

Idaan emerged from the building, walking toward him with a determined gait. Otah could see the ghost of her breath. He took a pose that offered greeting. It seemed too formal, but he couldn't think of one more fitting and he didn't want to speak.

"I'd guess they left before you reached Pathai," Idaan said. "They've left very little. A few jars of pickled nuts and some dry cheese. Otherwise, it all matches what she said. Someone's been here for months. The kitchen's been used. And the graves are still fresh."

"How many boys died here, do you think?" Otah asked.

"In the war, or when the Dai-kvo ran the place?" Idaan asked, and then went on without waiting for his reply. "I don't know. Fewer than have died in Galt since you and . . . the others left Saraykeht."

She had stumbled at mentioning Danat. He'd noticed more than once that it wasn't a name she liked saying.

"We have to find them," Otah said. "If we can't make her change this soon, the High Council will never forgive us."

Idaan smiled. It was an odd and catlike expression, gentle and predatory both. She glanced at him, saw his unease, and shrugged.

"I'm sorry," she said. "It's only that you keep speaking as if there was still a High Council. Or a nation called Galt, for that. If this Vanjit has done what for all the world it seems she's done, every city and town and village over there has been blinded for weeks now. It isn't winter yet, but it's cold enough. And even if they had gotten some of the harvest in before this, it would only help the people on the farms. You can't walk from town to town blind, much less steer one of these soup pots on wheels."

"They'll find ways."

"Some of them may have, but there'll be fewer tomorrow. And then the next day. The next," Idaan agreed. "It doesn't matter. However many there are, they aren't Galts anymore."

"No? Then what are they?"

"Survivors," Idaan said, and any amusement that had been in her voice was gone. "Just survivors."

They stood in silence, looking at nothing. The crows insulted one another, rose into the air, and settled again. The breeze smelled of new snow and the promise of frost.

Inside the stone walls, the armsmen had made camp. The kitchen was warm, and the smell of boiling lentils and pork fat filled the air. Ana Dasin and Ashti Beg sat side by side, talking to the air. Otah tried not to watch the two blind women, but he found he couldn't turn away. It was their faces that captured him. Their expressions, their gestures thrown into nothingness, were strangely intimate. It was as if by being cast into their personal darkness, they had lost some ability to dissemble. Ashti Beg's anger was carved into the lines around her mouth. Ana, by contrast, betrayed an unexpected serenity in every movement of her hands, every smile. Three empty bowls lay beside them, evidence of Ana's appetite. Their voices betrayed nothing, but their faces and their bodies were eloquent.

As the sun set, the cold grew. It seemed to radiate from the walls, sucking away the life and heat like a restless ghost. That night, they slept in the shelter of the school. Otah took the wide, comfortable room that had once belonged to Tahi-kvo, his first and least-loved teacher. The wool blankets were heavy and thick. The night wind sang empty, mindless songs against the shutters. In the dim flickering light from the fire grate, he let his mind wander.

It was uncomfortable to think of Eiah in this place. It wasn't only that she was angry with him, that she had chosen this path and not the one he preferred. All that was true, but it was also that this place was one part of his life and that she was another. The two didn't belong together. He tried to imagine what he would have said to her, had she and Maati and the other students in Maati's little school still been encamped there.

The truth he could not admit to anyone was that he was relieved to have failed.

The shadows at the fire grate seemed to grow solid, a figure crouching there. He knew it was an illusion. It wasn't the first time his mind had tricked itself into imagining Kiyan after her death. He smiled at the vision of his wife, but the dream of her had already faded. It was a sign, and since it was both intended for him and created by his mind, it was perfectly explicable. If killing his daughter was the price it took to save the world, then the world could die. He took little comfort in the knowledge.

In the morning, Danat woke him, grinning. A piece of paper flapped in the boy's hand like a moth as Danat threw open the shutters and let the morning light spill in. Otah blinked, yawned, and frowned. Dreams already half-remembered were fading quickly. Danat dropped onto the foot of Otah's cot.

"I've found them," Danat said.

Otah sat up, taking a pose that asked explanation. Danat held out the paper. The handwriting was unfamiliar to him, the characters wider than standard and softly drawn. He took the page and rubbed his eyes as if to clear them.

"I was sleeping in one of the side rooms," Danat said. "When I woke up this morning, I saw that. It was in a corner, not even hidden. I don't know how I missed it last night, except it was dark and I was tired."

Otah's eyes able now to focus, his mind more fully awake, he turned his attention to the letter.

Ashti-cha—

We have decided to leave. Eiah says that Maati-kvo isn't well, so we're all going to Utani so that she can get help caring for him. Please, if you get this, you have to come back! Vanjit is just as bad as ever, and I'm afraid without you here to put her in her place, she'll only get worse. Small Kae has started having nightmares about her. And the baby! You should see the way it tries to get away. It slipped into my lap last night after the Great Poet had gone to sleep and curled up like a kitten.

They've almost finished loading the cart. I'm going to sneak back in once we're almost under way so that she won't find it. You have to come back! Meet us in Utani as soon as you can.

The letter was signed Irit Laatani. Otah folded the paper and tapped it against his lips, thinking. It was plausible. It could be a trick to send them off to Utani, but that would mean that they knew where Otah and his party were, and the errand they were on. If that was the case, there was no reason for misleading them. Vanjit and her little Blindness could stop any pursuit if she wanted it. Danat coughed expectantly.

"Utani," Otah said. "They're going north, just the way you'd planned. This is where you tell me how clever you were for heading there at the first?"

Danat laughed, shaking his head.

"You were right, Papa-kya. Coming here was the right thing. If Maati wasn't ill, they'd have been here."

"Still. It does mean they've stopped hiding. That's a risk if they've only got one poet."

Danat took a questioning pose.

"This poet," Otah said. "She's their protection and their power. As long as she has the andat in her control, they think that they're safe. In truth, though, she can only defend against things she knows. As long as there is only one poet, a well-placed man with a bow could end her before she could blind him. And then none of them are defended."

"Unless there's a second binding. Another andat," Danat said, and Otah took a confirming pose. Danat frowned. "But if there had been, then Irit would have said so, wouldn't she? If Eiah had managed to capture Wounded?"

"I'd expect her to, yes," Otah said.

"Then why would they go?"

Otah tapped the letter.

"Just what the woman said. Because Maati's ill," he said. "And because Eiah decided that caring for him was worth the risk. If he's bad enough to need other physicians' help, they may well be going slowly. Keeping him rested."

"So we go," Danat said. "We go now, and as fast as we can manage. And attack the poet before she can blind us."

"Yes," Otah said. "Burn the books, stop them from binding the andat. Go back, and try to put the world back together again."

"Only . . . only then how do we fix the people in Galt? How do we cure Ana?"

"There's a decision to make," Otah said. "Doing this quickly and well means letting Galt remain sightless."

"Then we can't kill the poet," Danat said.

Otah took a long breath.

"Think about that before you say it," he said. "This is likely the only chance we'll have to take them by surprise. The Galts in Saraykeht are safe enough. The ones in their own cities are likely dead already. The others could be sacrificed, and it would keep us alive."

"And childless, so what would the advantage be?" Danat said. "Everything you'd tried to do would be destroyed."

"Everything I wanted to do has already been destroyed," Otah said. "There isn't a solution to this. Not anymore. I'm reduced to looking for the least painful way that it can end. I don't see how we take these pieces and make a world worth living in."

Danat was silent and still, then took Otah's hand.

"I can," Danat said. "There's hope. There's still hope."

"This poet? Everything Ashti Beg says paints her as angry and petty and cruel at heart. She hates the Galts and thinks little enough of me. That's the woman we would be trying to reason with. And if she chooses, there is more than Galt to lose."

Danat took a pose that accepted the stakes like a man at a betting table. He would put the world and everything in it at risk for the chance that remained to save Ana's home. Otah hesitated, and then replied with a pose that stood witness to the decision. A feeling of pride warmed him.

Kiyan-kya, he thought, we have raised a good man. Please all the gods that we've also raised a wise one.

"I'll go tell the others," Danat said.

He rose and walked for the door, pausing only when Otah called after him. Danat, at the doorway, looked back.

"It's the right choice," Otah said. "No matter how poorly this happens, you made the right choice."

"There wasn't an option," Danat said.

It had been clear enough that no matter what the next step was, it wouldn't involve staying at the school. Under Idaan's direction, the armsmen were already refilling the water and coal stores for the steamcarts, packing what little equipment they had used, and preparing themselves for the road. The sky was white where it wasn't gray, the snow blurring the horizon. Ashti Beg sat alone beside the great bronze doors that had once opened only for the Dai-kvo. They were stained with verdigris and stood ajar. No one besides Otah saw the significance of it.

Midmorning saw a thinning of the clouds, a weak, pale blue forcing its way through the very top of the sky's dome. The horses were in harness, the carts showing their billows of mixed smoke and steam, and everything was at the ready except Idaan and Ana. The armsmen waited, ready to leave. Otah and Danat went back.

Otah found the pair in a large room. Ana, sitting on an ancient bench, had bent forward. Tears streaked the girl's cheeks, her hair was a wild tangle, and her hands clasped until the fingertips were red and the knuckles white. Idaan stood beside her, arms crossed and eyes as bleak as murder. Before Otah could announce himself, Idaan saw him. His sister leaned close to the Galtic girl, murmured something, listened to the soft reply, and then marched to the doorway and Otah's side.

"Is there . . . is something the matter?" Otah asked.

"Of course there is. How long have you been traveling with that girl?"

"Since Saraykeht," Otah said.

"Have you noticed yet that she isn't a man?" Idaan's voice was sharp as knives. "Tell the armsmen to stand down. Then bring me a bowl of snow."

"What's the matter?" Otah demanded. And then, "Is it her time of the month? Does she need medicine?"

Idaan looked at him as if he had asked what season came after spring: pitying, incredulous, disgusted.

"Get me some snow. Or, better, some ice. Tell your men that we'll be ready in a hand and a half, and for all the gods there ever were, keep your son away from her until we can put her back together. The last thing she needs is to feel humiliated."

Otah took a pose that promised compliance, but then hesitated. Idaan's dark eyes flashed with something that wasn't anger. When she spoke, her voice was lower but no softer.

"How have you spent a lifetime in the company of women and learned nothing?" she asked, and, shaking her head, turned back to Ana.

True to her word, a hand and a half later, Ana and Idaan emerged from the school as if nothing strange had happened. Ana's outer robe was changed to a dark wool, and she leaned on Idaan's arm as she stepped up to the bed of the steamcart. Danat moved forward, but Idaan's scowl drove him back. The two women made their slow way to the shed, where Idaan closed the door behind them.

The men steering the carts called out to one another, voices carrying like crows' calls in the empty landscape. The carts stuttered and lurched, and turned to the east, tracking back along the path to the high road between ruined Nantani and Pathai, from which they'd come. Otah rode down the path he'd walked as a boy, searching his mind for some feeling of kinship with his past, but the world as it was demanded too much of him. He searched for some memory deep within him of the first time he'd walked away from the school, of leaving everything he'd known, rejected, behind him.

His mind was knotted with questions of how to find the poet, how to persuade her to do as he asked, what Idaan had meant, what was wrong with Ana, whether the steamcarts had enough fuel, and a growing ache in his spine that came from too many days riding horses he didn't know. There was no effort to spare for the past. Whatever he didn't remember now of his original flight from the school he likely never would. The past would be lost, as it always was. Always. He didn't bother trying to hold it.

They made better time than he had expected, starting as late as they had. By the time they stopped for the night, the high road was behind them. The fastest route to Utani would be overland to the Qiit, then by boat up the river. Any hope they had of overtaking Maati and Eiah would come on the roads, where the steamcarts gave Otah an advantage. They would have to sleep in the open more than if they had kept to wider roads, and the rough terrain increased the possibility of the carts breaking or getting stuck. Even of the boiler bursting and killing anyone too near it. But Idaan's voice spoke in Otah's mind of the next day, and the next, and the next, so he pushed them and himself.

Four of the armsmen rode ahead in the lowering gloom of night to scout out the next day's path. The others prepared a simple meal of pork and rice, Ashti Beg sitting with them and trading jokes. Danat's slow circling of their camp took the name of defense but seemed more to be avoiding the still-closed shed where Idaan and Ana rested. Otah sat alone near the steamcart's kiln, reflecting that it was very much like his son to shift between noble dedication in the morning and childish pouting as night came on. He had been much the same as a young man, or imagined that he had.

The door opened, Ana's laughter spilling out into the night. Idaan led the girl forward, letting Ana keep a careful grip on her. Her dark eyes and Ana's unfocused gray ones were both light and merry. Ana's hair had been combed and braided in the style of children in the winter cities. In the dim moonlight, it made Ana seem hardly more than a girl.

Idaan steered the girl to the cart's front and helped her sit beside Otah. He coughed once to make sure the girl knew he was there, but she seemed unsurprised at the sound. Idaan placed a hand on the back of the girl's neck.

"I'll go get some food," Idaan said. "My brother here should be able to keep you out of trouble for that long."

Ana took a pose that offered thanks. She did a creditable job of it. Idaan snorted, patted the girl's neck, and lowered herself to the ground. Otah heard her footsteps crushing the snow as she walked away.

"Ana-cha," Otah said. His voice was more tentative than he liked. "I hope you're well?"

"Fine," she said. "Thank you. I'm sorry I delayed things today. It won't happen again."

"Hardly worth thinking about," Otah said, relieved that her infirmity had passed. Grief, he suspected, over what the poet had done to her, to her family, her nation.

"I misjudged you," Ana said. "I know it seems like everything we do is another round of apology, but I am sorry for it."

"It might be simpler to agree to forgive each other in advance," Otah said, and Ana laughed. It was a warmer sound than he'd expected. A tension he hadn't known he felt lessened and he smiled into the glowing coals of the kiln. "It is fair to ask in what manner you judged me poorly?"

"I thought you were cold. Hard. You have to understand, I grew up with monster stories about the Khaiem and the andat."

"I do," Otah said, sighing. "I look back, and I suspect that more than half of the problems between Galt and the Khaiem came from ignorance. Ignorance and power are a poor combination."

"Tell me . . ." Ana said, and then stopped. Her brow furrowed, and in the dim light he thought she was blushing. Otah put his hand over hers.

She shook her head, and then turned her milky eyes to him. "You've forgiven me in advance if this is too much to ask. Tell me about Danat's mother."

"Kiyan?" Otah said. "Well. What do you want to know about her?"

"Anything. Just tell me," the girl said.

Otah collected himself, and then began to pluck stories. The night they'd met. The night he'd told her that he was more than a simple courier and she'd thrown him out of her wayhouse. The ways she had helped to smooth things as he learned how to become first Khai Machi and then Emperor. He didn't tell the hard stories. The conflict over Sinja's feelings for her, and Otah's poor response to them. The long fears they suffered together when Danat was young and weak in the lungs. Her death. Still, he didn't think he kept all the sorrow from his voice.

Idaan returned halfway through one story, four bowls in her hands like a teahouse servant juggling food for a full table. Otah took one without pausing, and Idaan squatted on the boards at Ana's feet and pressed another into the girl's hands. Otah went on with other little stories—Kiyan's balancing the combined populations of Machi and Cetani with Balasar Gice's crippled army in the wake of the war. Her refusal to allow servants to bathe her. The story of when the representative of Eddensea had mistaken something she'd said and thought she'd invited him to bed with her.

Danat arrived out of the darkness, drawn by their voices. Idaan gave him the last bowl, and he sat at Otah's side, then shifted, then shifted again until his back rested against Ana's shin. He added stories of his own. His mother's sharp tongue and wayhouse keeper's vocabulary, the songs she'd sung, all the scraps and moments that built up a boy's memory of his mother. It was beautiful to listen to. It wasn't something Otah himself had ever had.

In the end, Ana let Danat lead her back to her shelter, leaving Otah and his sister alone by the black and cooling kiln. The armsmen had prepared sleeping tents for them, but Idaan seemed content to sit up drinking watered wine in the cold night air, and Otah found himself pleased enough to join her.

"I don't suppose you'd care to explain to your poor idiot brother what happened today?" he said at length.

"You haven't put it together?" Idaan said. "This Vanjit creature has destroyed the only home Ana-cha had to go to. She's had to look long and hard at what her life could be in the place she's found herself, crippled in a foreign land, and it shook her."

"She's in love with Danat?"

"Of course she is," Idaan said. "It would have happened in half the time if you and her mother hadn't insisted on it. I think that's more frightening for her than the poet killing her nation."

"I don't know what you mean," he said.

"She's spent her life watching her mother linked with her father," Idaan said. "There are only so many years you can soak in the regrets of others before you start to think that all the world's that way."

"I had the impression that Farrer-cha loved his wife deeply," Otah said.

"And I had it that there's more than a husband to make a marriage," Idaan said. "It isn't her mother she fears being, it's Farrer-cha. She's afraid of having her love merely tolerated. I spent most of the day talking about Cehmai. I told her that if she really wanted to know what spending a life with Danat would be like, she should see what sort of man you were. If she wanted to know how Danat would see her, to find how you saw your wife."

Otah laughed, and he thought he saw the darkness around Idaan shift as if she had smiled.

"I'm sorry I didn't have the chance to know her," Idaan said. "She sounds like a good woman."

"She was," Otah said. "I miss her."

"I know you do," Idaan said. "And now Ana-cha knows it too."

"Does it matter?" Otah said. "All the hopes I had for building Galt and the Khaiem together are in rags around my knees. We're on a hunt for a girl who can ruin the world. What she's done to Galt, she could do to us. Or to all the world, if she wanted it. How do we plan for a marriage between Danat and Ana when it's just as likely that we'll all be starving and blind by Candles Night?"

"We're all born to die, Most High," Idaan said, the title sounding like an endearment in her voice. "Every love ends in parting or death. Every nation ends and every empire. Every baby born was going to die, given enough time. If being fated for destruction were enough to take the joy out of things, we'd slaughter children fresh from the womb. But we don't. We wrap them in warm cloth and we sing to them and feed them milk as if it might all go on forever."

"You make it sound like something you've done," Otah said.

Idaan made a sound he couldn't interpret, part grunt, part whimper.

"What is it?" he asked the darkness.

The silence lasted for the length of five long breaths together. When she spoke, her voice was low and rich with embarrassment.

"Lambs," she said.

"Lambs?"

"I used to wrap up the newborn lambs and keep them in the house. I even had Cehmai build them a crib that I could rock them in. After a few years, we had to switch to goats. I couldn't slaughter the lambs after all that, could I? By the end, I think we had sixty."

Otah didn't know whether to laugh or put his arms around the woman. The thought of the hard-hearted killer of his own father, his own brothers, cuddling a baby lamb was as absurd as it was sorrowful.

"Is it like this for everyone?" he asked softly. "Does every woman suffer this? Is the need to care for something that strong?"

"Strong? When it strikes, yes. But everyone? No," Idaan said. "Of course not. As it happened, it struck me. I assume Maati's students all feel strongly enough about it to risk their lives. But not every woman needs a child, and, thank the gods, the madness sometimes passes. It did for me."

"You wouldn't be a mother now? If it were possible, you wouldn't choose to?"

"Gods, no. I'd have been terrible at it. But I miss them," Idaan said. "I miss my little lambs. And that brings us back to Ana-cha, doesn't it?"

Otah took a pose that asked clarification.

"Who am I," Idaan asked, "to say that falling in love is ridiculous just because it's doomed?"

22

>+< The weeks spent at the school had let Maati forget the ways in which the world broadened when he was traveling, and also the ways in which it narrowed when he was traveling with company. Living in the same walls, the same gardens, and surrounded as he had been by only a few deeply familiar faces had begun to grate on him before they left, but there had still been a way to find a moment to steal away. On the road, all of them together, the chances for private conversation were few and precious.

Since the andat had spoken, he hadn't found himself alone with Eiah, or at least not so clearly so that he would risk speaking. He didn't want either of the Kaes or Irit to know what had happened. He was afraid that they would say something where Vanjit could hear them. He was afraid that Vanjit would find out what the andat had said and take some terrible action in her fear and in her own defense.

He was afraid because he was afraid, and he was half-certain that Vanjit knew he was.

They reached the lands surrounding the river sooner than he would have wanted; if the long days and nights on the road had kept him in close quarters with the others, the days ahead sharing a boat would be worse. He had to find a way to talk with Eiah before that, and the prospect of his lessening time made him anxious.

Cold and snow hadn't reached the river valley yet. It was as if their journey were moving backward in time. The leaves here clung to the trees, some of them with the gold and red and yellow still struggling to push out the last hints of green. As they approached the water, farms and low towns clustered closer and closer. The roads and paths began to cling to irrigation channels, and other travelers—most merely local, but some from the great cities—appeared more and more often. Maati sat at the front of the cart, his robes wrapped close around him, staring ahead and trying not to put himself anywhere that the andat could catch his eye.

He was, in fact, so preoccupied with the politics and dangers within his small party that he didn't see the Galts until his horses were almost upon them.

Three men, none of them older than thirty summers, sat at the side of the road. They wore filthy robes that had once been red or orange. The tallest had a leather satchel over his shoulder. They had stepped a few feet off the path at the sound of hooves, and the tall grass made them seem like apparitions from a children's epic. Their eyes were blue, the pupils gray. None of them had shaved in recent memory. Their gaunt faces turned to the road from habit. There was no expression in them, not even hunger. Maati didn't realize he had slowed the horses until he heard Eiah call out from the cart's bed behind him. At her word, he stopped. Large Kae and Irit, taking their turns on horseback, reined in. Vanjit and Small Kae moved to the side of the cart. Maati risked a glance at Clarity-of-Sight, but it was still and silent.

"Who are you?" Eiah demanded in their language. "What are your names?"

The Galtic apparitions shifted, blinking their empty eyes in confusion. The tall one with the satchel recovered first.

"I'm Jase Hanin," he said, speaking too loudly. "These are my brothers. It isn't plague. Whatever took our eyes, miss, it wasn't plague. We aren't a danger."

Eiah muttered something that Maati couldn't make out, then shifted a crate in the back. When he turned to look, she had her physician's satchel on her hip and was preparing to drop down to the road. Vanjit, seeing this as well, grabbed Eiah's sleeve.

"Don't," Vanjit said. The word was as much command as plea.

"I'll be fine," Eiah said. Vanjit's grip tightened on the cloth, and Maati saw their eyes lock.

"Vanjit-cha," Maati said. "It's all right. Let her go."

The poet looked back at him, anger in her gaze, but she did as he'd said. Eiah slipped down to the ground and walked toward the surprised Galts.

"You're a long way from anyplace," Eiah said.

"We were out in the low towns," the tall one said. "Something happened. We've been trying to get back to Saraykeht. Our mother's there, you see. Only it seems like we're put on the wrong path or stolen from as often as we're helped."

He tried what had once been a winning smile. Maati tied the reins to the cart and lowered himself to the road as well.

"Your mother?" Eiah said.

"Yes, miss," the Galt said.

"Well," she said, her voice cool. "At least you weren't a band of those charming liars out selling the promise of women in the low towns. What's in the satchel?"

The Galt looked chagrined and desperate, but he didn't lie.

"Names of men, miss. The ones who wanted wives from Galt."

"I thought as much," Eiah said.

"Don't help them," Vanjit said. She'd climbed to the front of the cart, but hadn't taken up the reins. From the way she held her body, Maati guessed it was a matter of time before she did. He saw the andat's black eyes peering over the cart at him and looked away. Eiah might as well not have heard her.

"We were going to do the right thing with them, miss," the tall man said. "There's a man in Acton putting together women who want to come over. We had an arrangement with him. All the money's been taken, but we still have the lists. God's word, we're going to keep our end of the thing, if we can just get back to Saraykeht."

"You stole from them," Eiah said, pulling a leather waterskin from her satchel. "They stole back from you. Seems to me that leaves you even. Here, drink from this. It's not only water, so don't take more than a couple of swallows, any of you."

"Eiah-kya," Irit said. Her voice was high and anxious, but she didn't say more than the name. Large Kae's mount whickered and sidestepped, sensing something uneasing in its rider's posture. Eiah might as easily have been alone.

"These . . . put out your hand. These are lengths of silver. I've put a notch in each of them, so you'll know if someone's trying to switch them. It's enough to pay for a passage to Saraykeht. The road you're following now, it will be about another day's walk to the river. Maybe longer. Call it two."

"Thank you, miss," one of the other two said.

"I don't suppose we could ride on the back of your cart?" the tall man said, hope in his smile.

"No," Maati said. There was a limit to what Vanjit would allow, and he wasn't ready for that confrontation. "We've spent too long at this. Eiah."

Without a word, without meeting his gaze, Eiah turned back, climbed into the cart, and went back to the wax writing tablets she'd spent her morning over. Maati climbed back up into the cart and started them back down the road, Vanjit at his side.

"She shouldn't have done that," Vanjit murmured. Soft as the words were, he knew Eiah would hear them.

"There's no harm in it," Maati said. "Let it pass."

Vanjit frowned, but let the subject go. She spent the rest of the day beside him, as if guarding him from Eiah. For her part, Eiah might have been alone with her tablets. Even when the rest of them sang to pass the time, she kept to her work, steady and focused. When the conversation turned to whether they should keep riding after sunset in hopes of reaching the river, she spoke for stopping on the road. She didn't want Maati to be tired any more than was needed. Large Kae sided with her for the horses' sake.

The women made a small camp, dividing the night into watches since they were so near the road. Vanjit sharpened their sight in the evenings but insisted on returning them to normal when dawn came. She, of course, didn't have a turn at watch. Neither did Maati. Instead, he watched the moon as it hung in the tree branches, listened to the low call of owls, and drank the noxious tea. Vanjit, Irit, and Small Kae lay in the bed of the cart, their robes wrapped tightly around them. The andat sat beside its poet, as still as a stone. Eiah and Large Kae had taken the first watch, and were sitting with their backs to the fire to keep their unnaturally sharp eyes well-adapted to the darkness.

You have to kill her, it had said, and when Maati had reared back, his fragile heart racing, the andat had only looked at him. Its childish eyes had seemed older, like something ancient wearing the mask of a baby. It had nodded to itself and then turned and crawled awkwardly away. The message had been delivered. The rest, it seemed to imply, was Maati's.

He looked at the bowl of dark tea in his hands. The warmth of it was almost gone. Small bits of leaf and root shifted in the depths. An idea occurred to him. Not, perhaps, a brilliant one, but they would reach the river and hire a boat in the morning. It was a risk worth taking.

"Eiah-kya," he said softly. "Something's odd with this tea. Could you . . . ?"

Eiah looked over at him. She looked old in the dim light of moon and fire. She came to the tree where he sat. Large Kae's gaze followed her. The sleepers in the cart didn't stir, but the andat's eyes were on him. Maati held out the bowl, and Eiah sipped from it.

"We need to speak," Maati said under his breath. "The others can't know."

"It seems fine. Give me your wrists," Eiah said in a conversational tone. Then, softly, "What's happened?"

"It's the andat. Blindness. It spoke to me. It told me to kill Vanjit-cha. This is all its doing."

Eiah switched to compare pulses in both wrists, her eyes closed as if she were concentrating.

"How do you mean?" she whispered.

"The babe was always clinging to Ashti Beg. It made Ashti-cha feel that it cared for her. Vanjit grew jealous. The conflict between them was the andat's doing. Now that it thinks we're frightened of it, it's trying to use me as well. It's Stone-Made-Soft encouraging Cehmai-cha into distracting conflicts. It's Seedless again."

Eiah put down his wrists, pressing her fingertips against his palms with the air of a buyer at a market.

"Does it matter?" Eiah murmured. "Say that the andat has been manipulating us all. What does that change?"

Eiah put down his hands. Her smile was thin and humorless. Something scurried in the bushes, small and fast. A mouse, perhaps.

"Is all well?" Large Kae called from the fire. In the cart, someone moaned and stirred.

"Fine," Maati said. "We're fine. Only adjusting something." Then, quietly, "I doubt it changes anything. Vanjit's more likely to side with Clarity-of-Sight than with us. If it is scheming against her—and, really, I can't see why it wouldn't be—it's better placed to get what it wants. It *is* her. It knows what she needs and what she fears."

"You think *she* wants to die?" Eiah asked.

"I think she wants to stop hurting. Binding the andat was supposed to stop the pain. Having a babe was supposed to. Revenge on the Galts. Now here she is with everything she wanted, and she still hurts."

Maati shrugged. Eiah took a pose of agreement and of sorrow.

"If she weren't a poet, I'd pity her," Eiah said. "But she is, and so she frightens me."

"Maati-kya?" Vanjit's voice came from the darkness over Eiah's shoulder. It was high and anxious. "What's the matter with Maati-kvo?"

"Nothing," Eiah said, turning back. Vanjit was sitting up, her hair wild, her eyes wide. The andat was clutched to her breast. Eiah took a reassuring pose. "Everything's fine."

Poet and andat looked at Maati with expressions of distrust so alike they were eerie.

THE RIVER QIIT HAD ITS SOURCE FAR NORTH OF UTANI. RAINS FROM THE mountain ranges that divided the cities of the Khaiem from the West-lands flowed east into the wide flats, gathered together, and carved their way south. Utani, the ruins of Udun, and then far to the south, the wide, silted delta just east of Saraykeht.

At its widest, the river was nearly half a mile across, but that was far-ther south. Here, at the low town squatting on the riverfront, the water was less than half that, its surface smooth and shining as silver. Eight thin streets crossed one another at unpredictable angles. Dogs and chickens negotiated their peace in bark and squawk, tooth and beak as Maati drove past. Two wayhouses offered rest. Another teahouse was painted in characters that made it clear there were no beds for hire there, and grudg-ingly offered fresh noodles and old wine. The air smelled rich with decay and new growth, the cold water and the dust of the road. There should have been children in the streets, calling, begging, playing games both innocent and cruel.

Maati drew the cart to a halt in the yard of the wayhouse nearest the riverfront itself. Large Kae dismounted and went in to negotiate for a room. After the incident with the andat, the agreement was that some-one would always be in a private room with the shutters closed and the door bolted, watching the andat. If all went as he intended it, they would be on the river well before nightfall, but still . . .

Vanjit's scowl had deepened through the day. Twice more they had passed men and women with pale skin and blind eyes. Two were beg-ging at the side of the road, another was being led on the end of a rope by an old woman. Eiah had not insisted on stopping to offer them aid. Happily, there were no Galtic faces at the wayhouse. Vanjit paused in the main room, her hand on Maati's shoulder. The andat was in her other arm, concealed by a blanket and as still as death.

"Maati-kvo," she said. "I'm worried. Eiah has been so strange since we left the school, don't you think? All the hours she's spent writing on those tablets. I don't think it's good for her."

"I'm sure she's fine," Maati said with what he hoped was a reassuring smile.

"And giving silver to those Galts," Vanjit said, her voice creeping higher. "I don't know what she means by that. Do you?"

Large Kae came in from a dark corridor and motioned them to follow.

Maati almost had to pull Vanjit to get her attention. She glared at Large Kae's back as they walked.

"It seems to me," Vanjit continued, "that Eiah is forgetting who are her allies and who are her enemies. I know you love her, Maati-kvo, but you can't let that blind you. You can't ignore the truth."

"I won't, Vanjit-kya," Maati said. The room was on the first floor. Fresh rushes on the floor. A small cot of stretched canvas. Oak shutters closed against the daylight. "You leave this to me. I'll see to it."

Large Kae left, murmuring something about seeing to the animals. When the door closed behind her, Vanjit let the blanket fall and set the andat on the cot. It cooed and burbled, waving its hands and grinning toothlessly. It was a parody of infantile delight, and seeing Vanjit's smile— pleasure and fear and anger all in the smallest stretching of her lips— made Maati's flesh crawl.

"You have to do something," she said. "Eiah-kya can't be trusted with the andat. You wouldn't . . ."

The baby shrieked and flopped to its side, trying to lower itself to the floor. Vanjit moved forward and lifted it back up before she went on.

"You wouldn't let someone you can't trust bind the andat. You wouldn't do that."

"Certainly, I'd try not to," Maati said.

"That's a strange answer."

"I'm not a god. I use the judgment I have. It isn't as if I can see into someone's heart."

"But if you think Eiah can't be trusted," Vanjit said, anger growing in her voice, "you *will* stop her. You have to."

Who am I speaking to? he wondered. The girl? The andat? Does Vanjit know what she's saying?

"Yes," Maati said slowly. "If she isn't fit to be a poet to wield the andat, it would be my duty to see that she does not. I will stop her. But I have to be sure. I can't do this thing until I'm sure there's nothing I can do that will mend her."

"Mend her?" Vanjit said and took a pose that scorned the thought.

"I won't kill someone unless there is no other way."

Vanjit stepped back, her face going pale. The andat's gaze shifted from one to the other and back, its eyes shining with unfeigned delight.

"I never said to kill her," Vanjit said, her voice soft.

"Didn't you?" Maati said as if making it an accusation. "You're sure of that?"

He turned and left the room, his hands trembling, his heart racing.

He'd been an idiot. He'd slipped. Perhaps making him say more than he'd intended had been the point; perhaps the andat had guessed that it could make him go too far. He paused in the main room, his head feeling light. He sat at one of the tables and lowered his head to his knees.

His heart was still pounding, and his face felt hot and flushed. The voices of the keeper and Irit seemed to echo, as if he were hearing them from the far end of a tunnel. He gritted his teeth, willing his body to calm itself, to obey him.

Slowly, his pulse calmed. The heat in his face lessened. He didn't know how long he'd been sitting at the little table by the back wall. It seemed like only moments and it also seemed like half the day. Both were plausible. He tried to stand, but he was weak and shaking. Like a man who'd just run a race.

He motioned to the keeper and asked for strong tea. The man brought it quickly enough. A cast-iron pot in the shape of a frog, the spigot a hollow tongue between its lips. Maati poured the rich, green tea into a carved wooden bowl and sat for a moment, breathing in the scent of it before trying to lift it to his lips.

By the time Irit arrived, he felt nearly himself again. Exhausted and weak, but himself. The woman sat across from him, her fingers knotted about one another. Her smile was too wide.

"Maati-kvo," she said and belatedly took a pose of greeting. "I've just come from the riverfront. Eiah has hired a boat. It looks like a good one. Wide enough that it isn't supposed to rock so much. Or get stuck on sandbars. They talked a bit about sandbars. In any case—"

"What's the matter?"

Irit looked out toward the main room as if expecting to see someone there. She spoke without looking at him.

"I'm not ever going to make a binding, Maati-kvo. I may have helped, I may not. But we both know I'm not going to do the thing."

"You want to leave," Maati said.

She did look at him now, her mouth small, her eyes large. She was like a picture of herself drawn by someone who thought poorly of her.

"Take your things," Maati said. "Do it before we get on the river."

She took a pose that accepted his orders, but the fear remained in the way she held her body. Maati nodded to himself.

"I'll tell Vanjit that I've sent you on an errand for me. That Eiah needed some particular root that only grows in the south. You're to meet us with it in Utani. She won't know the truth."

"Thank you," Irit said, relief in her expression at last. "I'm sorry."

"Hurry," Maati said. "There isn't much time."

Irit scuttled out, her hands fluttering as if they possessed a life of their own. Maati sat quietly in the growing darkness, sipped his tea, and tried to convince himself that his strength was coming back. He'd let himself get frightened, that was all. It wasn't as if he'd fainted. He was fine. By the time Eiah and Small Kae came to collect Vanjit and Clarity-of-Sight, he mostly believed it.

Eiah accepted the news of Irit's departure without comment. The two Kaes glanced at each other and kept loading their few remaining crates onto the boat. Vanjit said nothing, only nodded and took Clarity-of-Sight to the bow of the little craft to stare out at the water.

The boat was as long as six men laid end to end, and as wide across as five. It sat low in the water, and the back quarter was filled with coal and kiln, boiler and wide-slatted wheel ready to take to the river. The boatman who watched the fires and the rudder was older than Maati, his skin thin and wrinkled. The second who took duty whenever the old man rested might have been his son. Neither man spoke to the passengers, and the sight of the baby struggling in Vanjit's arms seemed to elicit no reaction.

Once they were all on and their belongings tied down, Eiah took a pose that indicated their readiness. The second called out, his voice almost a song. The riverfront clerk called back. Ropes were untied, the evil chuffing from the wheel grew louder, and the deep, violent slap of wood against water jerked them away from the bank and into the river. It seemed as if a breeze had come up, though it was likely only the speed of the boat. Eiah sat beside Maati, taking his wrists.

"We told them the child was the get of one of the utkhaiem on a Westlands girl. Vanjit is the nurse."

Maati nodded. It was as good a lie as any. At the bow, Vanjit looked back at the sound of her name. Her eyes were clear, but something in the set of her face made him think she'd been crying. Eiah frowned, pinching his fingertips until they went white, then waiting for the blood to pour back into them.

"She asked about your tablets," he said. "You have been busy with them. The binding?"

"I'm trying to cut deep enough that I can read it with my fingers," Eiah said quietly. "It's a better exercise than I'd expected. I think I've seen some ways to improve the grammar itself. It will mean another draft, but . . . How are you feeling?"

"What? Ah, fine. I feel fine."

"Tired?"

"Of course I'm tired. I'm old and I've been on the road too long and . . ."

And I have loosed a mad poet on the world, he thought. All the cruelties and tricks of the Dai-kvo, all the pain and loss that I suffered to be a poet was justified. If it kept people like Vanjit from the power of the andat, it was all justified. And I have ignored it.

As if reading the words in his eyes, Eiah glanced over her shoulder at Vanjit. The sun was shining off the water, surrounding the dark, huddled girl with a brilliant halo of gold and white. When Maati looked away, the image had scarred his eyes. It lay over everything else he saw, black where it had been light, and a pale shape the color of mourning robes where Vanjit had been.

"I'm making your tea," Eiah said, her voice grim. "Stay here and rest."

"Eiah-kya? We . . . we have to kill her," Maati said.

Eiah turned to him, her expression empty. He gestured to Vanjit's back. His hand trembled.

"Before your binding," he said, "we should be sure that it's safe for you. Or, that is, as safe as we can make it. You . . . you understand."

Eiah sighed. When she spoke again, her voice was distant and reflective.

"I knew a physician in Lachi. She told me about being in a low town when one of the men caught blood fever. He was a good person. Wellliked. This was a long time ago, so he had children. He'd gone out hunting and come back ill. She had them smother him and burn the body. His children stayed in their house and screamed the whole time they did it. She didn't sleep well for years afterward."

Her eyes were focused on nothing, her jaw forward as if she was facing someone down. Man or god or fate.

"You're saying it's not her fault," Maati said softly, careful not to speak Vanjit's name. "She was a little girl who had her family slaughtered before her. She was a lost woman who wanted a child and could never have one. What's wrong with her mind was done to her."

Eiah took a pose that disagreed.

"I'm saying no matter how little my physician friend slept, she saved those children's lives," Eiah said. "There are some herbs. When we stop for the night, I can gather them. I'll see it's done."

"No. No, I'll do the thing. If it's anyone, it should—"

"It will have to be quick," Eiah said. "She mustn't know it's coming. You can't do that."

Maati took a pose that challenged her, and Eiah folded his hands gently closed.

"Because you still want to save her," she said. Something about weariness and determination made her look like her father.

Otah, who had killed a poet once too.

23

>+< Otah rose in the mornings with stiff, aching joints and a pain in his side that would not fade. The steamcarts allowed each of them the chance to sleep for a hand or two in the late mornings or just after the midday meal. Without the rest, Otah knew he wouldn't have been able to keep pace with the others.

The courier found them on the road. His outer robe was the colors of House Siyanti and mud-spattered to the waist. His mount cantered alongside the carts now, cooling down from the morning's travel as its rider waited for replies. The man's satchel held a dozen letters at least, but only one had occasioned his speed. It was written on paper the color of cream, sewn with black thread, and the imprint in the wax belonged to Balasar Gice. Otah sat in his saddle, afraid to open it and afraid not to.

The thread ripped easily and the pages unfolded. Otah skimmed the letter from beginning to end, then began again, reading more slowly, letting the full import of the words wash over him. He folded the letter and slipped it into his sleeve, his heart heavy.

Danat drew closer, his hands in a pose that both called for inclusion and offered sympathy. The boy might not know what had happened, but he'd drawn the fact that it wasn't good.

"Chaburi-Tan," Otah said, beginning with the least of the day's losses. "It's gone. Sacked. Burned. We don't know whether the mercenaries turned sides or simply wouldn't protect it, but it comes to the same thing. The pirates attacked the city, took what they could, and set the rest alight."

"And the fleet?"

Otah looked at the roadside. Sun had melted the snow as far as its light could reach, but the shadows were still pale. Otah had known Sinja Ajutani for more years than not. The dry humor, the casual disrespect of all things pompous or self-certain, the knife-sharp and unsentimental analysis of any issue. When Kiyan died, they had been the only two men in the world who truly understood what had been lost.

Now, only Otah knew.

"What ships remain have been set to guard the seafront at Saraykeht," he said when he could speak again. "The thought is that winter will protect Yalakeht and Amnat-Tan. When the thaw comes in spring, we may have to revisit the plan."

"Are you all right, Papa-kya?"

"I'll be fine," Otah said, then he raised his hand and called the courier close. "Tell them I read it. Tell them I understood."

The courier made his obeisance, turned his mount, and rode away. Otah let himself sit with his grief. The other letters for him could wait. They had come from his Master of Tides, and from others he'd named to watch the Empire crumble in his absence. Two had been for Ana Dasin, and he assumed they were from her parents. The letters had made their way up from Saraykeht and then along the low roads, tracking Otah and his party for days. And each day had marked the ending of lives, in Galt especially, but everywhere.

He had known that Sinja might die. He'd sent the fleet out knowing it might happen, and Sinja had gone without any illusions of safety. If it hadn't been this and now, it would have been something else at some other time. Every man and woman died, in time.

And in truth, death wasn't the curse he'd set out to break. All his work and sacrifice had been only so that they could balance the constant withering of age with some measure of renewal. He thought of his own children: Eiah, Danat, and even long-dead Nayiit. They had each of them been wagers he'd placed against a cruel world. A child comes into the world, and its father holds it close and thinks, If all goes as it should, I will die first. This one, I can love and never mourn for. That was all he wanted to leave for Danat and Eiah. The chance of knowing a love that they would never be called to bury. It was the world as it was intended to be.

He didn't notice Idaan riding close to him until she spoke. Her voice was gruff, but he imagined he could hear some offer of comfort in it.

"It's past time to shift. Crawl up on that cart and rest awhile. You've been riding that thing for five hands together."

"Have I?" Otah said. "I didn't notice."

"I know. It's why I came," she said. After a moment's pause, she added, "Danat told us what happened."

Otah took a pose that acknowledged having heard her, but nothing more than that. There wasn't anything more that could be meaningfully said. Idaan respected it and let him turn his horse aside and shift to the steamcart where Ana Dasin and Ashti Beg sat, their sightless eyes fixed on nothing. Otah sat on the wide boards not far from them, but not so near that their conversation would include him. Ana laughed at something Ashti Beg had said. The older woman looked vaguely pleased. Otah lay back, his closed eyes flooded with the red of sun and blood. He willed himself to sleep, certain that it would elude him.

He woke when the cart jerked to a halt. He sat up, half-thoughts of snapped axles and broken wheels forming and falling apart like mist in a high wind. When he was awake enough to make sense of the world, he saw that the sun had sunk almost to the treetops, and the cart was sitting in the yard of a wayhouse. The memory of the morning's foul message flooded back into him, but not so deeply as before. It would rise and fall, he knew. He would be jarred by the loss of his friend again and again and again, but less and less and less. It said something he didn't want to know that mourning had become so familiar. He plucked his traveling robes into their proper drape and lowered himself to the ground.

The one thing he truly didn't regret about the journey was that his servants were all in Utani or Saraykeht. Walking into the low, warm main room of the wayhouse without being surrounded by men and women wanting to change his robes or powder his feet was a small pleasure. He tried to savor it.

"Half a day east of here," a young man in a leather apron was saying, but he was pointing north. "Must have been five or six days ago. Raised ten kinds of trouble, then left in the middle of the night. So far as I can see, no one's talked about anything else since."

"Did you see them?" Danat asked. His voice had an edge, but Otah couldn't see his face to know if it was excitement or anger.

"Not myself, no," the young man said. "But it's the ones you asked after. An old man with a physician, and nothing but women traveling with him. There was even some talk he was trying to start a comfort house or something of that kind, but that was before the baby."

"Baby?" The voice was Ana's.

"Yes. Little one, not more than eight months old from the size. So I'm told. I didn't see him either, but they all saw him over at Chayiit's place. Walked right out in the middle of the main room."

Otah slipped down at a bench by the fire grate. The fire was small but warm. He hadn't realized how cold he'd gotten.

"Those are the people," Danat said.

"Five, six days then," the young man said with a pleased nod. He glanced over at Otah, their eyes meeting briefly. The other man paled as Otah took a pose of casual greeting and then turned his attention back to the flames. The conversation behind him grew softer and ended. Danat came to sit at his side. Through the open door, the yard fell into evening as the armsmen finished unloading and leading away their horses.

"We've gotten closer," Danat said. "If they keep traveling as slowly as they have up to now, we'll overtake them well before Utani."

Otah grunted. There was a deep thump from overhead and voices lifted in annoyance. Danat's fingers laced his knee.

"I told Balasar that I would beg," Otah said. "I told him that I would bend myself before this new poet and beg if it meant restoring him and Galt."

"And now?"

"I don't believe I can. And more than that, having heard Ashti Beg talk about this Vanjit, it's hard work thinking it would help."

"Maati, perhaps. He holds some sway with her."

"But what can I say that would move him?" Otah asked, his voice thick. "We were friends once, and then enemies, and friends again, but I'm not sure we know each other now. The more I look at it, the more I'm tempted to set some sort of trap, capture the new poet, and give her over to blind torturers until she makes the world what it should be."

"And what about Eiah?" Danat asked. "If she manages her binding—"

"What if she does?" Otah said. "She's been against me from the start. She's gone with Maati, and between them they've sunk the fleet, burned Chaburi-Tan, blinded Galt, and killed Sinja. What would you have me say to her?"

"You'll have to say something," Danat said, his voice harder than Otah had expected. "And we'll be upon them soon enough. It's a thing you should consider."

Otah looked over. Danat's head was bowed, his mouth tight.

"You'd like to suggest something?" Otah asked, his voice low and careful. The anger in his breast shifted like a dog in sleep. Danat either didn't hear the warning or chose to ignore it.

"We're trading revenge," Danat said. "The Galts came from anger at our arrogance and fear of the andat. Maati and Vanjit have struck back now for the deaths during their invasion. This can't go on."

"It isn't in my power to stop it," Otah said.

262 >+< Daniel Abraham

"It isn't in your power to stop them," Danat said, taking a pose of correction. "Only promise me this. If you have the chance, you'll forgive them."

"Forgive them?" Otah said, rising to his feet. "You want them forgiven for this? You think it can all be put aside? It can't. If you ask Anacha, I will wager anything you like that she can't look on the deaths in Galt with calm in her heart. Would you have me forgive them for what they've done to her as well? Gods, Danat. If what they've done isn't going too far, nothing is!"

"He isn't worried for them," Idaan said from the shadows. Otah turned. She was sitting alone at the back of the room, a lit pipe in her hand and pale smoke rising from her lips as she spoke. "He's saying there are crimes that can't be made right. Trying to make justice out of this will only make it last longer."

"So we should let it go?" Otah demanded. "We should meekly accept what they've done?"

"It was what you told Eiah to do," Danat said. "She wanted to find a way to heal the damage from Sterile; you told her to let it go and accept what had happened. Didn't you?"

Otah's clenched fists loosened. His mind clouded with rage and chagrin. Idaan's low chuckle filled the room like a growl.

"Which of us is innocent now, eh?" she said, waving her pipe. "It's easy to counsel forgiveness when you aren't the one swallowing poison. It's harder to forgive them for having won."

"What would you have me do, then?" Otah snapped.

"In your place, I'd kill them all before they could do more damage," Idaan said. "Maati, Vanjit, Eiah. All of them. Even Ashti Beg."

"That isn't an option," Otah said. "I won't kill Eiah."

"So you won't end them and you won't forgive them," Idaan said. "You want the world saved, but you don't know what that means any longer. There isn't much time to clear your mind, brother. And you can't put your thoughts in line when you're half-sunk in rage."

Danat took a pose of agreement.

"It's what I was trying to say," he said.

"Lift yourself above this," Idaan said. "See it as if you were someone else. Someone less hurt by it."

Otah lifted his hands, palms out, refusing it all. His jaw ached, but the heat in his chest and throat, the blood in his ears, washed him out of the room. He heard Danat cry out behind him, and Idaan's softer voice.

He stalked out to the road. No one followed. His mind was a cacophony of voices, all of them his own.

Alone on the dimming road, he excoriated Maati and Eiah, Danat and Idaan, Balasar and Sinja and Issandra Dasin. He muttered all the venom that rose to his lips, and, in time, he sat at the base of an ancient tree, throwing stones at nothing. The rage faded and left him as empty as an old skin. The sun was gone and the sky darkening blue to indigo and indigo to starlit black.

Alone as he had not been in years, he wept. At first it was only the loss of Sinja, but then of the fleet and Chaburi-Tan. Eiah and his warring senses of guilt and betrayal. Galt, blind and dying. It ended where he had known it would. All rivers led to the sea, and all his sorrows to the death of Kiyan.

"Oh, love," he said to the empty air. "Oh, my love. Can this never go well?"

Nothing answered back.

The tears faded. The sorrow and rage, spent, left his heart and mind clearer. The tree at his back scratched, its bark as rough as broken stone. It offered no comfort, but he let himself rest against it. He noticed the scent of fresh earth for the first time, and the hushing of a breeze that stirred the treetops without descending to the path they covered. A falling star lit the sky and was gone.

He must, Otah thought, have looked like he was on the edge of murder the whole day for his son and his sister to face him down that way. He must have seemed like a man gone mad. It was near enough to the truth.

The night air was cold and his robes insufficient. He went back to the wayhouse more for warmth than the desire to continue any conversation. There was an odd silence in his mind now that felt fragile and comforting. He knew as he stepped into the yard that he wouldn't be able to maintain it.

Voices raised in anger filled the yard. Danat and the captain of the armsmen stood so close to each other their chests nearly touched, each of them shouting at the other. Idaan stood at Danat's right, her arms crossed, her expression deceptively calm. The captain had his armsmen arrayed behind him, lit torches in their hands. Otah made out words like *protection* and *answerable* from the captain and *disrespect* and *mutiny* from Danat. Otah rubbed his hands together to fight off the numbness and made his way toward the confrontation. The captain saw him first and stopped talking, his face flushed red by blood and torchlight. Danat took a moment longer, then glanced over his shoulder.

"I suppose this is to do with me," Otah said.

"We only wanted to see that you were safe, Most High," the captain said. The words were strangled. Otah hesitated, then took a pose of apology.

"I needed solitude," he said. "I should have told you before I left. But if I'd been clear-minded, I likely wouldn't have needed to leave. Please accept my apology."

There was little enough the man could do. Moments later, the armsmen were scattering back to the wayhouse or the stables. The smell of doused torches filled the air like a forest on fire. Danat and Idaan stood side by side.

"Should I apologize to you as well?" Otah asked with a half-smile.

"Isn't called for," Idaan said. "I was only keeping your boy near to hand in case you reconsidered my death order."

"Next time, maybe," Otah said, and Idaan grinned. "Is there anything warm to drink in this place?"

The young keeper brought them the best food the wayhouse had to offer—river fish baked with red pepper and lemon, sweet rice, almond milk with mint, hot plum wine, and cold water. They arrayed themselves through the main room, all other guests being turned away by the paired guards at every door. Ana and Ashti Beg were in a deep conversation about the strategies they'd developed in their new sightlessness. Danat sat nearer the fire, watching them with a naked longing in his expression that would have made Ana blush, Otah thought, had she been able to see it. Otah and Idaan sat together at a low table, passing the chipped lacquer bowls back and forth. The armsmen who weren't on duty had taken a back room, and their voices came in occasional outbursts of hilarity and song.

It could have been the image of peace, of something approaching a family passing a road-wearied night in warmth and companionship. And perhaps it was. But it was other things as well.

"You look better," Idaan said, freshening the wine in his bowl. Fragrant steam rose from it, astringent and rich with the scent of the fruit.

"I am for now," Otah said. "I'll be worse again later."

"Have you made up your mind, then?" she asked. He sighed. Ashti Beg illustrated some point with a wide, vague gesture. Danat placed a new length of pine on the fire.

"There isn't an answer," Otah said. "They have all the power. All I can do is ask them to reconsider. So I suppose I'll do that and see what happens next. I know that you think I should go in and kill them all—"

"I didn't say that," Idaan said. "I said it was what I would do. My judgment on those matters is . . . occasionally suspect."

Otah sipped his wine, then put the bowl down carefully.

"I think that's the nearest you've ever come to apologizing," he said.

"To you, perhaps," Idaan said. "I spent years talking to the dead about it. They didn't have much to say back."

"Do you miss them?"

"Yes," Idaan said without hesitation. "I do."

They lapsed into silence again. Danat and Ashti Beg were in the middle of a lively debate over the ethics of showfighting, Ana listening to them both with a frown. Her hand pressed her belly as if the fish was troubling her.

"If Maati were here tonight," Otah said, "and demanded that he be named emperor, I think I'd give it to him."

"He'd hand it back in a week," Idaan said with a smile.

"Who's to say I'd take it?"

They left in the morning, the horses rested or changed for fresh, the carts restocked with wood and coal and water. Ana looked worse, but kept a brave face. Idaan stayed with her like a personal guard, to Danat's visible annoyance. A cold wind haunted them, striking leaves from the trees.

News of the Emperor's party came close to overwhelming stories of the mysterious baby at the wayhouse. No couriers came to trouble Otah with word of fire or death. Twice, Otah dreamed that Sinja was riding at his side, robes soaked with seawater and black as a bat's wing, and he woke each time with an obscure feeling of peace. And with every stop, they found the poets had passed before them more and more recently.

Three days ago. Then two.

When they reached the river Qiit, tea-dark with newly fallen leaves, just the day before.

24

>+< The cold caught up with them in the middle of the day, a wind from the west that rattled the trees and sent tiny whitecaps across the river's back. They had covered a great stretch of river in their day's travel, but night meant landing. The boatman was adamant. The river, he said, was a living thing; it changed from one journey to the next. Sandbars shifted, rocks lurked where none had been before. The boat was shallow enough to pass over many dangers, but a log invisible in the darkness could break a hole in the deck. Better to run in the daylight than swim in the dark. The way the boatman said it left no room for disagreement.

They camped at the riverside, and awakened with tents and robes soaked heavy by dew. Morning light saw them on the water again, the boiler at the stern muttering angrily to itself, the paddle wheel punishing the water.

Maati sat away from the noise, huddled in two wool robes, and watched the trees march from the north to the south like an army bent on sacking Saraykeht. Large Kae and Small Kae sat in the stern, making conversation with the boatman and his second when the men would deign to speak. Vanjit and Eiah turned around each other, one in the bow, the other in the center of the craft, both maintaining a space between them, the andat watching with rage and hunger in its black eyes. It was like watching an alley-mouth knife fight drawn out over hours and days.

It was hard now to remember the days before they had been splintered. The years he had spent in hiding had seemed like a punishment at the time. Living in warehouses, giving the lectures he half-recalled from his own youth and half-invented anew, trying to understand the ways in which a woman's mind was not a man's and how that power could be channeled into grammar. He had resented it. He recalled crawling onto a cot, exhausted from the day's work. He could still picture the expressions of hunger and determination on their faces. He had not seen it then, but it had all of it been driven by hope. Even the sorrow and mourning that came after a binding failed and they lost someone to the andat's grim price had held a sense of community.

Now they had won, and the world seemed all cold wind and dark water. Even the two Kaes seemed to have set themselves apart from Vanjit, from Eiah, from himself. The nights of conversation and food and laughter were gone like a pleasant dream. They had created a women's grammar and the price was higher than he could have imagined.

Murder. He was planning to murder one of his own.

As he had expected, the boat was too small for any more private conversations. He had managed no more than a few moments with Eiah when none of the others were paying them attention. Something in Vanjit's wine, perhaps, to slow her mind and deepen her sleep. She mustn't know that the blow was coming.

He could see that it weighed on Eiah as much as it did upon him. She sat carving soft wood with a knife wherever Vanjit was not, her mouth in a vicious scowl. The wax tablets that had been her whole work before he'd come to her lay stacked in a crate. The latest version of Wounded, waiting for his analysis and approval. He imagined the two of them would sit nearer each other if it weren't for the fear that Vanjit would suspect them of plotting. And he would not fear that except that it was truth.

For their own part, Vanjit and Clarity-of-Sight held to themselves. Poet and andat in apparent harmony, watching the night sky or penetrating the secrets of wood and water that only she could see. Vanjit hadn't offered to share the wonders the andat revealed since before they had left the school, and Maati couldn't bring himself to ask the favor. Not knowing what he knew. Not intending what he intended.

When evening came, the boatman sang out, his second joining the high whooping call. There was no reason for it that Maati could see, only the habit of years. The boat angled its way to a low, muddy bank. When the water was still enough, the second dropped over the side and slogged to the line of trees, a rope thick as his arm trailing behind him. Once the rope had been made fast to the trees, he called out again, and the boatman shifted the mechanism of the boiler from paddle wheel to winch, and the great rope went taut. It creaked with the straining, and river water flowed from the strands as if giant hands were wringing it. By the time the boatman stopped, the craft was almost jumping distance from the shore and felt as solid as a building. It made Maati uncomfortable, afraid that they had grounded it so well that they wouldn't be able to free it in the morning. The boatman and his second showed no unease.

A wide plank made a bridge between boat and shore. The boatman wrestled it into place with a stream of perfunctory vulgarity. The second, his robes soaked and muddied, trotted back onto the deck.

"We're doing well, eh?" Maati said to the boatman. "The distance we went today must have been four days' ride."

"We'll do well enough," the boatman agreed. "Have you in Utani before the last leaf drops, that's certain."

Large Kae went across to the shore, two tents on her wide back. Eiah was just behind her with a crate of food to make the evening meal. The twilight sky was gray streaked with gold, and the calls of birds gave some hint to where the boatman's songs had found their start. On another night, it would have been beautiful.

"How many days do you think that would be?" Maati asked, trying to keep his tone light and friendly. From the boatman's perfunctory smile, it wasn't an unfamiliar question.

"Six days," the boatman said. "Seven. If it's been raining to the north and the river starts running faster, it could go past that, but this time of year, that's rare."

Vanjit shifted past them, brushing against Maati as she stepped onto the plank. The andat was curled against her, its head resting on her shoulder like a tired child might.

"Thank you," Maati said.

They made camp a dozen yards inland, where the ground was dry. It was habit now. Routine. Eiah dug the fire pit, Small Kae gathered wood. Large Kae put the sleeping tents in place. Irit would have started cooking, but Maati knew well enough how to take her part. A few bowlfuls of river water, crushed lentils that had been soaking since morning, slivers of salted pork, an onion they'd hauled almost from the school. It made for a better soup than Maati had first expected, though the gods all knew he was tired of it now. It would keep them alive until morning.

Vanjit stepped out of the shadows just as Maati filled a bowl for the boatman, the andat on one hip, a satchel on the other. Everyone was aware that she hadn't helped to make camp. No one complained. In the firelight, she looked younger even than she was. Her eyes flashed, and she smiled.

Vanjit sat at Maati's side, accepting the next full bowl. The andat rested at her feet, shifting its weight as if to crawl away but then shifting back. The boatman and his second went back to their boat, bowls steaming in their hands. It was, Maati supposed, all well for passengers to sleep on the shore, but someone needed to stay with the boat. Better for them as well. It would have been awkward, explaining why the baby's breath didn't fog.

When they had gone, Eiah rose to her feet. The darkness under her eyes was dispelled by her smile. The others looked up at her.

"I would like to announce a small celebration," she said. "I've been reworking the binding for Wounded, and as of today, the latest version is complete."

Small Kae smiled and applauded. Large Kae grinned. Eiah made a show of pulling a wineskin from her bags. They all applauded now. Even Vanjit. But Eiah's gaze faltered when her eyes met Maati's, and his belly soured.

Something in her wine to deepen her sleep. She mustn't see the blow coming.

"Yes," Maati said, trying to hide his fear. "Yes, I think celebration is in order."

"You've seen the new draft?" Vanjit asked as Eiah poured the wine into bowls. "Is it ready?"

"I haven't been through it all as yet," he said. "There are some changes that make me optimistic. By Udun, I'll have a better-informed opinion."

The two Kaes were toasting each other, the fire. Eiah came to Maati and Vanjit. She pressed bowls into their hands, and went back to pour one for herself. Maati drank quickly, grateful for something to do that would occupy his hands and his mind. If only for a moment.

Vanjit swirled her wine bowl, looking down at it with what might have been serenity.

"Maati-kvo," Vanjit said. "Do you remember when I first came to you? Gods, it seems like it was a different life, doesn't it? You were outside Shosheyn-Tan."

"Lachi," Eiah said from across the fire.

"Of course," Vanjit said. "I remember now. I met Umnit at a bathhouse, and we'd started talking. She brought me to Eiah-cha, and Eiah brought me to you. It was that abandoned house, the one with all the mice."

"I remember," Maati said. The two Kaes exchanged a glance that Maati didn't understand. Vanjit laughed, throwing back her head.

"I can't think what you saw in me back then," she said. "I must have looked like something the dogs wouldn't eat."

"They were lean times for all of us," Maati said, forcing a jovial tone.

"Not for you," she said. "Not with Eiah to look after you. No, don't you pretend that she hasn't supported us all from the start. Without her, we would never have come this far."

Eiah took a pose that accepted the compliment and raised her wine bowl, but Vanjit still didn't drink from her own. Maati willed her to drink the poison, to end this.

"I think of who I was then," Vanjit said, her voice soft and contemplative. She sounded like a child. Or worse, like a grown woman trying to sound childish. "Lost. Empty. And then the gods touched my shoulder and turned me toward you. All of you, really. You've been the only family I've ever had. I mean, since the Galts came."

At her feet, Clarity-of-Sight wailed as if heartbroken. Vanjit turned to it, her brow furrowed in concentration. The andat squirmed, shuddered, and became still. The tension in Maati's shoulders was spreading to his throat. He could see Eiah's hands clutching her bowl.

"The only family I've had," Vanjit said, as if finding her place in a practiced speech. And then softly, "Did you think I wouldn't know?"

Large Kae put down her bowl, her gaze shifting from Eiah to Vanjit and back. Maati shifted to the side, his throat almost too tight for words.

"Know what?" he asked. The words came out stilted and rough. Even he wasn't convinced by them. Vanjit stared at him, disappointment in her expression. No one moved, but Maati felt something shifting in his eyes. The andat's attention was on him, the tiny face growing more and more detailed with each heartbeat.

Vanjit held out the poisoned wine bowl. The color was wrong. No human would ever have seen the difference, but with the andat driving his vision and hers, there was no mistaking it. The deep red had a greenish taint that no other bowl suffered.

"What . . . what's that?" Maati squeaked.

"I don't know," Vanjit said in a voice that meant she did. "Perhaps you should drink it for me, and we could see. But no. You're too valuable. Eiah, perhaps?"

"I'm sorry. Did I not clean the bowl well enough?" Eiah asked.

Vanjit threw her bowl into the fire, flames hissing and smoke rushing up in a cloud. There was rage in her expression.

"Vanjit," Eiah said. "I don't think . . ."

Vanjit ignored them, untying her satchel with a fast scrabbling motion. When she lifted it, blocks of wax spilled out, gray and white, like rotten ice. Maati saw bits of Eiah's writing cut into them.

"You were going to kill me," Vanjit said.

Eiah took a pose that denied the charge. The firelight flickered over Vanjit's face, and for a moment, Maati thought the poet might believe the lie. He cleared his throat.

"We wouldn't do that," he said.

Vanjit turned to him, her expression empty and mad. At his feet, the andat made a sound that might have been a warning or a laugh.

"Do you think he only speaks to you?" Vanjit spat.

Maati sputtered, falling back a step when Vanjit lunged forward. She only scooped up the andat, turned, and ran into the darkness.

Maati scrambled after her, calling her name with a deepening sense of despair. The trees were shadows within the night's larger darkness. His voice seemed too weak to carry more than a few paces before him. It couldn't have been more than half a hand—less than that, certainly—when he stopped to catch his breath. Leaning against an ancient ash, he realized that Vanjit was gone and he was lost, only the soft rushing of the river away to his left still there to guide him. He picked his way back, trying to follow the route he had taken and failing. A carpet of dry leaves made his steps loud. Something shifted in the branches overhead. The cold numbed his fingers and toes. The half-moon glimmering among the branches assured him that he had not been blinded. It was the only comfort he had.

In the end, he made his way east until he found the river, and then south to the wide mud where the boat still rested. It was simple enough to find the little camp after that. He tried to nurture some hope that he would step into the circle of firelight to find Vanjit returned and, through some unimagined turn of events, peace restored. The laughter and soft company of the first days of the school returned; time unwound, and his life ready to be lived again without the errors. He wanted it to be true so badly that when he stumbled into the clearing and found Eiah and the two Kaes seated by the fire, he almost thought they were well.

Eiah turned gray, fogged eyes toward him.

"Who's there?" she demanded at the sound of his approaching steps.

"It's me," Maati said, wheezing. "I'm fine. But Vanjit's gone."

Large Kae began to weep. Small Kae put an arm over the woman's shaking shoulders and murmured something, her eyes closed and tear-streaked. Maati sat at the fire. His bowl of soup had overturned.

"She's done for the three of us," Eiah said. "None of us can see at all."

"I'm sorry," Maati said. It was profoundly inadequate.

"Can you help me?" Eiah said, gesturing toward something Maati couldn't fathom. Then he saw the pile of wax fragments. "I think I have them all, but it's hard to be sure."

"Leave them," Maati said. "Let them go."

"I can't," Eiah said. "I have to try the thing. I can do it now. Tonight."

Maati looked at her. The fire popped, and she shifted her head toward the sound. Her jaw was set, her gray eyes angry. The cold wind made her robes flutter at her ankles like a flag.

"No," he said. "You can't."

"I have been studying this for weeks," Eiah said, her voice sharpening. "Only help me put these back together, and I can . . . ."

"You can die," Maati said. "I know you've changed the binding. You *won't* do this. Not until we can study it. Too much rides on Wounded to rush into the binding in a panic. We'll wait. Vanjit may come back."

"Maati-kvo—" Eiah began.

"She is alone in the forest with nothing to sustain her. She's cold and frightened and betrayed," Maati said. "Put yourself in her place. She's discovered that the only friends she had in the world were planning to kill her. The andat must certainly be pushing for its freedom with all its power. She didn't even have the soup before she went. She's cold and hungry and confused, and we are the only place she can go for help or comfort."

"All respect, Maati-kvo," Small Kae said, "but that first part was along the lines that you were going to *kill* her. She won't come back."

"We don't know that," Maati said. "We can't yet be sure."

But morning came without Vanjit. The sky became a lighter black, and then gray. Morning birds broke into their chorus of chatters and shrieks; finches and day larks and other species Maati couldn't name. The trees deepened, rank after ragged rank becoming first gray and then brown and then real. Poet and andat were gone into the wild, and as the dawn crept up rosy and wild in the east, it became clear they were not going to return.

Maati built a small fire from last night's embers and brewed tea for the four of them still remaining. Large Kae wouldn't stop crying despite Small Kae's constant attentions. Eiah sat wrapped in her robes from the previous night. She looked drawn. Maati pressed a bowl of warm tea into her hand. Neither spoke.

At the end, Maati took the belts from their spare robes and used them to make a line. He led Eiah, Eiah led Small Kae, and Small Kae led Large Kae. It was the obscene parody of a game he'd played as a child, and he walked the path back to the boat, calling out the obstacles he passed—log, step down, be careful of the mud. They left the sleeping tents and cooking things behind.

To Maati's surprise, the boat was already floating. The boatman and his second were moving over the craft with the ease and silence of long practice. When he called out, the boatman stopped and stared. The man's mouth gaped in surprise; the first strong reaction Maati had seen from him.

"No," the boatman said. "This wasn't the agreement. Where's the other one? The one with the babe?"

"I don't know," Maati called out. "She left in the night."

The second, guessing the boatman's mind, started to pull in the plank that bridged boat and sticky, dark mud. Maati yelped, dropped Eiah's lead, and lumbered out into the icy flow, grabbing at the retreating wood.

"We didn't contract for this," the boatman said. "Missing girls, blinded ones? No, there wasn't anything about this."

"We'll die if you leave us," Eiah said.

"That one can see after you," the boatman called, gesturing pointlessly at Maati, hip deep in river mud. It would have been comic if it had been less terrible.

"He's old and he's dying," Eiah said, and lifted her physician's satchel as if to prove the gravity of her opinion. "If he has an attack, you'll be leaving all the women out here to die."

The boatman scowled, looking from Maati to Eiah and back. He spat into the river.

"To the first low town," he said. "I'll take you that far, and no farther."

"That's all we can ask," Eiah said.

Maati thought he heard Small Kae mutter, *I could ask more than that*, but he was too busy pulling the plank into position to respond. It was a tricky business, guiding all three women into the boat, but Maati and the second managed it, soaking only Small Kae's hem. Maati, when at last he pulled himself onto the boat, was cold water and black mud from waist to boots. He made his miserable way to the stern, sitting as near the kiln as the boatman would allow. Eiah called out for him, following the sound of his voice until she sat at his side. The boatman and his second wouldn't speak to either of them or meet Maati's eyes. The second walked to the bow, manipulated something Maati couldn't make out, and called out. The boatman replied, and the boat shifted, its wheel clattering and pounding. They lurched out into the stream.

They were leaving Vanjit behind. The only poet in the world, her andat on her hip, alone in the forest with autumn upon them. What would she do? How would she live, and if she despaired, what vengeance would she exact upon the world? Maati looked at the dancing flames within the kiln.

"South would be faster," Maati said. The boatman glanced at him, shrugged, and sang out something Maati couldn't make out. The second called back, and the boatman turned the rudder. The sound of the paddle wheel deepened, and the boat lurched.

"Uncle?" Eiah asked.

"It's all fallen apart," Maati said. "We can't manage this from here. Tracking her through half the wilds south of Utani? We need men. We need help."

"Help," Eiah said, as if he'd suggested pulling down the stars. Maati tried to speak, but something equally sorrow and rage closed his throat. He muttered an obscenity and then forced the words free.

"We need Otah-kvo," Maati said.

25

>+<   "Will you go back?" Ana asked. "When this is over, I mean."

"It depends on what you mean by *over*," Idaan said. "You mean once my brother talks the poets into bringing back all the dead in Galt and Chaburi-Tan, rebuilding the city, killing the pirates, and then releasing the andat and drowning all their books? Because if that's what *over* looks like, you're waiting for yesterday."

Otah shifted, pretending he was still asleep. The sun of late morning warmed his face and robes, the low chuckle of the river against the sides of the boat and the low, steady surge of the paddle wheel became a kind of music. It had been easy enough to drowse, but his body ached and pinched and complained despite three layers of tapestry between his back and the deck. If he rose, there would be conversations and planning and decisions. As long as he could maintain the fiction of unconsciousness, he could allow himself to drift. It passed poorly for comfort, but it passed.

"You can't think we'll be chasing these people for the rest of our lives, though," Ana said.

"I'm hoping we live longer than that, yes," Idaan said. "So. If this ends in a way that lets me return to him, then I will. I enjoy Cehmai's company."

"And he'll take you back in, even after you've been gone this long?"

Otah could hear the smile in Idaan's voice when she replied.

"He's overlooked worse from me. Why do you ask?"

"I don't know," Ana said. And then a moment later, "Because I'm trying to imagine it. What the world will be. I've never traveled outside Galt before, except one negotiation in Eymond. I keep thinking of going back to it. Acton. Kirinton. But it's not there anymore."

"Not the way it was," Idaan agreed. "We can't be sure how bad it is, but I'll swear it isn't good."

The silence was only a lack of voices. The river, the birds, the wind all went on with their long, inhuman conversation. It wasn't truly silence, it only felt that way.

"I think about what I would do without all of you," Ana said. "And then I imagine . . . What would you do if a city caught fire and no one could see it? How would you put it out?"

"You wouldn't," Idaan said. Her voice was cool and matter-of-fact.

"I think about that," Ana said. "I think about it more now. The future, the things that can go wrong. Dangers. I wonder if that always happens when—"

Idaan had made a clicking sound, tongue against teeth.

"You're not fooling anyone, brother," Idaan said. "We all know you're awake."

Otah rolled onto his back, his eyes still closed, and took a pose of abject denial. Idaan chuckled. He opened his eyes to the great pale blue dome of the sky, the sun burning white overhead and searing his eyes. He sat up slowly, his back as bruised as if someone had beaten him.

Ashti Beg lay a few yards off, her arm curved under her to cradle her sleeping head. Two armsmen sat at either side of their boat with pairs at the stern and the bow, keeping watch on the changeless river. Danat had joined the watchers at the bow and seemed to be having a conversation with them. It was good to see it. Otah had been concerned after his disappearance at the wayhouse that Danat and the captain of the guard might have found themselves on bad terms. Danat seemed to be making it his work to see that didn't happen.

The boat itself was smaller than Otah would have chosen, but the kilns at the back were solid, the wheel new, and the alternatives had been few. When there are only three boats on the riverfront, even being emperor won't create a fourth. Ana and Idaan were sitting side by side on a shin-high bench, their hands clasped.

It was something Otah had noticed before, the tendency of Ana and Ashti Beg to touch people. As if the loss of their eyes had left them hungry for something, and this lacing of fingers was the nearest they could come.

"You both look lovely," Otah said.

"Your hair looks like mice have been building a nest in it," Idaan said.

Otah confirmed her assessment with his fingertips. The fact of the matter was that none of them was presentable. Too many weeks on the road bathing with rags and tepid water had left them looking disreputable. Somewhere just east of Pathai, they had been joined by a colony of lice that still took up their evenings. Otah imagined walking into the palaces at Utani as he now was and smiled.

He walked to the edge of the boat where a bucket and rope stood ready for moments like this. With the armsmen looking on, he lowered the line himself and hauled up the water. When he knelt and poured it over his head, it was as if he could feel ice forming in his mind. He whooped and shuddered, pulling his hair back. Idaan, behind him, was laughing. He made his way back to them, Ana holding out a length of cloth for him to take and dry himself.

And that was the nature of the journey. Tragedy lay behind them, and desperate uncertainty ahead. He was gnawed by his fears and his guilt and his sorrow, but his sister was there, laughing with him. His son. The river was cold and uncomfortable and beautiful. Every day meant more dead, and yet there was no way for them to move faster than the boat would carry them. Otah knew that as a younger man, he would have been sitting at the bow, frowning at the water as if by will alone he could make things into something they weren't. As an old one, he was able to put it all aside for as much as a hand at a time, holding his energy for the moment when it might effect a change and resting until then. Perhaps it was what the philosophers meant by wisdom.

Somewhere ahead, Maati and Eiah and the new poet were making their own way to Utani and, he thought, the proclamation of their victory. Perhaps Eiah would bind her andat as well, and return to the women of the Khaiate cities their wombs. There would be children again, a new generation to take the place of the old. All that would be sacrificed was Galt, and the world would be put back as it was. An empire now, instead of a scattering of cities, but with the andat, slaves of spirit and will, putting them above the rest of the world.

Until a new Balasar Gice found a way to bring it all down, and the cycle of suffering and desperation began anew.

"You've gone solemn," Idaan said.

"Steeling myself for failure," Otah said. "We'll be on them soon, I think. And . . ."

"You've been thinking about forgiveness," Idaan said. Otah looked at Ana, listening, rapt. Idaan shook her head. "The girl's strong enough to know the truth. There's no virtue in softening it."

"Please," Ana said.

Otah took a deep breath and let it slide out between his teeth. River water traced a cold path down his back. On the east bank, half a hundred crows took to the air, startled by something on the ground or just one another.

"If we lose Galt," Otah said, stopped, and began again, more slowly. "If we lose Galt, I don't believe I can forgive them. I know what you said, and Danat. I should. I should do whatever it takes to stop all this, even if it means agreeing that I've lost, but it's beyond me. I'm too old to forgive anymore, and . . ."

"And," Idaan said, making it sound like agreement.

"I don't understand," Ana said.

"That's because you haven't killed anyone," Idaan said. Otah looked up at her. Idaan's eyes were dark but not unsympathetic. When she went on, the words were addressed to Ana, but her gaze was fixed on his. "There are some things about my brother that few people know. His best friend, Maati, was one who knew his secrets. And because of Maati, Cehmai. And so I am also one of the few to know what happened all those years ago in Saraykeht."

To his surprise, Otah found himself weeping silently. Ana leaned forward, her brow fierce.

"What happened?" she asked.

"I killed a good man. An honorable, unwell man with a wounded soul," Otah said softly. "I strangled him to death in a little room off a mud-paved alley in the soft quarter."

"Why?" Ana asked.

The answers to that seemed so intricate, so complex, he couldn't find words.

Idaan could.

"To save Galt," she said. "If the man had lived, all of Galt would have at least suffered horribly, and likely been wiped from the map. Otah had the choice of condemning his city or letting thousands upon thousands upon thousands of your countrymen die. He chose to betray Saraykeht. He's carried it ever since. He's ordered men killed in war. He's sentenced them to death. But he's only ever ended one life himself. Seen something that had been a man become only a body. If you haven't done it, it's a hard thing to understand."

"That's truth," Otah said.

"And along with all the other insults and injuries and pain that he's caused. Along with the deaths," Idaan said, sorrow and amusement mixed in her voice, "Maati Vaupathai has taken away the thing that made Otah's slaughter bearable. He took away the reason for it. Galt is dying anyway."

"I also did it for Maati," Otah said. "If I hadn't, he'd be fighting against Seedless today."

"And I wouldn't have been born," Ana said. She put out a wavering hand to him, and Otah took it. Her grasp was stronger than he'd expected. There were tears in her milky eyes. "I won't forgive him either."

Idaan sighed.

"Well," his sister said, "at least we'll be damned for what we are."

The second sang something from the bow, a high trill that ended in words Otah couldn't make sense of. The paddle wheel, in the stern, shifted and creaked, the deck beneath him lurching. Otah stood, unsteadily.

"Sandbar," Danat called to him. "It's all right. We're fine."

"Ah, well then. You see?" Idaan said with a chuckle. "We're fine."

They stayed on the river as long into the twilight as they could. Otah could see the unease in the boatman's expression and hear it in his voice. Otah's assumption was that the boats would travel at nearly the same speed. The gap between his party and Maati's would only keep narrowing if he pushed farther past the point of safety than they were willing to do. He thought his chances good. Maati, after all, had all the power, and time was his ally. There was no reason that he should rush.

They put in at a riverfront town half a hand after sundown. A small, rotting peer. A pack of half-feral dogs baying at the boatman's second as he made the boat fast and stretched a wide, arching bridge between the deck and the land. A handful of lights in the darkness that showed where lanterns burned like fireflies in the night.

While the armsmen unloaded their crates and skipped stones at the dogs' feet, Otah led Ashti Beg across to solid land, Idaan and Ana close behind. In the night, the moon and stars obscured by almost-bare branches, Otah felt hardly more sure of himself than did Ashti Beg. But then a local boy appeared with a lantern dancing at the end of a pole to lead them to the wayhouse. They walked slowly despite the cold, as if sitting on the deck all day had been the most wearying work imaginable. Otah found himself walking to one side of the group, hanging back with Danat at his side. It wasn't until his son spoke that Otah noticed that he'd been herded there like an errant sheep.

"I'm sorry, Papa-kya," Danat said, softly. "I need to speak with you."

Otah took a pose that granted his permission.

"You spoke with Ana earlier," Danat said. "I saw she took your hand. It looked . . . it looked like she was crying."

"Yes," Otah said.

"Was it about me?" Danat asked. "Was it something I've done wrong?"

Otah's expression alone must have been enough to answer the question. Danat looked around, shame in his face.

"She's avoiding me," Danat said.

"She's blind, and we've been sunrise to sunset on a boat smaller than my bedchamber," Otah said. "How could she possibly avoid you?"

"It wasn't today. It's been . . . it's been weeks. I thought at first it was only that Idaan and Ashti Beg joined us. There were women here, and Ana-cha felt more comfortable in their company. But it's more than that, and . . ."

Danat ran a hand through his hair. In the dim light of the lantern, Otah could see the single crease in his brow, like a paint mark.

"I don't know what to say. She's done nothing in my presence to make me suspect she's anything but fond of you. If anything, she seems stronger for having come with us."

Danat raised his hands toward some formal pose, but skidded in the mud. When he regained his balance, whatever he'd intended to express was forgotten. Otah put a hand on the boy's shoulder.

The wayhouse was a series of low buildings built of fired brick. The stable squatted across a thin, stone-paved road, a single light burning at its side where, Otah assumed, a guard slept. The wayhouse keeper stood outside, her hands on her hips and a dusting of flour streaking her robe. The captain of the guard stood before her, his arms crossed, while the keeper turned her head from side to side like a cat uncertain which window to flee through. When she saw Otah walking toward them, her face went pale and she took a pose of welcome and obeisance that bent her almost double.

"There's a problem?" Otah asked.

"There aren't rooms," the captain said. "All filled up, she says."

"Ah," Otah said, but before he could say more the captain turned on him. Even in the dim light, he could see a banked rage in the man's eyes. The captain took a pose that requested an audience more formal than the occasion called for. Otah replied with one, equally formal, that granted it.

"All respect, Most High, I have done my best all this campaign to respect your wishes. You want to dunk your head in river water, I haven't objected. You run off into the wilderness for half an evening with no guard or escort, and I've accepted that. But if you are about to suggest that we put the Emperor of the Khaiem in a sleeping tent in a wayhouse courtyard because someone else *got here first*, I'm resigning my commission."

"Actually, I was going to suggest that we offer the present guests our tents and compensation for their rooms," Otah said. "It seemed polite."

"Ah. Yes, Most High," the captain said. It was hard to tell in the night whether the man was blushing.

"There's room in the stables," the keeper said. She had an eastern accent.

"Yalakeht?" Otah asked, and the woman blinked.

"I grew up there," she said, a note of awe in her voice. As if recognizing an accent were a sign of supernatural power.

"It's a good city," Otah said. "Would there be room enough for your present guests if we put my guardsmen in the stables as well?"

"We'll *find* space, Most High," the keeper said.

"Then I'll go negotiate rooms for us," Otah said, and to the captain, "It might be more impressive if I went in with a guard. They'll be less likely to mistake me for a fraud."

"I . . . yes, Most High," the captain said.

The air in the wayhouse was thickened by a chimney with a poor draw. Smoke haze gave the place a feeling of dread and poverty. The tables were dark wood, the floors packed earth. A dozen men and women sat in groups, a few in a smaller room to the side. All eyes were on the guard as they strode in and took formal stances. Otah stepped in.

The movement that stopped him was so slight it might almost not have existed and familiar enough to disorient him. A woman by the fire grate with her back to him shifted her shoulders. In anyone else, it would have been beneath notice. Otah stood, stunned, his heart thudding like it was trying to break free of his ribs. Idaan appeared at his side, her hand on his arm. He motioned her back.

"Eiah?" he said.

The woman by the fire turned to him. Her face was thin and drawn, older than time alone could explain. Her eyes were the same milky gray as Ana's.

"Father," she said.

26

The years had changed Otah Machi. The last time Maati had seen him, his hair had been black or near enough to pass. His shoulders had been broader, his eyebrows smooth. The man who stood before the smoking fire grate now was thinner, his skin loose against his face. His robes, though travel-stained, were of the finest cloth. They draped him like an altar; they made him more than a man. Or perhaps Otah Machi had always been something more than the usual and his robes only reminded them.

Danat, at his father's side, was unrecognizable. The ill, coughing boy confined to his bed had grown into a hale young man with intelligent eyes and his father's distant, considering demeanor. The others Maati had either seen recently enough that they held no disturbing sense of change or were strangers to him.

They had all come. Large Kae and Small Kae and Eiah, but to his discomfort also Idaan Machi, sitting on a bench with a bowl of wine in her hand and her face as expressionless as the dead. A Galtic girl sat apart, her head held high, sightless and proud to cover the disgust and horror she must feel at all Maati had done. Ashti Beg sat at her side, another victim of Vanjit's malice. After all that had happened, after all his many failures of judgment, seeing her among his arrayed enemies was still wrenching.

Otah's armsmen cleared the wayhouse. The conversation that should have taken place in the finest of meeting rooms in the high palaces instead found its place in a third-rate wayhouse, free of ceremony or ritual or even well-brewed tea. Maati felt himself trembling. He had the powerful physical memory of being a boy at the school, holding himself still and waiting for Tahi-kvo's lacquer rod to split his skin.

"Maati Vaupathai," the Emperor said.

"Most High," Maati replied, crossing his arms.

"I suppose I should start by asking why I shouldn't have you killed where you stand."

Eiah, beside him, twitched as if wasp-stung. Maati stared at his old friend, his old enemy, and all the conciliatory words that he had imagined in the last day vanished like a snuffed candle. There was rage in Otah's stance, and Maati found himself more than matching it.

"How dare you?" Maati said, his voice little more than a hiss. "How *dare* you? I thought, coming here, I would at least be treated with respect. I thought at the very least, that. And instead you stand me up like a common thief in a low-town courtroom and have me defend my life? Justify my right to breathe to the man who killed my son?"

"Nayiit has nothing to do with this," Otah said. "Sinja Ajutani, to contrast, died because of you. Every Galt who has starved since you exacted this sick, petty revenge is dead because of you. Every—"

"Nayiit has *everything* to do with this. Your sick love of all things Galtic has everything to do with it. Your disloyalty to the women you claim to rule. Your perfect calm in making me an outcast living in gutters for something you were just as guilty of. You are a hypocrite and a liar in everything you've done. I owe you nothing, Otah-kvo. *Nothing!*"

Otah was shouting something, but Maati's ears were rushing with blood and raw anger. He saw the armsmen shift forward, blades at the ready, but Maati was far past caring. Every injustice, every slight, every cupful of pent-up outrage spilled out, all made worse by the fact that Otah—self-righteous, entitled, and arrogant—was so busy shouting back that he wasn't hearing a word of what Maati was saying.

When he noticed through his rage that a third voice had entered the fray, he couldn't say how long it had been going.

"I said *stop!*" the Galt shouted again. "Stop it! Both of you!"

Maati turned to the girl, a sneer on his lip, but he was having a hard time catching his breath. Otah also was now silent, his imperial face flushed bright red. Maati felt the urge to offer up an obscene gesture, but he restrained himself. The girl stood in the space between the two, her hands outstretched. Danat stepped to her side. If anything, her anger appeared as high as either of her elders', but she was able to speak coherently.

"Gods," she said. "Is this really what we've been doing? Someone please tell me that the world is on its knees over something more than two old men chewing over quarrels from their boyhood."

"This is much, much more than that," Otah said. His voice, though severe, had lost some of its certainty.

"I wouldn't know from listening to that display," Idaan said. "Ana-cha has more sense than you on this, brother. Listen to her."

Otah had calmed down enough to look merely peeved. Maati held his fist to his chest, but his heart was slowing to its usual pace. Nothing had happened. He was fine. Otah, across from him, took a pose appropriate to the beginning of a short break in a negotiation. His jaw was tight and his stance only civil. Maati replied with one that accepted the proposal. He wanted to sit at Eiah's side, to talk with her about what to do next and how to go about it. It would have been a provocation, though, so instead, Maati retreated to the door leading out into the cold, black courtyard and the clean night air.

It had been a mistake. Otah was too proud and self-centered to help them. He was too wrapped up in anger that the world hadn't followed his one and only holy and anointed plan. They should have gone on to Utani, found someone in the utkhaiem who would support them. Or they should have gone after Vanjit themselves.

They should have done anything but this.

Voices came from behind him. Danat's, Otah's, Eiah's. They sounded tense, but they weren't shouting. Maati pressed his hands into their opposite sleeves and watched his breath steam like a soup kettle. He wondered where Vanjit was and how she was keeping warm. It seemed the woman had become two different people in his mind—one, the girl who had come to him in despair and been given hope again, the other a half-mad poet he'd loosed on the world. The impulses to kill her and to see to her care shouldn't have been able to exist in him at the same time, and yet there they were. He prayed she was dead, and he hoped she was well.

Between that and seeing Otah again, his head was buzzing like a hive.

"We've reached a conclusion," Idaan said from behind him. He turned. She was standing in the doorway, blocking the light. His belly itched where her assassin had stabbed him all those years before.

"Should I be grateful?" Maati asked. Idaan ignored the jab.

"If you and Otah can't play gently, and it's clear as the moon that you can't, we're going to go through channels. Eiah's talking with Danat. They sent me to speak with you."

"Ah, because we're such excellent friends?"

"Say it's because our relationship is simpler," Idaan said. Her voice took on the texture of cast iron. "Tell me what happened."

Maati leaned against the rough wall and shook his head. He'd become too excited, and now that he was calming, it was coming out in an urge to weep. He would not under any circumstances allow that in front of Idaan. Idaan, who'd tried to have Otah killed and had now become

his traveling companion. What more did anyone need to know to understand how far Otah had fallen?

"Maati," Idaan said, her voice still hard. "Now."

He began with leaving the school, Eiah's opinion of his health, Vanjit's escalating unreliability. The story took on a rhythm as he told it, the
words putting themselves in order as if he had practiced it all before.
Idaan didn't speak, but her listening was intense, drawing detail from
him almost against his will.

It was as if he were telling himself what had happened, offering a
kind of confession to the empty night, Idaan Machi—of all people in the
world, Idaan Machi—as his intercessor.

He reached the end—Vanjit's discovery of the poison, her escape, his
decision to find help. Somewhere in the course of things, he'd let himself slip to the ground, sitting with his legs stuck out before him and the
stone paving leaching the warmth from his body. Idaan squatted beside
him. He imagined that the manner of her listening had softened, as if
silences could differ like speech.

"I see," she said. "Well. Who'd have thought this would become
worse?"

"You led him to us," Maati said.

"I did my best," Idaan agreed. "It's been years since I put my hand to
this kind of work. I'm out of practice, but I did what I could."

"All to regain his imperial favor," Maati said. "I would never have
guessed that you'd become his toady."

"Actually, I started it to protect Cehmai," Idaan said as if he had offered her no insult. "With you stirring up the mud, I was afraid for him.
I wanted Otah to know that he wasn't part of it. And then, once I was at
the court . . . well, I had amends to make to Danat."

"The boy?"

"No. The one he's named for," Idaan said. She heaved a great sigh.
"But back to the matter at hand, eh? I understand how hard and confus-
ing it is to love someone you hate. I really do. And if you call me his
toady again, I swear by all the gods there ever were, I'll disjoint your fingers. Understood?"

"I didn't mean for it to happen like this," Maati said. "I wanted to
heal the world, not . . . not this."

"Plans go awry," Idaan said. "It's their nature. I'm going back in. Join
us when you're ready. I'll get something warm for you to drink."

Maati sat alone, growing colder. Behind him, the wayhouse ticked as
the day's heat radiated away. An owl gave its low coo to the world, and

the darkness around him seemed to lessen. He could make out the paving stones, the outline of the stable, the high branches rising toward the stars like thin fingers. Maati rested his head against the wall and let his eyes close.

The trembling had stopped. The anger was less immediate, chagrin slowly taking its place. He heard Eiah's calm voice, as solid as stone, from within. He should be with her. He should be at her side. She shouldn't have to face them by herself. He rose, grunting, and lumbered inside, his knees aching.

Otah was sitting in a low wooden chair, his fingers pressed to his lips in thought. He glanced up as Maati stepped into the room but made no other acknowledgment. Eiah, speaking, gestured to the space between Otah and Danat. Her voice had neither rancor nor apology, and Maati was reminded again why he admired her.

"Yes," she said, "the andat outplayed us. From the beginning with Ashti Beg to the end with me, we wanted to think of it as a baby. We all knew it wasn't. We all understand perfectly well that it was some part of Vanjit's mind made flesh, but . . ."

She raised her hands, palms out. Not a formal pose, but the gesture was eloquent enough.

"So what does it want?" Danat said. "If it truly wants Vanjit killed, why didn't it help you? That would have done all it wanted to do."

"It may want more than freedom," Idaan said, speaking over her shoulder as she pressed a warm bowl into Maati's hand. "There's precedent. Seedless wanted his freedom, but he also wanted his poet to suffer. Clarity-of-Sight may want something for Vanjit besides death."

"Such as?" Large Kae asked.

"Punishment," Eiah suggested. "Or isolation. Or . . ."

"Or a sense of family," Ashti Beg said, her voice oddly contemplative. "If we think of the babe as having more than one agenda, this could be its way of making a world that was only mother and child. Alienating all the rest of us."

"But it also wants its freedom," Maati said. Small Kae shifted on her bench at the sound of his voice, making room for him. He moved forward and sat. "Whatever else it wants, it must want that."

A puff of smoke escaped from the fire grate. Maati sipped the drink Idaan had given him—rum with honey and apple. It warmed his throat and made his chest glow.

"Is this really what we should care about?" the Galtic girl—Ana—asked. "I don't mean that as an attack, but it seems that we've established that the girl's less than sane. Is there something we gain by trying to guess at the shape of her madness?"

"We might have a better idea of where she's gone," Small Kae offered. "What she might do next?"

"Ana's right," Danat said. "We could roll dice about it, but there are some things we know for certain. She set out half a day's boat ride north of here a night ago. If she goes upriver, she'll need to hire a boat. If she goes down, she could hire one or build a raft and rely on the current. Or she can go east over land. What about the low towns? Could she have found shelter in a low town?"

The group was silent, then Danat said, "I'll get the keeper. She may know something of the local geography."

It was, Maati thought, a strangely familiar feeling. A handful of people sitting together, thinking aloud about an insoluble problem. The weeks at the school, sitting in the classrooms with chalk marks on the walls. All of them offering suggestion, interpretation, questions opened for anyone to answer if they could. He took an unexpected comfort from it.

The only one who didn't speak was Otah.

The conversation went on long into the night. The longer they took to find Vanjit, the greater her chance of escape. The greater her chance of dying alone in the wild. The Galtic girl and Small Kae had a long discussion of whether they were going to rescue Vanjit or if the aim was to kill her; Small Kae advocated a fast death, Ana wanted the chance to ask Vanjit to undo the damage to Galt. Danat counted the days to Utani, the days back, guessed at the size of the search party that could be raised.

"There is another option," Eiah said, her pearl-gray eyes focused on nothing. "I had a binding prepared. Wounded. If I can manage it, we would have another way to heal the damage done to Galt."

Ana turned toward Eiah's voice, raw hope on her face. Maati almost felt sorry to dash it.

"No," he said. "It can't be done. Even if you knew it well enough to perform it blind, we hadn't looked over the most recent version. And Vanjit ruined the notes."

"But if Galt could be given its eyes again . . ." Danat said.

"Vanjit could take them away again," Maati said. "Clarity-of-Sight and Wounded could go back and forth until eventually Eiah tried to heal someone just as Vanjit tried to blind them, and then the gods alone know what would happen. And that matters less than the fact that Eiah would die if she tried the thing."

"You don't know that," Idaan said.

"I'm not willing to take the risk," Maati said.

Otah listened, his brow furrowed, his gaze shifting now and again to the fire. It wasn't until morning that Maati and the others learned what the Emperor was thinking.

The morning light transformed the wayhouse. With the shutters all opened, the benches and tables and soot-stained walls seemed less oppressive. The fire still smoked, but the breeze moving through the rooms kept the air fresh and clear, if cold. The wayhouse keeper had prepared duck eggs and peppered pork for their morning meal, and tea brewed until it was rich with taste and not yet bitter.

They were not all there. Ashti Beg and the two Kaes had stayed up after many of the others had faded into their restless sleep. Maati had slipped into dream with the sound of their voices in his ears, and none of them had yet risen. Danat and Otah were sitting at the same table, looking like a painter's metaphor of youth and age. Eiah and Idaan shared his own table, and he did not know where the Galtic girl had gone.

"She didn't blind Maati. Why?" Otah asked, gesturing at Maati as if he were an exhibit at an audience rather than a person. "Why spare him and not the others?"

"Well, for Eiah it's clear enough," Danat said around a mouthful of pork. "She didn't want another poet binding the andat. As long as Vanjit's the only one, she's . . . well, the only one."

"And the two Kaes," Eiah said, "so that they couldn't follow her."

"Yes," Idaan said, "but that's not the question. *Why not Maati?*"

"Because . . ." Maati began, and then fell short. Because she cared for him more? Because she didn't fear him? Nothing he could think of rang true.

"I think she wants to be found," Otah said. "I think she wants to be found, in specific, by Maati."

Idaan grunted appreciatively. Eiah frowned and then nodded slowly.

"Why would she want that?" Maati asked.

"Because your attention is the mark of status," Eiah answered. "You are the teacher. The Dai-kvo. Which of us you choose to give your time to determines who is in favor and who isn't. And she wants to show herself that she can take you from me."

"That's idiotic," Maati said.

"No," Idaan said, her voice oddly soft. "It's only childish."

"It fits together if you've raised a daughter," Otah agreed. "It's just what Eiah would have done when at twelve summers. But if I'm right, it changes things. I didn't want to say it in front of Ana-cha, but if your poet's truly gone to ground, I can't believe we'd find her before spring. She can find new allies if she needs them, or use the andat to threaten people and get what she wants from them. At best, we might have her by Candles Night."

"But if she's waiting to *be* found," Danat said.

"Then it's a matter of guessing where she'd wait," Otah said. "Where she'd expect Maati to go looking for her."

"I don't know the answer to that," Maati said. "The school, maybe. She might make her way back there."

"Or at the camp where we lost her," Eiah suggested.

Silence fell over the room for a moment. A decision had just been made, and Maati could tell that each of them knew it. Utani would wait. They were hunting Vanjit.

"The camp's nearest," Danat said.

"You can send one of the armsmen north with a letter," Eiah said. "Even if we fail, it doesn't mean a larger search can't be organized while we try."

"I'll round up the others," Idaan said, rising from the table. "No point wasting daylight. Danat-cha, if you could tell our well-armed escorts that we're leaving?"

Danat swilled down the last of his tea, took a pose that accepted his aunt's instructions, and rose. In moments, only Otah, Eiah, and Maati himself were left in the room. Otah took a bite of egg and stared out into nothing.

"Otah-kvo," Maati said.

The Emperor looked over, his eyebrow raised in something equally query and challenge. Maati felt his chest tighten as if it were bound by wire. He sat silent for the rest of the meal.

To Maati's dismay, Ashti Beg, Large Kae, and Small Kae all preferred to stay behind. There was a logic to it, and the keeper was more than happy to take Otah's silver in return for a promise to look after them. Still, Maati found himself wishing that they had come.

The Emperor's boat was, if anything, smaller than the one Maati had hired. One of the armsmen had been sent north with letters that Otah had hastily drafted, another to the south. Half of the rest were set to finding a second boat and following with the supplies, and yet the little craft felt crowded as they nosed out into the river.

Otah stood at the bow, Danat at his side. Idaan had appointed herself shepherd of Eiah and Ana, the blinded women. Maati sat alone near the stern. The sky was pale with haze, the river air rich with the scent of decaying leaves and autumn. The kiln roared to itself, and the wheel slapped the water. Far above, two vees of geese headed south, their brash unlovely voices made beautiful by distance.

His rage was gone, and he missed it. All his fantasies of Otah Machi apologizing, of Otah Machi debased before him, melted like sugar in water when faced with the man himself. Maati felt small and alone, and perhaps that was merely accurate. He had lost everything now except perhaps Eiah. Irit was gone, and the wisest of them all for fleeing. He couldn't imagine Large Kae and Small Kae would return to him. Ashti Beg had left once already. And then Vanjit. All of his little family was gone now.

His family. Ashti Beg's voice returned to him. Vanjit and Clarity-of-Sight and the need for family.

"Oh," he said, almost before he knew what he meant. And then, "*Oh.*"

Maati made his unsteady way to the bow, touching crates with his fingertips to keep from stumbling. Otah and Danat turned at the sound of his approach, but said nothing. Maati reached them short of breath and oddly elated. His smile seemed to surprise them.

"I know where she's gone," he said.

27

>+<   Udun had been a river city. A city of birds.

    Otah remembered the first time he'd come to it, a letter of introduction from a man he had known briefly years before limp in his sleeve. After years of life in the eastern islands, it was like walking into a dream. Canals laced the city, great stone quays as busy as the streets. Great humped bridges with stairs cut in each side rose up to let even the tallest boats pass. On the shores, tree branches bent under the brightly colored burden of wings and beaks and a thousand kinds of song. The street carts sold food and drink as they did everywhere, but with each paper basket of lemon fish, every bowl of rice and sausage, there would be a twist of colored cloth.

    Open the cloth, and seeds would spill out, and then within a heartbeat would come the birds. Fortunes were told by which birds reached you. Finches for love, sparrows for pain, and so on, and so on. Wealth, birth, death, love, sex, and mystery all spelled out in feathers and hunger for those wise enough to see or credulous enough to believe.

    The palaces of the Khai Udun had spanned the wide river itself, barges disappearing into the seemingly endless black tunnel and then emerging again into the light. Beggars sang from rafts, their boxes floating at the side. The firekeepers' kilns had all been enameled the green of the river water and a deep red Otah had never seen elsewhere. And at a wayhouse with a little garden, there had been a keeper with a fox-sharp face and threads of white in her black hair.

    He had entered the gentleman's trade there, become a courier and traveled through the world, bringing his messages back to House Siyanti and sleeping at Kiyan's wayhouse. He knew all the cities and many of the low towns as they had been back then, but Udun had been something precious.

    And then the Galts had come. There were tales afterward that the river downstream from the ruins stank of corpses for a year. Thousands

of men and women and children had died in the bloodiest slaughter of
the war. Rich and poor, utkhaiem and laborer, none had been spared.
What survivors there were had abandoned their city's grave, leaving it to
the birds. Udun had died, and with it—among unnumbered others—the
poet Vanjit's parents and siblings and some part of her soul.

And so, Maati argued, it was where she would return now.

"It's plausible," Eiah said. "Vanjit's always thought of herself as a victim. This would help her to play the role."

"How far would it be from here?" Danat asked.

Otah, his mind already more than half in the past, calculated. They
were six days south of Utani on this steamcart for water. Udun had been
a week's ride or ten days walking south from Utani. . . .

"She could reach it in three days," Otah said, "if she knew where she
was headed. There are more than enough streams and creeks feeding
the river here. Water wouldn't be a problem."

"If we go there now, we might reach it before she does," Idaan said,
looking out over the river.

"The camp's still the better wager," Danat said. "It's where she
parted ways with them. They left their sleeping tents, so there's shelter
of a sort. And it doesn't require walking anywhere."

Maati started to object, but Otah raised his hand.

"It's along the way," Otah said. "We'll stop there and look. If she's
been to the camp, we should be able to tell. If not, we won't have lost
more than half a day."

Maati straightened as if the decision were a personal insult, turned
and walked back to the stern of the boat. Time had not been gentle to the
man. Hard fat had thickened his chest and belly. His skin was gray where
it wasn't flushed. Maati's long, age-paled hair had an unhealthy yellow,
and his movements were labored as if he woke every morning tired. And
his mind . . .

Otah turned back to the water, the trees, the soft wind. The white
haze of sky was darkening as the day wore on, the scent of rain on the air.
The others—Idaan, Danat, Eiah, Ana—moved away quietly, as if afraid
their conversation might move him to violence. Otah breathed in and
out, slow and deep, until both his disgust and his pity had faded.

Maati had lost the right to feel anger when his pupil had killed Galt,
and any sentimental connection between Otah and his once-friend had
drowned outside Chaburi-Tan. If Maati thought that stopping at the
camp was a poor decision, he could make his case or he could choke on
it. It was the same to Otah.

In the event, they lost more than half a day. Maati identified the wrong stretches of river twice, and Eiah had no eyes to correct him. When at last they found the abandoned campsite, a soft, misting rain had started to fall and the daylight was beginning to fail them. Maati led the way into the small clearing, walking slowly. Otah and two of the armsmen were close behind. Eiah had insisted that she come as well, and Idaan was helping her, albeit more slowly.

"Well," Otah said, standing in the middle of the ruins. "I think we can fairly say that she's been here."

The camp was destroyed. The thick canvas sleeping tents lay in shreds and knots. Stones and ashes from the fire pit had been strewn about, and two leather bags lay empty in the mud. One of the armsmen crouched on his heels and pointed to a slick of black mud. A footprint no longer than Otah's thumb. Idaan's steps squelched as she paced near the ruined fire pit. Maati sat on a patch of crushed grass, his hem dragging in the mud, his face a mask of desolation.

"Back to the boat, I think," Otah said. "I can't see staying on here."

"We may still beat her to Udun," Idaan said, prying the gray wax shards that had been Eiah's binding from the muck. "She spent a fair amount of time doing this. Tents like those are hard to cut through."

One of the armsmen muttered something about the only thing worse than a mad poet being a mad poet with a knife, but Otah was already on his way back to the river.

The boatman and his second had fitted poles into thick iron rings all along the boat's edge and raised a tarp that kept the deck near to dry. As darkness fell and the rain grew heavier, the drops overhead sounded like fingertips tapping on wood. The kiln had more than enough coal. The wide-swung doors lit the boat red and orange, and the scent of pigeons roasting on spits made the night seem warmer than it was.

Maati had returned last, and spent the evening at the edge of the light. Otah saw Eiah approach him once, a few murmured phrases exchanged, and she turned back to the sound of the group eating and talking in the stern. If Idaan hadn't risen to lead her back, he would have. The boatman's second handed her a tin bowl, bird's flesh gray and steaming and glistening with fat. Otah shifted to sit at her side.

"Father," Eiah said.

"You knew it was me?"

"I'm blind, not dim," Eiah said tartly. She plucked a sliver of meat from her bowl and popped it into her mouth. She looked tired, worn thin. He could still see the girl she had been, hiding beneath the time and age. He felt the urge to stroke her hair the way he had when she was an infant, to be her father again.

"This is, I assume, when you point out how much better your plan was than my own," she said.

"I didn't intend to, no," Otah said.

Eiah turned to him, shifting her weight as if she had some angry retort that had stuck in her throat for want of opposition. When he spoke, he was quiet enough to keep the conversation as near to between only the two of them as the close quarters would allow.

"We each did our best," Otah said. "We did what we could."

He put his arm around her. She bit down on her lip and fought the sobs that shook her body like tiny earthquakes. Her fingers found his own, and squeezed as hard as a patient under a physician's blade. He made no complaint.

"How many people have I killed, Papa-kya? How many people have I killed with this?"

"Hush," Otah said. "It doesn't matter. Nothing we've done matters. Only what we do next."

"The price is too high," Eiah said. "I'm sorry. Will you tell them that I'm sorry?"

"If you'd like."

Otah rocked her gently, and she allowed him to do it. The others all knew what they were saying, if not in specific, then at least the sketch of it. Otah saw Danat's concern, and Idaan's cool evaluating glance. He saw the armsmen turn their backs to him out of respect, and at the bow, Maati turned his back for another reason. Otah felt a flicker of his rage come back, a tongue of flame rising from old coals. Maati had done this. None of it would have happened if Maati hadn't been so bent by his own guilt or so deluded by his optimism that he ignored the dangers.

Or if Otah had found him and stopped him when that first letter had come. Or if Eiah hadn't made common cause with Maati's clandestine school. Or if Vanjit hadn't been mad, or Balasar ambitious, or the world and everything in it made from the first. Otah closed his eyes, letting the darkness create a space large enough for the woman in his arms and his own complicated heart.

Eiah murmured something he couldn't make out. He made a small interrogative sound in the back of his throat, and she coughed before repeating herself.

"There was no one at the school I could talk with," she said. "I got so tired of being strong all the time."

"I know," he said. "Oh, love. That, I know."

Otah slept deeply that night, lulled by exhaustion and the soft sounds of familiar voices and of the river. He slept as if he had been ill and the fever had only just broken. As if he was weak, and gaining strength. The dreams that possessed him faded with his first awareness of light and motion, less substantial than cobwebs, less lasting than mist.

The air itself seemed cleaner. The early-morning haze burned off in sunlight the color of water. They ate boiled wheat and honey, dried apples, and black tea. The boatman's second made his call, the boatman responded, and they nosed out again into the flow. Maati, sulking, kept as nearly clear of Otah as he could but kept casting glances at Eiah. Jealous, Otah assumed, of the conversation between father and daughter and unsure of her allegiance. Eiah for her part seemed to be making a point of speaking with her brother and her aunt and Ana Dasin, sitting with them, eating with them, making conversation with the jaw-clenched determination of a horse laboring uphill.

The character of the river itself changed as they went farther north. Where the south was wide and slow and gentle, the stretch just south of Udun was narrower—sometimes no more than a hundred yards across—and faster. The boatman kept his kiln roaring, the boiler bumping and complaining. The paddle wheel spat up river water, slicking the deck nearest the stern. Otah would have been concerned if the boatman and his second hadn't appeared so pleased with themselves. Still, whenever the boiler chimed after some particularly loud knock, Otah eyed it with suspicion. He had seen boilers burst their seams.

The miles passed slowly, though still faster than the poet girl could have walked. Every now and then, a flicker of movement on the shore would catch Otah's attention. Bird or deer or trick of the light. He found himself wondering what they would do if she appeared, andat in her arms, and struck them all blind. His fears always took the form of getting Danat and Eiah and Ana to safety, though he knew that his own danger would be as great as theirs and their competence likely greater.

The spitting waterwheel slowly drove them toward the bow. Near midday, the captain of the guard brought them tin bowls of raisins and bread and cheese. They all sat in a clump, and even Maati haunted the edges of the conversation. Ana and Eiah sat hand in hand on a long, low bench; Danat, cross-legged on the deck. Otah and Idaan kept to leather and canvas stools that creaked when sat upon and resisted any attempt to rise. The cheese was rich and fragrant, the bread only mildly stale, and the topic a council of war.

"If we do find her," Idaan said, answering Otah's voiced concerns, "I'm not sure what we do with her. Can she be made to see reason?"

"A month ago, I'd have said it was possible," Eiah said. "Not simple, but possible. I'm half-sorry we didn't kill her in her sleep when we were still at the school."

"Only half?" Danat asked.

"There's Galt," Eiah said. "As it stands now, she's the only one who can put it back. It's harder for her to do that dead."

Danat looked chagrined, and, as if sensing it, Idaan put a hand on his shoulder. Eiah squeezed Ana's hand, then gently bent it at the wrist, as if testing something.

"She's alone. She's hurt and she's sad. I'm not saying that's all certain to work in our favor," Maati said, "but it's something." Otah thought he sounded petulant, but none of the others appeared to hear it that way.

Eiah's voice cut the conversation like a blade. Even before he took the sense of the words, Otah was halfway to his feet.

"How long?" Eiah asked.

Her hands were around Ana's wrists, her fingers curled as if measuring the girl's pulses. Eiah's face was pale.

"Ah," Idaan said. "Well. Sitting those two together was a mistake."

"Tell me," Eiah said. "How far along?"

"A third, perhaps," Ana said softly.

"We hadn't mentioned it to the men," Idaan said. "I understand the first ones don't always take."

It took him less than a breath to understand.

"Ah," Otah said, a hundred tiny signs falling into place. Ana's weeping at the school, her avoidance of Danat, the way she'd kept to herself in the mornings and eaten with Idaan.

"What?" Danat asked, baffled.

"I'm pregnant," Ana said, her voice calm and matter-of-fact, her cheeks as bright as apples with her blush. The whole boat seemed to breathe in at once.

"And how long has *this* been going on?" Otah demanded, shifting his gaze to the dumbstruck Danat at his feet. His son blinked up, uncomprehending. It was as if Otah had asked in an unknown language.

"You're joking," Idaan said. "You have a boy who's just ended his twentieth summer and a girl not two years younger, an escort of professional armsmen as chaperone, and a steamcart with private quarters built on its back. What did you expect would happen?"

"But," Otah began, then found he wasn't sure what he intended to say. *She's blinded*, or *They aren't wed*, or *Farrer Dasin will say it's my fault for not keeping better watch over them*. Each impulse seemed more ridiculous than the last.

"I'm going to be a father," Danat said as if testing out the words. He turned to look up at Otah and started to grin. "*You're* going to be a grandfather."

Eiah was weeping openly, her arms around Ana. A clamor of voices and a whoop from the stern said that whatever hope there might have been that the thing would be kept quiet once they returned to court was gone. Otah sat back, his stool creaking under his weight. Idaan took a pose of query that carried nuances of both pity at his idiocy and congratulations. Otah started laughing and found it hard to stop.

It had been so long since he'd felt joy, he'd almost forgotten what it was like.

The rest of the day was spent in half-drunken conversation. Otah was made to retell the details of Danat's birth, and of Eiah's. Danat grew slowly more pleased with himself and the world as the initial shock wore thin. Ana Dasin smiled, her grayed eyes taking in nothing and giving out a pleasure and satisfaction that seemed more intimate in that she couldn't see its reflection in the faces around her.

Stories came pouring out as if they had only been waiting for the chance to be told. Idaan's spectacularly failed attempts to care for a younger half-sister when she'd been little more than fourteen summers old. Otah's work in the eastern islands as an assistant midwife, and the awkward incident of the baby born to an island mother and island father and with a complexion that sang to the stars of Obar State. Eiah spilled out every piece of secondhand wisdom she'd ever heard about keeping a new babe safe in the womb until it was ready to be born. At one point the armsmen broke into giddy song and, against Danat's protests, lifted him onto their shoulders, the deck shifting slightly under them. The sun itself seemed to shine for them, the river to laugh.

Maati alone seemed not to recover entirely from the first surprise. He smiled and chuckled and nodded when it fit the moment, but his eyes were reading letters in the air. He looked neither pleased nor displeased, but lost. Otah saw his lips moving as Maati spoke to himself, as if trying to explain something to his body that only his mind knew. When the poet hefted himself up and came to take Ana's hand, it was with a formality that might have been mixed feelings on his part or only a fear that his kind thoughts would be unwelcome. Ana accepted the formal, some-what stilted blessing, and afterward Eiah took Maati's hand, pulling him down to sit at her side.

Even braided together, Otah's anger and distrust and sorrow couldn't overcome the moment. The blood and horror of the world lifted, and a future worth having peeked through the crack.

It was only much later, when the sun fell carelessly into the treetops of the western bank and shadows darkened the water, that the celebra-tion faltered. The boat passed a brickwork tower standing on the river-bank, ivy almost obscuring the scars where fire had burned through timber and stripped the shutters from the empty windows. Otah watched the structure with the eerie feeling that it was watching back. The river bent, and a great stone bridge came into sight, gaps in its rail like miss-ing teeth. Birds as bright as fire sang and fluttered, even in the autumn cold. Their songs filled the air, the familiar trills greeting Otah like the wail of a ghost.

The ruins of the river city. The corpse of a city of birds.

They had come to dead Udun.

28

>+< Maati tramped through the overgrown streets, Idaan walking silently at his side. The hunter's bow slung over her shoulder was meant more as protection from feral dogs than to assassinate Vanjit, though Maati knew Idaan could use it for either. To their left, an unused canal stank of stale water and rotting vine. To the right, walls stood or leaned, roofs sagged or had fallen in. Every twenty steps seemed to offer up a new display of how war and time could erase the best that humanity achieved. And above the ruins, rising like a mountain over the city, the ruined palaces of the Khai Udun were grayed by the moisture in the air. The towers and terraces of enameled brick as soft as visions.

He had lost Eiah too.

Squatting on the boat as they made their way upriver, he had watched her turn to Otah, watched her become his daughter again where before she had chosen the role of outcast. She had lost faith in Maati's dream, and he understood why. She had delighted in the Galtic girl's condition as if it weren't the very thing that they had feared and fought against.

Maati had wanted the past. He had wanted to make the world whole as it had been when he was a boy, none of his opportunities squandered. And she had wanted that too. They all had. But with every change that couldn't be undone, the past receded. With every new tragedy Maati brought upon the world, with each friend that he lost, with failure upon failure upon failure, the dim light faded. With Eiah returned to her father's cause, there was nothing left to lose. His despair felt almost like peace.

"Left or right?" Idaan asked.

Maati blinked. The road before them split, and he hadn't even noticed it. He wasn't much of a scout.

"Left," he said with a shrug.

"You think the canal bridge will hold?"

"Right, then," Maati said, and turned down the road before the woman could raise some fresh objection.

It was only a decade and a half since the war. It seemed like days ago that Maati had been the librarian of Machi. And yet the white-barked tree that split the road before them, street cobbles shattered and lifted by its roots, hadn't existed then. The canals he walked past had run clean. There had been no moss on the walls. Udun had been alive, then. The forest and the river were eating the city's remains, and it seemed to have happened in the space between one breath and the next. Or perhaps the library, the envoys from the Dai-kvo, the long conversations with Cehmai-kvo and Stone-Made-Soft had been part of some other lifetime.

The sound was low and violent—something thrashing against wood or stone. Maati looked around him. The square they'd come to was paved in wide, flat stones, tall grass a yellow gray at the joints. A ruined fountain with black muck where clear water had been squatted in the center. Idaan's bow was in her hands, an arrow between her fingers.

"What was that?" Maati asked.

Idaan's dark eyes swept over the ruins, and Maati tried to follow her gaze. They might have been houses or businesses or something of both. The sound came again. From his left and ahead. Idaan moved forward cat-quiet, her bow at the ready. Maati stayed behind her, but close. He remembered that he had a blade at his belt and drew it.

The buck was in a small garden with an iron fence overgrown now with flowering ivy. Its side was cut, the fur black with dried blood and flies. The noble rack of horns was broken on one side, ending in a cruel, jagged stump. As Idaan stepped near, it moved again, lashing out at the fence with its feet, and then hung its head. It was an image of exhaustion and despair.

And its eyes were gray and sightless.

"Poor bastard," Idaan said. The buck raised its head, snorting. Maati gripped the handle of his blade, readying himself for something, though he wasn't certain what. Idaan raised her bow with something akin to disgust on her face. The first arrow sunk deep into the neck of the once-proud animal. The buck bellowed and tried to run, fouling itself in the fence, the vines. It slipped to its knees as Idaan sank another arrow into its side. And then a third.

It coughed and went still.

"Well, I think we can say how your little poet girl was planning to get food," Idaan said, her voice acid. "Cripple whatever game she came across and then let it beat itself to death. She's quite the hunter."

She slung the bow back over her shoulder, walking carefully into the trampled garden. Flies rose from the beast in a buzzing cloud. Idaan ignored them, putting her hand on the dead buck's flank.

"It's a waste," she said. "If I had rope and the right knife we could at least dress him and eat something fresh tonight. I hate leaving him for the rats and the foxes."

"Why did you kill him then?"

"Mercy. You were right, though. Vanjit's in the city somewhere. That was a good call."

"I'm half-sorry I said anything," Maati said. "You'd kill her just as quickly, wouldn't you?"

"You think you can romance her into taking back her curse. I'm no one to keep you from trying."

"And then?"

"And then we follow the same plan each of us had. It's the one thing we agree upon. She's too dangerous. She has to die."

"I know what I intended. I know what Eiah and I were planning. But that was the andat's scheme. I think there may be another way."

Idaan looked up, then stood. The bow was still in her hand.

"Can you give her her parents back?" she asked. "Can you give her the brothers and sisters she lost? Udun. Can you rebuild it?"

Maati took a pose that dismissed her questions, but Idaan stepped close to him. He could feel her breath against his face. Her eyes were cold and dark.

"Do you think that Galt died blind because of something you can remedy?" she demanded. "What's happened, happened. You can't will her to be the woman you hoped she was. Telling yourself that you can is worse than stupidity."

"If she puts it to rights," Maati said, "she shouldn't have to die."

Idaan narrowed her eyes, tilted her head.

"I'll offer you this," she said. "If you can talk the girl into giving Galt back its eyes—and Eiah and Ashti Beg. Everyone. If you can do that and also have her release her andat, I won't be the one who kills her."

"Would Otah let her live?" Maati asked.

"Ask him and he might," Idaan said. "Experience suggests he and I have somewhat different ideas of mercy."

At midday, they returned to their camp. The boat was tied up at an old quay slick with mold. The scent of the river was rich and not entirely pleasant. Two of the other scouting parties had returned before them; Danat and one of the armsmen were still in the city but expected back shortly. Otah, in a robe of woven silk under a thicker woolen outer robe, sat at a field table on the quayside, sketching maps of the city from memory. Idaan made her report, Maati silent at her side. He tried to imagine asking Otah for clemency on Vanjit's behalf. If Maati could persuade her to restore sight to everyone she'd injured and release the andat, would Otah honor Idaan's contract? Or, phrased differently, if Maati couldn't save the world, could he at least do something to redeem this one girl?

He didn't ask it, and Idaan didn't raise the issue.

After Danat and the armsmen returned, they all ate a simple meal of bread and dried apples. Danat, Otah, and the captain of the guard consulted with one another over Otah's sketched maps, planning the afternoon's search. Idaan tended to Ana; their laughter seemed incongruous in the grim air of their camp. Eiah sat by herself at the water's edge, her face turned up toward the sun. Maati went to her side.

"Did you drink your tea this morning?" she asked.

"Yes," he lied petulantly.

"You need to," she said. Maati shrugged and tossed the last round of dried apple into the water. It floated for a moment, the pale flesh looking nearly white on the dark water. A turtle rose from beneath and bit at it. Eiah held out her hand, palm up, fingers beckoning. Maati was vaguely ashamed of the relief he felt taking her hand in his own.

"You were right," Maati confessed. "I still want to save Vanjit. I know better. I do, but the impulse keeps coming back."

"I know it does," Eiah said. "You have a way of seeing things the way you'd prefer them to be rather than the way they are. It's your only vice."

"Only?"

"Well, that and lying to your physician," Eiah said, lightly.

"I drink too much sometimes."

"When was the last time?"

Maati shrugged, a smile tugging at his mouth.

"I used to drink too much when I was younger," he said. "I still would, but I've been busy."

"You see?" Eiah said. "You had more vices when you were young. You've grown old and wise."

"I don't think so. I don't think you can mention me and wisdom in the same breath."

"You aren't dead. There's time yet." She paused, then asked, "Will they find her?"

"If Otah-kvo's right, and she wants us to," Maati said. "If she doesn't want to be found, we might as well go home."

Eiah nodded. Her grip tightened for a moment, and she released his hand. Her brow was furrowed with thought, but it was nothing she chose to share. *Don't leave me,* he wanted to say. *Don't go back to Otah and leave me by myself. Or worse, with only Vanjit.* In the end, he kept his silence.

His second foray into the city came in the middle of the afternoon. This time they had set paths to follow, rough-drawn maps marked with each pair's route, and Maati was going out with Danat. They would come back three hands before sunset unless some significant discovery was made. Maati accepted Otah's instructions without complaint, though the resentment was still there.

The air was warmer now, and with the younger man's pace, Maati found himself sweating. They moved down smaller streets this time, narrow avenues that nature had not quite choked. The birds seemed to follow them, though more likely it was only that there were birds everywhere. There was no sign of Vanjit or Clarity-of-Sight, only raccoons and foxes, mice and hunting cats, feral dogs on the banks and otters in the canals. They were hardly a third of the way through the long, complex loop set out for them when Maati called a halt. He sat on a stonework bench, resting his head in his hands and waiting for his breath to slow. Danat paced, frowning seriously at the brush.

It struck Maati that the boy was the same age Otah had been in Saraykeht. Not as broad across the shoulders, but Otah had been Itani Noygu and a seafront laborer then. Maati himself had been born four years after the Emperor, hardly sixteen when he'd gone to study under Heshai and Seedless. Younger than Ana Dasin was now. It was hard to imagine ever having been that young.

"I meant to offer my congratulations to you," Maati said. "Ana-cha seems a good woman."

Danat paused. The reflection of his father's rage warmed the boy's face, but not more than that.

"I didn't think an alliance with Galt would please you."

"I didn't either," Maati said, "but I have enough experience with losing to your father that I'm learning to be generous about it."

Danat almost started. Maati wondered what nerve he had touched, but before he could ask, a flock of birds a more violent blue than anything Maati had seen burst from a treetop down the avenue. They wheeled around one another, black beaks and wet eyes and tiny tongues pink as a fingertip. Maati closed his eyes, disturbed, and when he opened them, Danat was kneeling before him. The boy's face was a webwork of tiny lines like the cracked mud in a desert riverbed. Fine, dark whiskers

304   >+<   Daniel Abraham

rose from Danat's pores. His eyelashes crashed together when he blinked, interweaving or pressing one another apart like trees in a mudslide. Maati closed his eyes again, pressing his palms to them. He could see the tiny vessels in each eyelid, layer upon layer almost out to the skin.

"Maati-cha?"

"She's seen us," Maati said. "She knows I'm here."

In spite of the knowledge, it took Maati half a hand to find her. He swept the horizon and from east to west and back again. He could see half-a-hundred rooftops. He found her at last near the top of the palaces of the Khai Udun on a balcony of bricks enameled the color of gold. At this distance, she was smaller than a grain of sand, and he saw her perfectly. Her hair was loose, her robe ripped at the sleeve. The andat was on her hip, its black, hungry eyes on his own. Vanjit nodded and put the andat down. Then, with a slow, deliberate motion, she took a pose of greeting. Maati returned it.

"Where? Where is she?" Danat asked. Maati ignored him.

Vanjit shifted her hands and her body into a pose that was both a re-buke and an accusation. Maati hesitated. He had imagined a thousand scenarios for this meeting, but they had all involved the words he would speak, and what she would say in return. His first impulse now was to-ward apology, but something in the back of his mind resisted. Her face was a mask of self-righteous anger, and, to his surprise, he recognized the expression as one he himself had worn in a thousand fantasies. In his dreams, he had been facing Otah, and Otah had been the one to beg for-giveness.

Like a voice speaking in his ear, he knew why his hands would not take an apologetic pose. *She is here to see you abased. Do it now, and you have nothing left to offer her.* Maati pulled his shoulders back, lifted his chin, and took a pose that requested an audience. Its nuances didn't claim his superiority as a teacher to a student but neither did they cede it. Vanjit's eyes narrowed. Maati waited, his breath short and anxiety plucking at him.

Vanjit took a pose appropriate to a superior granting a servant or slave an indulgence. Maati didn't correct her, but neither did he respond. Van-jit looked down as if the andat had cried out or perhaps spoken, then shifted her hands and her body to a pose of formal invitation appropriate for an evening's meal. Only then did Maati accept, shifting afterward to a pose of query. Vanjit indicated the balcony on which she stood, and then made a gesture that implied either intimacy or solitude.

Meet me here. In my territory and on my terms. Come alone.

Maati moved to an accepting pose, smiling to himself as much as to the girl in the palaces. With a physical sensation like that of a gnat flying into his eye, Maati's vision blurred back to merely human acuity. He turned his attention back to Danat.

The boy looked half-frantic. He held his blade as if prepared for an attack, his gaze darting from tree to wall as if he could see the things that Maati had seen. The moons that passed around the wandering stars, the infinitesimal animals that made their home in a drop of rain, or the girl on her high balcony halfway across the city. Maati had no doubt she was still watching them.

"Come along, then," he said. "We're done here."

"You saw her," Danat said.

"I did."

"Where is she? What did she want?"

"She's at the palaces, and there's no point in rushing over there like a man on fire. She can see everything, and she knows to watch. We could no more take her by surprise than fly."

Maati took a deep breath and turned back along the path they'd just come. There was no reason to follow Otah's route now, and Maati wanted to sit down for a while, perhaps drink a bowl of wine, perhaps speak to Eiah for a time. He wanted to understand better why the dread in his breast was mixed with elation, the fear with pleasure.

"What does she want?" Danat asked, trotting to catch up to Maati.

"I suppose that depends upon how you look at things," Maati said. "In the greater scheme, she wants what any of us do. Love, a family, respect. In the smaller, I believe she wants to see me beg before I die. The odd thing is that even if she had that, it wouldn't bring her any lasting peace."

"I don't understand."

Maati stopped. It occurred to him that if he had taken the wrong pose, made the wrong decision just now, he and the boy would be trying to find their way back to camp by smell. He put a hand on Danat's shoulder.

"I've asked Vanjit to meet with me tonight. She's agreed, but it can only be the two of us," Maati said. "I believe that once it's done I'll be able to tell you whether the world is still doomed."

29

 "No," Otah said. "Absolutely not."

"All respect," Maati said. "You may be the Emperor, but this isn't your call to make. I don't particularly need your permission, and Vanjit's got no use for it at all."

"I can have you kept here."

"You won't," Maati said. The poet was sure of himself, Otah thought, because he was right.

When Danat and Maati had returned early, he had known that something had happened. The quay they had adopted as the center of the search had been quiet since the end of the afternoon meal. Ana and Eiah sat in the shadow of a low stone wall, sleeping or talking when Eiah wasn't going through the shards of her ruined binding, arranging the shattered wax in an approximation of the broken tablets. The boatman and his second had taken apart the complex mechanism connecting boiler to wheel and were cleaning each piece, the brass and bronze, iron and steel laid out on gray tarps and shining like jewelry. The voices of the remaining armsmen joined with the low, constant lapping of the river and the songs of the birds. At another time, it might have been soothing. Otah, sitting at his field table, fought the urge to pace or shout or throw stones into the water. Sitting, racking his brain for details of a place he'd lived three decades ago, and pushing down his own fears both exhausted him and made him tense. He felt like a Galtic boiler with too hot a fire and no release; he could feel the solder melting at his seams.

If they had followed his plan, Danat and Maati would have returned to the quay from a path that ran south along the river. They came from the west, down the broad stone steps. Danat held a naked blade forgotten in his hand, his expression set and unnerved. Maati, walking more slowly, seemed on the verge of collapse, but also pleased. Otah put down his pen.

"You've found her?"

"She's found us," Maati said. "I think she's been watching us since we stepped off the boat."

The armsmen clustered around them. Eiah and Ana rose to their feet, touching each other for support. Maati lumbered into the center of the quay as if it were a stage and he was declaiming a part. He told them of the encounter, of Vanjit's appearance, of the andat at her side. He took the poses he'd adopted and mimicked Vanjit's. In the end, he explained that Vanjit would see him—would see *only* him—and that it was to happen that evening.

"She doesn't know you," Maati continued, "and what little she does know, she doesn't have a use for. To her, you're the man who turned against his own people. And I am the teacher who gave her the power of a small god."

"And then plotted to kill her," Otah said, but he knew this battle was lost. Maati was right: neither of them had the power here. The poet and her andat were their masters whether he liked it or not. She could dictate any terms she wished, and Maati was important to her in a way that Otah himself was not.

It was a meeting with the potential to end the world or save it. He would have given it to a stranger before he trusted it to Maati.

"What are you going to tell her?" Ana asked. Her voice sounded hungry. Weeks—months now—Ana had been living in shadows, and here was the chance to make herself whole.

"I'll apologize," Maati said. "I'll explain that the andat manipulated us, playing on our fears. Then, if Vanjit will allow it, I'll have Eiah brought so that she can offer her apologies as well."

Eiah, standing where Otah could see her face, lifted her chin as if something had caught her attention. Something ghosted across her face— alarm or incredulity—and then was gone. She became a statue of herself, a mask. She had no more faith in Maati than he did. And, to judge from her silence, no better idea of what to do either.

"She has killed thousands of innocent people," Otah said. "She's crippled women she had numbered among her friends. Are you sure that apologizing is entirely appropriate?"

"What would you have me do?" Maati asked, his hands taking a pose that was both query and challenge. "Should I go to her swinging accusations? Should I tell her she's not safe and never will be?"

The voice that answered was Idaan's.

"There's nothing you can say to her. She's gone mad, and you talk about her as if she weren't. Whatever words you use, she's going to hear what she wants. You might just as well send her a puppet and let her speak both parts."

"You don't know her," Maati said, his face flushing. "You've never met her."

"I've *been* her," Idaan said dismissively as she walked down the steps to the now-crowded quay. "Give her what she wants if you'd like. It's never made her well before, and it won't make her well now."

"What would you advise?" Otah asked.

"She'll be distracted," Idaan said. "Go in with a bowman. Put an arrow in the back of her head just where the spine touches it."

"*No,*" Maati shouted.

"No," Eiah said. "Even if killing her is the right thing, think of the risk. If she suspects, she can always lash out, and we haven't got any protection against her."

"There doesn't need to be anyone there for her to be suspicious," Idaan said. "If she's frightened by shadows, the end is just as bloody."

"So we're giving up on Galt," Ana said. Her voice was flat. "I listen to all of you, and the one thing I never hear mentioned is all the people who've died because they happened to be like me."

Maati stepped forward, taking the girl's hand. Otah, watching her, didn't believe she needed comfort. It wasn't pain or sorrow in her expression. It was resolve.

"They don't think they can move her to mercy," Maati said. "I will do everything I can, Ana-cha. I'll swear to anything you like that I will—"

"Take me with you," Ana said. "I'm no threat to her, and I can speak for Galt. I'm the only one here who can do that."

Her orders were met by silence until Idaan made a sound that was equally laughter and cough.

"She told me to come alone," Maati said. "If she sees me leading a blind Galt to her—"

"Vanjit has the right to see her mistakes," Otah said. "She's done this. She should look at it. We all should look at what we've done to come here."

Maati looked at him as if seeing him for the first time. There was a deep confusion in the old poet's face. Otah took a pose that asked a favor between equals. As a friend to a friend.

"Take Ana," Otah said.

Maati's jaw worked as if he were chewing possible replies.

"No," he said.

Otah took a pose that was at once a query and an opportunity for Maati to recant. Maati shook his head.

"I have trusted you, Otah-kvo. Since we were boys, I have had to come to you with everything, and when you weren't there, I tried to imagine what you might have done. And this time, you are wrong. I know it."

"Maati—"

"Trust me," Maati hissed. "For once in your life *trust me*. Ana-cha must not go."

Otah's mouth opened, but no words came forth. Maati stood before him, his breath fast as a boy's who had just run a race or jumped from a high cliff into the sea. Maati had defied Otah. He had betrayed him. He had never in their long history refused him.

For a moment, Otah felt as if they were boys again. He saw in Maati the balled fists and jutting chin of a small child standing against an older one, the bone-deep fear mixed with a sudden, surprising pride in his own un-expected courage. And in Otah's own breast, an answering sorrow and even shame.

He took a pose that acknowledged Maati's decision. The poet hesitated, nodded, and walked to the riverside. Idaan leaned close to Ana, whispering all that had happened which the girl could not see.

Kiyan-kya—

Sunset isn't on us yet, but it will be soon. Maati is sulking, I think. Everyone's frightened, but none of us has the courage to say it. I take that back. Idaan isn't afraid. Just after Maati refused to take Ana Dasin with him to this thrice-damned meeting, Idaan came to me and said that she was fairly certain that if Vanjit kills us all, she'll die of starvation herself within the year. Vanjit's hunting ability hasn't impressed her, and Idaan has a way of finding comfort in strange places.

Nothing has ever come out the way I expected, love. It seemed so simple. We had men who could sire a child, they had women who could bear. And instead, I am sending the least reliable man I know to save everything and everyone by talking a madwoman into sanity. If I could find any way not to do this, I'd take it. I appealed to what Maati and I once were to each other when I tried to convince him to accept Ana's company. It was more than half a lie. In truth I can't say I know this man. The boy I knew in Saraykeht and the man we knew in Machi has become a stew of bitterness and blind optimism. He wants the past back, and no sacrifice is too high. I wonder if he never saw the weakness and injustice and rot at the heart of the old ways, or if he's only forgotten them.

If I had it all to do again, I'd have done it differently. I'd have married you sooner. I'd never have gone north, and Idaan and Adrah could have taken Machi and had all this on their heads instead of my own. Only then we'd have been in Udun, you and I, and I would have had your company for an even shorter time. There is no winning this game. I suppose it's best that we can only play it through once.

You wouldn't like what's become of Udun. I don't like it. I remember Sinja saying that he kept your wayhouse safe during the sack, but I haven't had the heart to go and look. The river still has its beauty. The birds still have their song. They'll still be here when the rest of us are gone. I miss Sinja.

There's something I'm trying to tell you, love. It's taking me more time than I'd expected to work up the courage. We all know it. Even Maati, even Ana, even Eiah. None of us can speak the words; not even me. You're the only one I can say this to, because, I suppose, you've already died and so you're safe from it.

Love. Oh, love. This meeting is all we can do, and it isn't going to work.

MAATI LEFT IN TWILIGHT. THE STARS SHONE IN THE EAST, THE DARKNESS RIS-ing up like a black dawn as the western sky fell from blue to gold, from gold to gray. Birdsong changed from the trills and complaints of the day to the low cooing and complexities of the night. The river seemed to exhale, and its breath was green and rotting and cold. Maati had a small pack at his side. In the light of the failing day and the flickering orange of the torches, he looked older than Otah felt, and Otah felt ancient.

He tried to see something familiar in Maati's eyes. He tried to see the boy he'd gone drinking with in dark, lush Saraykeht, but that child was gone. Both of those children.

"I will do my best, Otah-kvo," Maati said.

Otah bit back his first reply, and then his second.

"Tomorrow's going to be a very different day, Maati-cha," Otah said. Maati nodded. After so much and so long, there should have been more. Sinja appeared for a moment in the back of Otah's mind. There had been no last good-bye for him. If this was to be the ending between the two of them, Otah thought he should say something. He should make this part-ing unlike the others that had come before. "I'm sorry it's come to this."

Maati took a pose that agreed but kept the meaning as imprecise as Otah had. One of the armsmen called out, pointing at the looming threat of the Khai Udun's palaces. In a wide window precisely above the river, a light had appeared, glittering like gold. Like a fallen star.

Ana and Danat were in a corner of the quay, their arms wrapped around each other. Idaan stood among the armsmen, her expression grim. Eiah sat alone by the water, listening. Otah saw Maati's gaze linger on her with something like sorrow.

With a lantern in his unsteady hand, Maati walked off along the ruined streets that ran beside the river. Otah guessed it would take him half a hand to reach the palaces.

"All right," Idaan said. "He's gone."

Otah turned to look at her, some pale attempt at wit on his lips, and saw that the comment hadn't been meant for him. Idaan crouched beside Eiah. His daughter's face was turned toward nothing, but her hands were digging through the physician's satchel. Danat glanced at Otah, confusion in his eyes. Eiah started drawing flat stones from her bag and laying them gently on the flagstones before her.

No, he was wrong. Not stones, but triangles of broken wax. The contents of old, broken tablets with symbols and words inscribed on them in Eiah's hand.

"You could try being of help," Idaan said and gestured toward the shards at his daughter's knees. "There's a piece that goes right here I haven't been able to find."

"You did enough," Eiah said, her hands shifting quickly, fitting the breaks together. Already the wax was taking the shape of five separate squares, the characters coming together. "Just going to the campsite and bringing back the bits you did was more than I could have asked."

"What is this?" Otah asked, though he already knew.

"My work," Eiah said. "My binding. I hoped I'd have time. Before we actually came across Vanjit-cha, there was the chance she was spying on us. She'd always planned to kill me by distracting me during the binding. But now, and for I think at least the next hand and a half, her attention is going to be on Maati-kvo. So . . . ."

Idaan shook her head, clearing some thought away, and gestured to the captain of the guard.

"We'll need light," she said. "Eiah may be able to work puzzles in the dark, but I'm better if I can see what I'm doing."

"I thought you couldn't do this," Otah said, kneeling.

"Well, I haven't managed it yet," Eiah said with a wry smile. "On the other hand, I've studied to be a physician. Holding things in memory isn't so difficult, once you've had the practice. And there's enough here, I think, to guide me through it, no matter what Maati-kvo believes."

Idaan made a low grunt of pleasure, reached across Eiah and shifted a stray chunk of wax into place. Eiah's fingers caressed the new join, and she nodded to herself. Armsmen brought the wild, flickering light close, the waxwork lettering seeming to breathe in the shadows.

"Maati's warnings," Otah said. "You can't know what will happen if you pit your andat against hers."

"I won't have to," Eiah said. "I've thought this through, Papa-kya. I know what I'm doing. There was another section. It was almost square with one corner missing. Can anyone see that?"

"Check the satchel," Idaan said as Otah plucked the piece from the hem of Eiah's robe. He pressed it into her hand. Her fingertips traced its surface before she placed it at the bottom of the second almost-formed tablet. Her smile was gentler than he'd seen from her since he'd walked into the wayhouse. He touched her cheek.

"Maati doesn't know you're doing this, then?" Otah asked.

"We didn't think we'd ask him," Idaan said. "No disrespect to Eiah-cha, but that man's about half again as cracked as his poet."

"No, he isn't mad," Eiah said, her hands never slowing their dance across the face of the broken tablets. "He's just not equal to the task he set himself. He always meant well."

"And I'm sure the two dozen remaining Galts will feel better because of it," Idaan said acidly. And then, in a gentler voice, "It doesn't matter what story you tell yourself, you know. We've done what we've done."

"I wish you would stop that," Eiah said.

Idaan's surprise was clear on her face, and apparently in her silence as well. Eiah shook her head and went on, her tone damning and conversational.

"Every third thing you say is an oblique reference to killing my grandfather. We all know you did the thing, and we all know you regret it. None of this is anything to do with that. Papa-kya and Maati love each other and they hate each other, and it doesn't pertain either. Maati's overwhelmed by the consequences of misjudging Vanjit, and he might not be if he weren't hauling Nayiit and Sterile and Seedless along behind him."

Idaan looked like she'd been slapped. The armsmen were crowded so close, Otah could hear the low flutter of the torches burning, but the men pretended not to have heard.

"The past doesn't matter," Eiah said. "A hundred years ago or last night, it's all just as gone. I have a binding to work, and I'd like to make the attempt before Vanjit blinds Maati and walks him off something tall. I think we have something like half a hand."

They worked together in silence, three pairs of hands putting the wax into place quickly. There were still sections missing, and some parts of the tablets were shattered so thoroughly that Eiah's markings were all but lost. His daughter passed her fingertips slowly over each of the surfaces, her brow furrowed, her lips moving as if reciting something under her breath. Whether it was the binding or a prayer, Otah couldn't guess.

Idaan leaned close to Otah, her breath a warm and whispering breeze against his ear.

"She takes the tact from her mother's side, I assume?"

His tension and fear gave the words a hilarity they didn't deserve, and he fought to contain his laughter. The quay was dark around them; the torches kept his eyes from adapting to the darkness. It was as if the world had narrowed to a few feet of lichen-slicked flagstone, a single unshuttered window in the distance, and countless, endless, unnumbered stars.

"All right," Eiah said. "I can't be disturbed while I do this. If we could have the armsmen set up a guard formation? It would be in keeping with my luck to have a stray boar stumble into us at the wrong moment."

The captain didn't wait for Otah's approval. The men shifted, Idaan and Danat with them. Only Otah stayed. As if she saw him there, Eiah took a querying pose.

"You may die from this," he said.

"I'm aware of it," she said. "It doesn't matter. I have to try. And I think you have to let me."

"I do," Otah agreed. Smiling, she looked young.

"I love you too, Papa-kya."

"May I sit with you?" he asked. "I don't want to distract you, but it would be a favor."

He brushed the back of her hand with his fingertips. She took him by the sleeve of his robe and pulled him down to sit beside her. The fingers of her left hand laced with his right. For a moment, the only sounds were the gentle lapping of the river against the stone, the diminished hush of torch fire, the cooing of owls. Eiah leaned forward, her fingertips on the first tablet. Otah let go, and both of her hands caressed the wax. She began to chant.

The words were only words. He recognized a few of them, some phrases. Her voice went out on the cool night air as she moved slowly across each of the shattered tablets. When she reached the end, she went back to the beginning.

Though there were no walls or cliffs to sound against, her voice began first to resonate and then to echo.

30

>+< Maati traveled through the darkness alone. The sense of unreality was profound. He had refused Otah Machi, Emperor of the Khaiem. He had refused Otah-kvo. For years, perhaps a lifetime, he had admired Otah or else despised him. Maati had broken the world twice, once in Otah's service, and now, through Vanjit, in opposition to him. But this once, Otah had been wrong, and he had been right, and Otah had acknowledged it.

How strange that such a small moment should bring him such a profound sense of peace. His body itself felt lighter, his shoulders more nearly square. To his immense surprise, he realized he had shed a burden he'd been carrying unaware for most of his life.

Maati traveled through the darkness of Udun alone, because he had chosen to.

The brown vines and bare branches stirred in a soft breeze. The flutter of wings came from all around him, from nowhere. The air was cold enough to make his breath steam, and the voice of the river was a constant hush. With each step, some new detail of his path would come clear: an axe consumed by rust, a door still hanging from rotten leather hinges, the green-glowing eyes of some small predator. Cracks appeared in the paving stones, running out before him as if his passage were corrupting the city rather than revealing the decay already there.

He and Vanjit carried a history together. They had known each other, had helped each other. She would see that it was the andat's intervention that had turned him against her. The palaces of the Khai Udun grew taller and taller without ever seeming to come close until, it seemed between one breath and the next, he stepped into a grand courtyard. Moss and lichen had almost obscured the swirling design of white and red and gold stones. Maati paused, his lantern held over his head.

Once, it would have been a breathtaking testament to power and ingenuity and overwhelming confidence. Columns rose into the black air.

Statues of women and men and beasts towered over the entranceway, the bronze lost under green and gray. He walked alone into a welcoming chamber too vast for his lantern to penetrate. There was no ceiling, no walls. The river was silent here. Far above, wings fluttered in still air.

Maati took a deep breath—dust and rot and, after a decade and a half of utter ruin, still the faint scent of smoke. It smelled like the corpse of history.

He walked forward over parquet of ebony and oak, the pattern ruined and pieces pried up by water and time. He expected his footsteps to echo, but no sound he made returned to him.

A light glimmered high up and to his left. Maati stopped. He lowered his lantern and raised it again. The glimmer didn't shift. Not a reflection, then. Maati angled toward it.

A great stone stairway swept up in the gloom, a single candle burning at its top. Maati made his way slowly enough to keep from tiring. The hall that opened before him was not as numbingly huge as the first chamber; Maati could make out the ceiling, and that the walls existed. And far down it, another light.

The carpets underfoot had rotted to scraps years before. The shattered glass and fallen crystal might have been the damage of the elements or of the city's fall. The next flight of stairs—equally grand and equally arduous—could only have been a testament to that first violence, long ago. A human skull rested at the center of every step, shadows moving in the sockets as Maati passed them. He hoped the Galts had left the grim markers, but he didn't believe it.

Here, Vanjit was saying, *each of these is a life the soldiers of Galt ended*. They were her justification. Her honor guard.

He should have guessed where the candles were leading him. The grand double doors of the Khai's audience chamber stood closed, but light leaked through at the seams. After so long in the dark, he half-expected them to open onto a fire.

In its day, the chamber must have inspired awe. In its way, it still did. The arches, the angles of the walls, the thin ironwork as delicate as lace that held a hundred burning candles—everything was designed to draw the eyes to the dais, the black lacquer chair, and then out a wide, unshuttered window that reached from ceiling to floor. The Khai would have sat there, his city arrayed out behind him like a cloak. Now the cloak was only darkness, and in the black chair, Clarity-of-Sight cooed.

"I didn't think you'd come," Vanjit said from the shadows behind him. Maati startled and turned.

Exhaustion and hunger had thinned the girl. Her dark hair was pulled back, but what few locks had escaped the bond hung limp and lank, framing her pale face.

"Why wouldn't I?"

"Fear of justice," Vanjit said.

She stepped out into the candlelight. Her robes were silken rags, scavenged from some noble wardrobe, fourteen years a ruin. Her head was bowed beneath an invisible weight and she moved like an old woman bent with the pain for years. She had become Udun. The war, the damage, the ruin. It *was* her. The baby—the inhuman thing shaped like a baby—shrieked with joy and clapped its tiny hands. Vanjit shuddered.

"Vanjit-cha," Maati said, "we can talk this through. We can . . . we can still end this well."

"You tried to murder me," Vanjit said. "You and your pet poisoner. If you'd had your way, I would be dead now. How, Maati-kvo, do you propose to talk that through?"

"I . . ." he said. "There must . . . there must be a way."

"What was I supposed to be that I wasn't?" Vanjit asked as she walked toward the black chair with its tiny beast. "You knew what the Galts had done to me. Did you want me to get this power, and then forget? Forgive? Was this supposed to be the compensation for their deaths?"

"No," Maati said. "No, of course not."

"No," she said. "Because you didn't care when I blinded them, did you? That was my decision. My burden, if I chose to take it up. Innocent women. Children. I could destroy them, and you could treat it as justice, but I went too far. I blinded you. For half a hand, I turned it against you, and for *that*, I deserved to die."

"The andat, Vanjit-kya," Maati said, his voice breaking. "They have always schemed against their poets. They have manipulated the people around them in terrible ways. Eiah and I . . ."

"You hear that?" Vanjit said, scooping up Clarity-of-Sight. The andat's black eyes met hers. "This is your doing."

The andat cooed and waved its arms. Vanjit smiled as if at some unspoken jest, shared only between those two.

"I thought I would make the world right again," Vanjit said. "I thought I could make a baby. Make a family."

"You thought you could save the world," Maati said.

"I thought *you* could," she said in a voice like cold vinegar. "Look at me."

"I don't understand," he said.

"Look."

Her face sharpened. He saw the smudge of dust along her cheek, the stippled pores along her cheek, the individual hairs smaller than the thinnest threads. Her eyes were labyrinths of blood mapped on the whites, and the pupils glowed like a wolf's where the candlelight reflected from their depths. Her skin was a mosaic, tiny scales that broke and scattered with every movement. Insects too small to see scuttled through the roots of her hair, her eyelashes.

Maati's stomach turned, a deep nausea taking him. He closed his eyes, pressing his palms into the lids.

"Please," he said, and Vanjit wrenched his hands away from his face.

"Look at me!" she shouted. "Look!"

Reluctantly, slowly, Maati opened his eyes. There was too much. Vanjit was no longer a woman but a landscape as wide as the world, moving, breaking, shifting. Looking at her was being tossed on an infinite sea.

"Can you see my pain, Maati-kvo? Can you see it?"

No, he tried to say, but his throat closed against his illness. Vanjit pushed him away, and he spun, a thousand details assaulting him in the space of a heartbeat. He fell to the stone floor and retched.

"I didn't think you would," she said.

"Please," Maati said.

"You've taken it from me," Vanjit said. "You and Eiah. All the others. I was ready to do anything for you. I risked death. I did. And you don't even know me."

Her laugh was short and brutal.

"My eyes," he said.

"Fine," Vanjit said, and Maati's vision went away. He was once again in the fog of blindness. "Is that better?"

Maati reached toward the sound of her voice, then stumbled. Vanjit kicked him once in the ribs. The surprise was worse than the pain.

"There is nothing you have to teach me anymore, old man," she said. "I've learned everything you know. I understand."

"No," Maati said. "There's more. I can tell you more. I know what it is to lose someone you love. I know what it is to feel betrayed by the ones you thought closest to you."

"Then you know the world isn't worth saving," Vanjit said.

The words hung in the air. Maati tried to rise, but he was short of breath, wheezing like he'd run a race. His racing heart filled his ears with the sound of rushing blood.

"It is," he said. "It's worth . . ."

"Ah. There's Eymond. Everyone in Eymond, blind as a stone. And Eddensea. There. Gone. Bakta. But why stop there, Maati-kya? Here, the birds. All the birds in the world. There. The fish. The beasts." She laughed. "All the flies are blind. I've just done that. All the flies and the spiders. I say we give the world to the trees and the worms. One great nation of the eyeless."

"Vanjit," Maati said. His back hurt like someone had stabbed him and left the blade in. He fought to find the words. "You mustn't do this. I didn't teach you this."

"I did what you told me," she said, her voice rising. The andat's cry rose with her, an infantile rage and anguish and exultation at the world's destruction. "I did what you wanted. More, Maati-kvo, I did what you couldn't do yourself, and you hated me for it. You wanted me dead? Fine, then. I'll die. And the world can come with me."

"No!" Maati cried.

"I'm not a monster," Vanjit said. Like a candle being snuffed, the andat's wail ceased. Vanjit collapsed beside him, as limp as a puppet with cut strings.

There were voices. Otah, Danat, Eiah, Idaan, Ana. And others. He lay back, letting his eyes close. He didn't know what had happened. For the moment, he didn't care. His body was a single, sudden wash of pain. And then, his chest only ached. Maati opened his eyes. An unfamiliar face was looking down at him.

The man had skin as pale as snow and flowing ink-black hair. His eyes were deep brown, as soft as fur and as warm as tea. His robe was blue silk embroidered with thread of gold. The pale man smiled and took a pose of greeting. Maati responded reflexively. Vanjit lay on the floor, her arm bent awkwardly behind her, her eyes open and empty.

"Killed her," Maati said. "You. Killed her."

"Well. More precisely, we wounded her profoundly and then she died," the pale man said. "But I'll grant you it's a fine point. The effect is much the same."

"Maati!"

He lifted his head. Eiah was rushing toward him, her robes pressed back like a banner by her speed. Otah and Idaan followed her more slowly. Ana and Danat were locked in a powerful embrace. Maati lifted his hand in greeting. When she drew near, Eiah hesitated, her gaze on the fallen girl. The pale man—Wounded—took a pose that offered congratulations, and there was irony in the cant of his wrists. Eiah knelt, touching the corpse with a calm, professional air.

"Oh, yes," the andat said, folding its hands. "Quite dead."

"Good," Eiah said.

"*He* isn't standing," Idaan said, nodding toward Maati.

Eiah's attention shifted to him and her face paled.

"Just need. To catch my breath."

"His heart's stopping," Eiah said. "I knew this would happen. I told you to drink that tea."

Maati waved his hand, shooing her concerns away. Danat and Ana had come. He hadn't noticed it. They were simply there. Ana's eyes were brown and they were beautiful.

"Can't we . . . can't we do something?" Danat asked.

"No," said the andat in the same breath that Eiah said, "Yes. I need my satchel. Where is it?"

Danat rushed back to the great doors, returning half a moment later with the physician's satchel in his hands. Eiah grabbed it, plucked out a cloth bag, and started shuffling through sheaves of dried herbs that to Maati looked identical.

"There's another bag. A yellow one," Eiah said. "Where is it?"

"I don't think we brought it," Danat said.

"Then it's back at the quay. Get it now."

Danat turned and sprinted. Gently, Eiah took Maati's hand. He thought at first she meant to comfort him, but her fingers pressed into his wrist, and then she reached for his other hand. He surrendered himself to her care. He didn't have a great deal of choice. Idaan squatted at his side, Otah sitting on the dais. The andat rose, stepping back by Ana's side as if out of respect.

"How bad?" Idaan asked.

"He hasn't died. That's what I can offer for now," Eiah said. "Maati-kya, open your mouth. I don't have time to brew this, but it will help un-til I can get the rest of my supplies. It's going to be sweet first and then bitter."

"You've done it," Maati said around the pinch of leaves she put on his tongue.

Eiah looked at him, her expression startled. He smiled at her.

"You bound it. You've cured the blindness."

Eiah looked up at her creation, her slave. It nodded.

"Well, no," she said. "I mean, yes, I bound him. And I did undo Van-jit's damage to Ana and myself. And then you, when I saw that she'd done it."

"Galt?" Ana asked.

"I hadn't . . . I hadn't even thought of it. Gods. Is there anything different to be done? I mean, a whole nation at once?"

"You have to do everything," Maati said. "Birds. Beasts. Fish. Everyone, everywhere. You have to hurry. It's only a thought." The herbs were making his mouth tingle and burn, but the pain in his breast seemed to ebb. "It's no different."

Eiah turned to the andat. The kind, pale face hardened. No matter how it seemed, the thing wasn't a man and it wasn't gentle. But it was bound to her will, and a moment later Eiah caught her breath.

"It's done," she said, wonder in her voice. "They've been put back. The ones who are left."

Ana stepped forward and knelt, wordlessly enfolding Eiah in her arms. From where he lay, he could see Eiah's eyes close, watch her lean into the embrace. The two women seemed to pause in time, a moment that lasted less than two long breaths together but carried the weight of years within it. Eiah raised her head sharply and the andat twitched. Idaan leaped up, yelping. All eyes turned to her as she pressed a flat palm to her belly.

"That," she said, "felt very odd. You should warn someone when you're planning something like that."

"Sterile?" Otah asked. His voice was low. There was no joy in it.

"Repaired," Eiah said. "We can bear again. Galts can father children and we can bear them."

"I don't suppose you could leave me as I was?" Idaan asked.

"So we've begun again," Otah said. "It is all as it was. We've only changed a few names. Well—"

Wounded cut him off with a low bark of a laugh. Its eyes were fixed upon Eiah. Otah looked from one to the other, his hands taking a querying pose. Woman and slave both ignored him.

"Everyone?" the andat asked.

"Everyone, everywhere," Eiah said. "It's only a thought, isn't it? That's all it needs to be."

"What are you doing?" Ana asked. It seemed like a real curiosity.

"I'm curing everyone," Eiah said. "If there's a child in Bakta who split her head on a stone this morning, I want it fixed. A man in Eymond whose hip was broken when he was a boy and healed poorly, I want him walking without pain in the morning. Everyone. Everywhere. Now."

"Eiah Machi," the andat said, its voice low and amused, "the little girl who saved the world. Is that how you see it? Or is this how you apologize for slaughtering a whole people?"

Eiah didn't speak, and the andat went still again. Anger flashed in its eyes and Maati's hand went out, touching Eiah's. She patted him away absently, as if he were no more than a well-intentioned dog. The andat hissed under its breath and turned away. Maati noticed for the first time that its teeth were pointed. Eiah relaxed. Maati sat up; his breath had almost returned. The andat shifted to look at him. The whites of his eyes had gone as black as a shark's; he had never seen an andat shift its appearance before, and it filled him with sudden dread. Eiah made a scolding sound, and the andat took an apologetic pose.

Maati tried to imagine what it would be like, a thought that changeable, that flexible, that filled with violence and rage. *How did we ever think we could do good with these as our tools?* For as long as she held the andat, Eiah was condemned to the struggle. And Maati was responsible for that sacrifice too.

Eiah, it seemed, had other intentions.

"That should do," she said. "You can go."

The andat vanished, its robe collapsing to the floor in a pool of blue and gold. The scent of overheated stone came and went, a breath of hell on the night air. The others were silent. Maati came to himself first.

"What have you *done*?" he whispered.

"I'm a physician," Eiah said, her tone dismissive. "Holding that abomination the rest of my life would have gotten in the way of my work, and who told you that you were allowed to sit up? On your back or I'll call in armsmen to hold you down. No, don't say anything. I don't care if you're feeling a thousand times better. Down. Now."

He lay back, staring up at the ceiling. His mind felt blasted and blank. The enameled brick was blurred in the torchlight, or perhaps it was only that his eyes were only what they had been. The cold air that breathed in through the window too gently to even be a breeze felt better than he would have expected, the stone floor beneath him more comfortable. The voices around him were quiet with respect for his poor health or else with awe. The world had never seen a night like this one. It likely never would again.

She had freed it. Gods, all that they'd done, all that they'd suffered, and she'd just *freed* the thing.

When Danat returned, Eiah forced half a handful of herbs more bitter than the last into his mouth and told him to leave them under his tongue until she told him otherwise. Idaan and one of the armsmen hauled Vanjit's body away. They would burn it, Maati thought, in the morning. Vanjit had been a broken, sad, dangerous woman, but she deserved better than to have her corpse left out. He remembered Idaan saying something similar of the slaughtered buck.

He didn't notice falling asleep, but Eiah gently shook him awake and helped him to sit. While she compared his pulses and pressed his fingertips, he spat out the black leaves. His mouth was numb.

"We're going to take you back down in a litter," she said, and before he could object, she lifted her hand to his lips. He took a pose that acquiesced. Eiah rose to her feet and walked back toward the great bronze doors.

The footsteps behind him were as familiar as an old song.

"Otah-kvo," Maati said.

The Emperor sat on the dais, his hands between his knees. He looked pale and exhausted.

"Nothing ever goes the way I plan," Otah said, his tone peevish. "Not ever."

"You're tired," Maati said.

"I am. Gods, that I am."

The captain of the armsmen pulled open the doors. Four men followed, a low weaving of branches and rope between them. Eiah walked at their side. One of the men at the rear called out, and the whole parade stopped while the captain, cursing, retied a series of knots. Maati watched them as if they were dancers and gymnasts performing before a banquet.

"I'm sorry," Maati said. "This wasn't what I intended."

"Isn't it? I thought the hope was to undo the damage we did with Sterile, no matter what the price."

Maati started to object, then stopped himself. Outside the great window, a star fell. The smear of light vanished as quickly as it had come.

"I didn't know how far it would go."

"Would it have mattered? If you had known everything it would take, would you have been able to abandon the project?" Otah asked. He didn't sound angry or accusing. Only like a man who didn't know the answer to a question. Maati found he didn't either.

"If I asked your forgiveness . . ."

Otah was silent, then sighed deeply, his head hanging low.

"Maati-kya, we've been a hundred different people to each other, and tonight I'm too old and too tired. Everything in the world has changed at least twice since I woke up this morning. I think about forgiving you, and I don't know what the word means."

"I understand."

"Do you? Well, then you've outpaced me."

The litter came forward. Eiah helped him onto the makeshift seat, rope and wood creaking under his weight, but solid. The gait of the armsmen swayed him like a branch in the breeze. The Emperor, they left behind to follow in the darkness.

31

>+< The formal joining of Ana Dasin and Danat Machi took place on Candles Night in the high temple of Utani. The assembled nobility of Galt along with the utkhaiem from the highest of families to the lowest firekeeper filled every cushion on the floor, every level of balcony. The air itself was hot as a barn, and the smell of perfume and incense and bodies was overwhelming. Otah sat on his chair, looking out over the vast sea of faces. Many of the Galts wore mourning veils, and, to his surprise, the fashion had not been lost on the utkhaiem. He worried that the mourning was not entirely for fallen Galt, but also a subterranean protest of the marriage itself. It was only a small concern, though. He had thousands more like it.

The Galtic ceremony—a thing of dirgelike song and carefully measured wine spilled over rice, all to a symbolic end that escaped him—was over. The traditional joining of his own culture was already under way. Otah shifted, trying to be unobtrusive in his discomfort despite every eye in Utani being fixed on the dais.

Farrer Dasin wore a robe of black and a red ocher that suited his complexion better than Otah would have expected. Issandra sat at his side in a Galtic gown of yellow lace over a profoundly celebratory red. Danat knelt before them both.

"Farrer Dasin of House Dasin, I place myself before you as a man before my elder," Danat said. "I place myself before you and ask your permission. I would take Ana, your blood issue, to be my wife. If it does not please you, please only say so, and accept my apology."

The whisperers carried his words out through the hall like wind over wheat. Ana Dasin herself knelt on a cushion off to her parents' right and Danat had been sitting to Otah's left. The girl's gown had been an issue of long and impassioned debate, for the swell of her belly was unmistakable. With only a few minor modifications, the tailors could have done much to hide it. Instead, she had chosen Galtic dress with its tight fit-tings and waist-slung ribbons, which would make it clear to the farthest spectator in the temple that summer would come well after the child. Etiquette masters from both courts had gone at the issue like pit dogs for the better part of a week. Otah thought she looked beautiful with her gar-land of ribbons. Her father apparently thought so as well. Instead of the traditional reply, *I am not displeased*, Farrer looked Danat square in the eyes, then turned to Ana.

"Bit late for asking, isn't it?" Farrer said.

Otah laughed, giving his implicit permission for all the court to laugh with him. Danat grinned as well and took a pose of gratitude somewhat more profound than strictly required. Danat rose, came to Otah, and knelt again.

"Most High?" he said, his mouth quirked in an odd smile. Otah pre-tended to consider the question. The court laughed again, and he rose to his feet. It felt good to stand up, though before it was all finished, he'd be longing to sit down again.

"Let it be known that I have authorized this match. Let the blood of the House Dasin enter for the first time into the imperial lineage. And let all who honor the Khaiem respect this transfer and join in our cele-bration. The ceremony shall be held at once."

The whisperers carried it all, and moments later a priest came out, in-toning old words whose meanings were more than half forgotten. The man was older than Otah, and his expression was as serene and joyous as that of a man too drunk to stagger. Otah took a welcoming pose, accepted one in return, and stepped back to let the ceremony proper begin.

Danat accepted a long, looped cord and hung it over his arm. The priest intoned the ritual questions, and Danat made his answers. Otah's back began to spasm, but he kept still. The end of the cord, cut and knotted, passed from Danat to the priest and then to Ana's hand. The roar that rose up drowned out the whisperers, the priest, the world. The courts of two nations stood cheering, all decorum forgotten. Ana and Danat stood together with a length of woven cotton between them, grin-ning and waving. Otah imagined their child stirring in its dark sleep, aware of the sound if not its meaning.

Balasar Gice, wearing the robe of a high councilman, was at the front of the crowd, clapping his small hands together with tears running down his cheeks. Otah felt a momentary pang of sorrow. Sinja hadn't seen it. Kiyan hadn't. He took a deep breath and reminded himself that the moment wasn't his. The celebration was not of his life or his love or the binding of his house to a wayhouse keeper from Udun. It was Danat's and Ana's, and they at least were transcendent.

The rest of the ceremony took twice as long as it should have, and by the time the procession was ready to carry them out and through the streets of Utani, the sunset was no more than a memory.

Otah allowed himself to be ushered to a high balcony that looked down upon the city. The air was bitterly cold, but a cast-iron brazier was hauled out, coals already bright red so that Otah could feel the searing heat to his left while his right side froze. He huddled in a thick wool blanket, following the wedding procession with his eyes. Each street they turned down lit itself, banners and streamers of cloth arcing through the air.

Here is where it begins, he thought. And then, Thank all the gods it isn't me down there.

A servant girl stepped onto the balcony and took a pose that announced a guest. Otah wasn't about to stick his hands out of the blanket.

"Who?"

"Farrer Dasin-cha," the girl said.

"Bring him here," Otah said. "And some wine. Hot wine."

The girl took a pose that accepted the charge and turned to go.

"Wait," Otah said. "What's your name?"

"Toyani Vauatan, Most High," she said.

"How old are you?"

"Twenty summers."

Otah nodded. In truth, she looked almost too young to be out of the nursery. And yet at her age, he had been on a ship halfway to the eastern islands, two different lives already behind him. He pointed out at the city.

"It's a different world now, Toyani-cha. Nothing's going to stay as it was."

The girl smiled and took a pose that offered congratulations. Of course she didn't understand. It was unfair to expect her to. Otah smiled and turned back to the city, the celebration. He didn't see when she left. The wedding procession had just turned down the long, wide road that led to the riverfront when Farrer stepped out, the girl Toyani behind them bearing two bowls of wine that plumed with steam and a chair for the newcomer without seeming awkward or out of place. It was, Otah supposed, an art.

"We've done it," Farrer said when the girl had gone.

"We have," Otah agreed. "Not that I've stopped waiting for the next catastrophe."

"I think the last one will do."

Otah sipped his wine. The spirit hadn't quite been cooked out of it, and the spices tasted rich and strange. He had been dreading this conversation, but now that it had come, it wasn't as awful as he'd feared.

"The report's come," Otah said.

"The first one, yes. Everyone on the High Council had a copy this morning. Just in time for the festivities. I thought it was rude at the time, but I suppose it gives us all more reason to get sloppy drunk and weep into our cups."

Otah took a pose of query simple enough for the Galt to follow.

"Every city is in ruins except for Kirinton. They did something clever there with street callers and string. I don't fully understand it. The outlying areas suffered, though not quite as badly. The first guesses are that it will take two generations just to put us back where we were."

"Assuming nothing else happens," Otah said. Below, a fanfare was blaring.

"You mean Eymond," Farrer said. "They're a problem, it's true."

"Eymond. Eddensea, the Westlands. Anyone, really."

"If we had the andat . . ."

"We don't," Otah said.

"No, I suppose not," Farrer said, sourly. "But to the point, how many of us are aware of that fact?"

In the dim light of the brazier's coals, Farrer's face was the same dusky red as the moon in eclipse. The Galt smiled, pleased that he had taken Otah by surprise.

"You and I know. The High Council. That half-bastard council you put together when you headed out into the wilderness. Ana. Danat. A few armsmen. All in all, I'd guess not more than three dozen people actually know what happened. And none of them is at present working for Eymond."

"You're saying we should pretend to have an andat?"

"Not precisely," Farrer said. "As many people as already know, the story will come out eventually. But there might be a way to present it that still gave other nations pause. Send out letters of embassage that say the andat, though recovered, have been set aside and deny the rumors that certain deaths and odd occurrences are at all related to a new poet under the direction of the Empire."

"What deaths?"

"Don't be too specific about that," Farrer said. "I expect they'll supply the details."

"Let them think . . . that we have the andat and are hiding the fact?" Otah laughed.

"It won't last forever, but the longer we can stall them, the better prepared we'll be when they come."

"And they do always come," Otah said. "Clever thought. It costs us nothing. It could gain us a great deal. Issandra?"

Farrer leaned back in his chair, setting his heels on the parapet and looking up at the stars, the full, heavy moon. For the space of a heartbeat, he looked forlorn. He drank his wine and looked over at Otah.

"My wife is an amazing woman," he said. "I'm fortunate to have her. And if Ana's half like her, she'll be running both our nations whether your son likes it or not."

It was the opening to a hundred other issues. Galt and the cities of the Khaiem were in a state of profound disarray. Ana Dasin might be the new Empress, but that meant little enough in practical terms. In Galt the High Council and the full council were each in flux, their elections and appointments in question now that their cities were little more than abandoned. Otah would be hated for that destruction or else beloved for the mending of it.

"It is the point, isn't it? If we are two nations, we're doomed," Farrer said, reading his concerns. "We have too many enemies and not enough strengths between us."

"If we're one . . . how do we do that? Will the High Council be ruled by my edict? Am I supposed to cede my power to them?"

"Compromise, Most High," Farrer said. "It will be a long process of compromise and argument, idiotic yammering debate and high melodrama. But in its defense, it won't be war."

"It won't be war," Otah repeated. Only when the words had come out into the night air, hanging as if physical, did he realize he had meant it as an agreement. One nation. His empire had just doubled in size, tripled in complexity and need, and his own power had been cut at least by half. Farrer seemed surprised when he laughed.

"Tomorrow," Otah said. "Call the High Council tomorrow. I'll bring my council. We'll start with the report and try to build something like a plan from there. And tell Issandra that I'll have the letters of embassage sent. Best get that done before there's a debate about it, ne?"

They sat for a time without speaking, two men whose children had just joined their families. Two enemies planning a house in common. Two great powers whose golden ages had ended. They could play at it, but each knew that it was only in their children, in their grandchildren, that the game of friendship could become truth.

Farrer finished his wine, leaving the bowl by his chair. As he walked out, he put a hand on Otah's shoulder.

"Your son seems a fine man," he said.

"Your daughter is a treasure."

"She is," Farrer Dasin said, his voice serious. And then Otah was alone again, the night numbing his feet and biting his ears and nose. He pulled the blanket around himself more tightly and left the balcony and the city and the celebrations behind him.

The palaces were as quiet and busy as the backstage at a performance. Servants ran or walked or conducted low, angry conversations that died at Otah's approach. He let the night make its own path. He knew the bridal procession had returned to the palaces by the number of robes with bits of tinsel and bright paper clinging to the hems. And also by the flushed faces and spontaneous laughter. There would have been celebration on into the night, even if they hadn't scheduled the wedding on Candles Night. As it was, Utani as a whole, from the highest nobility to the lowest beggar, would sleep late and speak softly when they woke. Otah doubted there would be any wine left by spring.

But there would be babies. He could already name a dozen women casually who would be giving birth when the summer came. And everywhere, in all the cities, the conditions were the same. They would miss a generation, but only one. The Empire would stumble, but it need not fall.

Even more than the joining of the Empire and Galt, the night was the first formal celebration of a world made new. Otah wished he felt more part of it. Perhaps he understood too well what price had brought them here.

He found Eiah where he knew he would. The physicians' house with its wide, slate tables and the scent of vinegar and burning herbs. Cloth lanterns bobbled in the breeze outside the open doors. A litter of stretched canvas and light wood lay on the steps, blood staining the cloth. Within, half a dozen men and two women sat on low wooden benches or lay on the floor. One of the men tried to take a pose of obeisance, winced in pain, and sat back down. Otah made his way to the rear. Three men in leather aprons were working the tables, servants and assistants swarming around them. Eiah, in her own apron, was at the back table. A Galtic man lay before her, groaning. Blood drenched his side. Eiah glanced up, saw him, and took a pose of welcome with red hands.

"What's happened?" Otah asked.

"He fell out of a window and onto a stick," Eiah said. "I'm fairly sure we've gotten all the splinters out of him."

"He'll live, then?"

"If he doesn't go septic," Eiah said. "He's a man with a hole in his side. You can't ask better odds than that."

The wounded man stuttered out his gratitude in his own language while Eiah, letting him hold one of her hands, gestured with the other for an assistant.

"Bind the wound, give him three measures of poppy milk, and put him somewhere safe until morning. I'll want to see his wound again before we send him back to his people."

The assistant took a pose that accepted instruction, and Eiah walked to the wide stone basins on the back wall to wash the blood from her hands. A woman screamed and retched, but he couldn't see where she was. Eiah was unfazed.

"We'll have forty more like him by morning," she said. "Too drunk and happy to think of the risks. There was a woman here earlier who wrenched her knee climbing a rope they'd strung over the street. Almost fell on Danat's head, to hear her say it. She may walk with a cane the rest of her life, but she's all smiles tonight."

"Well, she won't be dancing," Otah said.

"If she can hop, she will."

"Is there a place we can speak?" Otah asked.

Eiah dried her hands on a length of cloth, leaving it dark with water and pink with blood. Her expression was closed, but she led the way through a wide door and down a hall. Someone was moaning nearby. She turned off into a small garden, the bushes as bare as sticks, a wide-branched tree empty. If there had been snow, it would have been lovely.

"I'm calling a meeting with the Galtic High Council tomorrow," he said. "And my own as well. It's the beginning of unification. I wanted you to hear it from me."

"That seems wise," Eiah said.

"The poets. The andat. They can't be kept out of that conversation."

"I know," she said. "I've been thinking about it."

"I don't suppose there are any conclusions you'd want to share," he asked, trying to keep his tone light. Eiah pulled at her fingers, one hand and then the other.

"We can't be sure there won't be others," she said. "The hardest thing about binding them is the understanding that they can be bound. They burned all the books, they killed every poet they could find, and we remade the grammar. We bound two andat. Other people are going to try to do what we did. Work from the basic structures and find a way."

"You think they'll do it?"

"History doesn't move backward," she said. "There's power in them. And there are people who want power badly enough to kill and die. Eventually, someone will find a way."

"Without Maati? Without Cehmai?"

"Or Irit, or Ashti Beg, or the two Kaes?" Eiah said. "Without me? It will be harder. It will take longer. The cost in lives and failed bindings may be huge."

"You're talking about generations from now," Otah said.

"Yes," Eiah said. "Likely, I am."

Otah nodded. It wasn't what he'd hoped to hear, but it would do. He took a pose that thanked Eiah. She bowed her head.

"Are you well?" he asked. "It isn't an easy thing, killing."

"Vanjit wasn't the first person I've killed, Father. Knowing when to help someone leave is part of what I do," Eiah said. She looked up, staring at the moon through the bare branches that couldn't shelter them, even from light. "I'm more troubled by what I could have done and didn't."

Otah took a pose that asked her to elaborate. Eiah shook her head, and then a moment later spoke softly, as if the words themselves were delicate.

"I could have held all our enemies at bay just by the threat of Wounded," she said. "What army would take the field, knowing I could blow out their lives like so many candles? Who would conspire against us knowing that if their agents were discovered, I could slaughter their kings and princes without hope of defense?"

"It would have been convenient," Otah agreed carefully.

"I could have slaughtered the men who killed Sinja-kya," Eiah said. "I could have ended every man who had ever taken a woman against her will or hurt a child. Between one breath and the next, I could have wiped them from the world."

Eiah turned her gaze to him. In the cool moonlight, her eyes seemed lost in shadow.

"I look at those things—all the things I might have done—and I wonder whether I would have. And if I had, would they have been wrong?"

"And what do you believe?"

"I believe I saved myself when I set that perversion free," she said. "I only hope the price the rest of the world pays isn't too high."

Otah stepped forward and took her in his arms. Eiah held back for a moment, and then relaxed into the embrace. She smelled of herbs and vinegar and blood. And mint. Her hair smelled of mint, just as her mother's had done.

"You should go see him," she said. He knew who she meant.

"Is he well?"

"For now," she said. "He's weathered the attacks so far. But his blood's still slowing. I expect he'll be fine until he isn't, and then he'll die."

"How long?"

"Not another year," she said.

Otah closed his eyes.

"He misses you," she said. "You know he does."

He stepped back and kissed her forehead. In the distance, someone screamed. Eiah glanced over his shoulder with disgust.

"That will be Yaniit," she said. "I'd best go tend to him. Tall as a tree, wide as a bear, and wails if you pinch him."

"Take care," Otah said.

His daughter walked away with the steady stride of a woman about her own business, leaving the bare garden for him. He looked up at the moon, but it had lost its poetry and charm. His sigh was opaque in the cold.

Maati's cell was the most beautifully appointed prison in the cities, possibly in the world. The armsmen led Otah into a chamber with vaulted ceilings and carved cedar along the walls. Maati sat up, waving the servant at his side to silence. The servant closed the book she'd been reading but kept the place with her thumb.

"You're learning Galtic tales now?" Otah asked.

"You burned my library," Maati said. "Back in Machi, or don't you recall that? The only histories your grandchild will read are written by *them*."

"Or by us," Otah said. "We can still write, you know."

Maati took a pose that accepted correction, but with a dismissive air that verged on insult. So this was how it was, Otah thought. He motioned to the armsmen to take the prisoner and follow him, then spun on his heel. The feeble sounds of protest behind him didn't slow his pace.

The highest towers of Utani were nothing in comparison to those in Machi; they could be scaled by stairways and corridors and didn't require a rest halfway along. Under half the height, and Otah liked them better. They were built with humanity in mind, and not the raw boasting power of the andat.

At the pinnacle, a small platform stood high above the world. The tallest place in the city. Wind whipped it, as cold as a bath of ice water. Otah motioned for Maati to be led forward. The poet's eyes were wild, his breath short. He raised his thick chin.

"What?" Maati spat. "Decided to throw me off, have you?"

"It's almost the half-candle," Otah said and went to stand at the edge. Maati hesitated and then stepped to his side. The city spread out below them, the streets marked by lanterns and torches. A fire blazed in a courtyard down near the riverfront, taller than ten men with whole trees for logs. Otah could cover it with his thumbnail.

The chime came, a deep ringing that seemed to shake the world. And then a thousand thousand bells rang out in answer to mark the deepest part of the longest night of the year.

"Here," Otah said. "Watch."

Below, light spread through the city. Every window, every balcony, ever parapet glowed with newly lit candles. Within ten breaths, the center of the Empire went from any large city in darkness to something woven from light, the perfect city—the *idea* of a city—made for a moment real. Maati shifted. When his voice came, it was little more than a whisper.

"It's beautiful."

"Isn't it?"

A moment later, Maati said, "Thank you."

"Of course," Otah replied.

They stood there for a long time, neither speaking nor arguing, concerned with neither future nor past. Below them, Utani glowed and rang, marking the moment of greatest darkness and celebrating the yearly return of the light.

We say that the flowers return every spring, but that is a lie.

CALIN MACHI, ELDEST SON OF THE EMPEROR REGENT, KNELT BEFORE HIS father, his gaze downcast. The delicate tilework of the floor was polished so brightly that he could watch Danat's face and seem to be showing respect at the same time. Granted, Danat was reversed—wide jaw above gray temples—and it made the nuances of expression difficult to read. It was enough, though, for him to judge approximately how much trouble he was in.

"I've spoken to the overseer of my father's apartments. Do you know what he told me?"

"That I'd been caught hiding in Grandfather's private garden," Calin said.

"Is that true?"

"Yes, Father. I was hiding from Aniit and Gaber. It was a part of a game."

Danat sighed, and Calin risked looking up. When his father was deeply upset, his face turned red. He was still flesh-colored. Calin looked back down, relieved.

"You know you're forbidden from your grandfather's apartments."

"Yes, but that was what made them a good place to hide."

"You're sixteen summers old and you're acting twelve of them. Aniit and Gaber look to you for how to behave. It's your duty to set an example," Danat said, his voice stern. And then he added, "Don't do it again."

Calin rose to his feet, trying to keep his rush of joy from being obvious. The great punishment had not fallen. He was not barred from the steam caravan's arrival. Life was still worth living. Danat took a pose that excused his son and motioned to his Master of Tides. Before the woman could glide over and lead his father back into the constant business of negotiating with the High Council, Calin left the audience chamber, followed only by his father's shouted admonition not to run. Aniit and Gaber were waiting outside, their eyes wide.

"It's all right," Calin said, as if his father's lenience were somehow proof of his own cleverness. Aniit took an exaggerated pose of congratulations. Gaber clapped her hands. She was young, though. Only fourteen summers old and barely marriageable.

"Come on, then," Calin said. "We can pick the best places for when the caravan comes."

The roadway had been five years in the building, a shallow canal of smooth worked iron that began at the seafront in Saraykeht and followed the river up to Utani. The caravan was the first of its kind, and the common wisdom in the streets and teahouses was evenly divided between those who thought it would arrive even earlier than expected and those who predicted they'd find splinters of blown boilers and nothing else.

Calin dismissed the skeptics. After all, his grandmother was arriving from her plantations in Chaburi-Tan, and she would never put herself on the caravan if it was going to explode.

The sweet days of early spring were short and cold. Frost still sent white fingers up the stones of the palaces in the morning and snow lingered in the deep shadows. A hundred times Calin and his friends had gone through the elaborate ritual of how they would greet the caravan, rehearsing it in their minds and conversations. The event, of course, was nothing like what they'd planned.

When word came, Calin was with his tutor, an ancient man from Acton, working complex sums. They were seated in the sunlight of the spring garden. Almond blossoms turned the tree branches white even before the first leaves had ventured out. Calin frowned at the wax tablet on his knees, trying not to count on his fingers. Hesitating, he lifted his stylus and marked his answer. His tutor made a noncommittal sound in the back of his throat and Gaber appeared at the end of the arcade, running full out.

"It's here!" she screamed. "It's here!"

Before any adult could object, Calin joined her flight. Tablet, stylus, and sums were forgotten in an instant. They ran past the pavilions that marked palaces from merchants' compounds, the squares and open markets that showed where the great compound gave way to the haunts of common labor. The streets were thick with humanity, and Calin threaded his way through the press of bodies aided by his youth, the quality of his robes, and the boyish instinct that saw all obstacles as ephemeral.

He reached the Emperor's platform just before the caravan arrived. Wide plumes of smoke and steam stained the southern sky, and the air smelled of coal. Danat and Ana were already there, seated in chairs of carved stone with silk cushions. Otah Machi—the Emperor himself— sat on a raised dais, his hands resting like fragile claws on the arms of a black lacquer chair. Calin's grandfather looked over as he arrived and smiled. Danat's expression was distracted in a way that reminded Calin of doing sums. His mother was craning her neck and trying not to seem that she was.

It hardly mattered. The crowd that pressed and seethed around the yard at the caravan road's end had eyes only for the great carts speeding toward them, faster than horses at full gallop. Calin sat at his mother's feet, his intended perch nearest his friends forgotten. The first of the carts came near enough to make out the raised dais, twin of his grandfather's, and the stiff-backed white-haired woman sitting atop it. Calin's mother left all decorum, and stood, waving and calling to her mother.

Calin felt his father's hand on his shoulder and turned.

"Watch this," Danat said. "Pay attention. That caravan reached us in half the time even a boat could have. What you're seeing right now is going to change everything."

Calin nodded solemnly as if he understood.

It is true that the world is renewed. It is also true that that renewal comes at a price.

CEHMAI TYAN SAT ACROSS THE MEETING TABLE FROM THE HIGH COUNCIL'S special envoy. The man was nondescript, his clothing of Galtic cut and unremarkable quality. Cehmai didn't like the envoy, but he respected him. He'd known too many dangerous men in his life not to.

The envoy read the letters—ciphered and sent between a fictional merchant in Obar State and Cehmai himself here in Utani. They outlined the latest advance in the poetmaster's rebuilding of the lost libraries of Machi, which also had not happened. Cehmai sipped tea from an iron bowl and looked out the window. He couldn't see the steam caravan from here, but he had a good view of the river. It was at the point he liked it most, the water freed by the thaw, the banks not yet overgrown by green. No matter how many years passed, he still felt a personal affinity with earth and stone.

The envoy finished reading, his mouth in a smile that would have seemed pleasant and perhaps a bit simple on someone else.

"Is any of this true?" the envoy asked.

"Danat-cha did send a dozen men into the foothills north of Machi," Cehmai said, "and Maati-kvo and I did spend a winter there. Past that, nothing. But it should keep Eddensea's attention on sneaking through to search for it themselves. And we're in the process of forging books that we can then 'recover' in a year or so."

The envoy tucked the letters into a leather pouch at his belt. He didn't look up as he spoke.

"That brings a question," the man said. "I know we've talked about this before, but I'm not sure you've fully grasped the advantages that could come from leaning a little nearer the truth. Nothing that would be effective. We all understand that. But our enemies all have scholars working at these problems. If they were able to come close enough that the bindings cost them, if they paid the andat's price—"

Cehmai took a pose of query. "Wouldn't that be doing your work for you?" he asked.

"My job is to see they don't succeed," the envoy said. "A few mysterious, grotesque deaths would help me find the people involved."

"It would give away too much," Cehmai said. "Bringing them near enough to be hurt by the effort would also bring them near to succeeding."

The envoy looked at him silently. His placid eyes conveyed only a mild distrust.

"If you have a threat to make, feel free," Cehmai said. "It won't do you any good."

"Of course there's no threat, Cehmai-cha," the envoy said. "We're all on the same side here."

"Yes," the poetmaster said, rising from his chair with a pose that called the meeting to its close. "Try to keep it in mind."

His apartments were across the palaces. He made his way along the pathways of white and black sand, past the singing slaves and the fountain in the shape of the Galtic Tree that marked the wing devoted to the High Council. The men and women he passed nodded to him with deference, but few took any formal pose. A decade of joint rule had led to a thousand small changes in etiquette. Cehmai supposed it was small-minded of him to regret them.

Idaan was sitting on the porch of their entranceway, tugging at a length of string while a gray tomcat worried the other end. He paused, watching her. Unlike her brother, she'd grown thicker with time, more solid, more real. He must have made some small sound, because she looked up and smiled at him.

"How was the assassin's conference?" she asked.

The tomcat forgot his string and trotted up to Cehmai, already purring audibly. He stopped to scratch its fight-ragged ears.

"I wish you wouldn't call it that," he said.

"Well, I wish my hair were still dark. It is what it is, love. Politics in action."

"Cynic," he said as he reached the porch.

"Idealist," she replied, pulling him down to kiss him.

Far to the east, an early storm fell from clouds dark as bruises, a veil of gray. Cehmai watched it, his arm around his lover's shoulder. She leaned her head against him.

"How was the Emperor this morning?" he asked.

"Fine. Excited to see Issandra-cha again as much as anything about the caravan. I think he's more than half infatuated with her."

"Oh please," Cehmai said. "This will be his seventy-ninth summer? His eightieth?"

"And you won't still want me when you've reached the age?"

"Well. Fair point."

"His hands bother him most," Idaan said. "It's a pity about his hands."

Lightning flashed on the horizon, less that a firefly. Idaan twined her fingers with his and sighed.

"Have I mentioned recently how much I appreciate you coming to find me? Back when you were an outlaw and I was still a judge, I mean," she asked.

"I never tire of hearing it," Cehmai said.

The tomcat leaped on his lap, dug its claws into his robe twice, kneading him like bread dough, and curled up.

For even if the flower grows from an ancient vine, the flowers of spring are themselves new to the world, untried and untested.

EIAH MOTIONED FOR OTAH TO SIT. SHE WAS GENTLE AS ALWAYS WITH HIS crippled hands. He sat back down slowly. The servants had brought his couches out to a wide garden, but with the coming sunset he'd have to be moved again. Eiah tried to impress on her father's servants that what he needed and what he wanted weren't always the same. She'd given up convincing Otah years earlier.

"How are you feeling?" she asked, sitting beside him. "You look tired."

"It was a long day," Otah said. "I slept well enough, but I can never stay in bed past dawn. When I was young, I could sleep until midday. Now that I have the time and no one would object, I'm up with the birds. Does that seem right to you?"

"The world was never fair."

"Truth. All the gods know that's the truth."

She took his wrists as if it were nothing more than the contact of father and daughter. Otah looked at her impatiently, but he suffered it. She closed her eyes for a moment, feeling the subtle differences of his pulses.

"I heard you woke confused again," she said. "You were calling for someone called Muhatia-cha?"

"I had a dream. That's all," Otah said. "Muhatia was my overseer back when I was young. I dreamed that I was late for my shift. I needed to get to the seafront before he docked my pay. That was all. I'm not losing my mind, love. My health, maybe, but not my mind. Not yet."

"I didn't think you were. Turn here. Let me look at your eyes. Have the headaches come back?"

"No," Otah said, and she knew by his voice he was lying. It was time to stop asking details. There was only so much physician's attention her father would permit. She sat back on the couch, and he let out a small, satisfied breath.

"You saw Issandra Dasin?" she asked.

"Yes, yes. She spent the better part of the afternoon here," Otah said. "The things they've done with Chaburi-Tan are amazing. I was thinking I might go myself. Just to see them."

"It would be fascinating," Eiah agreed. "I hear Farrer-cha's doing well?"

"He's made more out of that city than I could have. But then I was never particularly brilliant with administration. I had other skills, I suppose," Otah said. "Enough about that. Tell me about your family. How is Parit-cha? And the girls?"

Eiah let herself be distracted. Parit was well, but he'd been kept away from their apartments three nights running by a boy who worked for House Laarin who'd broken his leg falling off a wall. It had been a bad break, and the fever hadn't gone down quickly enough to suit anyone. It seemed as if the boy would live, and they were both happy to call that a success. Of Otah's granddaughters, Mischa was throwing all her free time into learning to dance every new form that came in from Galt, and wearing the dance master's feet raw in the effort. Gaber had talked about nothing besides the steam caravan for weeks, but Eiah suspected it was more Calin's enthusiasm than her own. Gaber assumed that Calin rose with the sun and set with the moon.

Eiah didn't realize how long she'd been telling the small stories of her family until the overseer came out with an apologetic pose and announced that the Emperor's meal was waiting. Otah made a show of rubbing his belly, but when Eiah joined him, he ate very little. The meal was fresh chicken cooked in last year's apricots, and it was delicious. She watched her father pluck at the pale flesh.

He looked older than his years. His skin had grown as thin as paper; his eyes were always wet. After his hands had fallen to their weakness, the headaches had begun. Eiah had tried him on half a dozen different programs of herbs and baths. She wasn't convinced he'd followed any of them very closely.

"Stop," Otah said. Eiah took a pose that asked clarification. He frowned at her, his eyebrows rising as he spoke. "You're looking at me as if I were a particularly interesting bloodworm. I'm fine, Eiah-kya. I sleep well, I wake full of energy, my bowels never trouble me, and my joints don't ache. Everything that could be right about me is right. Now I'd like to spend an evening with my daughter and not my physician, eh?"

"I'm sorry, Papa-kya," she said. "It's only that I worry."

"I know," he said, "and I forgive you. But don't let tomorrow steal what's good about tonight. The future takes care of its own. You can write that down if you like. The Emperor said it."

The flower that wilted last year is gone. Petals once fallen are fallen forever.

IDAAN ROSE BEFORE THE DAWN AS SHE ALWAYS DID, PARTING THE NETTING silently and stealthily walking out to her dressing chamber so as not to disturb Cehmai. She was not so important a woman that the servants wouldn't leave her be or that armsmen were needed to hold the utkhaiem and councilmen at bay. She was not her brother. She picked a simple robe of dusty red and rich blue and fastened all the ties herself. Then sandals and a few minutes before a mirror with a brush and a length of stout ribbon to bring her hair into something like order.

No one had assigned her the daily task of carrying breakfast to the Emperor. It was one she'd simply taken on. After two weeks of arriving at the kitchens to collect the tray with its plates and bowl and teapot, the servant who had been the official bearer simply stopped coming. She'd usurped the work.

That morning, they'd prepared honey bread and raisins, hot rice in almond milk, and a slab of roast pork with a pepper glaze. Idaan knew from experience that she would end with the pork and the honey bread. The rice, he might eat.

The path to the Emperor's apartments was well-designed. The balance between keeping the noises and interruptions away—not to mention the constant possibility of fire—and getting the food to him still warm meant a long, straight journey almost free from the meanderings to which the palaces were prone. Archways of stone marked the galleries. Tapestries of lush red and gold hung on the walls. The splendor had long since ceased to take her breath away. She had lived in palaces and mud huts and everything in between. The only thing that astounded her with any regularity was that so late in her life, she had found her family.

Cehmai alone had been miraculous. The last decade serving in court had been something greater than that. She had become an aunt to Danat and Eiah and Ana, a sister to Otah Machi. Even now, her days had the feel of relaxing in a warm bath. It wasn't something she'd expected. For that, it wasn't something she'd thought possible. The nightmares almost never came now; never more than once or twice in a month. She was ready to grow old here, in these halls and passageways, with these people. If anyone had the poor judgment to threaten her people, Idaan knew she would kill the idiot. She hoped the occasion wouldn't arise.

She knew something was wrong as soon as she passed through the arch that led to Otah's private garden. Four servants stood in a clot at the side door, their faces pale, their hands in constant motion. With a feeling of dread, she put the lacquer tray on a bench and came forward. The oldest of the servants was weeping, his face blotchy and his eyes swollen. Idaan looked at the man, her expression empty. Whatever strength remained in him left, and he folded to the ground sobbing.

"Have you sent for his children?" Idaan asked.

"I . . . we only just . . ."

Idaan raised her eyebrows, and the remaining servants scattered. She stepped over the weeping man and made her way into the private rooms. All together, they were smaller than Idaan's old farmhouse. It didn't take long to find him.

Otah sat in a chair as if he were only sleeping. The window before him was open, the shutters swaying slow and languorous in the breeze. The motion reminded her of seaweed. His robe was yellow shot with black. His eyes were barely open and as empty as marbles. Idaan made herself touch his skin. It was cold. He was gone.

She found a stool, pulled it to his side, and sat with him one last time. His hand was stiff, but she wrapped her fingers around his. For a long while, she said nothing. Then, softly so that just the two of them could hear, she spoke.

"You did good work, brother. I can't think anyone would have done better."

She remained there breathing the scent of his rooms for the last time until Danat and Eiah arrived, a small army of servants and utkhaiem and councilmen at their backs. Idaan told Eiah what she needed to know in a few short sentences, then left. The breakfast was gone, cleared away. She went to find Cehmai and tell him the news.

Flowers do not return in the spring, rather they are replaced. It is in this differ-ence between returned *and* replaced *that the price of renewal is paid.*

"No," Ana said. The ambassador of Eymond lifted a finger, as if beg-ging leave to interrupt the Empress. He made a small noise at the back of his throat. Ana shook her head. "I said no. I meant no, Lord Ambas-sador. And if you raise your finger to me again like I was a schoolgirl talk-ing out of turn, I will have it cut off and set in a necklace for you."

The meeting room was as silent as a grave. Even the candle flames stood still. The dark-stained wood of the floor and beautifully painted abstract frescoes of the walls seemed out of place, too rich and peaceful for the moment. A back room at a teahouse was the better venue for this kind of negotiation. Ana enjoyed the contrast.

She knew when she first heard of Otah Machi's death that she was going to have to be responsible for holding the Empire together until Danat regained his balance. She hadn't yet lost a parent. Her husband and lover now had neither of his. The lost expression in his eyes and the bewildered tone in his voice made her heart ache. And so when their partners and rivals in trade took the opportunity to renegotiate treaties in hopes of winning some concession in the fog of grief, Ana found her-self taking it personally.

"Lady Empress," the ambassador said, "I don't mean disrespect, but you must see that—"

Ana raised her finger, the mirror of the man's gesture. He went silent.

"A necklace," she said. "Ask around if you'd like. You'll find I have no sense of proportion. None."

Very quietly, the ambassador took the scroll up from the table between them and put it back in its satchel. Ana nodded and gestured to the door. The man's spine could have been made of a single, unarticulated iron bar as he left. Ana felt no sympathy for him.

The Master of Tides came in a moment later, her face amused and alarmed. Ana took what she thought was the proper pose to express continuity. The Khaiate system of poses was something that was best born into and learned from infancy. She did her best, and no one had the audacity to correct her, so Ana figured she was close enough.

"I believe that is all for the day, Most High," the Master of Tides said.

"Excellent. We got through those quickly, didn't we?"

"Very quickly," the woman agreed.

"Feel free to offer any other audiences the choice of meeting with me or waiting for my husband until after the mourning rites."

"I will be sure to sketch out the options," the woman said in voice that assured Ana that she would make room in her schedule to help Danat with his father's arrangements.

Ana found her mother in the guests' apartments. Her return trip had been postponed, the steam caravan itself waiting for her. The blue silk curtains billowed in the soft breeze; the scent of lemon candles lit to keep the insects away filled the air. Issandra sat before the fire grate, her hands folded on her lap. She didn't rise.

Ana would never have said it, but her mother looked old. The sun of Chaburi-Tan had darkened her skin, making her hair seem brilliantly white.

"Mother."

"Empress," Issandra Dasin said. Her voice was warm. "I'm afraid our timing left something to be desired."

"No," Ana said. "It wouldn't have mattered. Tell father that I appreciate the invitation, but I can't leave my family here."

"He won't hear it from me," Issandra said. "He's a good man, but time hasn't made him less stubborn. He wants his little girl back."

Ana sighed. Her mother nodded.

"I know his little girl is gone," Issandra said. "I'll try to make him understand that you're happy here. It may come to his visiting you himself."

"How are things at home?" Ana asked. She knew it was a telling question. She started to take a pose that unasked it but lost her way. It wasn't part of their conversation anyway.

"The word from Galt is good. The trade routes are busier than Far-rer's seafront can accommodate. He's filling his coffers with silver and gems at a rate I've never seen," Issandra said. "It consoles him."

"I am happy here," Ana said.

"I know you are, love," her mother said. "This is where your children live."

They talked about small things for another hour, and then Ana took her leave. There would be time enough later.

The Emperor's pyre was set to be lit in two days. Utani was wrapped in mourning cloth. The palaces were swaddled in rags, the trees hung heavy with gray and white cloth. Dry mourning drums filled the air where there had once been music. The music would come again. She knew that. This was only something that had to be endured.

She found Danat in his father's apartments, tears streaking his face. Around him were spread sheets of paper as untidy as a bird's nest. All of them were written upon in Otah Machi's hand. There had to be a thousand pages. Danat looked up at her. For the length of a heartbeat, she could see what her husband had looked like as a child.

"What is it?" Ana asked.

"It was a crate," Danat said. "Father left orders that it be put on his pyre. They're letters. All of them are to my mother."

"From when they were courting?" Ana asked, sitting on the floor, her legs crossed.

"After she died," Danat said. Ana plucked a page from the pile. The paper was brittle, the ink pale. Otah Machi's words were perfectly legible.

Kiyan-kya—

You have been dead for a year tonight. I miss you. I want to have some-thing more poetic to say, something that will do you some honor or change how it feels to be without you. Something. I had a thousand things I thought I would write, but those were when it was only me. Now, here, with you, all I can say is that I miss you.

The children are starting to come back from the loss. I don't know if they ever will. I have no experience with this. I had no mother or father. As a child, I had no family. I don't have any experience losing a family.

The closest thing I have to solace is knowing that, if I had gone first, you would have suffered all this darkness yourself. That I have to bear it is the price of sparing you. It doesn't make the burden lighter, it doesn't make the pain less, it doesn't take away any of the longing I have to see you again or hear your voice. But it does give the pain meaning. I suppose that's all I can ask: that the pain have meaning.

I love you. I miss you. I will write again soon.

Ana folded the letter. Thousands of pages of letters to the Empress who had died. The last Empress before her.

"I don't know what to do," Danat said.

"I love you. You know I love you more than anything except the children?"

"Of course."

"If you burn these, I will leave you. Honestly, love. You've lost enough of him. You have to keep these."

Danat took a deep shuddering breath and closed his eyes. His hands pressed flat on his thighs. Another tear slipped down his cheek, and Ana leaned forward to smooth it away with her sleeve.

"I want to," Danat said. "I want to keep them. I want to keep *him*. But it was what he asked."

"He's dead, love," Ana said. "He's dead and gone. Truly. He doesn't care anymore."

When Danat had finished crying, his body heavy against her own, the sun had set. The apartments were a collection of shadows. Somewhere in the course of things, they had made their way to Otah Machi's bed— a soft mattress that smelled of roses and had, so far as Ana could tell, never been slept in. She stroked Danat's hair and listened to the chorus of crickets in the gardens. Her husband's breath became deeper, more regular. Ana waited until he was deeply asleep, then slipped out from under him, lit a candle, and by its soft light gathered the letters and began to put them in order.

And as it is for spring flowers, so it is for us.

THE WORLD ITSELF SEEMED TO HAVE CONSPIRED TO MAKE THE DAY SOMBER. Gray clouds hung low over the city, a cold constant mist of rain darkening the mourning cloths, the stones, the newly unfurled leaves of the trees. The pyre stood in the center of the grand court, stinking of coal oil and pine resin. The torches that lined the pyre spat and hissed in the rain.

The assembly was huge. There weren't enough whisperers to take any words he said to the back edges of the crowd. If there was a back. As far as he could see from his place at the raised black dais, there were only faces, an infinity of faces, going back to the edge of the horizon. Their murmuring voices were a constant roll of distant thunder.

The Emperor was dead, and whether they mourned or celebrated, no one would remain unmoved.

At his side, Ana held his hand. Calin, in a pale mourning robe and a bright red sash, looked dumbstruck. His eyes moved restlessly over everything. Danat wondered what the boy found so overwhelming: the sheer animal mass of the crowd, the realization that Danat himself was no longer emperor regent but actually emperor, as Calin himself would be one day, or the fact that Otah was gone. All three, most likely.

Danat rose and stepped to the front of the dais. The crowd grew louder and then eerily silent. Danat drew a sheaf of papers from his sleeve. His farewell to his father.

"We say that the flowers return every spring," Danat said, "but that is a lie. It is true that the world is renewed. It is also true that that renewal comes at a price, for even if the flower grows from an ancient vine, the flowers of spring are themselves new to the world, untried and untested.

"The flower that wilted last year is gone. Petals once fallen are fallen forever. Flowers do not return in the spring, rather they are replaced. It is in this difference between *returned* and *replaced* that the price of renewal is paid.

"And as it is for spring flowers, so it is for us."

Danat paused, the voices of the whisperers carrying his words out as far as they would travel. As he waited, he caught sight of Idaan and Cehmai standing before the pyre. The old poet looked somber. Idaan's long face carried an expression that might have been amusement or anger or the distance of being lost in her own thoughts. She was unreadable, as she always was. He saw, not for the first time, how much she and Otah resembled each other.

The rain tapped on the page before him as if to recall his attention. The ink was beginning to blur. Danat began again.

"My father founded an empire, something no man living can equal. My father also took a wife, raised children, struggled with all that it meant to have us, and there are any number of men and women in the cities or in Galt, Eymond, Bakta, Eddensea, or the world as a whole who have taken that road as well.

"My father was born, lived his days, and died. In that he is like all of us. All of us, every one, without exception. And so it is for that, perhaps, that he most deserves to be honored."

The ink bled, Danat's words fading and blurring. He looked up at the low sky and thought of his father's letters. Page after page after page of saying what could never be said. He didn't know any longer what he'd hoped to achieve with his own speech. He folded the pages and put them back in his sleeve.

"I loved my father," Danat said. "I miss him."

He proceeded slowly down the wide stairs to the base of the pyre. A servant whose face he didn't know presented Danat with a lit torch. He took it, and walked slowly around the base of the pyre, cool raindrops dampening his face, his hair. He smelled of soft rain. Danat touched flame to tinder as he went, the coal oil flaring and stinking.

The fire roared. Smoke rose through the falling rain, carrying the body of Otah Machi with it. And pale petals of almond blossoms floated over the crowd and the pyre, the palaces and the city, like the announcement that spring had come at last.

ABOUT THE AUTHOR

The Price of Spring is the fourth and final novel of the Long Price Quartet by **Daniel Abraham**. The first three are *A Shadow in Summer, A Betrayal in Winter,* and *An Autumn War.* His short fiction has been published in the anthologies *Vanishing Acts, Bones of the World, The Dark,* and *Logorrhea,* and been included in Gardner Dozois's *Year's Best Science Fiction* and *The Year's Best Fantasy & Horror* edited by Ellen Datlow and Kelly Link & Gavin J. Grant, as well. His story "Flat Diane" won the International Horror Guild Award for best short story. His novelette "The Cambist and Lord Iron" was short-listed for the Hugo and World Fantasy awards. He is also the coauthor of *Hunter's Run* with Gardner R. Dozois and George R. R. Martin. He lives in New Mexico with his family.